Why

MOUNTAINS STAND

CLIMBING HIGHER

Why the
MOUNTAINS STAND

CLIMBING HIGHER

BOOK 3

ASHLYN McKAYLA OHM

Words from the Wilderness

WHY THE MOUNTAINS STAND
Copyright © 2024 by Ashlyn McKayla Ohm

For information, contact
www.wordsfromthewilderness.com

Cover design by Hannah Linder Designs
Formatting template by Derek Murphy

ISBN (paperback): 979-8-9853344-6-3
ISBN (ebook): 979-8-9853344-7-0
Library of Congress Control Number: 2023920803

Unless otherwise noted, Scriptures are drawn from GOD'S WORD®, © 1995 God's Word to the Nations. Used by permission of Baker Publishing Group.

First Edition: April 2024
Hot Springs, Arkansas

10 9 8 7 6 5 4 3 2 1
29 28 27 26 25 24

I have seen the scars. The story's carved
Upon this sharp-edged land. Here the ice
In glaciers great, groaned against the hills,
A world forever changed. And thus for me—
The fears that froze my past reshaped my soul,
An unfamiliar wilderness within. But I've learned
That mountains do not rise without this pain,
That gentle hands write healing in my scars.
So I stand
To trade a flatland faith for truer trust,
And shout the tale of what His love has wrought;
I'm climbing ever higher toward His heart.

△△ △△ △△

CHAPTER 1

Thirty-six thousand feet. Almost as high as her hopes.

Addisyn Miles glanced out the window of the jet, down to where the Rocky Mountains jumbled themselves into snow-crowned craters and shadowed slants of valleys. As a former professional figure skater, she'd spent many hours in the air, flying between training camps and competitions. After the first few flights, she'd stopped paying attention to the scenery.

But today was different…because the mountains below her were the ones that would lead her home. And no competition had held higher stakes than what was coming next.

A fresh wave of adrenaline tingled through her at the thought. Addisyn drew a steadying breath and glanced at the passenger next to her—a grandmotherly sort of woman who'd been sleeping since they'd lifted off the runway in Denver. Her beaded necklace rose and fell in time with her peaceful breaths.

If only Addisyn could tap into some of that tranquility.

Maybe reading the text again would help. Careful not to jostle the sleeping woman's arm, she fished her phone from her pocket and swiped to Darius's last message. The one he'd sent after she'd let him know she was boarding in Denver.

Only six and a half hours. I can't wait to see you, love.

She'd reread the message a dozen times, but it still made her heart swoop. She could hear just how his adorable West Coast accent would have wrapped around the words, could see how his smile would have tipped up toward his eyes. And at the end of this plane trip, he'd be waiting. The man who'd swept her off her feet while she was visiting his small Canadian town in search of healing after the end of her skating career.

A gusty sigh broke through her thoughts. Addisyn glanced over just in time to see the grandmother's eyes blink open. "Well, my lands. That was quite the nap." She yawned, then straightened in her seat and peered at Addisyn. "I believe I was too tired to introduce myself when we boarded, dear. I'm Patty."

"Hi, Patty." Addisyn had never been fond of in-flight conversation, particularly when her nerves were strung tight, but she managed a smile. "I'm Addisyn."

The woman's eyebrow quirked. "Addisyn. Now there's an unusual name." She continued before Addisyn could decide if that was good or bad. "How much longer until Vancouver?"

"Less than two hours." Addisyn noticed for the first time that the hem of the woman's scarlet sweater was embroidered with cats. Ugh. She barely repressed a shudder. Who wanted to adorn their clothing with those creepy creatures?

Patty studied her with the laser-beam look of someone puzzling out a riddle. "Not from Canada, are you?"

"Um—no. How did you—"

"Oh, the accent, dear. American through and through." She tapped her chest proudly. "I'm from Alberta, born and raised. I can always spot a foreigner."

A *foreigner*? "Well—yes. I'm visiting."

"You have family there, then?"

"No." Patty's curious gaze showed no sign of wavering. Addisyn sighed in surrender. "My boyfriend." Even the old woman's prying couldn't stop the way her soul sang at the thought of him.

"Your boyfriend? Bet there's a story there." Patty settled into her seat as if ready to hear it.

"Well—yeah. We met when I was in Canada before, and we started dating, and—well, the rest is history, I guess." The memories flashed against the windows of the plane, and once more she was in the coffee shop in Whistler, and he was shining that unhurried smile at her for the first time. How had it already been over a year since then?

"That's it? There has to be more to that story."

Of course there was more—much more. The way Darius had helped her disentangle from the abusive relationship in which she'd been trapped—the way he'd supported her in her search for the sister with whom she'd lost connection—the way his gentle faith in a Light greater than every shadow had sustained her during the chill of her darkest nights.

But all of that was too sacred to share with a stranger on a plane, and Addisyn merely shrugged. "That's the gist of it. We've been dating long-distance."

"Is he cute?"

Her embarrassment spilled over in a nervous laugh. "Yes. He's—quite handsome."

"Hmm." Patty leaned back in her seat.

Could she dare hope the woman's stream of questions had dried up? Addisyn was just turning back to her phone when Patty leaned forward again. "So the boyfriend lives in Vancouver?"

Addisyn glanced at the time on her phone screen. Ninety minutes left in the flight. Was there any chance Patty would go back to sleep? "Actually, he lives in Whistler."

"How long are you visiting for?"

"The summer. Darius—that's my boyfriend—his aunt and uncle operate the Bearstooth Athletic Center in the Callaghan Valley."

"Callaghan country?" Patty pressed her lips together. "Rough land, up there. Me, I've got no interest in being there. Not with all the bears."

Addisyn's heart lurched. "Bears?"

"Now where did you think that *Bearstooth* name came from?" Patty gave an exaggerated shiver. "That whole area is infested with them. Don't go outside after dark."

Great. Addisyn swallowed hard. "Okay—well—I'll just be commuting there to work." She sighed, resigning herself to unrolling the entire explanation. "I used to be a professional figure skater, and Darius's uncle has hired me to work there as an assistant coach this season."

"Really?" Patty's eyebrows shot up. "Pretty young to be a coach, aren't you?"

And just what did age have to do with anything? Addisyn narrowed her eyes. "I'm sorry?"

"Just seems like you would need some experience to do a job like that." She nodded mysteriously like some wise-woman guru. "My late husband, God rest his soul, played hockey for years and then started coaching. He always said the first thing his athletes did was teach him everything he didn't know."

Okay, this woman was really getting under her skin. She fought to keep her irritation out of her voice. "I do have experience. As I said, I was a competitive skater."

Patty gave a dry chuckle. "Athletic experience is one thing. But my husband always said coaching wasn't about the sport. It was about being a leader." She zeroed in on Addisyn. "Would you consider yourself a leader, Addisyn?"

Her palms were sweating on the slick fake leather. "Well—I mean—I don't think that's important." She heard the awkwardness in her laugh. "Like I said, I'm just an assistant."

"Doesn't matter." Patty shook her head. "People are looking for leaders, Addisyn. And what you know about the sport—well, it's not as important as what's in your heart. I watched my husband coach his athletes for forty years, and let me tell you, that man touched more lives in the locker room than on the rink. But—" She shrugged. "You'll see soon enough. Trust me, by the time you're my age, you'll have learned a thing or two about dealing with people."

Addisyn refrained from pointing out that Patty seemed to still have a ways to go in that department.

"Well, anyway." Patty tugged a faded vinyl purse from under her seat. She rummaged through it and produced a plastic sandwich bag full of crumbled walnut pieces. "Want any?"

"Um—no, thank you."

"You sure? Lots of magnesium in these, you know. They help when you're deficient, like me."

So far, the only essential nutrient in which Patty seemed deficient was tact. "I'm sure. But thank you."

"Okay. You don't know what you're missing." Patty crunched her walnuts with evident enjoyment, the conversation apparently— hopefully—over.

Addisyn turned back to the window. Bears? Prior to Darius's invitation, she'd been living with her older sister in the Colorado Rockies, where people existed in tandem with wildlife—elk in the park downtown, foxes trotting through backyards, even the low sob of a wolf some long winter evenings.

Her sister accepted, even appreciated, the overlap of the human and animal worlds. But then, Avery had always been the outdoorsy one. Addisyn preferred to be a bit more insulated from the wildlife around her. It had been bad enough going outside in the mornings not knowing if an elk would be standing on the porch. Having to batten down in a bear-infested valley was more than she'd bargained for.

Clouds were rolling in, and the mountains now looked more like sharpened teeth. She swallowed and glanced away from the view.

Would you consider yourself a leader?

Of course not. She was the one that had staggered over her bad choices for the last few years. Heat flooded her face. Was Patty right? With all her failures, did she really have any right to be in a position of authority? *Was* she too young?

She pressed her lips together. She was being ridiculous. She did not have to explain herself to anyone. Especially some nosy woman who wore clothes covered in cats. The seeds of doubt Patty had planted just wouldn't bear fruit. Coaching didn't require you to be a role model on a pedestal, right? She wasn't looking to "*touch lives*"; she just wanted to do a decent job training athletes. Ninety percent of that would be technical know-how, and she'd been on the ice since she was seven years old. That was fifteen years of experience, regardless of her age, and anyway Patty was probably one of those people who considered anyone under the age of sixty to be an inexperienced young kid.

Plus, this had been Darius's idea. He'd suggested the opportunity to her and coordinated everything with his aunt and uncle, even arranging housing for her. He wouldn't have taken the trouble if he didn't think she would succeed.

He hadn't mentioned bears either.

The thought of Darius soothed away the last of her worry. No matter what obstacles might arise, she'd have him. Not just all-too-short visits to each other's worlds or FaceTime calls that were a lukewarm substitute for reality.

That was enough to melt every drop of doubt.

A crackling voice over the loudspeaker made Addisyn jump. "Ladies and gentlemen, we welcome you to Vancouver. The local time is one thirty, and…"

The plane banked low, the city gridlock circling outside the window and the mountains a hint on the horizon. When the plane doors opened, Addisyn was the first one standing. "Bye, Patty. Nice talking to you." She didn't wait for a reply before she shrugged her carryon over her shoulder and pushed toward the front of the plane.

The skybridge unrolled like a magical portal to her new world, and peace washed away Addisyn's fears. Just as she exited security, her phone buzzed in her pocket. She slid it out to see a text from Avery.

Just checking on you. Flight ok?

Her heart hurt for just a moment. It was a little disorienting to realize that for the first time, she was truly on her own. The sister who'd been her constant rock was fifteen hundred miles away. Her thumbs flew through her response.

Hey, A! Flight was great. I'm here.

She sent the message and waited. Almost immediately Avery's reply dropped onto the screen.

Good. Tell Darius hi for me.

Addisyn narrowed her eyes. The short, curt message was nothing like her sister's usual warm personality. But really, Avery had been acting a little strange the whole time she'd helped Addisyn pack and plan for this trip. Quieter than normal, somehow.

Well, now was not the time for Avery to be acting weird. Addisyn needed her sister during this transition. More than she was willing to admit, in fact. Addisyn sighed and slipped her phone back into her pocket. She'd try to call her sister later. Anyway, it was entirely possible that Avery was just busy at work or out hiking somewhere.

"Addisyn!"

Her heart jerked at the voice that could sweep all other concerns from her mind. She spun, scanning the crowd, and there he was, jogging toward her. "Darius!"

Two more strides, and the soothing strength of his embrace wrapped around her. "Addisyn." He breathed her name. "You're here."

"I am." She pulled back just enough to gaze into his familiar face—the dark brown hair that brushed his shoulders, the beard that framed his smile, the blue-green eyes the color of the Pacific inlet on sunny days. A shyness she hadn't expected tangled her tongue. "Darius—you—I've missed you."

"I've missed you too." He stepped back and reached for the Styrofoam cup he'd set on the railing before hugging her. "Here."

"You remembered."

"Of course I did." His eyes held a meaning far deeper than the gesture. "Cuban latte. Your favorite."

The heat from the cup warmed her face. "Our favorite."

"Right." He settled his arm protectively across her shoulders. "Let's get the rest of your bags." He glanced suddenly over her head. "Who's that?"

"Addisyn?"

Oh, no. Addisyn grimaced at the all-too-familiar tone. "Uh—she sat next to me on the plane."

"Is this the boyfriend?" Patty ambled up with a smirk. "Well, Addisyn. I don't blame you for crossing international borders for this one. He's just as good-looking as you said."

Heat glowed to her cheeks, and she risked a glance at Darius only to catch his grin. She cleared her throat. "Yes. He's special."

"Well, good luck, Addisyn." Patty's expression turned more serious. "I hope you learn how to lead."

"What did she mean by that?" Darius cocked his head as she disappeared into the crowd.

"Oh—" For a moment, uncertainty squeezed her again, but she shrugged it away. No crazy old woman could dampen her spirits—not when she was standing at the gateway of a whole new world. She smiled and reached for Darius's hand, tugging him into the concourse. "Nothing. Just a conversation we had on the flight. Let's get my bags."

△△   △△   △△

LIKE AVERY'S OWN well-worn pair of hiking boots, the routine was a familiar fit. A predictable path over the mountains of her life.

Avery tapped her pencil on the clipboard and gave a satisfied nod. Monday—inventory day—was over. Stretching her arms as much as she could in the narrow space, she glanced at the boxes around her. The whole week's worth of new merchandise at the outdoors store. All meticulously marked, priced, and recorded.

Since she'd come to Estes Park over a year and a half ago and begun working at Laz Jobe's outdoors store, the days had marched through each week with a purposeful predictability. Monday was inventory day, when she brought order out of the chaos of new shipments that were crammed into the back room during the rest of the week. Tuesday was bulk restocking, Wednesday was promotion and advertising, and Thursday was placing new orders. On Friday morning, she helped Laz with the end-of-week accounting.

It was all as routine as the rotation of the earth. Which was fine. She'd always sought structure, after all. But on Friday afternoons, she stepped out of the sequence and headed instead to volunteer at Skyla Wingo's raptor center—which was rapidly becoming her favorite part of the week.

"Miz Avery?" Laz's hearty voice boomed into the back room.

"In here!" Avery turned toward the doorway just as Laz ducked inside. A burly fellow who stood well over six feet tall, he seemed to absorb all the air in the small space.

"Past five thirty, girl."

"I know." Avery gestured at the inventory sheet. "I wanted to finish up inventory."

Laz's bushy eyebrows drew together. "Them boxes'll still be there tomorrow, Miz Avery. Ain't no reason to stay at work for 'em."

As if it mattered what time she arrived home. Avery simply gave a lukewarm smile. "It's fine. I promise."

"I dunno, girl." Laz tipped his head to one side, an almost fatherly concern wrinkling his forehead. "Seems to me 'zif yer here more than yer not these days."

He was right, but she couldn't tell him why. Not without explaining the hollow ache that had begun to bleed through the pages of her life. Instead she just shrugged. "If you would come into the twenty-first century and run this store out of a computer instead of a notebook—"

Laz flung up his hands. "Don't start on me, gal. I'd rather trust paper than them fancy machines."

The argument was yet another piece of the predictability of the store, and she'd long ago given up on ever winning it. She just smiled and handed him the inventory pages. "Well, here's the *paper*, if you want to look over it."

Laz folded the papers without a second glance and stuffed them into the pocket of his shirt. "Thank you, Miz Avery, but I trust you. You know I got no hankerin' to spend more time on the bizness side o' things than's absolutely necess'ry."

Avery laughed and ducked past him into the front of the store. "That's what I'm here for."

"The Good Lord dropped you here, that's for sure." Laz shook his head admiringly as he followed her. "I been runnin' this store for ten years, an' you know a heckuva lot more than I do 'bout it now."

"Not true, but I'm happy to help."

"Heard anythin' from yer sister?"

Addisyn. The reason Avery didn't mind sitting in a stuffy closet packed with cardboard boxes an hour past closing time. Her smile slipped. "She's fine." Or so she assumed, since Addisyn's only communication since she'd left was a quick text she'd sent from the airport. Two days ago.

"Good." Laz sighed. "Didn't think I'd miss seein' her perky face around here, but I sure 'nuff do."

He wasn't the only one. Avery forced the shadow from her mind and glanced instead at her black Lab, smiling as the dog uncoiled from her relaxed position in a late shaft of sun. "Mercy, did you have a good day?"

"Don't she always. Jes' lay in the sun and sleep." Laz snorted, watching the dog stretch each back leg, then jerked his thumb toward the clock on the wall. "Now, it's a quarter to six, girl. Git!"

"All right." Avery snapped her fingers at Mercy and waved at Laz. "See you tomorrow, Laz."

A blast of surprisingly cool air—a downdraft over the snow fields up high—struck her in the face as she crossed the gravel parking lot and slipped into her battered truck, where the temperature wasn't much better. Avery rubbed her hands together and turned the key in the ignition. Years of driving the cranky contraption had taught her that it would be a good five minutes before the air emerging from the vents bore any faint resemblance to heat.

Sure enough, she was nearly to the end of Marys Lake Road before the inside of the truck began to warm. A brief spatter of rain speckled her windshield, and she shook her head. She loved these Colorado mountains in all their moods, but even she had to admit that they had their less-than-hospitable moments. The chilly winds crackling down from the High Peaks today were heavy with the damp cold of the melting snowpack. Storms had been rolling through every afternoon, and even now, the clouds swung so sullenly low that the fourteen-thousand-foot heads of the High Country were invisible. It was the kind of evening when traffic was light and tourists were few, the kind of evening when most people were happy to get home.

Most people—but not her.

What kind of weather was Addisyn receiving in British Columbia? She had said the temperatures were milder there. Better hiking weather. Although Ads would probably be holed up in an ice rink anyway, not out in the mountains the way Avery loved to be.

The bittersweet ache nipped at her, and Avery sighed. Addisyn had never fit well into Avery's simple mountain life. She'd tried, for Avery's sake, but there was no denying that the compass on her soul had always pulled her farther north—to other mountains and a different country and, most of all, to Darius.

Which was great. Really. Addisyn had overcome the struggles of her past and stepped into a bright new future. Just what Avery had always wanted for her—so why couldn't she be happier about it?

She was still mindlessly following the curves of the road and contemplating her sister when she saw the tree. She slammed the brake so suddenly that Mercy tumbled into the floor.

"Are you okay, girl?" Avery watched Mercy scramble back into the seat, then leaned on the steering wheel. "Well, we didn't need one more thing, did we?"

A fallen ponderosa pine was barricading the narrow road, blocking both lanes. Avery pulled over on the shoulder and shoved the truck into park before she dialed Laz. "A pine tree across Marys Lake Road." She squinted for a landmark in the deepening dusk. "Just past that llama farm."

"Be right there." Laz didn't sound harried. Incidents like this were part of life in the mountains. "Jes' stay patient."

Fifteen minutes later, he still hadn't arrived, and that patience was draining away. What could be taking Laz so long? She hadn't been more than a few miles from the store.

It was getting darker, and the anxiety of being stranded—especially if a storm was truly coming—made every shadow longer. Maybe she should just try to move it herself. She flipped her flashers on and grabbed her leather gloves from the console, then patted Mercy. "Wait here, puppy."

Thunder growled on the far horizon as she jogged toward the tree, sizing up the situation strategically in the headlights. This close, it was far bigger than she'd realized. At least eighteen inches in diameter and spiky with broken limbs. She tugged on a large branch, but it snapped in her hand. No way would she be able to clear a path.

She stepped back and studied the tree again. Apparently it had simply uprooted—not surprising. This time of year, the ground was wet, soggy with snowmelt. Couple that with the winds they'd had yesterday, and the tree simply hadn't been strong enough. Now it was toppled on its side, its root ball reaching uselessly into the air.

A wave of pity replaced her impatience. Avery walked to the root ball and rubbed the muddy tendrils gently. "I'm sorry. You don't have anything to hang onto, do you?"

Suddenly the pieces clacked together with clarity. For weeks now, ever since Addisyn had started planning her Canadian trip, Avery had been troubled by a feeling she couldn't quite name. Now, here it was—the feeling of being uprooted.

She gazed at the root ball, but it wasn't the dangling dirt she was seeing. Instead, she was three years old, and her mother, with hands that already seemed far too eager to let go, was setting a bundled blanket in Avery's arms. *"See here, Avery? Meet your new baby sister."*

And then the baby in the blanket was a curious toddler, with wide eyes and a laugh that could light the darkness, and for the first time Avery had somewhere to lavish the love that was so often stymied by her home life. And then Addisyn was older, growing fast, and Avery was helping her with homework and driving her downtown and laughing with her over silly movies. Everything had fallen to her, especially after their mother was no longer in the picture.

And it had all culminated the summer after Avery's graduation from high school. She'd dropped every dream she'd had and instead focused all her energy on escaping their dysfunctional family and keeping Addisyn safe in the process. She'd thrown herself into the chaos of New York City, an adult at seventeen, trying to give Addisyn a stability neither of them had ever had. Every move, every plan, every sacrifice had been for Addisyn's sake.

But now, Addisyn was gone, flown off into a future where Avery was only peripheral. And Avery was as unanchored as the uprooted tree.

Nothing to hold onto.

A beefy pickup roared behind her, diesel belching into the air. "Miz Avery?" Laz shouted out the window. "You okay?"

She hadn't realized she was crying. Quickly she swiped the tears away before she turned to face him. "Yes!"

"Okay, stand clear!" He was already out of the truck and maneuvering a bulky chainsaw from the bed. "I'll have 'er out of here in no time."

Within thirty minutes, the tree was cleared. Laz shook his head sadly as he tossed a last limb into the ditch. "Sure do hate to see trees fall."

Avery swung back into the cold, empty truck that waited to take her back to a cold, empty house. She glanced one more time at the uselessly grasping root ball and swallowed hard.

"Me too."

△△ △△ △△

DARIUS HADN'T DRIVEN Callaghan Road in years, and he'd forgotten how much of an interesting driving experience it was. The narrow route slashed northward into the mountains, winding among their snowy shoulders and dangling near the valley edges. The nausea that churned within him as he drove, therefore, was completely explainable. Except the curvy road probably wasn't to blame.

Uncle Trent had started asking him to come by the center for "*a meeting*" since last week, and at first Darius had managed to put him off. But with Addisyn in town three days now, he'd run out of time to postpone the task. He'd finally be seeing his uncle—Addisyn's new boss—for the first time in—how many years?

He rode his brakes around a curve and fought the urge to make a U-turn. It was downright cowardly of him. Not to mention ridiculous. He'd already talked to his uncle on the phone to arrange the details of Addisyn's position at the center. A face-to-face meeting couldn't be that much worse. And the very fact that the man had offered Addisyn the position showed he'd been impressed by her performance with Darius at that benefit event in January. So surely he was softening some. Right?

Of course, Darius had learned long ago to never try to predict Uncle Trent. It was the very reason he hadn't brought Addisyn along today. He'd made some excuse, told her to rest after her trip, but the truth was he knew what a landmine this encounter could be.

He scratched his beard. He still hadn't gotten around to explaining the tension within his family. Partly because he couldn't decide whether to debrief her up front or simply let her get to know them without preconceived notions.

There was the sign. He'd remembered it with fading paint and several dents from a hailstorm. But now it was a sleek, modern piece with red lettering and a white bear silhouette against the blue background. BEARSTOOTH ATHLETIC CENTER. CALLAGHAN VALLEY.

He turned onto the driveway—now paved—and coasted slowly up to the main offices. Wow. The place had been impressive when his father had worked here, but since taking over in the last few years, Uncle Trent had clearly outdone himself. The basketball courts had been resurfaced, there was a new walking trail around the lake, and several new buildings had been added.

But he couldn't admire the improvements now, not if he wanted to be on time for his meeting with Uncle Trent. And if he were a single minute late, his uncle would no doubt exhibit the same lack of mercy he'd shown years ago.

He swung out of the car and marched through the front doors. Was that his cousin behind the front desk? "Hi, Tina."

She glanced up and raised her eyebrows. "Darius. Hi."

With her bold mascara and sharp-pressed office clothes, she was a far cry from the moody teenager he remembered. Even her hair was a different color. How long had it been since he'd seen her? "I didn't realize you were working here now."

"There's a lot you've missed." Her tone wasn't sharp or sarcastic, just a statement of fact.

Darius swallowed hard. "Yeah...so..."

Tina's gaze dropped back to her computer screen. "Dad said you were coming in today. He's in the office two doors down."

Well, apparently the moodiness was still the same. Darius sighed and stuffed his hands into his pockets. "Okay. Thanks."

He headed down the hall, past a glass trophy case, and tapped lightly at the second door. "Hello?"

A man's gruff voice all but growled from inside. "Come in."

The urge to turn and walk away overwhelmed him. Darius pushed the door open and forced a smile. "Uh—hey, Uncle Trent."

His uncle stood and studied him. Still as tall and powerful as ever, although there were some new lines on his face and the gray corners at his temples were wider. "Darius." He held out his hand. His grip still felt like a vise. Silence seeped awkwardly into the cracks between them before Uncle Trent cleared his throat. "Haven't seen you in a while."

"Yeah." Words dangled just out of his reach. "Um, the place looks great."

"Thank you." Uncle Trent stayed standing, even though the office had several chairs.

A couple more empty seconds dripped by. Darius swallowed. "So—uh—you asked to see me—"

"Right." Uncle Trent picked up a pen from his desk and drummed it on his open palm. The same nervous tic Dad had turned to during stress. "Is the girl here?"

The girl? Darius forced himself to keep his irritation hidden. "Addisyn, Uncle Trent. And yes, she's here. She flew in Saturday."

Uncle Trent nodded. "And that's what we need to discuss."

His uncle wanted to talk about Addisyn? Darius's wariness doubled. "Okay…"

Uncle Trent sighed in a way that didn't sound promising. "When I saw you two perform in January, I assumed Addisyn was more—qualified. In fact, I based my offer to her on that assumption. And on your recommendation." His tone didn't indicate that recommendation had carried much weight. "But then I did some research this week. Her competition history is rather unimpressive to me."

This was happening. He could see it. His uncle was going to back out on the offer—now, with Addisyn already in the country. Darius's heart slammed into triple time. "Uncle Trent. I promise you, Addisyn is very qualified."

"So you say." Uncle Trent sighed, the lines in his face deepening. "But at the same time, I see her competition history. She's been off the ice for an entire season, Darius. And even before that, I see that she's had two major injuries, and she never made it to Nationals in America." He hesitated. "As you know, I have to have standards for the training staff who work here."

Oh, yes. He knew all about his uncle's impossible standards—the ones he hadn't been able to meet for years. "But she's a very talented skater. Her technique is super solid. And—" He couldn't begin to list all the qualities that would make Addisyn an ideal coach. "She's very smart, and she works hard, and she has such a passion for the ice. It's not her fault that she had to miss—"

"Darius, she just doesn't have the experience." Uncle Trent's voice was still locked behind the same wall that had risen between them for years. "I don't know that she has the qualifications to be working as a representative of this center."

His urgency doubled. Addisyn had left her whole life in America, coming here on the promise of a job that he'd arranged. He couldn't let it all fall through. "But—she's competed her whole life—"

"Just because someone can compete doesn't mean they're of high caliber."

The comment was a slap across the face. Darius sucked in a breath. "Look, Uncle Trent. I know how you feel about me, okay?" His eyes burned, but he blinked the frustration back. "And—I get that. But don't—don't take it out on Addisyn. Just take me out of the equation and look at her like you would anybody else." *Anybody that hadn't been recommended by your so-called sorry nephew.*

Uncle Trent opened his mouth, then sighed and ran a hand over his face. "It's not that." His voice sounded almost apologetic for half a second. Maybe not quite that long. "Look, Darius, you're very talented. Sure, you've had your—" he waved his hand vaguely—"issues." Darius braced for the usual remarks about his failures, but instead his uncle paused. The weight of the moment stretched between them before he spoke again. "Darius, I have a question, and I expect a straight answer."

"Of course."

"What's your connection with Addisyn, exactly?"

Oh boy. He'd downplayed their relationship when he'd first talked to his uncle about the opportunity, not wanting Addisyn to be forced beneath his family's microscope, but the time for that was over. Darius cleared his throat. "She's my girlfriend."

This time the silence stretched so wide that Darius expected to tumble into it.

"Didn't know you were dating anyone." Uncle Trent's voice was even more guarded than before.

How would the man have known, with the distance he'd created between them? Darius bit back the retort, ignoring the heat that crept over his face. "Yes."

Uncle Trent was back to drumming the pen on his palm. Faster this time. "So, are you two—"

"We're serious, if that's what you're wondering."

Uncle Trent tilted his head, a challenge in his eyes. "Then don't you think you're possibly being biased about her qualifications by your emotions?"

Just like Dad, Uncle Trent said the word as if it were a dangerous pathogen. Darius bristled. "Uncle Trent, my *emotions* have nothing to do with this." How could he make the man understand that his connection with Addisyn went deeper than some sentimental fling? "She's been—she's a huge part of helping me get where I am. Without her, I would have never given myself another chance." His voice cracked, and he cleared his throat. "I know she would do well here, sir. I'm asking you to please just give her an opportunity."

The pen accelerated for a few more seconds. Then his uncle sighed. "Okay. I'll give her a chance."

Relief sagged through him. "Thank you, Uncle—"

"But—" His uncle held up a warning finger. "She had better be just as qualified as you claim. And she had better be more competent than I have reason to believe she is, given her record."

If Addisyn's ability was the metric, Uncle Trent didn't need to worry. Addisyn was a natural on the ice—flawless and graceful. When the man saw her the first time, he'd have to agree. "She's very talented. That won't be an issue."

"Yes, well, another thing." The creases between his eyes deepened. "I expect her to conduct herself in a way that doesn't cause problems here at the center. This is a professional facility, and any time I believe she's not up to the standard I expect for my workers, out she goes. Understood?"

He hated the way Uncle Trent could always make him feel powerless. "You won't have a problem with Addisyn, Uncle Trent. I'll be responsible for her." He had no problem signing off on anything Addisyn did.

"All right, then." His uncle sighed. "Tell her to be here day after tomorrow. Thursday. Eight o'clock. She can get to work then."

And with that, he dropped into his desk chair and swiveled back toward his workspace.

Well, so the meeting was over. Darius was halfway across the threshold when his uncle spoke again, his tone slightly shifted. "Darius?"

"Yes?" He turned warily.

His uncle coughed, as if the words were caught in his throat. "Vera wanted me to ask you something."

Aunt Vera, who'd never stopped clinging to her useless hopes for a reunited family. "Yes?"

"She, well, she wanted you to come for dinner tomorrow night."

Dinner? After all these years? The hope he'd thought was dead stubbornly quivered to life. "I—thank you. May I bring Addisyn?"

His uncle's lips flattened slightly, but he nodded. "I suppose so."

"Then—yes. That'd be—that'd be great."

"Right. Six o'clock?"

"Six o'clock is perfect." Darius cleared his throat. "We'll be there."

As he hurried out of the office, his concerns were much lighter than before. As soon as his uncle saw Addisyn on the ice, he'd stop underestimating her. In fact, there was no need to even tell Addisyn about the man's misgivings. He'd hate to put more pressure on her.

But best of all, he'd been offered an opportunity even greater than Addisyn's. The opportunity to maybe take the first step back toward the thing he'd lost six years ago.

A family.

CHAPTER 2

There was no reason to be nervous, but as she dug through the clothes stuffed into her luggage, adrenaline throbbed through Addisyn's veins. She glanced at the clock on the wall. Almost five o'clock. Half an hour before Darius would pick her up for dinner with his family.

The thought doubled her already racing pulse. A monumental moment, and she was still scrambling through jumbled luggage in a cramped hotel room. Mostly because she had no idea what to wear.

What about navy slacks? And then she could add a nice blouse and maybe a blazer. Yeah, that would work, right?

She had to dig through three different bags to assemble the whole outfit, but once she'd donned all the components, she frowned. The outfit looked too—professional. Like the clothes Avery used to wear to her secretary job at the law office. Darius had downplayed this event as just a *"family dinner."* If his family were like him, they'd be down-to-earth, outdoorsy folks. The dinner might even be a back-porch campfire or a home-cooked meal in a rustic living room.

No, the outfit was the wrong vibe entirely. She unzipped another bag and grabbed her nice jeans and Whistler sweatshirt. Pair the combination with the suede boots Avery had given her years ago, and the outfit would be great.

She swapped her outfit and squinted at herself in the narrow strip of cloudy hotel-room mirror. Well, now she looked too casual. Regardless of Darius's views, this evening was significant. She'd be the object of double-duty scrutiny—both the new employee and Darius's girlfriend. She couldn't look as if she'd just wandered off the ski slopes.

Urgency snarled itself around the moment. She glanced at the clock again. Ten after five. Only twenty minutes before Darius came, and she hadn't even started on her hair and makeup.

She needed help. Time to call Avery. She grabbed her phone but paused with her finger on the icon. Wasn't becoming independent part of the whole point for being in Canada? She couldn't expect to ever learn how to make it on her own if she kept running back to Avery at every turn.

Besides, her sister's wardrobe consisted almost entirely of outdoorsy graphic tees and identical pairs of hiking pants in earth tones. She wasn't the best resource for fashion questions.

Addisyn lifted her chin and tossed the phone back onto the bed. Okay. She could do this. She tilted her head to the side, her creative spark returning. The jeans were still a good choice. She'd just switch out the sweatshirt for her pink cardigan with the cowl neck. Add earrings and leave her hair loose, and she'd surely be presentable for any family dinner situation.

She was waiting on the front steps of the hotel when Darius's Traverse rounded the corner. He parked in front of the building and hurried up the steps to meet her. "Addisyn!" His eyes sparked as he surveyed her. "Don't you look pretty tonight."

Warmth tingled through her, but worry remained. "Do you think it's too casual?"

"What?" His forehead crinkled with confusion. "No. You look great."

"Okay. Thank you." A guy's fashion advice was questionable at best, but his own khaki pants and flannel button-down weren't any more formal than what he normally wore. Surely her outfit would be fine.

"All right." Darius opened the passenger door for her. "Let's go."

The afternoon sunlight still glowed on the mountains as Darius drove out of the busy downtown area, but the lengthening valley shadows stretched long before them. Darius smiled at her. "You ready for tonight?"

"Yes." Another wave of misgiving washed over her, but Addisyn shrugged it off.

"Guess you'll start work tomorrow. You'll love the Callaghan." Darius smiled. "It's up in the mountains. Very rugged and beautiful. It's actually where the skiing and snowboarding were held during the Vancouver Olympics. Now it's an outdoor sports area."

He still hadn't mentioned bears. Surely Patty had been wrong. "It sounds nice."

"Oh, it is." A flicker of pain passed over Darius's face. "I used to go out there all the time when I was a child. Before my parents—" He cleared his throat.

It had been six years since Darius had lost his parents in a car crash, but the pain was there every time he mentioned them. Addisyn swallowed down the ache she felt for him. "I know."

"Anyway." He shrugged, clearly pulling himself out of the memory. "You'll love it. The athletic center is huge. My family started it over twenty years ago."

"That's so neat." Addisyn angled herself in the seat to face him. "Tell me more about your family."

"Well—" Darius flipped on his blinker and turned out of the crowded downtown onto a much quieter street. "It'll just be three tonight. Uncle Trent, Aunt Vera, and my cousin Tina. She's in university, but she lives at home and works part-time at the center."

"Cool." This was the first she'd heard about a cousin close to her age, and Addisyn smiled. Already she'd be making a new friend.

"Grant's my other cousin, but he lives pretty far north of here. All the way to Jade City, so I don't see him often. He's great. More like a brother. And Aunt Vera—she's nice. Always the peacemaker. Now, Uncle Trent is—" Darius made a slightly uneasy face. "A little—you know, a little exacting."

Exacting. Hard to read behind that word choice. "Well, I guess a coach would have to be detail-oriented."

"Yes, well—" He hesitated, seeming to form the sentence with care. "He's very much like my dad. Dad was his younger brother, you know."

"Really?"

"Yeah." Darius shrugged. "They were both skating coaches and both had a competitive streak a mile wide. And then when he and I—" He stopped, frowned, tried again. "My uncle and I—my uncle has some issues with me. We haven't talked much since my parents died, really."

How could anyone have *issues* with Darius? He was the kindest and gentlest man she'd ever met. "Darius—I didn't know."

"It's okay." His expression said it was anything but. "I've accepted it, more or less. Uncle Trent is just—he's difficult to please."

Addisyn swallowed. "Then—will he maybe not like me?"

"What? Of course he'll like you." His voice turned reassuring. "He'll love you, Addisyn. How could he not?" He smiled, although it looked forced. "Anyway, I suppose every family has to work through things like that."

His words twisted a knife inside, and Addisyn dropped her eyes to her lap. "Well—yeah." Now wasn't the time to remind him that she was far from an expert on the dynamics of a healthy family. Not when her concept of the word had been for so long condensed to just her and Avery.

A loneliness she'd never recognized before beat its wings against the inside of her soul. She'd never truly missed having family—not really. After the upbringing she'd had, the very word usually made her cringe. But listening to Darius describe his folks gave her a different view—a conglomeration of aunts and uncles and cousins and grandparents, stories separate but braided together in a tapestry of loyalty and love.

Oh, if only she could experience that too. If only his family would welcome her with open arms, and she'd find her place by his side among the people he cared most about. But if Darius's uncle was that difficult—

"Hey." Darius linked his fingers through hers, his thumb brushing the back of her hand. "Don't worry. They'll love you. Okay?"

She couldn't be too worried, not with his hand in hers. "Okay."

"We're almost there."

Addisyn glanced around. Thick ranks of evergreens guarded the road like sentries, broken only by spacious estates sprawling back from the road. Did Darius's family live in *this* neighborhood?

He slowed to a stop in front of a stone-and-iron gate. "Here we are." He rolled down his window and punched in a code on a freestanding keypad. The gate swung open. "Nice place, right?"

On a slight hill overlooking the road was a soft gray chalet that managed to combine both modern and rustic elements. Three stories rose against the hillside with wraparound porches and floor-to-ceiling windows that sparkled in the mellowing sunlight. How many millions of dollars were represented by the marriage of the expansive house and coveted location?

Addisyn's stomach dropped. "Your—your family lives here?"

"Yeah." Darius still seemed matter-of-fact. "This house has been in the family for a while."

If only she could snap her fingers and be back in her hotel room. She'd go for the navy pants and blazer in a heartbeat. Why, oh why, had she worn jeans?

"Addisyn?" Darius flashed her a concerned look as they rolled up the driveway. "Are you okay?"

"Of course." The words were a reflex, because she was not okay. She hadn't even walked through the door yet, and already her expectations had tilted sideways. But she found her smile. "Let's go."

A pair of twin copper sconces flanked the double front doors. Darius pressed the buzzer, and almost immediately the door flung open to reveal a woman with wavy blonde hair and more jewelry than an Egyptian princess. "Hello, Darius!" Her gaze flicked to Addisyn. "Oh, and you must be Addisyn Miles."

"Yes." Addisyn shook the woman's hand and summoned what Avery had always called her ice-rink smile. "It's so good to meet you, Mrs. Payne."

"Please, call me Vera. And so you're Darius's girlfriend." She tilted her head. "He never mentioned until yesterday that he was seeing someone."

What? In all the time he'd arranged her coaching opportunity, Darius hadn't told his family about their relationship? Addisyn kept the ice-rink smile in place, but her heart dropped like a stone.

Darius shifted beside her. "Aunt Vera, may we come in?"

"Oh, of course." Vera waved them inside and led them down a long hallway, her heels clacking on the rich stone flooring.

Darius leaned closer. "Addisyn, it's not how it sounds, actually I—"

"Here we are." Vera waved them into an elegant room, and Addisyn fought to keep her eyes from widening all over again. The tongue and groove ceiling stretched to an entire wall of windows, out of which the snowcapped mountains glistened in a pristine view. A tufted leather sectional was flanked by two matching armchairs, and a collection of taper candles flickered from a bronze stand on the iron coffee table. Flames snapped inside an embedded fireplace on the opposite wall, where two people stood talking. The whole scenario seemed somehow—staged. Like one of those shiny photos on the cover of a lifestyle magazine.

"Trent, Tina, Darius is here." Vera clapped her hands lightly, her bracelets clattering, and paused for emphasis. "And his girlfriend."

The air in the room hung heavy as the man and girl who'd been talking by the fireplace studied her. Addisyn swallowed and glanced down at the suede boots she'd been so proud of. They looked shockingly shabby against the hardwood floor. Oh, why had she come?

And then Darius's fingers twined through hers, strong and comforting. "Hey, everyone." He nodded at the room at large. "This is Addisyn."

She still didn't know why he hadn't told his family about her, but she couldn't dwell on that now. Addisyn squeezed his hand, drawing in his confidence, and forced herself to smile. "Hello." The desire to be accepted thumped in her chest.

"Hello, Addisyn." A serious man with graying hair and a hard-edged expression held out his hand. "I'm Trent Payne."

The man had a powerful grip. No resemblance to Darius in his face. "Nice to meet you, sir. Thank you for offering me the opportunity to coach for you this summer."

"I hope it's not too much for you." The man tossed an unreadable glance at Darius. "Darius tells me you'll do fine."

"She will." Darius squeezed her shoulder reassuringly, but Addisyn could feel her ice-rink smile slipping again. He hoped it wouldn't be too much for her? What was that supposed to mean?

Before she could decide how to react, Trent gestured to the girl behind him. "This is my daughter, Tina."

Addisyn smiled. "Hi, Tina."

"Hi." The girl flipped her dark reddish hair—far too metallic to be natural—over her shoulder and studied Addisyn with a guarded expression. "Huh."

"Well, anyway." Vera cleared her throat just before the moment could turn awkward. "Let's all head into the dining room."

△△　△△　△△

THE DINING ROOM was just as opulent as the rest of the house. Elegant iron chairs circled a glass-topped table with layered cowhide rugs underfoot. Just the crystal bowl of brass pinecones on the sideboard had probably cost more than Addisyn's plane ticket to Canada.

"Everyone go ahead and gather. I'll bring the food." Vera disappeared through a pair of swinging doors before Addisyn could offer to help.

"Addisyn—" Darius shuffled up beside her. "Look, I know what you're thinking, but there's a reason I didn't—"

"Never mind, Darius." She kept her emotions in check. She couldn't blame him, really. It was clear she didn't fit here. "We can talk about it later."

She turned away before he could see her hurt and slid into an empty seat next to Tina, who was absorbed in her phone, her thumbs flicking over the screen. Addisyn watched her for a moment, but the girl never looked up. "Hey, Tina."

"Hey." The girl darted an uninterested glance at Addisyn. "So, you're Darius's girlfriend."

"Yes." Although their relationship suddenly seemed wobbly. She changed the subject. "Darius said you're in college."

"We call it university here." Tina set her phone on the table and glanced again at the screen before focusing on Addisyn. "But yeah. I'm a business major."

"Business. That's impressive."

Tina just shrugged. "Whatever. Not like I had a choice." She pinched a piece of bread roll from the serving dish and popped it into her mouth. "Dad wanted me to work at the center. I'm not an athlete, and I don't have enough patience to be a coach, so that left the business office."

"Do you like it?"

Tina's snort was pure sarcasm. "You'll find out soon enough that *liking* something is irrelevant around here."

The moment hovered uneasily between them, but just then, Vera appeared, balancing platters of food that belonged in an upscale restaurant. "All right, everyone. Let's gather."

Trent droned out a table grace, and Addisyn cracked her eyelid open just enough to see Vera sweep into the seat beside her—the one she'd hoped Darius would take. And Darius, with unease hunched across his shoulders, gingerly took the chair beside Trent. Well, great.

"So, Addisyn." Vera fixed her with an appraising gaze as soon as the grace ended. "What do you think of our humble home?"

Humble was not the word Addisyn would have selected, but at least she had a conversation starter. "It's quite lovely. Darius said you have lived here a long time."

"Oh, yes." Vera helped herself to some salad, then passed the bowl to Addisyn. "Ever since Trent's parents passed away. Before that, we lived closer to Vancouver." She eyed Addisyn. "Perhaps you have heard of Monaco Steel? My father was one of the founders."

What on earth was Monaco Steel? "Well, this is a beautiful home." She surveyed the china platters of food. Who had prepared all this abundance? Tina whose phone hadn't left her hand? Vera with her ten pounds of jewelry? As wealthy as these people apparently were, they might have hired a cook for the occasion.

"What about your home?" Tina slanted a curious glance Addisyn's way. "Dad says you're from America." She said it as if the States were a wildly exotic land.

"Well, yes." Addisyn shifted slightly. These chairs were downright uncomfortable. Not surprising in a house where looks obviously trumped livability.

Vera passed the platter of rolls down the table. "I must say I was surprised when Trent told me you were from America. I always thought Darius would find a nice Canadian girl. But love is strange."

Addisyn blinked. Before she could respond, Tina spoke again. "Where at in America?"

"I'm from New York originally." She had three forks to choose from. Seriously? "But most recently, I lived in Colorado."

"Colorado?" The first hint of interest flickered in Tina's expression. "Is it like it is on *Sierra Song*?" Apparently seeing Addisyn's blank look, she sighed. "The TV show. Haven't you seen it?"

"No…" There was no television set in Avery's cabin. And Addisyn hadn't missed it.

"It's about this family on this ranch in Colorado. The daughter is, like, this fabulous model, come home to help save the farm or whatever, and she's in love with this hot cowboy. And they get attacked by wolves and stuff." Tina shrugged. "So? Is that realistic?"

Not even close. "Um, not really." Addisyn shrugged. "There are ranches, but I didn't live in that part. My sister has a house in the mountains."

"You never saw a wolf?"

"Well…no. But I did see elk and moose. One time there was a fox too."

Tina frowned. "Boring."

"Well, anyway." Vera was obviously the peacekeeper of the family. She leaned forward and smiled at Addisyn. "Darius can show you the guesthouse tomorrow. I'm sorry I didn't have a chance to get it ready this evening, but I guess you'd rather see it in the daylight anyway."

"The guesthouse?"

"Back there." She gestured vaguely behind the house. "That's where you'll be staying."

"Oh. Okay." She'd had no idea the *housing* his family had promised was on their own property. She should have known. Right under their watchful gaze.

"You'll need the code to get into the gate." Tina gave a satisfied smirk. "Six-letter combination. I set it myself. It's GO AWAY."

Vera's laugh was awkward. "Tina loves to joke around."

Except this was probably not a joke. Addisyn smiled tightly. "Okay." She glanced across the table at Darius, who hadn't contributed a word to the discussion so far. "Darius, maybe you can help me move my stuff over tomorrow."

"Absolutely. And I can't wait for you to see the center." Darius glanced uneasily at his uncle. "I almost didn't recognize it yesterday. Uncle Trent has made a lot of improvements since I was there."

"Which was six years ago." Trent sliced his salmon with a vigor. "When you were skating."

Darius's eyes fell to the table. "Right."

Trent deliberately folded his napkin. "Darius was an admirable athlete, Addisyn. You know, he won his gold medal when he was fifteen. The youngest age qualifying for the Olympics."

"Yes. It's quite impressive." Of course she knew about Darius's Olympic achievements. Did Trent really think Darius wouldn't have shared such an enormous part of his story?

"Same path as his grandfather. A three-time gold medalist." Trent's eyes flicked back to Darius. "It is indeed unfortunate that Darius lost out on continuing the legacy."

Darius's fingers tightened on his fork. "I know."

Vera cleared her throat. "Trent."

The sight of Darius's drooping expression set protectiveness pounding in her soul. Before her brain could hijack her heart, Addisyn leaned forward. "Well, it seems to me that Darius is very successful. With or without skating."

A shocked silence dropped like a curtain over the table, and suddenly panic pulled at her. What was she doing, snapping back at the man who would be her new boss?

Trent's eyes narrowed. "I guess that would depend on the definition of success."

Across the table, Darius was sending her some urgent message with his eyes, but she couldn't back down now. "Making a life doing what you love is success to me."

"See, I'd have to disagree." Trent's tone had dropped fifteen degrees. He laid his silverware down and pinned her with his gaze. "Success is found in persistence. Decisions that produce results and make a lasting impact." He stroked his chin. "Which reminds me of something I intended to ask you. You trained in New York, I believe you said?"

Trying to tug the microscope from Darius had only swiveled it onto her. "Yes."

"With the New York Figure Skaters' Agency, if I read correctly."

How deeply had he pried into her past? Addisyn twisted her napkin in her lap. "Yes. I did."

"I saw you perform with Darius, you know, a couple months back."

Trent buttered his roll. "I must say, your technique is solid. It was quite a nice routine. Not up to professional levels, of course."

Where was he going with this? Addisyn glanced helplessly at Darius, but he was simply watching the exchange with an uneasy look. "It was only a benefit performance. Nothing too rigorous."

"Right. Of course, the assistant coaching you'll be doing will require you to be at professional level."

What was he insinuating? "Mr. Payne, I've been skating since I was seven years old. I was the youngest member from my skating guild to medal at the Eastern Regionals, and I even competed in the—"

"Yes, so I found online." Trent brushed away her words as if they were merely dust on the table. "A good start, certainly. But coaching requires a different skill set."

She'd only wanted to defend Darius, and now she was sparring with his uncle while the whole table watched. "My technique is strong, and—"

"More than technique." Trent took a sip of his water before continuing. "Coaching requires confidence. Leadership." His eyes drilled into her. "Have you had any experience with coaching at all, Miss Miles?"

Why didn't Darius say something? Anything? "No. But I—I performed very well by all the U. S. Standards, and so—"

"Well, as you may have noticed—" Trent's smile didn't reach his eyes—"our standards are higher in Canada."

And in a sudden, sick moment, it came together clear. This family hadn't asked her here tonight to satisfy their curiosity about Darius's girlfriend or to form a meaningful connection or to welcome her to their world. No, they'd wanted to meet her for one reason only: because they were certain she wouldn't measure up.

The thought slammed into her soul with a pain she hadn't expected. This wasn't a homecoming; it was a court trial.

She had to say something, had to make her plea, but the disappointment was lodged in her throat. "Um—" She shrugged nervously. "I've never coached professionally, but I did spend a summer helping with the students at my local—"

Something soft and slick curled around her ankle under the table, and a shriek burst out before she could stop it. She shoved her chair back by reflex, nearly toppling as she grabbed the edge of the table.

"Addisyn?" Darius was on his feet.

"Something—" Before she could finish, the largest cat she had ever seen stalked from under the table and peered up at her with slanted green eyes.

A cat? Seriously? The room rang with a complete and utter silence as Addisyn stared helplessly from the cat to the people around the table. The ones she had naively assumed would welcome her.

"Addisyn, say hello to Canuck the Cat." Tina's smirk held a devilish satisfaction. "Do they not have cats in America?"

Canuck sideswiped her and slipped back under the table, leaving a swath of silver hairs across her good jeans.

WOW. WHAT A night.

Darius took a deep breath as he navigated the lonely, silent road away from his family's house. He glanced over at Addisyn, but she was staring out the passenger window at where the snowcapped mountains rose with a ghostly glow in the dusk. She hadn't said two words since they'd left his family's house.

He tapped his thumbs nervously on the steering wheel. Okay, so she was upset. And he could understand why. But what was a guy supposed to do in a situation like this? Leave her alone? Ignore the tension? Ask questions?

He cleared his throat, the sound loud in the ominous silence. "So—um—I know you're upset—"

"Upset?" She flashed him a look that stopped just short of exasperated. "You didn't tell them about—about us."

He'd seen that coming. "I don't talk to them that often." *Or at all.* "It just—it never came up. Anyway, I thought Uncle Trent was more likely to take you seriously as a skater than as my girlfriend."

"But I'm going to be here the whole summer. He had to know eventually."

She was right. He hadn't wanted to share his love life with his all-but-estranged family, but had it really been better for it to come out this way? He rubbed his forehead. Who would have known that mediating between his girlfriend and his family would be harder than training for the Olympics?

"So—" Her voice cracked. "Were you—embarrassed?"

"Embarrassed?"

"Because of me." Even in the fading daylight, he could see tears in her eyes. "Is that—is that why you didn't say anything to them? Because you didn't want them to know that—"

Was that what she thought? "No, no!" He pulled to the edge of the road and put the car in park, then twisted in the seat to face her. "That wasn't it at all. You're right. I should have said something earlier, but—"

"It doesn't matter." Her voice broke again, and she swiped her sleeve under her eyes. "Not after tonight." A strange kind of sadness wrapped around her words. "Your family doesn't like me."

"That's not true." He kept his voice calm, searching for the positives of the evening. "Now, Aunt Vera talked to you a lot during dinner. And I saw you and Tina talking too."

Addisyn bit her lip. "Yes—but even then—I mean, Vera said she was surprised you were dating an American girl."

Could Aunt Vera, just for once, not make such stupid offhand comments? "She didn't mean it like that. It's just that they've always had this dumb joke that I could only marry a good Canadian girl. My mom and my aunt used to laugh about it all the time."

"Okay." Addisyn didn't look convinced. "Trent doesn't seem to be impressed with me."

Uncle Trent. The elephant in the room. Again. "He's—he's slow to trust people." An understatement.

She nodded, but the tightness in her face didn't ease.

"What else is wrong?"

For a moment it seemed that Addisyn wouldn't answer him. Then she took a deep breath. "It's you."

"What?"

"I mean—when you heard him at dinner—why didn't you say

31

something?"

The question hung in the air between them, a finger pointing accusingly at him. The same frustration he'd felt all evening rose again. "Because—" Again he was back there, in the dark days after his accident, and his uncle's anger was burning away the little bit of fight he'd had left. "I wanted to say something. I did. But it would have made everything worse." Not just for him, but for her.

There was an uncertainty in her eyes he hadn't seen before. "I sort of felt like—like you weren't on my side."

"Addisyn, you know I'm on your side." He took her hands, gently rubbed her cold fingers. Searching her expression for the trust he'd always seen there. "I know it didn't seem like it, but the problem is—well, he's—you know, you're going to be working under him, and—"

"In fact, I ended up defending *you*." Her chin tilted in a slight challenge. "You seemed—I don't know, scared of him."

Scared? His soul stiffened. He pulled his hands away. "I'm not scared of him."

"Well, it looked like it tonight." Her voice was rising, her emotions starting to flare. "Why do you let him say stuff like that about you?"

"Look, I'm used to it." He heard the edge to his voice, but he couldn't force it away. "It doesn't bother me anymore."

"But you—you let him bully me. And that's after you didn't mention our relationship for an entire year."

"Addisyn, I didn't *let* him do anything." Once again, that familiar helplessness was snapping manacles onto his soul. Even now, his uncle was straitjacketing him. "It's just that it's not a good idea to start your job there by making him upset." Well, *more* upset, anyway.

"So that's it?" Addisyn's words were strung tighter and higher. "I just walk on eggshells all summer because you won't—"

"No!" She was tying herself into a knot he couldn't talk her out of. He blew out a breath. "Look, there's a reason I couldn't say anything. Let me explain instead of overreacting and—"

"Overreacting?" The hurt on Addisyn's face hardened to outrage, and he cringed. "How can you say that?"

What a terrible choice of words. "No, no, wait!" Darius waved his hands between them as if he could shoo away his clumsy statement. "That's not—that's not what I meant. I shouldn't have said that."

"Never mind." Addisyn slumped down in her seat. "It's late. Can you please take me back to the hotel?"

"Addisyn, please—"

"Darius." She folded her arms across her stomach as if pulling into herself. "The hotel. Please."

No good would come from continuing to argue with her here. His explanation would have to wait. He sighed and pulled back onto the road. "Okay."

The tension tangled the air between them, pulling the knots tighter with every mile toward Whistler. Why wouldn't Addisyn let him explain why he'd stayed silent tonight? Couldn't she realize that he was on her side? He'd been the liaison between her and Uncle Trent, arranging the details of the training opportunity, orchestrating the housing, even convincing his uncle to give her a chance during the conversation yesterday.

He glanced over at her. She was still huddled in the seat, her head bowed, and guilt trickled in to replace his attempts at rationalization. She wasn't angry with him—not really. She was only hurting and confused. With good reason, really. And whether she would let him explain or not, he had to try. He couldn't let her keep doubting him.

They were outside the hotel now, and Darius guided the car into a parking space. "Listen." He reached across the console and grabbed Addisyn's hands before she could reach for the door handle. "I'm so sorry, Addisyn. I shouldn't have said that to you."

The hurt in her eyes eased somewhat, and she worked her fingers between his. "Okay." She angled her head. "I'm sorry too. For saying you weren't on my side."

"No, I mean—I can see why you thought that." He sighed, the helplessness handcuffing him again. "Look, I wanted to say something tonight. But—" How much could he say? "It would have only made things worse. I've seen what happens when Uncle Trent gets upset. And—like I said, we have some issues, so if I'd gotten involved—" The mental image wasn't pretty. "I know it doesn't look like it, but I was trying to protect you."

"Oh." Her eyes softened just a little. "I thought—maybe you agreed with him."

That's what she'd been believing? The idea broke his heart. "Oh, Addisyn, no. Of course not." He shifted closer to her. "I'm sorry for what he said to you. But trust me—it's better to just stay out of his way. Go along with him, don't make him mad."

She sighed. "I understand. I'll try."

"Okay." He ducked his head, finding her gaze. "Anyway, the first time Uncle Trent sees you on the ice, he'll have no choice but to take you seriously. You have plenty of ability, and you're a natural leader. Perfect combination."

The comment should have made her smile, but instead the uncertainty in her eyes doubled. "I don't know, Darius." She bit her lip. "What if I'm not good at this? What if I'm not—"

Uncle Trent's words must still be pricking at her. Which Darius understood all too well. "You are." He circled his thumbs soothingly on the backs of her hands. "You're brave and smart and compassionate." He smiled, trying to see past her fear. "Like I said. A leader."

She glanced awkwardly away. "Well. Thank you." The ghost of a smile flitted over her lips. "Also, you didn't tell me they had a cat."

His laughter mixed with hers. "Another regrettable oversight. I honestly had forgotten about him. He's Tina's baby."

"I didn't expect him." Addisyn twisted her lips. "I didn't expect a lot about tonight."

The disappointment in her voice draped heavy over him. "I'm sorry about my part in it." He tilted his head. "Forgive me?"

Her expression softened, and she slid closer to him. "Okay." Her smile was small, but at least it was there. "It's really hard to stay mad at you anyway."

He breathed in the relief and grinned. "Because of my dazzling good looks?"

She laughed softly and swatted him on the shoulder. "Because I know you." Her face turned more serious. "I know you have my back."

She was once again allowing him to hold her trust, and this time he'd be careful not to drop it. "You're right." He stroked his thumb across her cheek, grateful that she didn't pull away. "I'll always have your back."

He bent forward and brushed his lips against hers, a tender kiss that mingled apology and promise. "I love you, Addisyn Miles." He pulled back just far enough to see that her eyes were bright again. "And the cat will warm up to you soon enough."

Her laugh was the sound of restoration. "Okay." A shyness crept into her tone. "Thank you, Darius. I love you too."

He watched her hurry up the hotel steps and blow him one last kiss on the threshold. Only when she was safely inside did he head toward his house, her kiss still resting on his lips like a blessing.

She'd forgiven him, and he didn't take that for granted. But what he hadn't told her was that the night had thrown him off kilter too. His uncle's remarks had sliced like barbed wire.

I guess that would depend on the definition of success…

After his accident, he'd been so broken. One bad choice, and he'd been left drowning in regret and wounded in body and soul. And there, in the darkest time of his life, Uncle Trent had turned his back. He'd unleashed his disappointment like a mountain avalanche and walked away, leaving Darius to pick up the pieces.

Alone.

I think you're afraid of him.

The words rubbed raw against the scars, and Darius locked his jaw. Addisyn was wrong. He wasn't afraid of the man. Not in the slightest. But he couldn't bear the thought of Addisyn being hurt by Uncle Trent the way he had been. And if he had to lie low, hold his tongue, and look like a coward to protect her—so be it.

That would be his goal for the summer. Keeping her soul from being snagged on Uncle Trent's rough edges. And one day, if he kept doing the right thing—maybe he'd finally break free from his uncle's image of him as the loser who'd let the whole family legacy come crashing down. If he could have another chance, he'd work harder and try better than anyone else could. And then his uncle would have to choke down his own words.

Every last bitter one.

The lights of Whistler were in view. He took a deep breath and let the glow from the city dispel the dusk settling in the car. Yes, he'd made a mistake years ago. But this was his time of redemption.

And nothing could stand in his way.

CHAPTER 3

Addisyn went to bed in her hotel room still completely off-balance. First was Darius's family, of course. Between the ridiculously posh house, Tina's prickly personality, and Trent's decision to spend the entire dinner belittling her, all her hopes of acceptance and approval had plummeted faster than a downhill skier on Whistler Blackcomb.

And then of course that stupid cat had to ambush her ankles. A Russian Blue, Tina had informed her with evident pride. As though that meant anything. A cat was a cat as far as Addisyn was concerned. Slinky, slippery, and sly.

Rather like his owner.

But the worst part had been the friction with Darius. She'd only been in Whistler for forty-eight hours, and she'd already proven her inability to handle any turbulence in their relationship. She'd jumped to conclusions without talking to him, lashed out before she'd ever given him a chance to explain. What was the matter with her?

And what about Trent? If he was as volatile as Darius claimed, how could she possibly meet his standards for the whole summer?

For just a moment, she could hear it again, the echo of Brian's voice. *You're weak, Addisyn. You've always been weak—*

She flinched and forced the accusation away, but she couldn't ignore the truth of the words. What had possibly made her think she was qualified to do this? Especially since she was recently escaped from her own disaster?

She closed her eyes and let Darius's words float around her mind again. *Brave and smart and compassionate…a natural leader.*

Brave and smart and compassionate? Those were words to describe Avery. Her older sister had always been effortlessly capable, a woman who could see into a person's soul and care for injured animals and hike ten miles without ever losing her breath. But Addisyn…well, if that was really how Darius viewed her, then he was in for a letdown when he realized the truth.

She tossed on the narrow hotel bed until eleven o'clock, her emotions stairstepping higher and higher the more she considered the situation. Finally she swung her legs over the edge of the bed and grabbed her phone. Regardless of her vow to be independent, she needed to talk to her sister. Avery would have advice—she always did. And most importantly, she'd be able to read past Addisyn's words straight into her heart.

But then she'd glanced at the clock, and her plan had crumbled. Colorado was a time zone later, and Avery had always been an early riser. She would have been in bed long ago.

Addisyn flopped back down on the bed and stared at the blotchy water stain on the ceiling until exhaustion dragged her eyelids down. By the time she awakened, her frustration and fear had sailed away on the buoyancy of the early morning. Things were fine with Darius. They'd sorted through that last night. And while she still wouldn't agree with that *overreacting* comment…there might be some truth. It was understandable that Trent would want to confirm her credentials, and perhaps she'd simply misinterpreted his questions through the haze of her own anxiety. She'd drive up to the center for her orientation day, and she'd see for herself that everything was fine.

She continued her internal pep talk the whole time she dressed and ate breakfast in the hotel dining room and then climbed into the car Darius was letting her borrow—a sporty Jeep Escape that had belonged to his parents. Ten years old, but under forty thousand miles on it. She put the car in drive and grinned at the power of the four-wheel acceleration. Well, Avery would love a car like this, wouldn't she? And speaking of, she really did need to call her sister. Maybe she could call tonight and fill Avery in on how her first day at the center had gone.

Assuming, of course, that it was a success.

She programmed the address Darius had given her into her phone's

GPS and set off, driving west out of Whistler and up the narrow Callaghan Road. Just past the intersection, a rectangular yellow road sign waved a warning.

BEAR CROSSING NEXT 5 MILES. USE CAUTION.

Oh no.

The road burrowed further into the mountains the longer she drove, but after months of driving in the Colorado Rockies, she wasn't concerned anymore by sharp turns or steep edges, and the little car held its own. And the scenery was absolutely exquisite—pine forests that lifted their arms in praise, rock cliffs that cut against the achingly blue sky, and of course the snowy stencil of the highest mountains all above her.

The beauty only increased when the athletic center finally came into view. As elaborate as the house had been last night, she'd expected Bearstooth to be grand. But Darius's description and her own imagination hadn't prepared her for how expansive it was.

The driveway ended next to a cluster of buildings that, like the house, fit harmoniously into the environment, huddled under the protective arms of pine trees. Early morning sunlight glinted off a lake in one direction, and the hollow bounces of basketballs came from two courts behind what must be the offices. The Canadian flag snapped smartly in the breeze above a shady picnic area. Even at this early hour, the place was already bustling with people carrying gym bags into the buildings, unloading climbing gear from their cars, or strolling down the dirt paths that branched toward the rest of the activities.

When Addisyn stepped through the door, her awe only doubled. Her images of "athletic centers" involved spartan gym facilities that blasted power rock and smelled permanently of sweat and disinfectant. But this place had a much more peaceful vibe—soothing, even. Soft folk music twanged from a speaker system, the decor was mainly nature photographs, and one entire wall was floor-to-ceiling windows through which sunshine splashed against the hardwood floors.

"Addisyn. Hi." Trent nodded at her from behind a stone counter that ran the length of the back wall.

"Hi." Addisyn flashed her brightest smile, determined to undo all that had gone wrong last night. "The center is beautiful."

"Thanks. It's the work of a lifetime." Unless it was just her imagination, he seemed more relaxed here in his natural habitat. He was even dressed more casually: black jogging pants and a sweatshirt coupled with a Vancouver Canucks ball cap. He glanced at his watch. "I thought I could give you a quick tour first, but something's come up. A family matter."

A family matter? Oh no, were there *more* relatives she didn't know about yet? "I'm sorry."

"It will be okay. I just have to make some phone calls. I'll have Tina show you around instead."

Addisyn kept her smile in place. "Oh. Perfect."

"Tina?" He frowned toward one of the hallways and raised his voice. "Addisyn's here. I want you to show her around."

"Okay, just a second!" The answer was muffled, but there was no hiding the irritation in her tone.

A catchy tune invaded the stillness, and Trent snatched his cell phone from his pocket. "She'll be out in a moment. See you later."

With that he was gone, sneakers squeaking as he hurried down a different hallway. Addisyn sighed and leaned against the counter. No telling how long *a moment* would be for Tina.

A soft chirp near the doorway caught her attention. She turned just in time to see Canuck creep over the threshold and jog toward her, his tail quirked in a question mark.

The cat came with Tina to the center? Somehow she wasn't surprised. "Hey, boy." Addisyn grimaced as he twined around her ankles, leaving another swath of silver hairs in his wake. But at least someone here was friendly. "You're a pretty cat." She'd barely begun to stretch her hand toward him when he swiped at her fingers. "Ouch!"

"He doesn't like to be petted by anyone but me."

Tina's grating voice was already familiar. Addisyn gritted her teeth and shoved her stinging hand into her pocket. "Okay. Good to know."

"He's very particular." Today Tina was wearing dark green leggings and an oversized sweatshirt that said WHO CARES? "He doesn't even let me pet him all the time."

Oh, there were so many potential responses to that statement. Like why have an animal that couldn't be touched. Or who could blame him for wanting to avoid Tina. Addisyn smashed her lips together. "I won't bother him."

"All right. I guess I should go over the rules with you." Tina tapped the countertop. "You're scheduled for afternoon sessions. Tuesday, Wednesday, Thursday. Sign in here when you arrive. Lanyards are in that bottom drawer. Be here by one o'clock because I start scheduling athletes at one thirty, and if the coach isn't there, it's not my problem. Got it?"

Tina's tone alone made Addisyn want to arrive at two o'clock each afternoon. "Got it."

"And employee parking is around back. Don't take up space in that front lot."

"Okay." Addisyn kept a poker face. As soon as the tour was over, she'd run out and move the car. Hopefully before Tina or Trent connected it with her.

"And then there are the bear country rules."

Addisyn's heart rate notched up. "Bear country?"

"We have a lot of bears come through the center." Tina's tone was still bored. "It happens this deep in the mountains." She slid a glance at Addisyn. "But I assume you already know the bear country protocol, since you lived in Colorado."

She couldn't admit that she'd let Avery worry about issues like that. "Oh, uh, well—"

Tina sighed elaborately. "Don't go out after dark. Don't leave your windows open. And when you're outside, put all your trash in those bad boys." She tipped her head toward the set of industrial-looking dumpsters visible outside the window. "And don't leave anything smelly in your car. No food or perfume or air freshener." She shrugged one shoulder. "Guy last year left a hamburger wrapper in his car with the window open. A bear came up and pretty much wrecked his car. Broke in the window and ripped up the upholstery. Even gnawed on the steering wheel."

If the girl was exaggerating, she was hiding it well. Addisyn gulped. Definitely not the most promising beginning. "I'll remember that."

"K. Well, I guess you're supposed to get the tour or something." Tina threw a rebellious look in the direction Trent had gone, then strode across the lobby. "Let's get going."

Addisyn jogged a couple steps to catch up to Tina, who was speed-walking down the corridor as if eager to get the tour over with. "This seems like a neat place."

"It's okay." She pointed to a glass door on their right without slowing her pace. "Weight rooms are in there. Hot tubs across the hall. PT rooms behind that."

"PT?"

"Physical therapy." Tina's tone indicated that should have been an obvious acronym. "And then there's the business offices. Where I work when I'm not in reception. Budgeting, accounting, booking, all that."

"That sounds—" *Boring.* "Important."

"It's a job." Tina stopped in front of a door topped by a glowing EXIT sign. "I had to do my part to keep up the precious family legacy." Sarcasm brittled her tone. "I learned a long time ago that you're not worth anything in this family if you're not athletic."

Before Addisyn had the chance to respond, Tina shoved the door open, revealing a gorgeous wooden balcony built around the trunks of three of the largest pine trees. Addisyn drew a breath of the spicy evergreen air. "Oh—wow."

"This is the outdoor adventure area." Tina was already clattering down the steps on the side of the deck to descend to ground level. She nodded toward the lake. "Canoeing and fishing are down there. Volleyball and basketball courts are up on the hill. And then behind us—" she jerked a thumb over her shoulder—"climbing gym and meditation garden. Yoga classes and all that."

The directions spun dizzily around her. She'd never remember a fraction of this. "When Darius described this place as an athletic center— I guess I didn't realize how big it was."

"That was Dad's idea." Tina veered down another gravel path. "He started this center with his younger brother—my Uncle Zach—twenty years ago." She glanced toward Addisyn. "Darius's dad."

Darius's father had been a founder of this place? Addisyn stared at Tina. "I didn't know that."

"Yeah, and at first it was basically a glorified gym. A training place for the pros. But it was Dad's idea to make it into something bigger. He calls it an 'outdoor sports destination.' He came up with this long-term expansion program and did fundraising and everything."

"So—" Should she even ask the question? But Tina was Darius's cousin, after all. "Why doesn't Darius work here? If his dad started it—"

Tina pressed her lips together. "He used to, a long time ago. Before his accident. But now he and Dad have issues. You'd have to talk to him about that." She shrugged as if the matter were closed and marched toward a smaller building. "Now, I guess this is the part that interests you, huh? Let me show you the rink."

△△ △△ △△

WHEN TINA PUSHED open the heavy door, all of Addisyn's irritation and uncertainty dissolved. The room was entirely filled with a state-of-the-art ice rink, lit by fluorescent fixtures and ringed by modern aluminum bleachers.

Tina was watching her, so she couldn't show the depth of her delight. "Wow." She trailed her fingertips along the railing, drinking in the vision of that polished, perfect ice. "This is gorgeous."

"Yeah, I guess you'll be coaching here." Tina shrugged. "If you're up for it."

And just like that, her delight turned sour again. "Up for it?"

"Up for dealing with Dad all summer." Tina flipped her hair over her shoulder. "Trust me, he's not impressed."

"What do you mean?"

Tina shrugged with a snide smile. "You heard him last night, didn't you?" Before Addisyn could respond, she grabbed a stack of papers off the railing around the rink. "Here. The coaching roster."

Addisyn skimmed the sheet. Seven names, all at the junior level. Easy, so far. She glanced at the coach's name and frowned. "Mark Tesson?"

Tina shrugged. "Our resident coach."

"So—" The sinking feeling was back, stronger this time. "Where's my roster?"

"I guess you'll just be helping him."

Addisyn gripped the paper. "Wait a minute. I was supposed to take

43

half of the total clients for—"

"All I know is Dad came in this morning and told me to switch your clients to Mark." Tina made a face. "I had to rework that whole chart and print new copies. It took forever."

So Trent had taken all her clients away from her before she'd even started? "Why?"

"Because Dad still makes me use this dinosaur software program, so every time I try to edit a spreadsheet, I have to first save it as a—"

"No, why did he take my clients away?"

"Oh. That." Tina shrugged. "Look, I don't make the decisions, okay? He's probably just worried about your experience. Especially after last night."

The same insecurity from dinner was creeping up behind her again, but Addisyn clenched her jaw, shoving it back. "Look, I get that I haven't coached before. But I know what I'm doing." The ice was the one place where she never made mistakes.

"Not my problem."

Should she scream or cry or maybe just shake Tina until her bad attitude fell off? "Well, you know what? It doesn't matter." Frustration all but choked her. She hadn't even started yet, and the cards were already stacked against her. "This isn't what I was promised. I'll talk to your dad."

"I wouldn't bother." Tina gave a sardonic smile. "Welcome to the family, Addisyn."

Before Addisyn could respond, the door scraped open, and Trent peered inside. "Tina? Addisyn?"

"Over here!" Tina's tone had magically transformed into innocence.

"Thought I might find you two in here." Trent's brow was furrowed with distraction. "Listen, the phone call was from—"

"Mr. Payne." Interrupting was probably a bad idea, but she had to know what was going on. "I'm sorry, but Tina has been explaining everything to me. Is it true that I won't be coaching? I was told that—"

"Just a moment." Trent held up his hand and turned to his daughter. "Tina, your cousin is coming here. She'll be spending the summer with us."

"*Kenzie's* coming *here*?" Tina's voice was just short of a yelp. "For the whole summer?"

"Tina!" Trent frowned at her. "She's going to be training here at the facility." He turned to Addisyn. "Kenzie is my sister's daughter. They live in Montreal, so we don't see them very often."

"Which is a relief." Tina crossed her arms.

Trent kept his focus on Addisyn. "She's been skating since she was ten."

"But why is she coming here?" Tina narrowed her eyes. "Isn't she still in school anyway?"

"She's finishing the semester online." Trent's tone carried a warning. "Her mom thought this would be a good environment for her. She'll be flying into Vancouver tomorrow afternoon. Anyway—" He cleared his throat. "You will be responsible for her coaching, Addisyn."

Addisyn blinked. He was giving her responsibility for his niece's coaching? After he'd expressed doubts about her qualifications? "I—what?"

"She needs some—" He hesitated. "Specialized coaching. She's coming back from a season of, uh, injury. I'll be her coach of record, but you'll be conducting day-to-day training for her."

None of this made sense, given the morning's news. "I—I'm sorry." She gripped the papers tighter. "Tina was just telling me that—my roster had been given to Mr. Tesson, so—"

"Right. An adjustment I made this morning, once I knew Kenzie was coming." Again, Trent seemed to be choosing the words he said from among many that he didn't. "As I said, she'll need a great deal of help. Careful monitoring, a rigorous training program. I felt that you should be the one to lead that effort."

Specialized coaching? She wasn't qualified to work as the head coach for a competitive skater, much less one already struggling. Trent knew that. Why was he putting her in this position?

Tina wrinkled her nose. "But didn't she go crazy or something? Back last—"

"Tina!" Trent shot her a final exasperated glance and looked at Addisyn. "Well? Can you handle that?"

There was a challenge in his eyes. Was that what this was? A test? Addisyn squared her shoulders. "I—of course." In two minutes, she'd gone from being all but fired to now managing the specialized coaching of a reportedly crazy girl coming back from injury. "I'll be, uh, happy to take on her case."

"Great." Trent rubbed his hands together. "Like I said, this is going to be a touchy season for her. You'll need to help her build back her stamina, technique, all of that."

"Well, what fun for you, Addisyn." Tina's smile reminded Addisyn of Canuck. "Like I was saying. Welcome to the family."

△△ △△ △△

BACK HOME AFTER another long day at work. Avery turned off her truck and propped her elbows on the steering wheel. Time to go inside the cabin.

She studied the home that had always been her mountain sanctuary, the place where she'd found the peace that had eluded her in her previous chaotic life. Tonight, it looked more sad than serene. Huddled against the mountainside, shivering in the still-cold winds. And so dark. No warm glow from the windows, no smoke curling from the chimney, no other headlights turning in the driveway. And most importantly—no Addisyn.

The faint heat that had lingered in the truck was rapidly draining away. Beside her, Mercy whined softly. Avery stepped out and jogged across the dry grass. As soon as she stepped into the hollow house, she began flipping light switches. Part of her still expected to see Addisyn somewhere—making a mess with some disastrous cooking attempt, sprawled on the couch with one of her dog-eared romance novels, or waiting to tell Avery all about her day.

Mercy leaned against her leg, and Avery rubbed her ears. "I know, girl. You miss Ads too, don't you?"

She was just hanging up her coat when John Denver's "Rocky Mountain High" twanged from her pocket. Could it be—yes! Addisyn was calling. "Hello?"

"Hey, Mountain Girl!"

Mountain Girl. The sort of nickname Avery would never have allowed from anyone else but cherished from her sister. She laughed and dropped into one of the dining room chairs. "Ads. I've been waiting to hear from you."

46

"I know. I've been meaning to call." Addisyn hesitated. "Things have been—busy."

Too busy for her. But she wouldn't allow the admission to hurt. "Yeah—I'm sure it's been hectic." She soothed her hand over Mercy's thick coat. "So how's Canada?"

"Everything's—good."

Did Addisyn's tone sound off? Probably it was just the distortion of the phone connection. "Well—the photos you texted me looked beautiful."

"Oh, yeah. The landscape is lovely here. And I want you to come visit. Remember? You said you would."

She had promised, back last fall, but now—now she didn't have the heart to see firsthand how little Addisyn needed her. "Well, work is very busy right now."

"Okay." Addisyn was quiet for a moment. "Maybe later in the summer?"

"Yeah...maybe."

"Are you still volunteering with Skyla?"

"Yes." The thought of Friday afternoons brought a rare spark of joy. "We have a lot of juvenile birds there right now. The young ones try to go out on their own, and then they get in trouble."

Only then did she consider the layers of meaning to her statement. She cringed. "I mean—"

"It's fine." Addisyn sounded awkward, but not angry. "I know you worry about me."

She always would, but she was trying so hard to keep her fingerprints off Addisyn's new life. "I—no." She forced the fib out. "Of course not."

"You're not worried about me at all?"

Why did Addisyn sound like that? Avery chose her next words carefully. "I know you'll do fine, Addisyn. There's no reason for me to worry about you."

"Oh. Okay." Before Avery could pursue the subject further, a door creaked shut in the background. "There, I'm in my hotel room now."

"The same place you stayed before, right?"

"Yep. The Gold Aspen. They haven't changed anything. Even down to the hideous black bear cushions on the lobby chairs."

Avery laughed. "Well, you won't be there long. Didn't you tell me you'll be living with Darius's family?"

"Yes." Again, hesitation in Addisyn's voice. "They have a guesthouse. Darius is going to help me move my stuff in tomorrow."

"So do you like them?"

"Uh—" Addisyn cleared her throat. "They're fine. Just, you know, I have to sort of get to know them. Trent—that's Darius's uncle—is a little, well, strict."

Strict? That sounded bad. "And he's your new boss, right?"

"Right, but it'll be fine." Addisyn's tone took on a little more emphasis. "Just fine."

It didn't sound fine. Maybe Addisyn should—

Avery sighed and rubbed her eyes. *Back off.* She had to break her big-sister habits. "Well. Okay." Time to switch to a less prickly subject. "So, have you started your job yet?"

"Not yet. It's, um, different from what I thought."

Oh, this sounded even worse. "Different?"

"Well—actually, I'll only have one athlete. Trent's niece. She needs some special assistance, because she's coming back from a season off, and so—"

"Wait a minute." Avery shook her head. "You were supposed to be helping with a lot of skaters, right? What happened to that plan?"

"I'm—I'm not really sure."

So Addisyn hadn't even started her job yet, and already the terms had changed. This could not be good. Avery bit her bottom lip to seal her objections inside as Addisyn related the rest of the story to her. Apparently Darius's uncle had cleared her caseload and given her only one skater. His niece—a special case.

"So, it will be really great, don't you think?" Addisyn's voice switched to her artificially perky tone—the one she'd used as a teenager to try to convince Avery that her report card was better than it looked. "I'll be in charge of all of her training. It will be fun."

Her flaky younger sister was going to be coaching a client by herself? Who in their right mind would put Addisyn in charge of anything? "That's a lot of responsibility, Ads."

"I know." Addisyn's tone turned defensive. "I'm good at skating, Avery. I know what I'm doing."

"But—I mean, I thought you didn't have the training to coach without—"

"Trent is still going to be her coach of record. I'm just doing the day-to-day stuff." Addisyn's voice hardened. "Look, Avery, skating is one thing I do know about, okay?"

"Of course, but skating is one thing. Coaching is a whole different situation." So many times her sister had folded on follow-through. "You have to be responsible and dependable and—"

"And you don't think I'm any of those things."

"No, that's not what I meant!" Avery rubbed her forehead. She was too tired from work to be having this conversation. "I mean—you'll do great. Of course. And if you're fine with the job changing—"

"I am." Addisyn's tone was clipped. "I know this is different from what Trent offered me first. But it's not going to be a problem. I'm fine."

"Okay." So much she wouldn't allow herself to say. "Good."

Long after the call ended, Avery stared out her windows into the thickening darkness beyond. She'd spent her life trying to help her sister find her wings, to push her past the dysfunction that had stitched a barbed-wire fence around their story. And she'd succeeded. Addisyn was now just fine. She'd said so herself.

So why did that hurt so much?

Maybe because she knew what was coming next. Of course she wanted to see Addisyn succeed, but still, it was ridiculous to imagine her curfew-skipping, rule-dodging, logic-defying sister helping to lead someone else. The very idea was absurd, especially when Ads was still so young, so in need of guidance herself.

But knowing Addisyn, she wouldn't rest until she'd at least tried her hand at this. She'd have to give it a go for a few months, and then maybe she'd realize the obvious. Maybe—the idea brought a spark of hope— maybe she'd even come back to Colorado. Because when everything went south, Avery would be there to pick up the pieces.

The way she always had been.

Outside the window, the mountains were fading into the twilight. A hard knot wedged itself into Avery's throat. Really, why borrow trouble about her younger sister's situation, job change or not? Because Addisyn was right—at least for now, she was doing just fine on her own.

More than Avery could say about herself.

CHAPTER 4

It was 7:58 when Addisyn stepped over the threshold of Bearstooth on Friday morning, carrying a stack of skating printouts and an extra-large thermos of coffee. Two minutes before Tina's shift apparently started. Tina had said that Kenzie's sessions wouldn't start until next week, but Addisyn had hoped she might earn a few extra brownie points by coming in to work anyway. For starters, she needed to familiarize herself with the rink. After that, maybe she could help Trent or something. Show him she wasn't as incapable as he thought.

After an hour of exploring the rink and planning for next week, she headed back to the main building to find Tina. Today the lobby was empty, and besides a few wads of cat hair floating next to the heat vent, there was no sign of Canuck either. Where had Tina said the offices were? Addisyn headed down the long hallway, glancing in each doorway until she saw Tina slouched behind a desk, Canuck draped across the arm of her chair. "Tina. Uh, good morning."

Tina glanced up from her computer. "Too cloudy to be a good morning. What do you need?"

Not the best start. "Well, I just came from the rink, and—there's a section of railing that's come loose. I was wondering if there's any way it could be replaced."

Tina shrugged. "Dad's already finalized the budget for this year. Sorry."

Her tone sounded anything but. "But if it's a repair—"

"Nope."

Canuck hopped delicately to Tina's desk, perching on the edge as if surveying his domain. Addisyn sighed. "Also, is there a place around here I can get new skate guards?" She pulled her old ones out of her pocket. "You can see—mine are wearing through." She'd meant to buy some better ones before she'd left Colorado, but she'd forgotten. Information she was not sharing with Tina.

"There's a place down in the Village, but they're pretty steep." Tina shrugged. "The skate shop in Vancouver would be a better choice."

Addisyn blinked. "Vancouver?"

"Yep." Tina stood and snatched the skate guards. "Let's just run by Skate Central this morning."

"This morning? I'm not going to be in Vancouver any time—"

"Yep, you are." Tina glanced at the clock and slung her purse over her shoulder. "I'm supposed to pick up Kenzie from the airport around noon. I'm taking you with me."

A three-hour-roundtrip drive to Vancouver and back in Tina's company did not sound fun. "Wait a minute. Why do *I* have to go?"

Tina made a face. "Because I'm not going to be stuck in a car all the way back to Whistler with nobody to talk to except my crazy cousin."

Addisyn straightened her shoulders and tried for Avery's older-sister tone. "I'm not going all the way down there just to keep you company."

"Whatever." Tina dropped the skate guards into Addisyn's hand and shouldered past her into the hall. "But I'm not shopping for you."

Canuck twitched his tail and positively smirked at her with those sly yellow eyes. Addisyn glared at him and hurried out of the office. "All right! I'm coming."

Tina was already out the door and heading for a black Lexus that gleamed like a commercial for car wax. "Brush your shoes off. I just vacuumed the floor mats on Wednesday. And these seats are real leather, so—" Her eyes darted to Addisyn's thermos.

Addisyn barely escaped an involuntary eye roll as she swung into the shotgun seat and jammed the thermos into the cupholder. "I know how to be careful. My sister used to have one of these cars." Although Avery had never turned hysterical over it. Not even that summer when Addisyn had dripped chocolate ice cream on the seat—and then sat in it by mistake.

"Your sister?" Tina threw her a curious glance as they backed out of the parking lot. "Didn't realize you had a sister."

"Yeah, Avery." Longing pinched her for a moment. Why had she never appreciated how fun car rides with Avery had been? "She's four years older."

"So what's she do?" Tina licked her thumb and rubbed at an invisible smudge on the dashboard.

"She works at an outdoors store. It's up in the mountains where she lives. She does a lot of hiking too."

Tina wrinkled her nose. "Huh. Sounds boring."

Okay, if Tina thought she could dis Avery, she had another think coming. "It's not boring! Avery's really cool. She knows all this stuff about mountains and birds and hiking."

She was braced for battle, but Tina gave a sudden, surprising grin. "Sister solidarity. I like that. Grant and I are pretty tight too. Even given his strange taste in music." She rolled her eyes. "Can you believe he only listens to songs that are at least twenty years old?"

Addisyn laughed. "Darius is that way too. It's the eighties for him."

"Maybe it's a guy thing."

Addisyn relaxed into the seat. Only ten minutes into the drive, but Tina seemed to be calming down the farther they traveled from work. Maybe Addisyn could hazard some questions of her own. "So——" She took a deep breath, sorting through all she wanted to ask. "Kenzie. She's your cousin?"

Tina grimaced. "Yeah. My dad and her mom are siblings. But we're not close or anything."

"How come?"

"Well, I mean——" Tina frowned and flipped down the visor. "She and her mom live in Montreal. We never see them. And, I don't know, she's just different. You'll see soon enough."

"And she'll be here the whole summer?"

"Yeah. I really don't get it. The last few years she trained at the ice school in Montreal." Tina shrugged. "Her mom's a single parent. Maybe she wants a break."

"You said she was crazy."

For the first time since Addisyn had met her, a hint of shame crept into Tina's expression. She shifted uncomfortably. "Well. Not crazy like padded walls and straitjackets, okay? But—there was something that happened last year. I don't really know what, but I know her mom called my dad every day crying and stuff and saying she didn't know what she was going to do with Kenzie."

"But you don't know what was going on?"

"Nope. It was NMP." When Addisyn stared at her, Tina shrugged. "Not My Problem. NMP. Get it?"

The acronym was exactly what she would have expected from Tina's brassy temperament. "Yeah. I get it."

They'd already reached the Callaghan Road intersection. Tina turned right onto 99, humming along with a sugary pop song on the radio, and Addisyn pondered Tina's information. Surely Kenzie couldn't be as bad as Tina believed.

Right?

As they crossed the Lions Gate Bridge, Tina glanced at the dashboard clock. "Ten forty-eight. That's exactly eighty-seven minutes. I can always make the drive from Whistler in under an hour and a half." Smugness oiled her tone as if she'd just announced some grand achievement.

"Okay." Addisyn had noticed Tina's speedometer creeping past the limit on a number of occasions, but no need to point that out. "When does Kenzie's flight get here?"

"Twelve fifteen." The skyscrapers soared above them, blocking them into the bustle of the big city. "We'll pick up Kenzie and then grab some lunch. First, I need to get gas."

Addisyn fingered the skate guards in her pocket. "And go to the skate store."

"Right."

Unsurprisingly, Tina hadn't left much margin in the schedule. After they finished at the gas station and the skate store, they were just pulling up at the airport when a giant red-and-blue jet roared to a nearby runway. "That's probably her flight." Tina hopped out of the car and led the way into the dome, shouldering through the swarms of people. "Help me watch for her, okay?"

"Watch for her?" Addisyn dodged a luggage cart, trying to stay in step with Tina. "I have no idea what she looks like."

"Easy." Tina rolled her eyes. "Just watch for the blonde girl who looks like a ghost." She surveyed the concourse, then pointed toward the escalators. "Hey, over there. That might be her."

Sure enough, a blonde girl had just stepped off the escalator. Hunched under an oversized purple backpack, she was scanning the crowds with the wary look of a turtle peering out of its shell.

Tina cupped her hands around her mouth. "Kenzie! Over here!"

The girl jerked like a startled rabbit, the worry on her face only tightening when she caught sight of them. Beside Addisyn, Tina huffed. "Yep. Still her charming self." As Kenzie shuffled closer, she raised her voice. "Hello, Kenzie."

"Hey." The girl's voice was whisper-soft, nearly buried under the layers of noise in the concourse. Tina leaned in to give her an awkward hug, but she remained stick-stiff, her gaze fixed on her scuffed sneakers.

Tina stepped back and frowned. "Kenzie, this is Addisyn Miles. She's Darius's girl, and she's going to be your coach."

Darius's girl? Addisyn forced a smile. "Hi, Kenzie. Nice to meet you." Okay, so that last statement might not be truthful.

Kenzie just nodded, still staring at the airport floor. Up close, she really did look like a misplaced ghost—ash-blonde hair and skin so fair it was nearly translucent. Even the watery blue of her eyes seemed washed out. Her jean shorts and baggy Soul Decision T-shirt draped loosely from her thin frame, as if she were poised to disappear.

"So." Tina removed her glasses, fiddling with the earpiece. "Let's grab your luggage."

Kenzie remained just as withdrawn while they wrangled her luggage off the baggage carousel and hauled everything back to the Lexus. Tina, apparently by sheer force of will, crammed the bags into the backseat, and Kenzie somehow squeezed herself beside them.

"Okay." Tina was wearing that uneasy expression again as they pulled away from the airport. As though Kenzie were a stick of dynamite with a fuse of unknown length. "Let's go grab lunch. Tim Hortons?"

"Sure." Addisyn glanced over her shoulder, but Kenzie was leaning back with her eyes closed.

Within a few minutes, Tina whipped the Lexus into a drive-thru line and pointed to the menu. "What do you want?"

Addisyn squinted at the brightly colored marquis. She wasn't yet familiar with the typical offerings of the famous Canadian chain. "What are you getting?"

"Roast beef and cheddar sub."

The car in front of them was edging forward. Addisyn nodded. "I'll have the same."

"Okay. We can split a bag of potato wedges, if you want."

"Sure." Addisyn glanced warily behind them. "Should we wake Kenzie up?"

Tina shrugged as she rolled her window down at the speaker post. "Look, I'm not taking any more trouble for her. I'll get three of everything and save hers till she wakes up."

The drive-thru line moved fast, and within minutes, they were back on the highway. When Addisyn pulled down the wrapper on her sandwich, the aroma of the meat and cheese filled the car. "Wow."

"I know, right?" Tina was eating and driving simultaneously and doing neither very well. "I'm telling you, these calories don't count."

A soft sound from the backseat made Addisyn glance over her shoulder. Kenzie blinked and slowly sat up, rolling her neck as if her head were too heavy to keep upright.

"Hey." Addisyn smiled at the girl and held out the remaining foil-wrapped sandwich. "We got you one."

Kenzie gingerly took the warm foil and stared at the packet suspiciously. "What—what is this?"

"Roast beef sub. Tim Hortons." Addisyn kept her voice upbeat. "It's good."

"What's on here?" Her tone was listless, as though she were already bored with the conversation.

"Oh—cheese, beef, tomato, lettuce, onion. A little bit of everything." Addisyn laughed, but Kenzie didn't join in.

Instead, she unwrapped a tiny corner of foil, took a cautious bite, chewed it reluctantly, and then laid the sandwich down on the seat beside her. "I don't want any more."

What an attitude. Didn't they at least deserve a thank-you for ordering on Kenzie's behalf? "You've got to be hungry. I know how airplane food is."

"I said I don't want it." Her voice was still flat. She leaned back and closed her eyes again. "Wake me up when we get to Whistler."

Addisyn watched her for a moment, but Kenzie's eyes remained stubbornly shut. When Addisyn turned back around in her seat, Tina was wearing an *I'm-not-surprised* face. "Well, there you have it." She poked the last bit of her sandwich in her mouth and wadded up the foil. When she'd finished chewing, she glanced in the rearview mirror, keeping her voice low. "Miss Congeniality. I had thought about hitting the outdoor market, but I guess we'll just make tracks back home."

"Is she always like that?" Addisyn also kept her words quiet, although there seemed no sense in minding her manners when certainly Kenzie had none to speak of.

"Pretty much. As far as I know." Tina shrugged. "Like I said, we're not too chummy."

But something in Tina's voice didn't match her flippant attitude. And when she glanced in the rearview mirror again, her brows pinched together in a complicated expression—worry and sadness and—was it a trace of guilt?

The next moment her eyes caught Addisyn's, and she blinked the expression away. "Well, at least I'm done with her when we get to Whistler." A hardness underlay her words. "From that point on, she's NMP."

△△ △△ △△

ALL THROUGH THE twists and turns of his life, the white roses had never changed.

Darius flipped on his blinker and put a steadying hand on the bouquet in his passenger seat as he made the turn. He'd already used the seatbelt to loosely secure the flowers as well as directed all the air vents away from them. Nothing would harm these roses. Not when they were for his parents.

The road unrolled ahead, trees flicking past the windshield, but instead he was watching his dad coming through the door every May 22, bringing Mom the roses she adored. In twenty-four years of marriage, they hadn't deviated from the routine. Even the year when Darius was twelve and training in Amsterdam for the month. There'd been no florists for a hundred miles of the remote location, but Dad had still managed to find a bouquet of white roses at an obscure floral vendor on a street corner.

The roses filled the car with their fragrance—the aroma of lost love and time run out and too many yesterdays. At the cemetery, Darius gently cradled the bouquet and made his way across the soft green grass until he was in front of the twin granite monuments. The engraving was as cold and lifeless as the stones. Names, Bible verses, dates that were much too close to each other. Details that couldn't begin to represent all that his parents had been and still were to him.

"Hey, Mom. Dad." His words were instantly swallowed into the cemetery silence. "I brought the roses." He gently tugged away the tacky plastic wrapping, careful to avoid the thorns, and propped the flowers on the ground between the monuments.

"I miss you guys." The little memories were prickling in his mind, the ones that jabbed more keenly than the thorns. The funky maple-leaf slippers his mother had worn despite Dad's teasing. The spicy warmth of the Christmas candles they'd burned every holiday season. The way his dad had been so exasperated during a Canucks playoff game that he'd jumped up from his recliner without thinking and spilled an entire bowl of queso all over the carpet.

Darius's eyes burned. He sniffed and scrubbed a hand over his face. He'd visited his parents' graves dozens, probably hundreds, of times over the last few years. Yet today, the weight of their loss settled across his shoulders in a way it hadn't since they were first—well, since he'd first lost them.

It was probably because of seeing his family the other night after so long. The people that were his last link to the past brought a measure of comfort, but at the same time, they were a backdrop against which his loss stood out in 3D. Especially when Uncle Trent looked so much like Dad.

He cleared his throat and refocused. He couldn't be distracted by his emotions, not when he had something specific to tell his parents today. "Sure do wish you were here. Although I know you're in a wonderful place."

He squinted up at the sky. Somewhere behind those low-hanging clouds, his parents were alive in a way they'd never been on Earth. Could they still hear him in Heaven? Did they watch the details of his life?

If so, what did they think about it?

"I've tried to do my best. You know I was—lost for a while there."

He couldn't bear to look at the monuments any longer, so he studied the flowers at his feet. So pale, so paltry. Nothing but drained-dry ghosts of a love that was past.

For a while after he'd lost it all, he'd practically been a ghost himself. He'd lived with one foot firmly in the past—in the whirlpool that had sucked away everything that had once given his life meaning.

But that was about to change.

He took a deep breath. "Mom and Dad...I'm trying to find a way to move forward." He waited, but the only response was a gentle wind shivering through the trees. "I—I'm in love with Addisyn. And—I'm going to marry her."

The words were like a tree of life, sprouting right there in the place of death, and the thought of her was healing and hope. From the moment she'd burst into his life, she'd been busy waking up his heart, chasing away his ghosts, inviting him outward into a world he'd shunned for so long. No longer would he pine in the ruins of the past. Not when Addisyn was tugging him forward into the future.

"And I'm changing some things." He pushed at the ground with his boot. "I'm finally sorting through all your stuff, for one thing." His laugh caught. "Mom, you'd scold me for keeping those boxes in the basement that long. It looked like a mess." The way all of his life had, until Addisyn.

"I'll always miss everything we had together. But...it's time for me to build my own life." Once more he gazed at the clouds. They were thinner now, a reminder that far above death and destruction, the light could not be stopped. "With her."

A bittersweet smile tugged at his lips. Oh, his parents would have loved Addisyn. Dad would have swapped skating stories with her, and

Mom would have copied down a dozen recipes and made sure she had a decent tea cozy—whatever those things were for. If only he'd been able to introduce her to his parents, instead of dour Uncle Trent.

Guess it depends on how you define success…

His uncle's words numbed like frostbite, and Darius flinched. He knew how his uncle defined it. By a standard so high that not even an Olympic medal had ever come close.

And suddenly his whole imagined future with Addisyn seemed as flimsy as a house of cards. After the ways he'd let his family down, what made him think he could be the kind of man Addisyn needed? He'd disappointed everyone else in his life. Would he let her down too?

He straightened his shoulders, shrugging off the ghosts. He wouldn't listen to his uncle's words. He'd made mistakes, sure. But this one thing he could do: he could love Addisyn Miles with his whole heart. And together, they'd build the kind of life his parents had always shared.

He took a step back from the graves. "I love you, Mom. I love you, Dad." His throat tightened at the fraying of the threads, the invisible turning of the page. "Thank you. For everything."

As he turned and walked to his car, he noticed something. For the first time ever when he left his parents' graves, he wasn't longing for the past.

Instead, he was ready for the future.

△△ △△ △△

NOON ON FRIDAY, and Avery was out the door. "Bye, Laz!" She poked her head into the back room and waved.

"Headin' out?" He grinned.

"Yes." Her smile leaped back, coming from the place in her heart that lived for Friday afternoons. "We've got three new juvenile hawks this week alone. Two Swainson's and a Red-tailed."

"Eh, spring's always the time." Laz peered at her. "You love them birds, don'tcha?"

"Yes." Finally, an answer that came easily.

"Hmm." He gazed at her with an odd expression of knowing, then

60

suddenly clapped his hands. "Waalll, then, git. Them birds are waitin' for you. Tell Chay and Miz Skyla I said howdy."

"Will do." Avery slung her crossbody over her shoulder and snapped her fingers at Mercy. "C'mon, puppy."

The drive to Chay and Skyla Wingo's raptor rehab center was a long one—farther down Marys Lake Road and up the winding, cliff-carved route that zigzagged over Lily Ridge into the wilder valley country of Allenspark. The narrow switchbacks, steep grade, and crowding cliffs would have made Avery nervous when she'd first come to Colorado, but after a year and a half in the mountains, roads like this could no longer intimidate her. Besides, for the joy of these Friday afternoons, she would have driven straight up the side of Storm Mountain if she'd had to.

Within half an hour, she was pulling up to the raptor center, parking between the gray ranch-style building and the rows of lattice-like flight cages that lined up like greenhouses at the edge of a tangled meadow. She hurried into the building, Mercy on her heels.

"Hey, Avery!" Hunched over a computer screen, Tyler waved from behind the counter in the office area.

"Hi, Tyler." A Colorado U grad pursuing a master's degree in conservation management, Tyler had been working at the center long before Avery started volunteering. Usually, though, he was in the business office. "What's up?"

"Checking some records." He brushed his straight brown hair out of his eyes. "Come take a look."

Avery peered over Tyler's shoulder as he clicked through a series of X-rays. "This is from that Barn Owl that came in back in February. Humerus and alula are both mended, and—" he circled the cursor around a bright white patch on one of the bones—"you can see the calcium fortification." He grinned at her and held up his hand for a high-five. "So she's ready to try flying again."

Avery slapped his palm. "That's wonderful!" No matter how many birds came through the center, she never tired of the moments when they were ready to soar skyward.

"Avery?" Skyla Wingo peered around the corner of the hallway, her dark hair swishing over one shoulder. "I thought I heard your voice."

"Hi, Skyla." Avery pointed to the screen. "Tyler was just telling me the news about the Barn Owl."

"Yes." Skyla's strong features softened into her rare smile. "It is a sacred thing. She had the will to fight, and so she has won. Can you help her in the flight cage?"

"Of course." The flight cage was Avery's favorite part of the job—while each raptor practiced flying between strategically placed perches in the lattice enclosure, she'd jog along with them, watching their flight and making notes of any deficiencies. The process was designed to help the birds build stamina and coordination, and witnessing their healing was a kind of miracle. "I'll take her this afternoon, in fact."

"Good." Skyla nodded. "I will come with you. This bird is very strong, and you may need more hands."

"I'd appreciate it." Avery glanced back at Mercy, who had already flopped down under Tyler's desk. "Mercy, stay here."

"She will." Tyler scratched the dog under the chin and smiled at Avery. "We'll look at X-rays together. She loves that."

Avery laughed and followed Skyla out of the building. An unseasonably chilly gust of wind rushed across the field. "Cold today."

"As always at the end of the snows." Skyla hefted the Barn Owl's carrier and glanced overhead at the steely clouds that clung to the sides of the mountains. "The spring does not come easily, ever."

"No." She herself was stuck between seasons. "I guess not."

"But still, the spring comes. Always." Skyla paused at the closest flight cage and nodded to Avery. "Please release the door for us."

The flight cages were sacred spaces. Even today, with the wind whistling down the long lattice tunnel and jostling the perches suspended from the ceiling, the empty space held all the promise of healing. Avery lifted the lid of the carrier and carefully retrieved the blinking owl, holding her by the ankles just as she'd learned months ago. "There, now." She kept her voice soothing. "Ready to try this?"

The owl strained skyward, stretching her wings. Avery smiled at Skyla. "She's ready."

"Indeed. Let us see."

Another gust rattled down the length of the cage. Avery crouched, ducking under the wind, and then in the moment of release she'd learned so well, she flung her hands free. The owl burst down the enclosure, wings churning the air. Twenty feet, and then she fluttered to a stop on one of the perches, head twisting to examine her new surroundings.

"She did great, Skyla!" The joy of these moments would never lose its luster. "Did you see anything?"

"Only strength, as you have said." Skyla nodded, her keen eyes trained thoughtfully on the bird. "No stiffness, do you think?"

Avery jogged toward the owl and clapped her hands, sending the bird swooping to the next perch. "Hmm—maybe a little, in that left wing? But that's just scar tissue, probably."

"I agree. Use of the wing will help." Skyla jotted down a notation on her clipboard. "Now it only remains to make her strong."

For the next half hour, they took turns jogging back and forth behind the owl, keeping her in the air long enough to rebuild power in her healing wings. After twelve laps, the bird clung stubbornly to one of the perches, and Avery trotted back toward Skyla, the sawdust crunching under her boots. "She's seeming tired."

"Very well." Skyla zipped her coat up higher. "We will let her rest for a moment and then try one more lap."

Avery leaned against the wall next to Skyla. A fresh gust of wind shook the enclosure, and the owl hunched slightly on her swaying perch, feathers ruffling. Skyla cleared her throat. "You have seemed lost to me these past days, Avery."

"Oh—" She shouldn't have been surprised that the intuitive woman had sensed her turmoil, but she wasn't ready to force her feelings into words. "I'm okay, just—"

"The stars are not in their patterns for you, I believe."

The gentle compassion of Skyla's tone worked its way into the cracks in her defenses. "Well—" How could she explain all that she was working through? "All my life, I've had a purpose."

"Yes." Skyla gazed at the healing bird. "Your sister."

"And now—" Again the wind whistled through the slats of the cage, colder this time. "She doesn't need me anymore."

"But the work does not end when the bird takes to wing."

"My work has ended." Avery swallowed down the ache. "She's—she's out on her own now. And she likes it that way."

"The trail ran straight, and now it does not." Skyla's voice was rich with empathy. "But you have walked a borrowed path, yes? And now you may at last find your own way forward."

"Maybe." No sense in telling Skyla that she had no idea what that path might be. Or if it even existed at all.

"Perhaps—" Skyla leaned forward, gazing intently toward the High Country with a questioning look. A few moments, and then she nodded. "Avery, I wonder if you might consider something to help me."

Avery blinked at the change of subject. "Um—sure."

"Chay and I take the ambassador birds to school groups frequently, you know."

"Yes." The ambassador birds, for a variety of reasons, weren't able to be released, but Skyla trained them to accompany her on educational outings in the community.

"We had a classroom visit scheduled for next Tuesday afternoon at the elementary school in Fort Collins, but Chay cannot go with me now. He is needed at the center in Denver to help with a release." Skyla ran her hand through her hair. "I wonder if you might go with me."

"Me?" Her doubts outpaced her excitement. "Skyla, that's kind of you to ask, but I've never done that, and—"

"You would do well." Skyla laid a hand reassuringly on her shoulder. "Please. It would be a great kindness of you to help me in this way."

"Well—" Laz would let her off work, once she told him the reason, and she had no additional excuses. "If you think I can help, of course I'll go. Or—I suppose I could fill in here, and maybe Tyler could go with you. He's had more experience."

"It is not Tyler I would ask. Because, for you, this is very—" Skyla paused, gazed skyward, found words again. "Sometimes, paths open of which we are not aware. We must hold the chance with care and listen to what the wind will say before we move forward." She turned searching eyes to Avery. "Do you understand?"

Not at all, but she trusted Skyla. "Okay. I'll be there."

A relief filled with subtle knowing relaxed Skyla's features. She nodded. "Thank you, Avery."

CHAPTER 5

Addisyn hadn't seen Kenzie since Friday afternoon. As soon as they'd arrived back in Whistler, Tina had dropped Addisyn off at the center and toted the uncommunicative cousin to the Payne house. And Kenzie hadn't put in an appearance on Saturday, when Darius had helped Addisyn transfer her belongings from the Gold Aspen to the cozy studio guesthouse—which was thankfully furnished in a far more down-to-earth style than the elaborate chalet.

But even though Addisyn hadn't seen Kenzie, she'd thought about the sullen girl ever since they'd met. Was she always that difficult? And if so, how was Addisyn supposed to coach her?

And the glance she'd shot Addisyn during Tina's introduction had been suspicious at best and hostile at worst. Why would Kenzie dislike her before they'd even met?

Addisyn was still distracted with the problem on Sunday morning, when Darius arrived to pick her up for church—his invitation. "Hey." He glanced at her expectantly as she slipped into his passenger seat. "You never told me what happened with Kenzie on Friday. You got to meet her, right?"

"Uh—yes." Addisyn bit her bottom lip. Kenzie was his cousin, after all. How much could she say? "She's a little bit, um, quiet."

"Probably shy." He frowned. "I guess. I don't really know what she's like anymore. Honestly, the last time I saw her or Aunt Tracy—that's her mom—was at my parents' funerals. So, six years ago."

Hmm. "What was she like then?"

"Kinda quiet, like you said. Mostly kept to herself. But back then, she would have been—what, ten? Eleven?" He shrugged. "Kids change."

"Yeah." Most likely that was the problem. Maybe Kenzie hadn't yet grown into her sulky personality when Darius knew her.

"Plus—" His face was suddenly shadowed. "At that time, I didn't pay much attention to her. I was—well, I had a lot to process."

The wound from his parents' deaths was still unhealed, and every time Addisyn glimpsed that raw place, she ached to bring him peace. But before she could choose the right words, he pulled into a gravel parking lot near the end of a narrow road and cut the engine. "Here we are."

Well, at first glance, the church didn't look too threatening. A stoop-shouldered brick building—seemingly too small for the number of cars in the lot—squatted underneath a dingy white metal roof. A leaning bronze statue of a cross draped with an anchor tilted next to the front doors. On the other side of the driveway, a wrought-iron fence encircled a huddle of headstones.

Darius pointed toward the cemetery. "My parents are buried there. My grandparents too." He glanced away and wrapped his fingers around hers. "Let's find seats."

There were still almost twenty minutes until the service was scheduled to start, but people were already settling into pews and chatting as if the whole morning were a social occasion. A group of women clacked by in heels and fussy dresses, and Addisyn cringed. She'd worn her jeans again, with a floral tunic top this time. Underdressing was apparently becoming her pattern.

"Here." Darius slid into a pew a few rows back from the low stage at the front of the room and patted the space beside him. Addisyn gingerly perched on the stiff wooden edge just as an older man made his way to them and clapped Darius on the back. "Darius, how you doing, son?"

"Great." Darius shook the man's hand. "Mr. Myers, this is my girlfriend, Addisyn Miles."

"Nice to meet you." Mr. Myers smiled. "Ready to be in the house of the Lord this morning?"

"I—yes, sir." Well, now she'd just lied. In a church, no less.

Fortunately the man turned his attention back to Darius. "I guess you heard that my nephew's coming back from Vancouver next fall, after he—"

The conversation was a collection of names and places that meant nothing to her. Addisyn slumped against the back of the pew and watched the announcements scroll by on the screen at the front of the room—a men's Bible study on Tuesday nights, a fundraiser for the children's ministry, a number you could call to leave a "prayer request." Few of the terms and concepts were familiar to her. This place clearly had its own culture.

Or maybe all churches did. After all, how would she know? She couldn't remember the last time she'd been inside one. Her atheist father had used God's name as nothing more than an expletive. Brian had frequently sneered at people of faith as fumbling fools who swapped logic for emotion. And even Avery, though her faith was as genuine as a gold nugget, didn't go to church. She'd always said she preferred to connect with God in the world He'd created rather than in the buildings people had made, and Addisyn could understand that viewpoint.

But regardless of how they lived it out, there was no denying that faith was a cornerstone for both Avery and Darius—undergirding their lives like the bedrock that lifted the mountains. And it was seeing both of them sink their souls into the solid ground that had first moved Addisyn to reach for the rock herself. But still, compared to Avery's and Darius's faith, her own was as feeble as a candle next to a wildfire.

"Well, I'm here." Tina suddenly flopped beside her with a dramatic sigh. "Wow. What a weekend."

So Darius's family went to this church too. Was there no escaping them? "Hey." Addisyn glanced around warily. "How's Kenzie?"

Tina rolled her eyes. "She's sick, apparently." She propped her ankle on her knee and yanked off one of her glossy black heels. "Ugh. Only ten minutes in, and my feet are already killing me."

Addisyn was still focused on the first part. "Wait, she's sick?" So she'd been exposed to Kenzie's germs for a ninety-minute car ride on Friday. Oh boy.

"Environmental. Sinus or something." Tina shrugged. "She tried Benadryl, but it doesn't seem to be helping. Probably the change of weather, especially this season. Spring runs hot and cold."

Addisyn refrained from pointing out that it wasn't the only one.

Tina rubbed her bare heels. "You don't think anybody will notice if I leave these off during church, do you?"

As if anyone were paying that much attention to Tina's footwear choices. "I think it will be okay."

"At least Mom and Dad won't see. They're sitting in the back." Tina made a face. "I don't really enjoy this anyway. Too stuffy for me." She eyed Addisyn. "What about you? Are you, like, a spiritual person?"

"I—well, I wouldn't say *spiritual*." That designation sounded too lofty, as if she were someone who actually felt a connection with the divine, the way Avery did. She glanced again at the pulpit, at the weathered cross carved deep into the heart of the wood. "Um—I've seen grace. More times than I ever expected. And that—changed me, I guess."

She braced for Tina to pounce on her less-than-theological explanation, but the girl nodded with a surprising hint of respect. "I like that. Good for you. I guess I'd say the same."

Addisyn was about to ask Tina another question when the lights dimmed, and the conversation dwindled as a man with a white goatee took the stage. "Good morning!" The crowd murmured a response, and he smiled. "Let's worship together."

Everyone stood as if by a common cue, so Addisyn scrambled to her feet as well. A small band filed onto the stage, and the music began—some unfamiliar song about love and salvation and the Lamb of God. The lyrics were on the screen, but how did all of these people know the tune? The best Addisyn could do was try to hum along.

The singing continued for fifteen minutes, with pauses between songs for prayers or Scripture readings. Addisyn was starting to tire of standing when Kenzie scuttled down the aisle and scooted in next to Tina. Her eyes were red, and she was sniffling. So she really was sick.

Or—had she been crying? No, surely not.

The singing stopped, and the white-bearded man launched into an eloquent prayer. "O God, today we come before You grateful for the gift of Your Presence. We ask Your blessing upon our brother and pastor today as He delivers the truth of Your Word, and we request that You…"

Addisyn tried to pay attention to the prayer, but she was stuck wondering about Kenzie. What did the girl have? Some highly contagious disease, no doubt. Wouldn't it help her case with Trent if she caught Kenzie's germs and had to take a sick day right off the bat?

She sniffed. No congestion. Good. But what about her throat? She swallowed. It did feel scratchy, didn't it? Or was she imagining things?

"...in Your holy Name. Amen."

The lights came up, and Addisyn blinked. She'd been busy freaking herself out over Kenzie's illness and completely zoned out during the prayer. Great.

Strike two at doing the Christian thing.

The pastor began by telling everyone to turn to Ephesians—a book of the Bible, apparently. Addisyn thumbed through the stiff pages of the little Bible Avery had given her for Christmas, but Ephesians seemed to be hiding in the tiny text. Finally she just gave up.

Maybe because she couldn't follow the verses, the pastor's sermon seemed complicated. He started out talking about being "seated in the heavenly realms with Christ Jesus," which sounded super abstract, and then rolled into holy living and harmonious relationships between believers. Addisyn glanced at Tina and Kenzie, tension like a forcefield between them. Harmony, indeed.

The pastor transitioned to something about cornerstones and temples made without hands, and Addisyn gave up. She slumped a little deeper into the pew and studied the people around her. Most of them were nodding soulfully or even making notes in the margins of their Bibles. Even Tina was staring at the pastor with an expression of concentration. Although maybe she was just concentrating on ignoring Kenzie.

Addisyn was really starting to understand why Avery lived out her faith beyond the confines of a church building. She couldn't imagine her free-spirited sister sitting through this ritual.

"For we are God's handiwork, created in Christ Jesus to do good works, which God prepared in advance for us to do." The pastor's voice boomed out suddenly, and Addisyn jumped.

"For every person in this room—" The man leaned forward over the pulpit, his words shaping into a storyteller's tone—"there is a path set for us by God. A pattern that is planned for us. A route of decisions and actions and consequences that we walk out every day of our lives."

Decisions and actions and consequences. Addisyn sank a little deeper into the pew. She was all too familiar with those. Although God didn't have much to do with the dumpster-fire choices she'd made.

"And that is the wonderful news for us today." The pastor stepped away from the pulpit and paced toward the edge of the stage. "Each move, each choice, each decision can become part of our story. A story of hope that God tells through our lives. And if we allow Him into our stories, then even our failures and regrets can have purpose as part of the glorious pattern."

Even our failures and regrets…

Brian's face flashed against her mind like a sudden slap. He'd been so much more than a skating coach, and she'd let him steal more from her than she'd ever regain. Was the pastor saying that the terrible decisions she'd made because of him could be redeemed? That even her greatest stumbles might have meaning one day?

Must be more of that *"everything happens for a reason"* business. Avery was fond of that quote. And sure, at times Addisyn had seen how God had woven things together in a way that was watertight against doubt. But Brian…Brian had been her own disastrous decision. So why would God be interested in making meaning out of her own bitter stupidity?

She hadn't realized that she'd been gripping the Bible, so tightly that she'd creased one of the pages. She shut the Book, and something harder than disbelief sank into her soul. Everything adding up into a beautiful story? No, that was a platitude to crochet on a throw pillow. Or a privilege reserved for people like Avery and Darius. Or maybe just wishful thinking, a nice fantasy to tell yourself when you were broken at the end of a long fall.

Because no matter how much Scripture that pastor could spin, one fact could wipe it all away: there was no way that the snarled knots of her choices with Brian could ever tie into a tapestry of truth.

△△   △△   △△

WHEN ADDISYN ARRIVED the next morning, Kenzie was already sitting on one of the bleachers at the rink, staring at her phone.

Well, if she was really this girl's coach, she needed to form at least some kind of rapport. Addisyn cleared her throat. "Hey, Kenzie."

Kenzie jumped and glanced up from her phone. "Oh. Hi."

Not promising. Addisyn put on her warmest smile. "Are you feeling better?"

Kenzie shook her head and sniffed. "Not really."

Sure enough, her eyes were still red and watery, and her face was even paler than it had been on Sunday. Addisyn frowned. "I'm sorry. You must be allergic to something."

Kenzie shrugged and sniffed again. "Benadryl's not helping. Uncle Trent's taking me to the doctor this afternoon."

"Well, I hope you feel better soon."

Kenzie just nodded, her pale blue eyes glazed. "Oh, and that railing is loose."

Addisyn clamped her jaw shut. "Yes. I told Tina." Enough said on that subject. She sat on the bleacher a cautious distance from Kenzie and reached for her skates. "So, uh, you're from Montreal, Tina said."

"Yes. Why?"

The edge to Kenzie's voice made her blink. "Well, I—I used to practice there. My coach—" The laces knotted in her hands at the thought of Brian. She cleared her throat. "My coach took me to Montreal one winter for a tournament. It's a lovely town."

"Yeah."

Forget it. She was done trying to break the glass of this girl's repellent personality. Addisyn stood and made her way to the rink. "Ready to get started?"

This was her world. Smooth ice and perfect conditions. Ice where she would soon stand and transfer her love of this sport to someone else for the first time. Adrenaline zinged through her. She had to get this right.

"Okay." She gripped the railing—which jiggled in her hand—and looked at Kenzie with a smile that hopefully hid her nerves. "Why don't you go on out there and give me some crossovers? Just to warm up."

Kenzie nodded as she finished threading her skates. Her first step onto the ice made Addisyn's heart sink. Any skater could perform this simple warm-up exercise blindfolded and handcuffed. Yet Kenzie's motions were jerky, halting, as if she were holding herself away from the ice.

"Kenzie, can you come here for a second?" Hopefully her tone reflected an encouragement she didn't feel.

Kenzie all but limped over to the railing and pulled herself to an awkward stop. "Yeah?"

"You're—" What was a nice way to say this? "You're kind of tight out there. Try to relax some."

Kenzie ducked her head. "My, um, my balance isn't very good yet. After—" She waved her hand vaguely in the air. "I'm trying to build back."

Right. She'd known that. She just hadn't realized how challenging this would be. "Okay. I understand. Let's do some long glides instead. Just loosen up, and don't think too much about it."

Kenzie turned and began the next exercise without a word. Addisyn watched her through narrowed eyes. Kenzie had blamed her problems on poor balance, but that didn't seem to be an issue. Sure, her movements were tentative, but she wasn't wobbling or leaning or grabbing for stability the way some novice skaters did.

No, her problem was something else. Something deeper. Something that was going to make this even more of a challenge than Addisyn had expected.

Kenzie eased to a stop at the railing. "Are those better?"

"Yes." The glides did look better. Not wonderful, but she was at least executing the motion. Probably all that could be expected for now. And anyway, she had to be as nervous as Addisyn was. Maybe anxiety was the only problem.

Addisyn took a breath and found her smile again. "Now, your uncle tells me you'll have auditions in August. So we'll need to start working on the choreography for your short program."

"I don't do any of my choreography."

Addisyn blinked. Brian had always taken the lead on creating her performances, but she'd still had a strong amount of input in the process. "Oh. Well, then this will be a good experience for you."

Kenzie's face tightened. "I don't know how."

I don't either. "It's not that hard." Hopefully. "Pick some music first. Do you have a piece you'd like to perform to?"

Kenzie thought for a moment. "'Blue Garden' is nice."

Okay. The Clearsound tune was overplayed, but it did have a strong melody. They could probably do something with an instrumental version. "All right, then 'Blue Garden' it is." Addisyn tapped the paper. "Now, I've made a list here for you." She'd worked on the outline all last evening. "These are steps you already know, but you'll need to master them again before August. So, with each one we'll start at a more basic level, and then we'll dial up the difficulty when you're comfortable."

Kenzie leaned closer, her expression intent for once. "Toe loop...Axel..."

Addisyn followed the line of jumps with her finger. "And Salchow, and a combination spin."

Kenzie bit her lip. "Triple Axel?"

"Well...yeah." Why did Kenzie look so worried? That number of rotations was quite standard, especially in Canada's competitive skating world. "Is there a problem?"

Kenzie glanced away. "I haven't done any of these jumps for almost a year."

Almost a *year*? Addisyn tried not to show her shock. "Oh...because...?"

"Because of my, um, health stuff." Kenzie folded her arms tightly around herself. "I lost—a lot of ground."

Kenzie hadn't skated in a year, and Trent expected her to be ready for auditions in two months? Addisyn grasped desperately for words. "Okay—well—" She cleared her throat. "No problem. You've got time to get ready." Actually she wasn't at all sure of that. "Let's just practice some of these steps now, okay?"

She slipped on her own skates and joined Kenzie on the ice, helping her mark through some of the easier movements, but the more they worked, the more tense Kenzie seemed to become. When Addisyn suggested a toe loop, she bit her lip. "I'm not ready to jump yet."

Not ready? Well, when would she be? Addisyn shook her head.

"Kenzie, you have to try this. Simplest jump, you know." She gestured down the rink. "Go down to the end and take some crossovers toward me, and then start the jump."

Kenzie took a deep breath and glided down to the end of the rink, then headed back, gathering speed as she approached the jump.

It was going to be a failure. Addisyn knew the minute she saw Kenzie tilt too far toward the inside of her blade. Her back leg didn't extend, and then she was on the ground. Spilled across the ice before Addisyn could react.

"Kenzie, you okay?"

Kenzie sat up and rubbed her elbow. "I'm done." She eased up painfully and pushed off to the edge of the rink, snapping on her skate guards.

Done? Just like that, she was giving up? "Wait a minute." Addisyn glided across the rink and caught up with Kenzie at the gate. "We're not done for today. You're not supposed to stop on a fall, you know."

"No." Kenzie shrugged. "I can't get it."

She gave up that easily? "It was your first try, Kenzie." There was an edge to her voice she didn't try to disguise. "You're going to fall when you skate. It's unavoidable."

"Well, I'm sick of falling."

And she was sick of putting up with this moody girl. "You know what, Kenzie? Nobody likes to fall. But it just comes with the territory." She crossed her arms. Enough tiptoeing around Kenzie's fragile feelings. "Now it seems to me that you give up too easily."

Kenzie's head snapped around. "If I gave up easily, I wouldn't be here." Her voice was low but cold as the ice. "Not after this last year."

"That's not what I'm seeing." Addisyn stabbed a finger at the ice. "When you get on that ice, you have to—"

"You have no idea what it's like!"

"*What?*"

Kenzie's voice soared. "You're some successful skater from America. Everything is easy for you! You can't possibly understand what it's like to be me."

Easy? Kenzie thought everything was *easy* for her?

Before Addisyn could respond, Kenzie swung her bag over her shoulder and marched for the entrance, slamming through the door and into the day beyond.

Addisyn sank onto the first row of bleachers and stared at the ice. That perfect smooth surface, now scarred by the tracks of the session.

Oh, she was off to a terrible start.

∧∧　　∧∧　　∧∧

ADDISYN TOOK HER time packing up her things and locking the rink. Anything to postpone navigating the fallout of her clash with Kenzie. Finally, she trudged back to the office and tentatively opened the door.

Behind the reception counter, Tina was stapling papers together with a vengeance while Canuck batted at the loose pages. "If you're looking for Kenzie, she was heading toward the meditation garden."

"Okay." Addisyn took a deep breath.

Tina flicked a stray staple toward Canuck. "So? Was I right?"

Addisyn fought the urge to roll her eyes as she watched Canuck spar with the pretend prey. Cats were so stupid. "Right about what?"

"That Kenzie's crazy."

Addisyn wasn't about to let Tina know how convincing that assertion was starting to sound. "Ornery, I'd say."

"Both." Tina raised her eyebrows. "Hey, by the way, I gave her a lift this morning, so can you take her to that doctor's appointment? I'm supposed to stay later here and help my coworker design some flyers on the computer."

Drive around with the sick girl. And especially after the exchange they'd just had. Oh, just great. Addisyn stiffened. "Um—"

"If you'd rather take my place with the flyer, that will work." Tina's eyes gleamed wickedly. "Jessica will be happy to have you. But get ready for her to ask about you and Darius in the first thirty seconds. She's had it bad for him forever."

Tina's personality had all the subtlety of sandpaper. Addisyn grimaced. "Okay. I'll take her to the appointment. Whatever I need to do."

"Whatever you need to do?" Tina rubbed Canuck's ears with a satisfied grin. "Well, that's great."

Before Addisyn could press the issue farther, the door blew open on a gust of cold air. Trent stepped in, rubbing his hands together. "Good news!"

Tina rolled a paper wad down the counter toward Canuck. "Don't tell me. You're giving me a raise."

Trent brushed past the comment. "I just talked to Dr. Smith. Kenzie won't need to see him this afternoon after all. He already knows what's causing her allergies."

"What?" Addisyn stared blankly at him.

He cut his eyes accusingly toward the counter. "Canuck."

"Canuck?" Tina crossed her arms. "He is a very clean—"

Trent held up his hand. "Dr. Smith says that cats often cause allergies. He believes if Kenzie's not around the cat, she'll be fine." He glanced at Addisyn. "Which is where you come in."

After the day of coaching she'd just had, Addisyn did not want to *come in* to anything involving Kenzie. "I'm sorry?"

"Well, the obvious solution is to let Canuck stay in the guesthouse with you for the duration of Kenzie's visit."

"What?" Tina's question was just short of a screech. She snatched up Canuck in a protective grip. "Canuck can't leave! He's very territorial. He'll be miserable without me all summer."

For once, Addisyn was on Tina's team. The idea of that cat twining everywhere, shedding hair on all her possessions, was unbearable. She cleared her throat. "I'm not sure that's the best option either. I'm not very knowledgeable about cats." And what little she did know wasn't favorable.

Tina looked at her with an expression that could have been gratitude. "Canuck is a Russian Blue, Dad. He's territorial and easily disrupted. Look at him. The very idea is disturbing him."

The cat was dangling limply from Tina's arms with a bemused expression. Trent pressed his lips together in a thinly veiled impatience. "And you have a better idea?"

"Well—" A slyness crept into Tina's expression. "Actually, I do.

Addisyn here was just telling me how she wanted to do anything she could to help Kenzie. Apparently, they've really built some rapport." She narrowed her eyes meaningfully at Addisyn. "*Whatever she needed to do*, I believe were her words."

Tina had braided her offhand remark into a noose. "Wait. That's not what—"

"So, you know, there's that extra bedroom in the guesthouse." Tina shrugged. "Canuck stays with me—where he belongs—and Kenzie moves in with Addisyn. Problem solved."

Problem solved? For Tina, maybe! Addisyn forced her voice to remain calm. "No. I mean—I don't think that's a good—" She pivoted toward Trent. Surely he'd realize how ridiculous this scheme was.

But instead, he was stroking his chin with a too-thoughtful expression. "It could work. And that way you could also keep an eye on her, help her settle in."

"Right, because I don't have time, unfortunately. You know, with my summer classes and all." Tina could have won an Academy Award with the regretful face she pulled. "Anyway, Addisyn, you're her coach. Only makes sense you'd be responsible for her."

She would strangle Tina. She would. That little snake, putting the welfare of her dumb cat above that of her cousin. Well, she wouldn't tolerate any more of—

"Addisyn, I certainly do appreciate your offer to help." For the first time, sincerity rang in Trent's tone. And he was looking at her with—gratitude?

She paused. Was this the angle to earn Trent's approval? "Uh—well—"

His forehead creased. "It is all right with you, isn't it?"

What could she say? Tina was a traitor and Kenzie was a time bomb, but Trent was treating her with the first signs of respect he'd exhibited since she'd arrived.

She'd regret this. She already did. But she couldn't forfeit the brownie points she'd apparently just earned. She swallowed the panic pressing at her voice. "Um, yes. Right. She can move in with me."

"Great." Trent's smile broke through his usual stony demeanor.

"Tina, let's go find your cousin. We'll need to move her stuff over."

"Okay." Tina plopped Canuck back on the counter and hurried after her dad, diligently evading Addisyn's glare. As the door closed behind them, Addisyn melted against the counter. "Canuck, what have I gotten myself into?"

The cat lifted his front leg and began washing his paw, studying her the entire time with an insolent indifference. Addisyn sighed and propped her head on her hand. "You know what? I bet you wouldn't have been such a terrible roommate."

CHAPTER 6

Addisyn had always believed that she was a rather decent roommate. After all, as a teenager, she'd shared a one-bedroom apartment with her sister for four years, and both of them had lived through it. So that had to say something.

That *something* was probably more about Avery's patience than her own good qualities, but she didn't stop to consider that for long.

Anyway, being a good roommate was fairly simple. Clearly label your food in the refrigerator, be mindful of the volume of your music, keep dirty laundry—literal and metaphorical—out of sight, and interact civilly with the other party.

But apparently Kenzie wouldn't be able to fulfill even the transactional nature of this arrangement. When Trent had explained the new plan to her, her face had pinched with aversion. *"I don't think that's a good idea. Addisyn probably doesn't want a roommate."*

Trent had smiled, apparently oblivious to the disdain in her tone. *"Addisyn's the one who offered."*

Kenzie's gaze had flicked to her with an odd current of distrust. A moment later, she'd shrugged. *"Okay. I guess so."*

I guess so? That was your response to someone willing to upend their entire home, life, and schedule because cat hair was your kryptonite?

And Kenzie's rudeness hadn't stopped there. She'd scowled at the empty room when she'd first walked in—no doubt it wasn't fancy enough or something. And while Trent had hurried back and forth between the houses to transfer all her belongings, she'd stayed in the room. Sulking, no doubt.

"I think there's just one more trip." Trent emerged from Kenzie's room and glanced at Addisyn almost apologetically. Almost. "I know she's a little, well, moody right now. But she'll settle down. She's been through a—a difficult time."

So by all means, she'd make sure everyone around her had a difficult time too. Addisyn just nodded with what she hoped was an understanding expression. "Of course."

"It will be good for her to be over here." He rubbed his nose. "I appreciate your willingness to be responsible for her."

Responsible. According to Avery, exactly what she'd never been. Addisyn squirmed beneath the weight of the word. She could barely be responsible for her car keys. Thinking she could answer for a troubled teenager was ludicrous.

"Of course, you won't have to do too much. She's old enough to look after herself. I just mainly want to make sure she's being—well—monitored." He waved his hand vaguely. "Making consistent progress, and all that."

And all *what?* Was she missing something here? Addisyn nodded, feeling her way forward in the unsettling conversation. "Right. Of course."

"Well, then." He reached for the doorknob. "I'll head to the house and grab her last bag."

The door closed behind him, and Addisyn released the exasperated sigh she'd held back. Responsible, indeed. She glanced cautiously toward the back room, but Kenzie's door was solidly shut. There weren't even any sounds of life—no moving around or unpacking boxes or playing music.

No, Kenzie was doing what she apparently did best—stewing in silence behind an impenetrable wall.

But then, maybe that was for the best. At least she wasn't blasting power rock or hammering pictures into the walls. Maybe Addisyn should just accept the silver linings wherever she could find them.

Well, if they were going to reach any kind of understanding, she'd have to make the first move. She took a deep breath and crept toward the closed door. "Kenzie?"

Silence sealed itself around the perimeter.

"Kenzie?" She swallowed. "Uh, it's me. Addisyn." *Well, of course.*

An elaborate sigh, and then the door cracked open, Kenzie peering out with a gaze that was far from welcoming. "I'm unpacking."

"Right. Of course." Although from what she could see over Kenzie's shoulder, all the luggage still looked intact. "Um—"

"Is something wrong?"

What was she supposed to say? *I'm your babysitter now?* "Uh, no. Not at all." She tried to keep her voice casual. "Your uncle says I'm supposed to, uh, help you." Okay, that sounded lame.

"I don't need help." The words were clipped short.

"Right, well—" Every path forward was blocked by a barred gate. "So do you need anything, or—"

"No."

Was there no way to crack open the girl's forcefield? "Um—what about, like, ground rules?"

Kenzie's already chilly expression dropped another ten degrees. "Ground rules?"

Avery's phrase, and she'd always hated it, so why was she reusing it now? "Well, I guess not really *rules*. Just—guidelines. Like, you know, a roommate code." Great. Just great. Thirty seconds with Kenzie, and she was already losing ground.

Kenzie appeared to weigh the idea for a moment. "Okay."

What could she tackle first? "So—I don't cook much." Addisyn paused, rethinking the statement. "Or at all."

"Okay." Kenzie's expression relaxed ever so slightly. "We can each do our own thing with food."

"Perfect." No awkward sit-down meals. "And, uh—music. We should each keep our volume down."

Kenzie shrugged and fished a pair of earbuds from her pocket. "I use these."

"Okay. Good." She should have really made some notes. Or thought her ideas through. "And—uh—" What was a catch-all rule Avery might use? "Don't do anything that's going to get me in trouble with your aunt and uncle, okay?"

The instant the words left her mouth, she knew they were wrong.

"Trouble?" Kenzie's eyes brewed a storm cloud. "What, you think I've got a boyfriend hidden under my bed or alcohol in my—"

"No! No." Addisyn waved her hands. If she was in charge, why was she on the defensive? "Sorry. I just had to, you know, lay the groundwork."

"That's not necessary." Kenzie's hand tightened around the earbuds. "Ask anyone. I'm a good girl." Her tone made it sound like a curse. "Anyway—" She lifted her chin. "I'm not going to be here long. My mom—she'll come for me. Probably any day."

That wasn't what she'd understood, but she wasn't about to cross Kenzie now. "Okay." Addisyn took a step backward. "Well, if you don't need—"

The door shut.

Wow. What a disaster. Addisyn scrambled back into the living room and dropped onto the couch. Seriously, how had everything gone so wrong? The last thing she needed was to be responsible for a stubborn teenager. Trent's niece, no less. And what had he said? Help her *make progress*?

She wasn't equipped for this. She was only six years older than Kenzie herself. And what did she know about helping teenagers—or anyone, for that matter?

A subtle shame wriggled through her. She was freshly escaped from her own mistakes—mistakes that haunted her still. And now she was supposed to help someone else?

That job belonged to Avery—the soul-reader, the truth-teller, the one with a compassion the size of Canada. None of those descriptions had ever fit Addisyn.

The door opened, and Trent marched in behind an overstuffed luggage case. He paused. "Is she settling in?"

"Uh—yeah." Addisyn shrugged evasively. "Unpacking."

"Hmm."

He glanced toward the door again, and this time he looked as apprehensive as she felt.

△△ △△ △△

THE NEW ROOM was stark. Plain. Nothing on the walls, no touches to make it hers. But at least it was simple and uncomplicated—the only part of her life Kenzie could say as much for.

The one bright spot was the crazy quilt, the squares somersaulting in shades of navy and scarlet. Kenzie perched on the side of the bed and fingered the intricate stitching. Grandma Del had made this, no doubt. Kenzie's last summer in BC—before Uncle Zach and Aunt Cynthy died— she'd begged to take the quilt home. Aunt Vera had been willing to give it to her, but Mom had said it was too bulky to bother with.

Now, the happiness of the funky design was no longer familiar.

"Well, this is it, Kenz." Uncle Trent tramped into the room, carting one last bag. "Anything else to bring?"

"No." Moving all her stuff hadn't taken long. Not when she'd barely unpacked any of it in Uncle Trent's house. Because—yeah, it was supposed to be a summer-length visit, but Mom might still send for her. You never knew.

"All right, then." Uncle Trent nodded. "I think this will work better for you. Especially with you and Addisyn both here together. She'll help you if you need anything, and you can ride with her to the center for practices."

That was Uncle Trent—measuring every situation with the yardstick of pure logic. Well, Addisyn was another complication, but she wasn't about to let him know that.

"If you need anything else—" Uncle Trent was turning for the door.

"Uncle Trent?" The words shot out before she could trap them behind her indifference.

"Yes?" He paused, glanced over his shoulder.

"Any—any word from—from my mom?" She jammed her hands into her pockets so he couldn't see her crossed fingers.

A flicker of something rawer than his businesslike expression shivered over his face. Pity, maybe. "No, Kenzie." He cleared his throat. "I'm sure she would love to hear from you, though. If you want to call."

"Okay. Yes." She wouldn't be ringing her mom anytime soon. But she'd learned long ago that agreement trumped argument. Saved time. And energy. And heartache.

Her uncle's steps echoed down the stairs, leaving her alone in the thickening silence. She dug into the front pocket of her purse and fished out her cell phone, holding down the power button until the screen lit to life. She swiped away all the social media notifications. No way was she ready for Instagram yet.

Instead, she tapped her missed calls. Mom hadn't contacted Uncle Trent. But maybe—

Three missed calls. Three voicemails. One a robotic scam message from a weird number in Ontario, one simply static, one a recorded reminder from her school about a field trip day. Which didn't apply, of course, to her.

Fine. She clicked the phone off and dropped it back into her bag, then glanced out the window, where the windows of her family's mansion flashed back the afternoon sun. From here, she could pick out Tina's room: second story, lefthand corner.

It still hurt that Tina hadn't sent Canuck away instead, but Kenzie couldn't blame her cousin. Canuck was more Tina's friend than she was now.

At one time, though, it had been different. Before everything had shattered like broken glass around her, before she'd wounded herself trying to crawl across the destruction to reach what had once been.

But this summer…well, this summer she had the chance to make it all right again.

A glimmer of hope sparked to life in the shadowed corners of her heart. She pushed off the bed and crossed the room to the window, leaning against the wide wooden sill.

The landscape hadn't changed. She'd noticed that right away when she'd arrived. There were a few more houses on Spring Creek than she'd remembered, but the acreage around the Payne land was still pristine. The ridge still rose behind the house, the trees marshaling in stern rows across the top under the severe gaze of the snow-shredded mountains.

And somewhere in those trees and ridges and mountains was the thing she'd held in her mind all through her flight across Canada. The thing that might finally hold the clue to undoing all the horrible events of the last few years.

The absurdity of the undertaking hit her all over again. She hadn't told anyone about The Project. Partly because it might jinx it. Partly because it sounded sort of lame, like something a little kid would do. But mainly because she couldn't stand for anyone to make fun of The Project. No, she was done with letting other people slice her with their sarcasm.

Although really, would she blame anyone for making fun of her if they heard about The Project? It had been six years, for crying out loud. She had no reason to believe what she was looking for was still there. Probably it had disappeared. Melted like the mountain snow, along with all the joy she'd had before. Maybe there was no way out of her wilderness after all.

Stop it. She shook her head. Thoughts like that were a big part of what had gotten her into this situation in the first place.

She squinted at the trees and forced herself to think strategically. She needed to check out the ridge behind the center first. Which was unfortunately going to be much harder now that Addisyn was apparently her keeper.

Kenzie frowned. She'd known the minute she'd laid eyes on Addisyn Miles that she was one of Those Girls. Girls who were pretty and popular and poised. Girls who knew what to do with clothes and hair and jewelry. Girls who could make you trust them, make you spill all the secrets during conversations at slumber parties and on the bus, and then twist all your words into weapons.

Girls who laughed with you…until they laughed at you.

What would it be like to be Addisyn? To have the whole world before you and no problems at all and never face a rainy day? She was from America, Aunt Vera had said. Pretty, smart, independent, talented. Working as a coach and dating Darius, who'd grown up to be a lot better-looking than Kenzie remembered. Perfect little fairytale, apparently.

Far too perfect to be trusted.

Addisyn's preachy little pep talk at the rink today had just confirmed it. Giving up, indeed. Anger sizzled through her at the memory. Oh, Addisyn could preach persistence from her high horse, but she didn't know the kind of pain Kenzie had pushed through for the last year—and longer. Or how important it was that she find a way to make everything right again.

Which was why The Project was so important. But instead of getting out there to find what she'd lost, here she was trapped under the same roof with the kind of girl she'd flown across the country to avoid. Terrific. As bad as her allergies had been, she'd almost rather suffer through the histamines than deal with Addisyn. But the doctor must have been right. Already she was breathing much easier, the itching in her throat easing.

Well, it would be fine. She'd just keep her well-practiced armor up and watch her words. Words were a doorway, she'd learned. Say enough of them, and people could walk right across your sentences into the secrets of your heart. Into the keep-out zone.

And Addisyn couldn't stop her from going up on the ridge. Probably she wouldn't even try. She was just like all the others. She didn't know how to handle Kenzie, she didn't want to learn, and she was already looking for someone else to whom she could shove off the responsibility.

It had always been that way.

Kenzie sank back down on the quilt and for the first time noticed a loose thread around one of the squares.

So even the quilt was unraveling.

△△ △△ △△

THE ANNOYING INSISTENCE of her alarm tugged Addisyn out of the blurry edges of sleep. She sat up and squinted in the morning sunshine spilling through the window. The next instant the events of the previous day crashed into the fragile bubble of her early morning calm. She flopped back onto the pillow with a groan.

Well, at least she'd survived an entire night with Kenzie. It had been—she glanced at her clock—a little over fifteen hours since the girl moved in? Not bad. Although who knew how many more weeks she had to go.

She dressed and crept cautiously down the hallway into the kitchen, but the silence was still undisturbed. Maybe she'd lucked out and Kenzie was one of those semi-nocturnal teens who scrolled on TikTok till 3 a.m. and then crashed until noon. One could hope.

She was just adding milk to a bowl of cereal when the back door

87

jerked open with no warning. She jumped, the milk sloshing across the counter. "Kenzie!" Okay, that had taken ten years off her life. "I didn't know you were up. You—" *Scared* was the wrong word.

The hood of Kenzie's sweatshirt shadowed her face. "I get up early."

Well, scratch that hope. "And you went outside?"

"Yeah." Kenzie's stance turned more rigid. "Is that a problem?"

"Well, it's just—can you let me know next time?"

"Why, so you can babysit me?"

"No!" She couldn't handle an altercation this early in the morning. Certainly not before breakfast. "I just didn't know that—"

"Never mind." Kenzie slouched down into one of the dining room chairs. "I get it."

The puddle of milk was expanding across the counter like misunderstanding. Addisyn swiped it up with a dishtowel and poured another bowl of cereal, the rattle of the wheat bran loud in the tension between them. "Um, here's some cereal. If you want it."

Kenzie dragged herself out of the chair as if Addisyn had presented her with an exhausting chore instead of a meal. "I hate this kind."

Well, that was the last straw. Addisyn was done trying to make conversation. She picked up her own bowl and sighed at the now-soggy contents, then glanced at the neon numbers on the microwave.

Fifteen hours and forty minutes.

Kenzie had already ruined the morning. And what about the rest of the day? Addisyn frowned as a thought struck her. They didn't have practice till the afternoon, so what was she supposed to do all morning? She couldn't very well leave Kenzie here by herself. Who knew what the girl might do. But the idea of tiptoeing around the house all morning, sidestepping Kenzie's personal storm system, was less than appealing.

Should she try to take the girl somewhere? She cringed at the thought. Wasn't that rewarding bad behavior? But did she care at this point? It wasn't like she'd been tasked with shaping Kenzie's moral values, thank goodness. If it got them both out of the house…

She braced herself to propose the idea, but even an argument would surely be better than the smothering silence. She cleared her throat. "So— we have practice at one thirty today. Do you want to go downtown this morning?"

"Downtown?" The first hint of interest flickered over Kenzie's face, but then suspicion slid it away. "Why?"

To keep them both sane? "Just for fun." Addisyn tried to keep her tone casual. If Kenzie suspected she wanted to go, the girl would never agree to it.

Kenzie appeared to weigh the idea while she slowly dragged her spoon through the contents of her bowl. Had she eaten any of it? "Does it have to be downtown?"

Aha, she was weakening. "Nope." What might be fun to a sixteen-year-old? "Um…we could go to the park, or drive up to the ski basin, or—" oh, could she hope—"get some coffee?"

Kenzie studied her cereal bowl again. "I don't drink coffee."

Hmm. Maybe that explained her bad mood.

"But—" She set the bowl aside and tilted her head at Addisyn with a testing gaze. "Can we go to the ridge?"

"The ridge?" Was that some store she hadn't heard of?

"Behind the center." Kenzie was actually making eye contact now. "There are hiking trails that go up the ridge there. Some really nice views."

Okay, not what she'd intended. "That's what you want to do?"

"Yeah."

Bears. Addisyn gulped. "Maybe—I don't know what the weather is supposed to be like, and—"

"It's sunny all week." Kenzie crossed her arms, her expression like a dare. "Look, you're the one who said—"

"I know, I know." Could it have been anything but hiking? She plunked her empty bowl in the sink a little more forcefully than necessary. "Let me grab a jacket, and we'll head out."

Tina had mentioned hiking trails the other day, but Addisyn would have never found the trailhead if not for Kenzie's directions. She had to keep going past the office, take a right behind the basketball courts, and then follow a pockmarked dirt road that even the Jeep seemed to find challenging. By the time the road looped back on itself in front of a wooden sign announcing the Bearstooth Trails, her muscles were already sore from the jolting drive.

"This is it." Kenzie scrambled out of the car. "Redfeather Ridge."

That narrow indentation between the trees was supposed to be a trail? And why were there no other cars in the parking lot? Because the bears had eaten all the other hikers, probably. "How far is it?"

"About a mile." Kenzie pointed upward. "You can kind of see the ridge itself."

Looking up at the ominously steep ridge—which had to be farther than a mile away—made Addisyn's neck hurt. And her stomach, too, although no need to mention that. "Oh. Sure."

"So? Are we going?" Kenzie folded her arms with an oddly challenging expression.

Probably she'd picked this trail for no other reason than to test Addisyn's mettle. Well, the best way to thwart her vindictiveness was to feign enjoyment. Addisyn pasted on a smile. "Of course."

Climbing the trail felt like trespassing. The trees crowded on both sides of the narrow rocky strip, their branches thick enough to blot out the sky. The air was still and heavy with the damp green scent of the Whistler rain forests. Addisyn shuddered at the uncanny feeling that the forest was swallowing them both. Who knew how many bears might be lurking back in these trees? She tried to quiet her ragged breathing—no need to sound like easy prey—but the altitude and the steep grade were wearing her down.

Annoyingly, Kenzie didn't seem to find the trail difficult at all. She was hiking ahead of Addisyn with a purposeful stride like Avery's. And her flimsy tennis shoes didn't slow her down, even on the rocky terrain.

Addisyn slipped on a mossy stone and just managed to catch her balance. She jogged a few steps to catch up to Kenzie. "Hey—" She tried to swallow her panting. "Are we still on the right trail?"

"Yeah." Kenzie wasn't even breathing hard. Infuriating. "I know where we're going." She hesitated for just a moment. "I hiked here a lot. Before."

Was that the first personal detail she'd ever shared? "Oh." She needed a way to keep the conversation going. If her oxygen-deprived brain would let her think of one. "So, you like being outside?"

"Yeah." Kenzie tilted her face to the pines as if drinking in their fragrance. "Especially here."

And here she'd thought Kenzie had chosen the hike just to spite her. Shame prickled over her. "So how often did you come here? Darius said you came here when—his parents—"

"I did, but I lived here before that." Kenzie hopped nimbly onto a crumbling log to navigate a muddy section. Too bad that her agility didn't seem to translate to the ice. "My mom worked at a law firm in Vancouver."

Her mom again. A big part of the mystery. "Well—then it's probably nice to be back."

Kenzie tunneled her hands into the pockets of her gray hoodie. "It's been a long time." But there was an uncertainty in her voice that didn't match the vibe of someone returning to a beloved place.

"So, uh—about how much farther up here?" Hard to make the question seem casual when she sounded as if she were bursting one of her lungs.

"Half a mile."

They were only halfway? Addisyn barely had enough dignity left to suppress a groan. "Right. Okay."

Evidently, Kenzie's ability to assess distances was as shaky as her social skills. The ridge took another thirty-two minutes to reach—not that Addisyn had kept track or anything—and finished with a short rock scramble that Kenzie had conveniently forgotten to mention.

"This is the top." Kenzie had, of course, shinnied up the rocks like a squirrel. "The view is beautiful."

The most beautiful thing Addisyn saw was the relatively flat ground. She crawled ungracefully over the last section of rocks and winced as she eased the kinks from her back. She glanced the direction Kenzie was pointing and blinked. "Wow."

The mountains sloped all around them, their shoulders bristly with pines. Directly below them, Bearstooth dotted the valley like a setup from a model maker's kit. Addisyn pulled out her phone to snap a few photos. "That really is a view."

"Uh huh." But Kenzie's brow was furrowed with distraction. She glanced around. "This is where I came before. I'm sure…"

She was talking mostly to herself, apparently. Addisyn took a sip from her water bottle, then glanced at her watch. Yikes. She'd really hoped to be able to go back home and take care of some housework before Kenzie's practice. "So, ready to go back?"

Kenzie's face hardened into what Addisyn was quickly learning to recognize as her stubborn look. "Can't we, um, can't we just wait for a minute?"

"Wait for what?"

"Just—I mean, we hiked all the way up here. Shouldn't we, like, enjoy the view?"

Nope. She'd already done more than could have been expected. "Kenzie, I've seen the view. Look, I really need to get back down and take care of—"

"Then go." Kenzie plopped down on a fallen log. "I know the trail better than you do anyway. I'll go back to the center when I'm ready and wait for this afternoon."

"No." Regardless of how tempting the offer was, she wasn't stupid. The last thing she needed was Kenzie rattling to Trent about how Addisyn had abandoned her in the woods. She leaned against a tree and sighed. "Fine. Ten minutes, and that's it."

"Okay."

No *thank you*, but she expected that by now.

Kenzie rummaged in her bag and pulled out some battered— *binoculars?* She scooted forward on her log and began scanning the valley with closed-off concentration. Well, what was that all about?

Nine more minutes.

The tree trunk was warm against Addisyn's back. A wind sifted through the rustling branches, and the aroma of pine swirled around her like a blessing. A sudden peace she hadn't expected worked its way through her. As much as she hated to admit it, there was something soothing about being up here, watching the cloud shadows leaving footprints on the sun-soaked valley below. The knots in her spirit loosened ever so slightly. Maybe this was why Avery loved the outdoors so much.

The thought of her sister lodged a lump in Addisyn's throat. Avery would have handled this whole adventure differently. She wouldn't be daunted by a steep trail. Or a tough skating job. Or a surly teen. No, she'd have led the hike with a joy and enthusiasm that would have already melted Kenzie's defenses.

But Avery had always been the strong one. The capable one. The responsible one. And Addisyn—well, Addisyn had always been the *other* sister. The one who'd ducked away from duty time and again. The one who'd followed her own chaotic course right into a darkness that had nearly drowned her. How many times had she washed up onto Avery's life raft?

Probably about as many times as she'd longed to be like her sister. To draw on some of that mysterious power that kept Avery rooted in something larger than even the mountains she loved so much.

"I'm ready."

Kenzie already had her backpack on? Addisyn blinked and glanced at her watch. Twelve minutes. She'd lost track of time. "Okay." Should she mention the binoculars, or were those some kind of secret? "Did you—see what you wanted to?"

Kenzie's shoulders slumped as if the mountain was bearing down on her. "No."

Addisyn picked her way down the rocky part. Not nearly as bad going this way. "So—what were you looking at?" She tried to sound compassionate and trustworthy. The way Avery would.

"Um—just something that was here before. When I came the last time."

"Something that was here?" Addisyn angled her head, trying to see past Kenzie's vague words. "Like—a treasure?"

Kenzie didn't laugh. "It doesn't matter." Once again, her expression was overcast, the brief light behind her eyes snuffed out again. "It's not here now."

Well, so much for being like Avery. Addisyn frowned and followed Kenzie onto the trail. But for the entire mile—or more—down, she couldn't help but wonder what Kenzie had been hoping to find again.

Or why it was so important that she'd remembered it after six years.

CHAPTER 7

Addisyn had rarely felt more ridiculous.

She shifted position, peering around the corner of the guest house at an awkward angle. The back door of the Payne house was still stubbornly closed. She huffed out an exasperated breath and pressed herself against the siding again. What was taking Tina so long this morning? She normally left at eight o'clock on the dot. Addisyn had come out at ten till, and she'd already been here for at least twenty minutes, shivering in the early-morning shadows on which the sun hadn't yet breathed.

But how else was she going to nab Tina? That backstabbing girl had conveniently managed to fly under the radar since she'd all but tricked Addisyn into taking Kenzie. Well, she wasn't getting off that easily. She'd foisted her cousin onto Addisyn. Now she could just see about undoing her deception and taking her back.

Because Addisyn wasn't spending one more day with Kenzie in her house. She'd thought at first that yesterday's hiking trip might forge a tenuous connection, but the girl's unguarded moment had been as brief as the fitful cloud shadows on the valley. Evidently, not finding whatever she'd been looking for had soured Kenzie's mood still further—something Addisyn hadn't believed possible. She hadn't said two words this morning, and as soon as they'd finished breakfast, she'd flopped down on the couch with her earbuds and phone. Built-in conversation repellent.

Oh, how naive Addisyn had been to balk at the idea of hosting Canuck for the summer. If Trent gave her that choice again, she'd welcome the cat with open arms and let him use her best pair of dress slacks for a scratching post before she'd opt for Kenzie.

The back door was still closed. Addisyn bit back a groan. Fortunately the curtains were drawn on the windows facing her. At least no one was watching her lurk around the backyard in what felt uncomfortably like the elaborate spy games she and Avery had played as kids. She could only imagine the explanation Trent would demand.

What else could she do to get Tina's attention? Spray-paint her precious Lexus? Catnap Canuck? No tactic was off the table at this point. Desperate times, and all that.

The door creaked open, and Addisyn jerked to alertness. *Target acquired.* Tina was sauntering out the back door, her hands—and attention—absorbed by Canuck and her cell phone. Unsuspecting victim. Perfect.

Addisyn pushed off from the guest house and sprinted across the backyard, the dew-drenched grass squeaking under her tennis shoes. "Tina!"

Tina jumped, her cell phone clattering to the sidewalk. "Nice. Now my phone's all wet." She plopped Canuck on the ground and scowled. "What were you doing? Playing hide-and-seek?"

Addisyn lifted her chin. She did not have to offer explanations for what she did on her property. Okay, not *her* property, but whatever. "Look, Tina." She tried for the air of authority that three years' age difference should give her. "I did not volunteer to be responsible for Kenzie."

"Guess I should have known you'd still be hung up on that." Tina made a show of drying her phone with the hem of her jacket. "You did say you would help however you could."

"That wasn't what I meant, and you know it."

"Details, details." Tina flicked a blade of grass from her phone screen. "Look, you're her coach."

"Right. Not her babysitter." Canuck coiled around Addisyn's ankle, and an idea struck. Hadn't she read somewhere that when cats smeared their faces on you like that, it was a sign of affection or something? She braced herself for a true Hail Mary move. "See this, Tina?"

"See what?" Tina took a step back and glanced at her watch. "Look, I'm going to be late."

"Canuck likes me now. So—I'm going to tell your dad that Kenzie can go back with you guys, and the cat can move in with me. That was the first plan anyway."

"What?" Tina's eyes popped open, her attention finally hooked. "No. Not happening."

"But she's your cousin." Addisyn heard the edge to her voice. "We don't get along, and she's not happy over there with me, and I just think—"

"Fine." Tina pushed past Addisyn to her car. Yanking open the door, she snatched up Canuck and plunked him down in the passenger seat. "I'll talk to Dad today."

It was that easy? "You will?"

"Sure." Tina ducked into the driver's seat, then narrowed her eyes. "I'll let him know that you have refused to do this one small thing to help the family. Maybe I'll even remind him that you came from America where you never made it to Nationals and—"

"Tina!" Addisyn leaped forward so she couldn't close the car door. "You wouldn't do that." But her tone sounded unconvinced. Even to herself.

Tina curled her lips into a more sinister version of a smile. "Would I?"

Well, apparently Tina had some desperate measures of her own up her sleeve. Addisyn gritted her teeth. "Okay."

"Okay, what?"

"Okay, Kenzie stays with me." Addisyn all but spit her surrender. "Deal?"

"Sure." Tina grinned and reached for her door handle. "See you this afternoon."

Addisyn stomped back to the house as Tina's little car jetted down the driveway. Oh, if only she could find a bear right now. She'd give him that obnoxious girl as breakfast and throw in the irritating cousin for dessert.

Time for Plan B. She slipped her phone from her pocket. She needed backup, and she knew where to get it.

She tapped the icon for a video call and waited. The call rang five times before Avery's face filled the screen, looking not altogether thrilled.

"Addisyn?"

"Hey, A." Addisyn sighed. "Listen, I've got a problem."

"Okay…um…" Avery glanced over her shoulder. "Can it wait? I'm at the store."

Sure enough, Addisyn could hear John Denver crooning in the background. Of course. Would she ever remember the time zone difference? She bit her lip. "I forgot."

"That's okay." The image scrambled, and then Avery reappeared, farther away this time. "There, I propped the phone up. I'm stocking shelves anyway. Doesn't take much concentration."

She still sounded oddly distracted. Addisyn frowned. "Are you okay?"

Avery hesitated. "Oh—yeah. I've just been…I've had a lot going on." She turned away from the camera and pulled out an armload of hiking shirts. "Uh, Skyla's having me go with her on a visit to a school group."

"Really?" When had this come about? "That's awesome! Why didn't you tell me?"

Avery shrugged, flopping the shirts onto the display rack in an uncharacteristically haphazard way. "I knew you were busy."

"Not too busy to hear something like that." What was off between them? If only she could see Avery's expression better on the tiny screen. "So, are you taking one of the birds? What are you going to talk about?"

"I'm taking our Swainson's Hawk, Elijah. And I don't know. Skyla gave me some bullet points to look over." Avery brushed off the conversational trail. "So. You said you had a problem."

"Well—" Avery's weird behavior had significantly shrunk her own gripe. "It's, uh, it's nothing major. Kenzie—that's Trent's niece—she's being—difficult."

Avery turned her attention back to the screen. "Really? Difficult how?"

That was more like the sister she knew, and the question was enough to start the whole tale tumbling down like a mountain stream. How Kenzie was prickly and unpredictable, how she mostly just took shelter in silence. How she'd couched herself deep within a barbed-wire barricade of sullenness. "Like, she's in the house right now just listening to music on her earbuds. Or pretending to. Probably she just uses that so I'll leave her alone.

I swear, it's like she's just a ghost. Just floats through the world and never interacts with it."

"Hmm." Avery reached for another armload of shirts.

"And the worst part is she doesn't even try." Recounting all of it sent her frustration foaming over again. "It's like she wants to see just how unapproachable she can be."

Avery glanced back toward the camera briefly. "Sounds tough."

"And she's a horrible roommate. Like, the worst. She won't even say good morning, let alone do anything fun." She really hadn't appreciated living with Avery enough. They'd had their share of conflicts at that time, but they'd also had dance parties and homemade pizza and wildly competitive Go Fish games.

"That's not good."

"No. It's not." She swirled her tirade into its grand finale. "And cat or no cat, it's not fair that I have to be the one to deal with her. She's their relative, which makes her their problem, but they just want to play hot potato with the responsibility. I'll keep coaching her, but I can't be under the same roof with her. And now I don't know how to get out of this."

There. She paused for breath, her words hanging in the air. Now was the time for Avery to take her turn sympathizing with Addisyn and condemning Kenzie and assuring Addisyn that her resentment was perfectly justified. But instead, Avery kept unfolding shirts with an odd expression.

"A? Did you hear me?"

"Oh! Yes." Avery blinked. "Yeah. She sounds pretty bad."

That was it? She'd unloaded ten minutes' worth of woes on Avery just for some lukewarm agreement? "So?" She wouldn't let her impatience show. "Any advice?"

"Well—" Avery tapped her chin. "Just keep being nice to her. Keep trying to build that connection."

"Avery, I *have* tried." Why wasn't her sister getting the picture? "I just told you."

"Well, then you'll have to try something different to reach her."

"Reaching her is not my job." Her tone was tightening. "I just need her to straighten up so she doesn't cost me my actual, real job."

Avery picked up the phone again and peered at the camera. "But— maybe there's a reason for how she's acting."

"The reason is that she doesn't care about anything except—"

"The reason could be that she's deeply hurting." For the first time, Avery seemed fully engaged with the conversation. "Maybe she just needs a friend."

And that right there was Avery. Always the do-gooding idealist. Addisyn stopped just short of an eye roll. "If she needs a *friend*—" she splashed some sarcasm on the word—"she should try being a little more approachable than a desert cactus." A bizarre sense of betrayal pressed at her. "I thought you would understand."

"I do." Avery frowned and shrugged. "Okay, well, then you do what you want to."

Do what you want to? Since when had Avery ever given her such uninterested advice? "You're—are you mad at me?"

"No! It's—" Avery stopped, sighed, tugged on her hair. "I'm sorry. I'm just—I'm distracted right now." She took a deep breath. "It hasn't been—"

Distracted? Resentment shriveled into hurt. "No, I get it. I'll call you back later. When you can actually listen to me." She ended the call before she could regret the last words and slumped against the siding again.

Distracted? Really?

Avery was never distracted. Her sister had always been able to multitask like a circus juggler. And what was there to be distracted by, just sticking shirts on shelves in an empty store?

A sudden lostness pressed close around her. She couldn't remember a time when Avery hadn't carefully gathered up the pieces of Addisyn's problems and stitched them all together with loving advice. The conversation today had been as disorienting as a compass that now pointed east.

And as unhelpful. What had Avery even offered her? Just some vague nonsense about trying to "*reach*" Kenzie. Good grief, she didn't need to save the girl's soul. She just needed her to straighten up enough to keep them both out of trouble.

Her phone buzzed in her hand. Avery.

I'll call you back this evening.

No *I'm sorry*. No *I love you*. No *I'm not mad* or *I still care* or *I'm going to help you*. No, because the phone call was simply an item to mark off Avery's to-do list.

And for the first time, Addisyn was on her own.

⩍ ⩍ ⩍

DARIUS HAD BEEN intentionally giving Addisyn some space for the last couple of days. He'd known how busy she'd be, starting her coaching with Kenzie and all, and he hadn't wanted to wedge one more thing into her schedule. But on Wednesday evening, he texted her as soon as he left the climbing center.

Off work. Want to watch a sunset?

Her reply slipped onto the screen only a couple of minutes later.

Yes!!! Kenzie and I just got home. Meet here?

Sure. He drove across town to his uncle's house. She was running down the steps of the guesthouse before he even put the car in park. "Hey." She slid into the passenger seat, slightly breathless, and let her head drop back into the headrest. "There. I can breathe now."

"Long day?" A brief movement fluttered in one of the guesthouse windows. Was Kenzie watching them?

"You could say that." Addisyn glanced at the house with a frown. "Let's go. I'll tell you about it on the way. Where are we going, anyway?"

He chuckled. "Guess I forgot to mention that part. We're heading to Alexander Falls."

"Sounds lovely." Her smile sparkled through the weariness that still tugged at her expression. "I can't wait to see it."

As they made the twenty-minute trip north, Addisyn filled him in on the details of Kenzie's training. "She's just...very uncertain. She's very timid when she skates, and so her movements are jerky and...oh, it's just a mess. And her attitude is still..."

"Still what?"

Addisyn opened her mouth, then closed it again. "She's a little

100

difficult. Maybe—do you think it's because Trent owns the center? So she thinks she's bulletproof?"

"Hmm…could be." The idea made sense. After all, Darius had seen firsthand the tension that could develop when family ties tangled with athletic ones. Maybe Kenzie assumed that she could play it both ways. Slack off at practice, then pull the family card and recruit Uncle Trent's support. Which might not be wrong. He frowned. "Well, be firm with her, Addisyn. Make sure she knows she can't get by with less than her best, family or no family." He'd heard his dad say words like that a hundred times.

Addisyn jerked her head in a firm nod. "I agree."

Darius pulled into the parking lot for the falls and cut his engine. "And her living with you is definitely going to help. Keep her grounded, out of trouble. That was really great of you to offer to take her." Honestly, after what Addisyn had said, he wasn't sure he'd have had the nerve to take on his apparently temperamental cousin. But that was just like Addisyn, after all. A heart the size of the Pacific.

Addisyn's words seemed caught halfway. "Oh, well—somebody had to." Her smile returned, a little too quickly, and she glanced away. "Come on. The sun won't wait."

Nights were still chilly this high in the mountains, and a brisk wind was scampering through the leaves as they made their way down the short trail to the observation deck. Darius pointed ahead to a rocky section. "Almost there. Watch your step here."

"Okay." She gave him a shy smile and slipped her hand into his.

He tugged her closer to him, close enough that he could catch a whiff of her floral perfume. He'd never get tired of how perfectly her hand fit in his, how every part of her heart fit the locks that had hung so long on the outside of his soul.

She lifted her face to the mountains around them, her cheeks pink from the wind, her hair tucked over her shoulder. "This is beautiful out here." Her voice had the special lilt it held when she was at peace.

"Yes." He watched her profile. "Beautiful."

"Is that the falls?"

He tore himself loose from his admiration. "Yes. Coming down the cliff over there." He could just glimpse the observation deck through the trees.

He led her across the suspension bridge and onto the wooden deck. "There we are." He leaned against the railing, glancing across the deep gorge to where Alexander Falls slid with a pounding roar over the cliff edge. "Impressive, right?"

"Absolutely." Addisyn shook her head in wonder. "I didn't realize it would be so big."

"It's full right now, with the snowmelt." Even at this distance, the spray floated in the air.

"And that's a long drop too." She studied the cliff.

"Uh huh. It's glacier-carved."

"Really?"

He sorted back through his high school geology lessons. "Yes. The glaciers once filled this whole area. Cut the valleys out and carved the mountains."

"Wow." Addisyn's voice held a reverence. "So the whole land was changed."

"Yeah." He glanced around at the familiar landscape and tried to imagine it groaning under the weight of all that ice.

"What happened to the glaciers?"

"Most melted at the end of the Ice Age. But there are still some around. Tantalus and Fitzwilliam...oh, and there's a monster one on Overlord Mountain." He nudged her shoulder. "I'll show you sometime. You can see them from several places on the highway or up at Alta Lake."

"I'd like that."

Long fingers of shadow crept down the ravine. In the afterglow of the setting sun, the western sky blushed pink. Addisyn blinked toward the last embers of the daylight. "Perfect view of the sunset. You were right."

"Yes." Darius took a breath, feeling the familiar ache. "My mom and dad used to come here and watch the sunset together."

"That's neat." She gently settled her hand on top of his where it rested on the railing. "They loved each other very much, didn't they?"

"Very much." A sudden panic pounded in his chest. Was this it? His chance to let her know what he dreamed of? "I, uh, I'm getting ready to clear out their stuff. From my house. I had it all packed in boxes, and now I'm going to sort it out, decide what's worth keeping."

The compassion in her eyes touched the old wounds like a balm. "I'm sure that will be hard."

"It will be. Harder than I thought." His throat pinched. "I mean, they've been—gone for six years. But…"

"But they were your best friends." She stroked the back of his hand, her touch like silk. "I'll come over sometime when you're working on it. Maybe I can help you."

He flipped his palm over, capturing her hand like the lifeline it was. "I'd love that. Thank you. And—" *Slow down.* He couldn't let his heart outrun his mind. "I think—I think it's time for me to move forward."

"Move forward?" Still no comprehension in her gaze.

"Yes." Each word was careful, like a footstep on the rocky ground. He couldn't afford to slip. "I—I have things I envision for my future, and—and I want to make room for those things."

Her expression changed slightly. Just a tiny ripple of unease. "That makes sense." She glanced back toward the embers of the dying sunset. "You've got a lot going on. I know this is a busy season at the climbing center."

Didn't she know it wasn't just the climbing center? "Well—" What could he say to make her understand him? "That, of course. But also—" He cleared his throat. "I want to have the kind of life my parents had."

"You'll find it, you know." A deep sadness suddenly hung from her smile. She swallowed. "You're a good man, Darius."

A good man. Yeah, ask Uncle Trent about that. "Well—thank you." He tried one more time. "I want a life with—with purpose. And—family."

"Family." Now she definitely looked off-balance. She pulled her hand free and brushed invisible dust from her sleeve. "Family is important. I mean, I only have Avery, but I don't know what I would do without her." Her words were coming fast, pulling her away from the topic. Away from him.

"Yes—of course—but—"

"Well, anyway." She pushed away from the railing. "It's getting late. Maybe we should go back."

Why was she responding this way? For just a moment, he had the childish urge to kick the deck in frustration. But he forced a smile instead. "Okay. Let's go back to the bridge and watch for the stars." Casual. He could be casual.

Addisyn led the way to the path, rehashing some story about Avery teaching her the constellations, but all Darius could think about was the odd moment they'd just had. Had Addisyn not understood his meaning?

Or had she understood all too well?

He'd never considered the possibility, and it opened a door to twenty new ways to worry. They were on the same page, weren't they? Addisyn loved him. He was sure of that. Their hearts already beat in unison, and she knew it as well as he did.

Right?

Of course that was right.

The bridge stretched before him, a pathway over the deepest unknowns. He forced himself to relax. She was just stressed right now, was all—adjusting to Canada and meeting his family and working with Kenzie. He would just talk with her again once things could settle down.

But one thing he was sure of: Addisyn Miles was the love of his life.

And he wouldn't wait much longer before he told her so.

△ △ △

AS ADDISYN FOLLOWED Darius down the path away from the falls, the weight of all those glaciers he'd talked about crushed down on her shoulders. She'd never expected the conversation to take that turn.

Wasn't that just like Darius? He'd brought her to a place made sacred by his yesterdays. Because he was thoughtful, caring, gentle. Because he was a man who made every move with heartfelt purpose. A man whose greatest desire was to walk the path his parents had forged.

His parents…who had loved each other very much.

She glanced down at the muddy path beneath her feet. She knew nothing about that kind of love. Neither how to receive it nor how to give it.

Really, where would she have learned? Her own family had been disastrously dysfunctional—an absent mother, an abusive father, a scattered handful of extended relatives who mostly looked the other way. And then, of course, she'd springboarded to Brian. Like a moth to a flame, she'd burned her soul against his cheap imitation of love.

She glanced over the edge of the bridge, the dark river crawling beneath them as if it held all those memories. She'd asked Brian one time, the question. He'd been taking her to some gala or function—he'd used every social function as a career opportunity—and as usual, he'd expected her to appear flawless. The perfect accessory to complete his polished facade.

She couldn't remember the event, but she could remember what she'd worn—a black off-the-shoulder dress that hugged her hips with those horridly stiff heels that she only wore because he liked them. She'd spent forty-five minutes perfecting her smoky eye makeup.

She'd walked into the front room, where he was waiting, and as always, she'd had the sense that she was bringing an offering, some appeasement that might not be enough. But his eyes had sparked with a greedy approval. *"Well."* He'd twined his arms around her waist, turned his head to inhale her perfume. *"You sure look hot tonight, baby."*

His standard compliment, but somehow that night it had rung so hollow. She'd suddenly longed for something more from him. Something that had nothing to do with the cut of her dress or the style of her hair or the aroma of her perfume. *"Brian—"*

He'd drawn back and frowned. *"What's wrong with you?"*

"Do you—do you love me?"

"Do I—what?" Confusion creased his face. "Of course I do, baby. I tell you all the time how pretty you are."

Which was true, and she hadn't been able to explain why that wasn't enough. *"But—but do you* love *me? Not just when I'm pretty, but—"*

"I don't understand what you're talking about." Brian had glanced at the clock, then back at her with an impatient edge to his voice. "Of course I love you, Addisyn. Why are you talking crazy tonight?"

Tears had trembled to the surface, but she'd blinked them back. She couldn't ruin the eye makeup, after all.

He'd sighed. Huffed, really. *"Come here."* He'd pulled her to him, his hands sliding to her waist, and pressed his lips to hers. A kiss was the farthest thing from what she was craving, but he'd pushed past her defenses until she'd finally kissed him back out of nothing more than defeat.

He'd drawn back with a triumphant smile. "*See?*" There'd been a hardness to his laugh. "*That right there is what I love about you, Addisyn Miles.*"

The nausea of the memory tied a knot in her stomach, and she stumbled. Darius caught her arm. "Whoa, there."

Her heart was pounding with a jarring urgency, old scars and new fears crosshatching each other. "Just—lost my footing." In so many ways.

"Are you okay?"

Always his first question. Even in the shadowed dusk, she could read a gentleness on his face that Brian had never known about. "Yes. I'm— fine."

"You're shivering." He wrapped his arms around her.

Her shivering had nothing to do with the cold. "I'm okay."

"We'll go back soon. I just wanted you to see the first stars come out. My dad—" He cleared his throat. "My dad always said you could see the whole universe from here."

He was so strong, even when he was hurting, and she loved him for it. Addisyn leaned back against his chest, into the warmth of his embrace. If only she could share some of his strength.

I want a life like my parents had…purpose…family…

What exactly had he meant by those words? The way he'd looked at her…it had almost seemed as if…

Shame trickled through her, dark and poisonous. Darius wanted— *deserved*—a life of love as vibrant as what his parents had shared. But if he thought she could ever hold up her half of a relationship like that, then he hadn't yet realized how broken she was.

There had only been two men in her life before Darius: the man she didn't even like to call her father, and Brian. With examples like that, all she'd learned were survival skills. How to sink out of sight during a tirade. How to recognize triggers. How to beg for forgiveness for imaginary sins. How to absorb blame over and over and over again.

But building a healthy relationship—that took courage. Peace. Forgiveness. Communication. Respect. All the unknown places where she'd never ventured.

"There's the first star." Darius's voice was a breath against her ear. "You get to make a wish."

She swallowed down the ache in her throat. There was no star that could give her what she longed for.

The sunset was a pale smear on the western horizon, the night closing in relentlessly. Fitting. Because sooner or later, Darius would see the truth about her.

And then all the light would fade just like that.

△△ △△ △△

AVERY HAD NEVER imagined herself in this role. Sitting in a colorful classroom, waiting to introduce a cluster of elementary kids to a majestic bird. She shifted her elbow slightly on the crayon-scuffed plastic table. The Swainson's Hawk clinging to that arm gave a soft whistle, his talons embedding deeper into the thick padding of her leather glove.

"Shh." Avery gripped the strap around his ankles more tightly and smoothed her free hand down his back. The last thing she needed was for the bird to suddenly decide to explore the classroom. Not that she really had to worry. This hawk—Elijah, Chay had named him—had been doing school tours for five years, ever since the loss of his left eye had rendered him unable to survive in the wild. He probably had more skill than she did at this point. And he definitely had more confidence.

"The children will be here in less than five minutes." Mrs. Hamm, the third-grade teacher, was chatting with Skyla, maintaining a respectful distance from Elijah. "I know they'll enjoy this. Goodness, the last time we had a science day this interesting was when our natural history teacher brought a terrarium of little frogs and accidentally knocked the lid off."

Skyla laughed, but the best Avery could do was a faint smile. She couldn't be amused by a funny story—not with her first audience just minutes away.

She should have never agreed to this. She'd spent her life avoiding attention as if it were a contagious disease. What if she didn't know the answers to the kids' questions? What if she couldn't handle Elijah?

And why had Skyla asked her to do this in the first place? Sure, she'd given the excuse of Chay being out of town, but she'd been making school visits with her husband for years. No doubt she could have handled the situation quite capably on her own. And Skyla did nothing by accident. She'd planned for Avery to be here, at the intersection of this time and place. Why?

Well, regardless of what Skyla was thinking, Avery couldn't worry with it right now. She needed to be focusing—remembering the notes she'd made, preparing to face the kids, and praying that Elijah's apparent interest in the ceiling fans would subside.

The door opened, and a cluster of kids trotted in, ricocheting to seats around the room. As they caught sight of Elijah, a ripple of hushed excitement tingled among them. Well, at least no one looked bored. Yet.

Mrs. Hamm stepped forward and clapped out a rhythm, waiting for the kids to clap it back to her before she spoke. "All right, students! We have an interesting science day today. Mrs. Skyla Wingo is here with her assistant from the Estes Valley Raptor Center, and they are going to be introducing you to a very special bird." She smiled and beckoned for Skyla to come forward.

"Greetings to you, students." Skyla's expression softened as she scanned the room. "It is such the honor to learn with all of you today. My friend Miss Avery Miles will be introducing you to this wonderful bird."

Friend. Skyla considered her a friend. The thought brought a bracing courage, and Avery took a deep breath. "Hi, everyone." She gave the room her biggest smile, refusing to focus on the unflinching gazes trained on her. "This is Elijah. He's a kind of bird called a Swainson's Hawk."

As if on cue, Elijah rippled his wings, and even Mrs. Hamm gasped in admiration.

Good job, boy. Avery swallowed the dryness in her mouth. So far, so good. "Elijah came to the Estes Valley Raptor Center five years ago when he was hit by a car." She'd worked to distill the terminology into kid-friendly language. "He doesn't have one of his eyes anymore, which makes it very difficult for him to find food. So now he lives at the center and visits schools like this one."

A little girl in the front row shot her hand up, and Avery nodded to her. "Go ahead."

"Can he still see?"

"Yes, absolutely." Thank goodness, an easy question to start with. "He likes to watch everyone around him with his good eye."

"He looks mean. Is he mean?" A more timid-looking girl on the right side of the room eyed Elijah uneasily.

"Not at all." Avery tried to infuse some extra encouragement into her smile. "He might look a little scary, but he's a very nice bird." She hesitated. "You know, sometimes that's true for people too, isn't it?"

Heads nodded around the room. Avery glanced at Skyla in time to see her approving smile.

"Will he let me hold him like that?" A boy with curly black hair bounced in his seat exuberantly.

Avery bit back a chuckle. "Well, probably not. He's been taught to sit like this only for people he knows. Plus—" she pretended to heft her arm with exaggerated strain—"he's a lot heavier than you would think."

The kids giggled, and the sound faded the last of her fear. She'd shrunk from this event, but now, her doubts and dread were giving way to the same rightness she felt when she ran with the raptors in the flight cages.

She explained more information and fielded questions from the kids for another thirty minutes, and then Mrs. Hamm came to her side. "All right, kids, it's time for your next class. Let's line up to thank Mrs. Wingo and Miss Miles."

"And Elijah!" The boy with the black hair clapped his hands.

Mrs. Hamm smiled. "And Elijah."

The kids filed past, each one thanking them and some asking a last question about Elijah. At the end of the line was a little girl with brown hair in two ponytails. "Bye, Elijah." She waved to the regal bird, then grinned shyly at Avery. "And thank you, Miss Miles. This is the best science day ever!"

"I'm glad you enjoyed it." A strange nostalgia pinched her heart. Something about the girl reminded her a bit of herself as a child. "Do you like being outside?"

"Oh, yeah. I go outside all the time." The girl's face drooped suddenly. "Well, I mean, I used to. In our old house. But now we live in town." She scowled. "No more birds. And too many people."

Okay, they were definitely kindred spirits. "Hmm." Avery cocked her head. "You know, hawks are actually seen in cities a lot."

"Really?" Hope sparked back to the girl's expression.

"Yes." Avery reached across the table with her free arm and grabbed one of her few remaining Urban Birds flyers. "Here. This will show you a lot of different birds you can still look for. Even in the city."

Awe spread across the girl's face. "Wow!" She thumbed through the flyer, her smile spreading. "I didn't know there were so many cool birds around here."

"Remember that, okay?" Avery waited until she had the girl's full attention. "There are wonders everywhere, all around us. Just keep looking for them."

"I will." Impulsively the girl threw her arms around Avery in the fierce hug of an eight-year-old. "Thank you, Miss Miles! Thank you for coming here and bringing Elijah to see us."

Avery's heart swelled. She tucked her free arm around the little girl and blinked back the emotion. "You're welcome."

The girl skipped out of the classroom, and Avery sat back, realization glowing like the first hints of dawn. This was why it mattered, what the center did. Yes, they were healing birds—but they were healing people too.

Today, a generation who would grow up suffocated by artificial lights and concrete jungles and mind-numbing screen time had experienced something different—something deeper. They'd had a chance to see a small part of the wonder that wrapped itself all around them. And maybe some of them would remember to chase that wonder. To keep looking up instead of giving in to a head-down life.

The excitement of the mission tingled all over her with a passion she'd never experienced. Now this—this she could get behind. If Skyla would let her, she'd gladly come along on the next school visit.

"You did well."

Three little words, yet coming from Skyla they were the highest compliment. Avery looked up hopefully. "I did?"

"Yes." Skyla began gathering up the flyers. "You pointed them upward. All we can ever do. And you did it in grace. You seem to love children."

"Oh, yes." A pang dampened her excitement for a moment. For a moment, she'd felt it again, that fulfillment she'd found in raising Addisyn. She sighed. "Kids are wonderful."

"Indeed. So much love and light. Such a large future. It is no wonder they connect so deeply with the birds."

Elijah hunched slightly on her glove. Probably ready to take a nap. Avery stood to carry him to his crate. "So—I'd love to do this again."

Skyla paused, her hands still full of flyers. "Indeed? Good, then." Her smile warmed her expression. "Because I certainly plan for you to have that chance."

CHAPTER 8

By the time Darius made it home from work the next Tuesday evening, a rainy dusk was peering with hostile eyes from beneath the tree limbs, and on the radio, John Mellencamp was crooning the story of Jack and Diane. Darius turned into his driveway and flipped the radio off. He couldn't focus on the music he normally loved. Not with the task he'd postponed for years now sitting squarely in front of him.

The house was soaked with shadows and unfriendly quiet. He snagged his coat on the hall rack and frowned as he flicked the light switch. He really needed to remember to leave the lights on if he was coming back late.

He paused for a moment, the silence buzzing in his ears. He'd lived in this house all his life. But once he'd inherited it after his parents' death—well, then it was just a shell. A sad, silent shell whose hollowness only reminded him of the great empty spaces that had been ripped in his story.

But someday—someday he'd quit coming home to an empty house where loneliness collected in the corners. Instead, Addisyn's presence would bring the barrenness to life like the first blossoms of spring. And instead of a generic place to eat and sleep and watch the occasional hockey game, this house would become the epicenter of their life together.

Longing squeezed his soul, and he took a deep breath. He was getting ahead of himself. Before he could let himself walk any further into this imaginary future, he had to pry open the past. And in the process of sorting through his parents' belongings, he needed to find the ring.

He could still picture it, his mother's beautiful engagement ring.

Silver band, engraved design, studded with a single solitaire diamond. When the time came—and it would soon—he'd be offering Addisyn that ring.

Now he just had to find it.

He brewed himself a cup of coffee—no way could he face this without caffeine to bolster him—and hurried down the creaking wooden stairs to the basement. He tugged the light chain and blinked in the glare of the bare bulbs that peered from the ceiling. He rarely came down here, and there wasn't much to see. A concrete floor, a threadbare couch that needed to be reupholstered, an old television set. That last year, his parents had been busy converting this to a cozy den area—a place to watch Canucks games and visit with friends and play endless rounds of the board games they'd loved. But then they died, leaving it unfinished.

Like so many other things.

He glanced away from the furniture toward the stack of cardboard boxes in the corner. Sad, that a whole lifetime of moments was reduced to the broken relics that could be crammed into those crates. At the time he'd packed those boxes, he'd been choking under the weight of grief. He'd just shoved everything in and dumped it all here.

Was he ready to step back into that unfinished space?

He took a steadying breath. He needed to focus. To think like a museum curator looking for a specific artifact instead of an aching son missing the people who had been his lifeblood. There was no telling which items were in which boxes. He'd just have to search until he found his mother's jewelry box.

He lifted the lid off the top box, holding himself back as if the past might explode from the contents. Instead, a dusty smell floated out, the scent of memories gone stale. Nothing but dog-eared books on coaching and skating and fitness, all with frayed corners and peeling covers. Darius pulled out *Gold-Medal Discipline* and flipped it open. His dad's writing leapt out—underlined phrases, scribbled notes in the margins. He glanced at one of the sections Dad had highlighted.

Therefore, a growth mindset, as thus described by Dr. Weston, is essential for athletes. Persistence and determination—two traits commonly believed to be inborn qualities—are now shown to be

practiced attitudes that enhance...

Persistence and determination. No wonder his dad had marked that section.

Darius slapped the book shut and dropped it back in the box, then wrestled the lid back on and reached for his Sharpie. BOOKS—DAD.

Okay, so now what? He didn't have any use for the books, but somehow he couldn't envision taking his dad's meticulous notes to Goodwill.

Oh, this was going to be even harder than he thought.

He slid the box aside—he'd decide later—and reached for the next one. This one was heavier, making him grunt as he lifted it. A glance under the lid revealed a dozen photo albums.

His shoulders relaxed just a fraction, and he flipped open the top album. The first photo landed squarely on the broken places in his soul. Dad. Aggressive blond crew cut, signature workout clothes, standing in the gym at Bearstooth. The consummate coach, gripping a forty-pound dumbbell in each hand. No wonder he'd always seemed larger than life.

The pages were stiff, heavy with memories. He thumbed through a few more before he saw himself for the first time. Talking with his dad in some candid shot at his regional championships the year before the Olympics.

Even through the pain of the memories, Darius gave a soft laugh to see the way he'd been at that age—a lanky kid with an awkwardly shaggy haircut that Mom had allowed for way too long. Addisyn would get a kick out of photos from this era.

His laugh faded as he looked at his dad. The man's expression was concrete, set hard with the lines of determination and drive. He was pointing downward, no doubt critiquing some aspect of Darius's performance.

Wanting something that Darius hadn't been able to give.

A strange blend of emotions swirled in his chest. Being coached by his dad had been wonderful; he would never regret it. But it had added another layer to their relationship, introduced a complexity that had sometimes been too much for either of them to navigate. Workouts and training and medals had sometimes overbalanced their dynamic.

Not that Darius could blame the man. Dad had seen gold within Darius, and he'd pushed his son to dig out the ore. And Darius had been just as eager to succeed. He'd thrived on the thrill of competing, and he'd been more than proud to continue the legacy that had flowed downstream to his life…a grandfather who was a gold medalist, a father who was a coach, a whole family circled around the Olympic Rings and the code of sportsmanship and the mysterious ice on which miracles happened.

He could see his dad again, standing by his side at his first trip to Nationals. *"Remember something, when you get on that ice."* The man had gripped his shoulder with an inescapable conviction. *"You're not out there for yourself. You're representing your country, and your sport, and…"* His dad's gesture had encompassed the section of the arena where the rest of Darius's relatives were waiting to see him compete. *"And this family."*

It had been a heavy trust to sling across the shoulders of an early teen, but he'd picked up the mantle without fear. *"I know, Dad."*

"Good." Dad had smiled, but his expression hadn't relaxed. He'd slapped Darius's shoulder with the no-nonsense fire of a coach. *"Go make us proud."*

The memory soured in the air around him. One Olympic medal, and then his career had disintegrated in shame. And now he was just the mountain climber and Uber driver. The weak link that had broken the entire chain of their heritage.

Ordinary house. Ordinary life. Ordinary future.

He'd never made them proud.

⁂

ADDISYN WAS STARTNG a load of laundry on Wednesday morning when Kenzie shuffled into the laundry room apprehensively. "Hey."

Wariness held her back. "Hey."

"I, uh, I need some help."

Oh, so now she was going to be Miss Sociable. Now that she needed something. "With what?" Addisyn didn't make a serious attempt to keep the frost out of her voice.

"Um—" Kenzie picked at her chipping fingernail polish. "I have a doctor's appointment this morning. I didn't find out till last night."

A doctor's appointment? "Are your allergies still bothering you?"

"No. This is for something else." Kenzie narrowed her eyes slightly, apparently already reading Addisyn's next question. "And I'm not contagious."

"Okay..."

Kenzie focused on her fingernails again. "Anyway, I, uh, I need a ride."

Addisyn punched the extra-rinse button on the washer and glanced at the clock on the wall. "You can't borrow Tina's car?"

Embarrassment peered through Kenzie's forced nonchalance. "I, uh, I can't drive."

Sixteen, and she couldn't drive? Avery had thrown Addisyn behind the wheel of her creaky old truck the day she'd turned fourteen. "Oh." What else could she say? "Well, maybe Tina could—"

"I texted her. She said to ask you."

Of course she had. And if Addisyn said no, Tina would be in Trent's ear before you could say *higher standards in Canada*. Addisyn shoved the detergent bottle back onto the shelf. "Okay. Sure, I'll give you a ride. What time is your appointment?"

A flash of relief swept over Kenzie's face. "Ten o'clock. I have the address." She tugged at the hem of her shirt. "It's a weekly thing, actually. My mom thought—my mom set it up for me."

So she would have to ferry Kenzie back and forth every *week*? And when would everyone quit expanding her job description? "Fine."

By nine thirty, she and Kenzie were heading through the downtown area, Kenzie studying directions on her phone. "Turn left at this light."

"Got it." Addisyn flipped on her blinker. It wasn't her business, but she couldn't help but wonder what was wrong with Kenzie. A sports injury, probably. If the appointment was weekly, she was most likely doing physical therapy.

But then, why wouldn't Trent have mentioned something like that? Weird.

"There it is." Kenzie pointed at a low brick building set back from the road. "Whistler Holistic Health."

"All right." Only fifteen minutes from the house. Maybe this wouldn't be too bad after all. Addisyn nosed into a parking space close to the door and left the car running. "What time should I be back to pick you up?"

"Probably an hour."

"Will do."

Kenzie didn't move. Addisyn shifted. "Um, it's 9:50."

"Yeah." She still seemed rooted in place.

Addisyn cleared her throat. "Is there a problem?"

Kenzie twisted her hands in her lap. "Can you—come in? Maybe help me with the paperwork?"

She'd already made her contribution by driving Kenzie there, but... She grabbed her purse. "All right."

Addisyn disliked the office from the moment they stepped foot in the lobby. The whole place was coldly clinical, with sterile white walls and stark metal chairs marching across rigidly geometric tile flooring. She was halfway to the reception desk before she realized Kenzie wasn't beside her. A glance over her shoulder revealed that the girl was still frozen by the door. "Kenzie, come on!"

Kenzie shrank back. "I—I can't—"

Addisyn sighed and backtracked. "Look, your appointment's in ten minutes."

"I—my stomach hurts."

Her breathing was hitching faster, and her face was even paler than normal. Was she—scared? A sliver of sympathy poked at Addisyn. "Hey, it's okay. Just come on and get checked in so—"

"But I don't know how to handle the insurance or—"

"All right." Addisyn took the lead toward the reception desk. "I'll take care of it."

She braced herself against the counter and smiled at the sour-looking woman behind the computer. "Hi. We're here to check in for an appointment."

"Name?" The woman could have been an older version of Tina.

Addisyn nudged Kenzie forward.

"McKenzie Howard." Kenzie's voice was soft, but at least she was speaking up.

"Howard—" The woman scanned her computer screen. "Here to see Dr. Drees?"

"Yes."

"All right." The woman thrust forward a clipboard practically sagging under an overabundance of paperwork. "Start on these forms for me, please. Since you're a first-time patient, we'll need a copy of the insurance card."

Addisyn braced herself, but Kenzie reached into the pocket of her coat and handed over the plastic. Well, she'd come at least partially prepared.

The woman glanced at it, typing in some numbers. "Fifty-dollar copay, please."

Kenzie's brow crinkled in confusion, and she glanced at Addisyn. "What's a copay?" She kept her voice low.

"Payment up front." Years of skating injuries had left Addisyn all too familiar with the insurance process.

"But—I thought the insurance paid everything."

Not even close. "The copay is sort of an upfront fee." They didn't have time for a lesson on the economics of healthcare. "Go ahead and give her the payment."

Kenzie bit her lip. "I don't, uh—"

Oh, so that was the problem. "Here." Addisyn pulled out her wallet and flipped through the cash she kept for emergencies. "Your uncle can pay me back later."

After the woman processed the payment, Addisyn scanned the paperwork with Kenzie and pointed out where she should sign. "Okay, so just fill out the rest of this while you wait. Are you all good?"

Kenzie's expression was next door to terror, but she nodded. "Uh huh."

"All right. I'll be back in an hour."

Addisyn was four steps away when Kenzie cleared her throat. "Hey, um—that was nice. What you did."

Addisyn blinked and turned back toward her. "What?"

She ducked her head a little sheepishly. "The money—you know. Just—thanks."

Kenzie was thanking her? "Oh, uh, it was nothing." Addisyn waved and turned away. "See you in an hour."

She stepped outside, blinking in the morning brightness, and glanced back at the four M.D. names painted on the glass door. Who had Kenzie said she was seeing? Dr. Drees, right?

Yeah, there it was. *Dr. Leann Drees. Doctor of mind-body health.*

Concern crinkled over her. She didn't know much about doctors. But suddenly she had the feeling that whatever was wrong with Kenzie went deeper than a sports injury.

As she walked to the car, she glanced back at the waiting room windows. But the glass was deeply tinted, and she couldn't see Kenzie clearly.

Maybe she never had.

IT HAD BEEN exactly an hour when Kenzie rushed out of the building and slid into the passenger seat of the car. Addisyn smiled in a way she hoped was encouraging. "So? How'd it go?" Although the speed of her exit from the building probably answered that question.

Kenzie let out a breath and leaned back with the expression of a war-weary refugee. "Dr. Drees was okay."

"So...are *you* okay?"

Kenzie fiddled with her seatbelt. "Sure."

She'd pulled even deeper into herself. Deep enough that she might never come up for air. Deep enough that Addisyn could almost—if she didn't think too much about the ways Kenzie had complicated her life—feel sorry for the girl.

What had Avery said? Keep trying to build that connection.

Not that her sister was right, but still... Addisyn cleared her throat. "Do you need anything?"

Kenzie snapped her head up, suspicion peering from every corner of her face. "Like what?"

"Like...uh..." Her thoughts stalled. "I don't know. You tell me."

Kenzie studied her for a long moment. "You mean, like, what would help me?"

Addisyn shrugged. "Yeah."

Kenzie leaned back in the seat. "I need to go back on Redfeather Ridge."

"What?" Addisyn hadn't meant her tone to come out that loud. She lowered her voice and tried again. "Why do you need to go back up there?"

Rosy embarrassment soaked into Kenzie's face. "I still need to check on—that thing. What was here before."

The conversation was dizzyingly random. "Yeah, but—you said you didn't see it the other day."

Kenzie made an uneasy face. "It might be there now."

What was this, something that might grow legs and march around the valley? Nope. They weren't doing this any longer, with Kenzie's riddles chasing their tails around the situation. Addisyn folded her arms. "Look, Kenzie. I'm not doing anything—" she jabbed the steering wheel for emphasis—"until you tell me what you're looking for and where you think it is and why it might be there now when it wasn't the other day."

Kenzie bit her lip and swept the car with a furtive glance, as if eavesdroppers might be lurking in the backseat. When she finally met Addisyn's gaze, her eyes held a challenge. "You'll think it's weird."

She'd already thought that about everything else Kenzie had done. "Try me."

"I'm looking for a spirit bear."

A—*what*?

Kenzie held her gaze evenly with no sign of retracting the statement. Addisyn opened her mouth, then closed it again. Desperately she shook herself loose from the shock. "A—a spirit bear?"

"Yes."

Addisyn's exhale was too confused to be a laugh. "Um—what is that?" Surely it was just a metaphorical name for some butterfly or mushroom and not an actual—

"A white bear." Kenzie leaned forward, her words tumbling over each other. "They're really rare, and they're entirely white, I mean, white like a polar bear. And I saw one last time, and—"

"Stop." Addisyn held up her hands. This had taken a hard left past *strange* into *certifiably nuts.* "A white bear?"

Kenzie gave her a steady look for a moment. As if measuring trust in her gaze. Then she took a deep breath. "When I was here before, I saw a white bear. From the ridge."

The ridge where they'd just been. Where Kenzie wanted to go again. Addisyn reflexively stiffened.

"You don't believe me?"

"Well—I mean—that does sound pretty—" What was a less offensive synonym for *crazy?*

Kenzie's eyes flared. "Look, I didn't make it up. And after I went home, I did some research. There really are white bears, and they're called spirit bears. Actually, they're just ordinary black bears with some kind of genetic quirk or something, but they're really rare and protected. There are even a whole lot of Native stories about them."

"And they're here, in Whistler?"

Kenzie hesitated. "Well, they're usually farther north. Like, along the coast. But it doesn't matter. I know what I saw. And now—" Her eyes were enormous, the intensity of her gaze startling. "I need to find it again."

Okay, this was outrageous. "What—when—" Her temples were starting to throb. "Why do you *need* to find this bear?" The statement felt ridiculous even saying it.

Kenzie pressed her lips together. "There's a legend—" She broke off and shook her head. "Look, it's personal, okay?"

Personal? Surely this was not her life. Surely she was not listening to a girl she could barely tolerate convincing her to search for some weird animal that sounded more like a myth. Addisyn crossed her arms. "And—they're really called spirit bears?"

"Yeah. Or some people call them ghost bears."

Ghost bears. Oh yeah, that made her feel better. She didn't want anything to do with a ghost or a bear, let alone the two together.

"Kenzie—" Where had this big-sister voice come from? She'd always hated that tone from Avery. She cleared her throat. "Look, I'm not doubting you"—although she was—"but—there's a lot of land around those trails. A lot of miles of dense forest." Filled with snakes and bears and wildcats and who knew what else. "And, you know, we can't possibly cover all of it."

"But we can go back to the ridge."

"And maybe that bear isn't—well, you know, they may not live that long, and if you saw it before, then—"

"The average bear lives nineteen years."

Scratch that tactic. "But—won't it be kind of like a needle in a haystack? I mean—"

"I have to try, Addisyn!"

The intensity in Kenzie's voice caught Addisyn off guard. The girl leaned forward, her expression caught with conviction for the first time. "Look, I know it's crazy, okay? And if I don't find it, I don't find it. But I can't just give up."

Addisyn wasn't normally the most rational person, but even she could hear reason screaming in her ear on this one. "Kenzie, I really don't think—"

"Never mind." Kenzie's voice was low, but there was a rock-hard granite to her tone. "I get it. You don't believe me, and you're not going to help."

"I didn't say—"

"This is what always happens." Ice crusted at the edges of Kenzie's words. "But I should have expected this. You don't know—" She stopped. Breathed out. Squinted out the windshield at the scowling office from which she'd just come. "You don't know how important it is to me."

The words knocked her sideways. She'd heard them before. The day she'd been convincing Avery to let her compete at Regionals the first time. Her sister's face had been lined with worry, anxiety doing the math on the entry fee and gas for the drive and a paycheck still eight days away. They'd argued for half an hour until Addisyn had reached for the same gauntlet Kenzie had just flung down.

"You don't know how important it is to me..."

And Avery had watched her with measuring eyes, then pulled her into a hug. *"Okay, Ads. I'll make it work."*

She'd filled out her entry form that night.

How many other sacrifices had Avery made? And for the most part, Addisyn had been as thankless as Kenzie.

She blinked back to reality. "Kenzie—" She would regret this moment, no doubt. But she took a deep breath and tried not to think about spirits or bears. "Listen. Only twice, okay?"

"Twice?"

"Twice back up the ridge. Once this week, once next week." Her legs already ached at the thought. "And then we're done, because we can't take up all your skating time with this." She pinned Kenzie with her gaze. "Okay?"

Kenzie opened her mouth, then closed it again. "You mean it?"

"Yes." The word dragged a grudge behind it, but something softened in Kenzie's eyes anyway.

"Really? Can we go tomorrow?"

Addisyn put the car in drive a little harder than necessary. "We'll see what the weather does." She'd start praying for rain now.

Oh, what had she just agreed to?

△△ △△ △△

ADDISYN STILL SEEMED out of sorts during practice. And she didn't say a word the whole time they drove back to the house. She'd driven with arms stiff and jaw locked and a thundercloud behind her eyes. Not that Kenzie could blame her.

She wasn't stupid. She knew how ridiculous the whole thing sounded. Especially to a girl like Addisyn. A girl who had everything she needed would never understand the way desperation clawed at your insides.

It would probably make more sense if she explained the legend. But she'd already shared more than she'd wanted to. If there had been any way to get to the trails without Addisyn's help, she would have never let the other girl in on the project. Yet another reason that stupid driver's license would come in handy. If she could ever get it, of course.

In the meantime, she'd keep the rest of her secrets in her pockets, even if they could have helped prove her sanity. Who cared anyway if Addisyn thought she was crazy? The older girl already disliked her—that much was obvious. Which was fine.

Addisyn pulled up to Uncle Trent's house and rolled down her window. "I wish Tina would change this code." The words were a disgusted mutter as she jabbed GO AWAY into the keypad. She glanced over her shoulder at Kenzie. "What do you think? Does she mean it?"

Kenzie glanced up at the lefthand window on the second story as they followed the driveway. Dark blinds were a tightly shut eyelid. "Uh huh. Definitely."

As soon as Addisyn put the car in park, Kenzie hurried into her bedroom. Only within the embrace of the four walls was there some sort of security. You were only safe when you were alone, anyway.

She flopped back down on the bed. She definitely wasn't hungry, and she didn't feel like facing Addisyn any more this evening. What about Instagram? She hadn't checked social media since she'd been in Whistler. But it might be interesting to see what everybody was up to.

She flicked onto the feed. The first picture was Erika Wilson with her parents, a Monopoly board spread on the table in front of them. **Family game night! Love these two.**

What would that be like? To have two parents so clearly devoted to each other and to you? Kenzie studied Erika's dad, the way he kept a protective arm around his daughter. Her own father—if you could call him that—had left her with nothing more than some jumbled little-kid memories. Mom had never said where he went after that, and Kenzie had never asked. She knew where he wasn't, and that was what mattered.

Next picture. Britt and Beth, pulling funny faces while clutching ice cream cones. **It's not #sistersummer until you have matching desserts!**

There was a glow on both their faces that Kenzie had almost forgotten. She frowned and drew her knees onto the bed. Funny thing was, Britt and Beth were both kind of on the fringes of school. Same way she was. But they were their own dynamic duo, and the loneliness that had been strangling Kenzie for so long never touched them. That's why having a sister would have been cool. Like a built-in bestie.

She flicked on through the feed. All the kids she knew, scrolling by in a highlight reel of happiness. Campfires and vacations and prom dates and pets. Smiles stacking on each other until her own loneliness pinched even tighter.

And then in the midst of the feed, suddenly there was Marie

Schwann's face. Like the snake in Paradise. Propped next to William Trott, making some pouty hot-girl face. Thanks to my bae @real_will for standing beside me during all these months of skating! Practices are easier when I can hang out with you afterwards.

Oh, and how exactly had Will *stood beside her?* From what Kenzie could tell, his biggest contribution had been appearing as Marie's accessory on Instagram. Still, maybe somebody should tell Will that his *bae* had a mean streak wider than the Christie Inlet and didn't try to hide it.

Kenzie should know.

She skimmed the rest of the caption. Mostly more gushing about Will, along with a sickening number of heart emojis, but the last sentence stopped her cold.

@montreal_skate_six here I come! #practicemakesperfect

Skate Six? Marie had applied too?

Her heart skittered into overdrive. Last time she'd checked—by eavesdropping in the locker room, mainly—she was the only one from her local club planning to apply. She'd figured even the snooty skating camp was beneath Marie, anyway.

But apparently not.

Panic pushed higher. She couldn't lose this chance. Going to the elite training camp was the kind of thing that could salvage any skater. Even one who'd been away from the ice for almost a year.

Which was why Kenzie had spent hours painstakingly completing her application, mailing it off just before she'd come to BC. The application was based on—she'd memorized the wording—*highest scores in all competitive events, aggregated from the past season.* Last season, her scores had been well above the eligibility requirements. Even with her—uh—setback, Uncle Trent expected her to be called for auditions in August.

So Marie wasn't a threat, right? The other girl's scores had never been close to hers. Unless…unless something had changed that she didn't know about…

Kenzie zoomed in on the picture and frowned, studying Marie's appearance for any clues of improved performance. She'd lost weight, hadn't she? Yeah…it looked like it. In those pants, at least. She'd always been pretty skinny, but now she was practically a human Barbie doll.

Anxiety squirmed through her. Marie was losing weight and working out and trying to nab that Skate Six spot. Meanwhile, Kenzie was—what? Holed up in the BC nowhere, trying to stagger back into a sport that was feeling more and more foreign. Every time she got on the ice, the anxiety drowned her once again. Her hands felt numb, and her legs shook so much she botched even the simplest moves. She didn't need the impatient look on Addisyn's face to tell her that she was failing.

The idea raked a frantic kind of urgency up her spine. Skating was an unforgiving sport, a discipline where the odds stacked higher every year. It was a race against time, a battle to cram as much competition as possible into the ever-shrinking window of youth. So what if she couldn't make up the ground she'd lost?

And if Marie got to go to Skate Six…after all she'd done…

Kenzie tossed her phone aside. She should have known better than to check Instagram. It always colored things even darker for her. And now the pain was only increasing, the anxiety thrumming its way through her with every fluttering heartbeat.

There was only one thing that helped when she felt like this. She grabbed the bag she kept by her bed—already her hands were unsteady— and fumbled frantically in the bottom. There. She yanked out the crumpled T-shirt, shaking it loose until the pill bottle fell in her lap.

The bottle was green, with a label crammed with fine print and some chemical names she couldn't pronounce. Her sweaty hands slipped on the childproof cap. She swiped her palm against her shorts, and the dose rattled out: two of the little orange ovals.

She hesitated just a moment. The pills were supposed to help with her problems, but sometimes she felt a little uneasy about taking them. Especially after last year. Uncle Trent would say that she shouldn't have kept ordering them online. She shouldn't have brought them with her to Whistler. And she shouldn't be staring at a dose in her palm right now.

Marie's face flashed back to her mind, and resolve turned her hesitation to steel. The girl for whom perfection was a plastic mask. The girl who'd found a way to bury her words inside Kenzie's brain until she'd driven Kenzie into exile from everything that mattered. The girl who was the reason she was in Whistler at all.

No! She'd do whatever it took to keep Marie from undercutting her any more than she'd already done. And that started with the pills.

She grabbed a bottle of water from her nightstand and twisted the cap off. One swallow, two, and the pills were gone. Her stomach lurched slightly, guilt sliding through the nausea.

But she had no reason to feel guilty. The pills had great reviews online. And there was nothing wrong with them, really. They were just medicine. No different than an aspirin or a Tylenol, right? And a lot of the kids she knew used them with no problems. As long as you didn't exceed the dosage. And she never did.

She heard movement on the porch. Was Addisyn coming back in? She grabbed the bottle and thrust it back into her bag, burying it under her T-shirts. She wasn't trying to hide the pills, exactly, but it was none of Addisyn's business either.

Outside, the last rays of sun flashed against Tina's window. At one time, she would have told her cousin everything. All the ways life had gone wrong, all the things that left her opening that green bottle every day. And Tina would have been sarcastic and straight-shooting, but somehow, she'd have found a way to hide hope between her snarky words.

But that, like so many other things, was gone.

Kenzie needed a distraction. And some fresh air. The pills always made her feel a little dizzy. She cracked the bedroom door open and glanced down the hall. Addisyn was nowhere to be seen, so she tiptoed through the entryway and outside into the cool evening.

She closed the door gently behind her and took a deep breath of the fresh air. There. The lightheadedness was settling. She wandered across the backyard, into the summer evening fragrant with cut grass and blooming plants.

It smelled like hope and life and joy. Everything she'd long since lost.

Before she could start crying, she saw it—a narrow trail that dodged between the trees, heading up the hill. She blinked, old memories creeping back. It was still there? Did that mean the fort was too?

She jogged up the trail, following as it unrolled itself to the foot of a grandfatherly oak. And sure enough, there it was, the rough wooden platform perched in a fork of the branches. The rope ladder was fraying now, but when she tugged on it, nothing gave way.

She scurried up, the rope burning her palms, avoiding the two broken rungs. And then she could crawl onto the weathered boards, the moss that clung to them damp against her legs. She leaned into the tree and breathed in the gentle peace of the Vancouver rainforest. Finally. A place that didn't rub her soul raw.

She closed her eyes and let the happier days float back through her heart. From elementary school on, she and Tina had used the place as their headquarters. They'd watched the Perseid meteor shower, swapping wishes with every shooting star. They'd played endless games of crazy eights—the warped deck of cards was probably still tucked into the tackle box at the back of the platform. And of course, they'd spun stories, though Tina's had veered toward the edge of Kenzie's comfort zone—ghosts and goblins and whatnot.

She gave a soft laugh in spite of herself. How many nights had she had nightmares after that one story? Something about an evil sea queen who rode a killer whale.

Kenzie had come alive in these woods. The best moments of her life had sown themselves into her soul while she'd run through the rainforest. And then there had been the white bear.

During spring break, it had been. Mom and she had moved to Montreal the winter before, but they'd come back for ten whole days. And she'd spent her time running wild with Tina—trying out the climbing wall, racing each other along the trails, and exploring the woods behind the center with the toy swords Uncle Zach had given them. And on the last day, the white bear had happened. She could still hold the memory like a keepsake, still replay the scene and watch the creature she'd never really believed in until then crashing down the hillside.

She'd planned to find it again that summer, when they were set to return. But instead, late one stormy night in the middle of April, Mom had received a phone call. Uncle Zach and Aunt Cynthia were dead. Killed in a car crash on the winding mountain roads.

They'd flown back for the funeral, but all the grown-ups were tense and sad, the air in the house heavy. Even Tina had seemed different. They hadn't gone back that summer. And then they hadn't gone again. And everything marvelous about the sighting of the white bear had drifted downstream in the wake of high school drama and health problems.

But she'd never forgotten that bear. Mainly because of the legend. She hadn't needed it then. But now…now she could only hope the stories were true.

So who cared if Addisyn thought the search was stupid? It was the first thing in a long time that had sparked even a pinprick of hope. Because if she could find the white bear, then maybe she could find something else.

The girl she once had been.

CHAPTER 9

Addisyn had never been thankful for BC's wet weather before, but now three straight days of steady rain brought immense relief. At least she had a reprieve before Kenzie dragged her into those woods to be eaten by spirit bears. The name alone made shivers tingle up her spine. Why Kenzie was so bent on this, she had no idea. It was getting harder to refute Tina's assertion that the girl was crazy.

It was still drizzling on Saturday evening when Addisyn drove across town to Darius's house. He lived in the Alpine Village, a quiet neighborhood that Addisyn had always loved. She passed the fire station and park and followed the woodsy streets until she saw his lights glowing through the fog. She parked in his driveway and pulled the hood of her jacket up as she dashed through the drizzle to the porch.

The little ranch-style house looked prettier than ever. Darius had pruned some of the overgrown bushes in the flower beds and replaced the ugly dented mailbox with a nice white model. He was even planning to paint the house in the fall. She'd gone with him to the home improvement store one evening and helped him pick out a lovely butter-yellow shade.

No answer to her knock. "Darius?" She cautiously pushed the door open. "I'm here."

Only the soft whoosh of the oven and some delicious smell, but then she heard sounds coming from the basement—muffled thumps and sliding, along with snatches of breathy singing. She smiled and headed down the steps.

Sure enough, there he was, stacking boxes with his back to her. She leaned against the doorway for a moment. She'd never get tired of watching him, the way his moves held an expert athleticism, the way his dark hair curled against his shoulders, the way he often sang, low and softly questioning under his breath. She'd spent enough time listening to his playlists that she recognized the tune he was singing now. Elton John. "I Guess That's Why They Call It the Blues."

The shame she'd felt at Alexander Falls burned hot up her neck again. He was the kind of guy she'd never even dreamed of. And she was only—

He turned and saw her, and the song broke off. "Hey."

The awkwardness of the situation suddenly tapped her on the shoulder. She'd walked into his house without permission! Why did she never think before she did anything? "I'm sorry—I knocked—but when you didn't come—the door was unlocked—"

He just laughed. "I'm glad you came on in. I can't hear anything from down here. Concrete ceiling, you know." He crossed the space between them and pulled her into his arms. "How's your day been?"

The way he always cared made her feel beyond special. "Okay. The usual."

"How's Kenzie doing?"

She hesitated. Should she mention the white bear to him? But what could she even say that wouldn't sound ridiculous? "She's…okay. Still a little, uh, tense." Probably the whole bear thing would be no big deal anyway. She'd take Kenzie on the ridge again, they wouldn't see it, and there. The end, right?

He frowned. "I guess it's hard for her to adjust."

"You could say that." She hadn't come here to talk about Kenzie. She looked over his shoulder at the boxes. "How many more do you have to sort through?"

"Believe me, I'm asking myself the same thing." Darius tugged off his beanie and ran his hand through his hair with a rueful expression. "I've gone through that stack so far."

That stack was a dismal little heap of no more than four boxes. Out of what looked like four hundred. Addisyn searched for something encouraging to say. "You're making good progress."

He shrugged. "Slower than I want to go."

"Well, there's no deadline, is there?"

"No…just…" An odd nervousness crept into his expression, and he looked away. "Just—I want this place ready for whatever comes next."

Before she could decipher the odd remark, he cleared his throat and jammed his beanie back on. "I did want to show you something, though." He grabbed a leather-bound book from the top of one of the boxes, then flopped down on the decrepit sofa and patted the place beside him. "Come look."

She perched next to him as he flipped the book open, and laughter burst out before she could stop it. "That's you?"

"Yep." He was grinning, clearly enjoying her reaction. "Am I rockin' it or what?"

"*Or what* is more like it." She was still laughing too hard to say more. Darius must have been thirteen or fourteen in the photo—a beanpole of a guy with a cringey haircut and a cheap suit standing beside a flower-clutching girl who looked almost as awkward as he did.

"Yep, that was the weird high-school dance thing they did at church every April." Darius rolled his eyes. "I was in ninth grade. Why I ever thought that haircut looked good, I can't imagine. Total dork phase."

"Well, you definitely grew out of it." As soon as the words slipped out, her face heated. To escape Darius's knowing grin, she pointed at the photo. "Who's the girl?"

"The associate pastor's daughter. My first crush." He leaned back, stretching his arms over his head. "I thought I had scored a big one, getting her to go to the dance with me."

She had no reason to be jealous. "You liked her?"

"Yeah, until that evening." He grimaced. "Turns out the most serious thing she'd ever thought of was what lipstick matched what eyeliner. I don't think we ever talked again after that night."

"Short-lived romance." She drew her knees up on the couch. "What about the others?"

He gave a soft laugh and slid closer to her, draping an arm around her shoulders. "Others?"

"Yeah." The warmth from his arm felt good. She pulled back just enough to let him see her teasing grin. "Come on. There must have been a lot of girls with eyes on you."

"No, not really. I was busy skating. Traveling to train and compete. Plus—" He shrugged. "I never met any girls that were interesting." His expression deepened. "Until you."

She couldn't let him see how his words affected her. "I'm honored." She kept her tone light.

"What about you?"

Her heart turned over. "Well—" The room was colder than before. "I didn't date anyone seriously before Brian."

"I don't mean date." His tone was still casual. "Who was your first crush?"

"Oh—" She bit her lip. Someday she'd tell him, but not today. "The usual, I suppose. Movie stars and singers. Guys that could stare right at the camera with a heart-stopping look."

"I can do that." Darius leaned forward and angled himself toward her with an exaggerated smolder drawn straight from the cover of *Teen Vogue*. "See?"

"Stop it!" She swatted him, but not before her giggle escaped.

"How am I doing?" The corners of his mouth were twitching. He was struggling to hold the pose.

She could have kissed him on the spot, but she just laughed instead. "Ten out of ten."

"So there. I'm as good as those guys."

She snuggled next to him and slipped her hand in his, the warmth from his side working through her. "You're better." She gazed at their linked hands, at the Olympic tattoo inked along the inside of his forearm. "Darius?"

"Yep?"

"Do you ever miss skating?"

He was quiet for a moment, no doubt examining the question, holding it up to the light. "Well, sometimes, I guess. I wish things had worked out differently with my injury."

She nodded. After the January event, they'd had the chance to audition as a competitive team, but Darius's injury hadn't been fully healed enough. He hadn't said much about it, but he hadn't needed to for her to feel his disappointment.

"But still, I don't think I miss it enough to want to go back." He shifted. "If you're competing—that's your whole life. You know that."

"Yes." She'd been there, lived the rigid life encircled entirely by the railing of the ice rink. For a moment she considered Kenzie. Was that really how the younger girl wanted to live?

"And now I have other important things in my life." He squeezed her hand. "Although I guess Uncle Trent will never understand that."

She bit her lip. She hadn't meant to ask, but since he brought it up… "What happened? With you and him?"

Darius studied the opposite wall. "My accident."

Oh. "When you fell? In Sochi?"

"Yes." His shoulders drooped slightly beneath an invisible burden. "He'll never stop blaming me."

"But that's behind you now."

"I know, but—" He shook his head. "The accident was from one stupid decision. I never touched alcohol before or since. And Uncle Trent will always hold me responsible. The way he sees it, I let down our whole family."

The pain in his voice made her desperate to comfort him. "Darius—" She gently traced his tattoo with her free hand. "Don't listen to him. He doesn't have a right to make you feel that way."

Darius shrugged one shoulder helplessly. "He's my family. And he's not wrong."

Why did he always defend Trent? Addisyn leaned back and frowned. As far as she was concerned, people who weren't willing to walk with you through your mistakes didn't deserve the title of *family*, regardless of what showed up on a DNA test. But then again, what right did she have to weigh in on Darius's relational dynamics? Goodness knew that except for Avery, her family tree was loaded with the proverbial nuts.

"But—" Hope tipped his words upward. "I just have to keep reminding myself of the truth. God's forgiven me. Now I live for Him."

He was so sincere, so rooted in his faith. The way she longed to be. "Darius?"

"Mmhm?"

"At church—the pastor talked about everything happening for a

134

reason. How do you know that's true?" She rushed on before he could answer. "And don't just tell me because the Bible says so, okay? Like, how do you really know?"

Darius nodded thoughtfully, accepting her question with gentle hands. "Well—I guess I'd say because you can see the pattern."

"What do you mean?" She waited for the words, the answer that might unlock the kind of faith that he and Avery shared.

"Because nothing happens by accident." Darius's every word shone with a trust she could only dream of. "I can't usually see it at the time, you know? But then I look back, and I see all the hundreds of choices—choices I thought were all mine—and I see how they make this—this pattern."

"But what if—" Shadows clashed in her mind. Brian's face. "Even the bad parts?"

"Even then." He glanced out the window, where dusk clouded beneath the trees. "The pattern is big enough, Addisyn. Grace brings it all together. We can't always see it, but that's where faith comes in."

His answer was strong, a rope to follow out of the dark. But still her steps were unsure.

"Now, I better check on our food in the oven." Darius squeezed her hand one last time, then stood and headed for the doorway. On the threshold he paused. "Addisyn?"

"Yeah?"

"There's one other really important part of the pattern that I can see." He came back to the couch, framed her face with his hands. "You and me."

He pressed his lips to hers in a kiss that reminded her all over again of how he surpassed her wildest dreams. When he pulled away, he brushed back a strand of her hair. "I love you, Addisyn Miles. Don't ever forget that."

"I love you too." She whispered the words, soft enough that they wouldn't be heard by her fears, and watched him head for the door. As his footsteps jogged up the stairs, she sank into the couch.

Nothing happens by accident...the pattern...

Was it true what Darius said? That divine hands wrote every story? Looking back, she could see some of the pieces at play. Finding the first slivers of light even in the midst of Brian's darkness. Rebuilding the bridge she'd burned with Avery. And of course, meeting Darius in what was too crazy to be a coincidence.

But there couldn't be any pattern in what Brian had done. There, the knots entwined around all her wrong choices. And Darius's talk of a faith to follow twisted itself into tangles.

Just more proof that he was too good for her.

The photo album was still open on the arm of the couch. She glanced at Darius's awkward teen picture again and couldn't help but smile. Dear Darius, who'd only loved her. But she was anything but a pastor's daughter.

Who was your first crush?

She closed her eyes, and there she was again, a lovestruck preteen kneeling on the floor in front of her family's TV, watching the skaters at the Vancouver Olympics. Especially the gorgeous fifteen-year-old who'd skated under the name of Andrew Payne.

She hadn't followed his career after the Olympics. She hadn't expected to cross paths with him. And she certainly hadn't expected to see his sterling soul or to fall in love with the way his heart beat with a rare kind of strength.

And in the meantime, she'd gambled her whole self on a broken relationship that was never anything but a losing game.

If only she could go back to that kid watching the TV. She'd tell that romantic young girl to never look twice at Brian. Instead, she'd plead with her to wait for the man who truly loved her.

The man whose place in the pattern was far more precise than hers.

△△ △△ △△

THE STORE WASN'T as busy the next Friday, the pace slow enough for Avery to leave early. She eagerly covered the miles to the center, wondering about the Barn Owl all the way. The bird's second trial flight was scheduled for today. Hopefully the deficiencies in her flight would be corrected by now.

The details were still on her mind as she breezed through the center door and almost bumped into Skyla. "Hi, Skyla! Have you tried the Barn Owl anymore? I—"

Her words broke off as she finally registered Skyla's expression. The woman's rare smile was shining until her face nearly glowed. "Avery, I have been waiting for you." She clasped her hands together, her words treading on each other's heels. "A blessing has come to us."

"A blessing?" Her pulse quickened. "What's going on?"

"Come." Skyla beckoned her into the main room. "Chay has gathered everyone."

Sure enough, Avery hurried after her to see the rest of the staff and volunteers huddled in a circle. She squeezed in next to Skyla. "What's happened?"

Skyla folded her hands in a prayer-like gesture. "Everyone, we have most joyous news to share." She glanced around the circle. "The center will be expanding."

"Expanding?" So—bigger flight cages? A new rehab area? Oh! Maybe a larger administration building. That would be amazing.

"Yes." Chay stepped up beside Skyla and slung an arm around her shoulders. "We—" he smiled proudly at his wife—"just received word that we've been awarded the Great Outdoors Grant. This is a funding opportunity through U of C. We applied for it several months back but weren't sure we had any chance of being selected. But today—" His grin burst through his words. "Today we received the email."

The circle erupted in spontaneous applause. "That sounds incredible." Across the room, Tyler leaned forward, appearing nearly as excited as Avery felt. "So—what does *expansion* mean, exactly?"

Chay turned to Skyla. "This part is your news, dear."

Skyla smiled at the group. "To explain what lies ahead, I must first remind you of something of which I have spoken often. You have heard me say that the world that has been created is so alive. Vibrant with power and beauty and more wonder than can ever be seen." A passion crackled behind her words. "So many people go through their lives head-down. They do not see the artistry. And so they miss the chance to be amazed, to see the miraculous, to—to be soul-healed."

Heads bobbed around the circle, Avery's among them. Every word mirrored her own beliefs, echoed the same breath-snatching awe she'd first found among the mountains.

Skyla straightened her shoulders. "Thus, this center exists for more than the healing of the wings. It has always been my intent, and Chay's, that one day, it would become a—a doorway, one might say." Skyla held both hands in front of her like a gate. "A connection point, so that people might come and behold the wonders that wait for us all. And in so doing, they might find rest for their souls."

Tyler tilted his head, as if trying to see Skyla's words. "You mean—like a museum? A conservatory?"

Chay shook his head. "More hands-on than that. The idea is outdoor education. Giving people a way to learn about the natural world. It's up to us to decide what that looks like, but most likely we'll be holding classes and guided nature walks, maybe creating interactive exhibits or observation areas. We're hoping to host school groups too."

"Will we quit doing bird rehab?" One of the older rehab techs, a burly guy named Tom, frowned.

"No, certainly not." Chay shook his head quickly. "This is just an expansion on top of what we already offer. And of course, the new programs will include the species ambassadors."

Skyla nodded. "In this way, we can offer so much more healing. Of course it teaches people to protect this world, because when they truly witness the wonder, they will be led to act. But beyond this, it is much good for them as well. Many hearts have been healed by seeking the Creator in what His hands have formed." Her eyes shifted to the clouds outside the window. "Including mine."

The idea was brilliant—a concept so desperately needed in a world that every day seemed to grow more callous to wonder. Avery could already imagine the people—children whose wide eyes were still undimmed, adults whose years of cynicism could be peeled back, teenagers who could look up from their technology to a world more thrilling than any glowing screen. All of them, they'd wander weary through the doors, but they'd leave with hope in their hands. And she'd be a part of the story—pointing their eyes to El Shaddai and His marvelous world.

She snapped her focus back. Skyla was still talking. "—fill some of the deficiencies, as well." Skyla smiled. "We can mend the flight cages, for one thing. And we can also bring more who share this vision."

Chay nodded. "We've had so much support from dedicated volunteers. But now, with the new funding, we'll be able to hire more staff and fill those positions permanently."

Hire more staff.

Her joy dissolved like snow in the spring sunshine. Of course. Why hadn't she remembered? She was only a volunteer. Just a placeholder until someone far more capable could take her place. And now that day had come.

Was there nowhere that needed her anymore?

No more Friday afternoons. No more running behind the birds. No watching the wonders of nature with the crowds who would come. Her eyes stung, and she shrank back. The circle had disintegrated into a chattering crowd, with Skyla and Chay still fielding excited questions. No one would notice if she left.

She backed out of the room and ducked through the doorway, blinking the disappointment away. Regardless of the raw edges of her emotions, she had a job to do. The birds were depending on her.

At least, until she was shuffled aside by someone better and smarter and more capable.

She headed straight for the Barn Owl, stilling her shaking hands enough to wrap the bird in a towel and complete the brief physical exam. She'd painstakingly memorized each step of the process. Knowledge she wouldn't need now.

The disappointment kept churning its way through her while she jogged behind the bird in the flight cage. The owl's movements were smoother, stronger. She'd be ready for release in another month. Would someone else already be handling her by then? How many Friday afternoons did Avery have left before she spent them only with the store? Nothing but the store.

"Avery?"

Avery swiped the dampness from her cheeks—surely she wasn't crying. "Skyla." She couldn't make eye contact, not without Skyla instantly reading her hurt. "Did you—did you need something?"

"That is the question I would ask you." Skyla stepped into the flight cage, perplexity written across her expression. "I did not realize you had left during the meeting." She glanced at the Barn Owl, and her expression eased slightly. "I should have known you would be with the wings."

Not for much longer.

Skyla watched as the owl settled onto a perch. "How is her flight?"

"Much better. Stronger." Avery forced herself to focus on the protocol. "Her lean to the left seems to have corrected. Both wings are pushing equally."

"Excellent." Skyla smiled. "You have done well, Avery, these last few months. But—now—"

Here it was. Skyla would thank her for her time and send her on her way—graciously, of course, but still. Avery braced herself. "Now—?"

"We discussed paths the other day." Skyla ran a hand through her hair, then resettled her wide-brimmed hat and leaned against the wall of the flight cage. "You seemed unsure."

"Well—yes." Why couldn't Skyla get to the point? Dancing around the blow wasn't helping either of them.

"And truly, that is a story I lived before."

Hadn't Skyla said something about that earlier? Something about her heart healing? But Avery couldn't picture the strong, confident woman lost and searching. "Really? What did you do?"

Skyla fingered her copper bracelet. "I met Chay, and through him, the birds. And I watched their wings until I myself held the strength to fly." She spread her hands. "And I would invite you to follow the wings as I have done."

Avery didn't dare read between the lines of her words. "You mean—"

"Avery, you carry a healing. You do not know this yet, perhaps, but I can see."

A healing? What did Skyla think she saw? Avery took a step back, ducking away from Skyla's gaze. "No, I—"

"Avery, please receive this." Skyla's voice rang rich with empathy. "I have watched you. At the center, with the birds, and with the hearts of the children last week. I know your strength. If you would give your gift at the center, we would be highly honored to have you."

"Skyla—" She couldn't begin to sort through all the questions, but— "You're—are you offering me a job?"

"Yes, with gratitude."

Every expectation slid sideways. Skyla was offering her a job? *Her*? A *job*? Here with the birds, where she could help and watch and—

The next instant reality rushed in and dumped her back to earth. "Skyla, that's so kind of you, but—I'm not—" *Not educated. Not trained. Not prepared. Not brave.* "Not—qualified."

"Qualified?" Skyla's eyebrows disappeared under the rim of her hat. "You hold the skills in your heart. Given time, they would find their way to your hands with no trouble. It is your gift."

There was that *gift* business again. Skyla had read her all wrong. "I've never worked in anything like this before—"

"And beginning must start at some time." Skyla pressed her palms together. "There is more, Avery, than the mending of wings. There is also the gift of watching the journey, of living the story with the birds, and then of sharing it with all. And that is the gift you possess. You can hold the birds, and you can tell their stories. The combination is indeed rare."

Oh, Skyla was wrong about her. The older woman was doing what she always did—seeing through the prism of her personality. Finding rainbows where there was only ordinary white light. Avery stared at her hands, watching her confidence slip so easily through her fingers. "I don't think—"

"I do not need an answer now. Think and pray and be still." Skyla turned her searching gaze on Avery. "Please, Avery. Hold this chance, and listen to what the wind will say. Can you promise me this?"

Could she do anything less for the woman she'd rapidly come to respect? Avery swallowed. "Of course."

Across the enclosure, the owl flung herself into the air again, wings forging forward. Avery scuffed her boot along the sawdust-scattered ground.

When had she lost that kind of courage?

⩲ ⩲ ⩲

"GOOD JOB, KENZIE." Addisyn nodded and leaned against the railing, jerking back in remembrance when it wobbled in protest. She clenched her jaw. No funds to replace a railing, indeed.

She refocused on Kenzie, who was warming up with gentle crossovers. "Keep your shoulders relaxed, okay?"

Kenzie just nodded, but her tight expression didn't relax. Addisyn's own face probably reflected that worry. Trent had informed her that he would be coming today for what he had diplomatically framed as a *progress check*.

Nitpicking session was probably more like it.

"How's she doing?"

Addisyn jumped slightly and turned. "Darius! You startled me."

"I'm sorry." His adorable crooked grin always made her heart swoop. "Uncle Trent ordered some new ropes for the climbing wall from us at iClimb. I delivered them and thought I'd stop by to see you and Kenzie."

Addisyn studied the girl in question. "I hope she does well."

"She will." His arm came around her shoulders. "She has you for a coach."

He tugged her closer to him, bending down, and she closed her eyes, waiting for his kiss. But the next moment the door creaked open again.

"Are we ready to get started?"

Darius's hand dropped as if she were on fire. No PDA in front of his uncle, apparently. Addisyn turned toward Trent with her ice-rink smile, ignoring the heat in her face. "Yes. We are."

Trent glanced between the two of them suspiciously and shook his head. "All right. Let's talk details."

Darius took a seat in the first row of the bleachers while Addisyn and Kenzie joined Trent at the edge of the ice. Fifteen minutes later, Trent had done nothing except watch Kenzie's movements with an unchanging expression and scribble notes on his clipboard, and Addisyn was ready to implode from the tension. Finally he sighed and waved Kenzie over. "Still tight. What's up?"

Kenzie ducked her head. "I'm not very confident yet."

"I can see that." He included Addisyn in his scowl. "All right, we need to work on this." He pinned Addisyn with his gaze. "Are you developing choreography for her?"

"Uh—" *Shoot.* How had she forgotten that? "We've picked out music.

She's using 'Blue Garden' for her free skate."

Trent paused with a scowl. "Too common. Get something different."

What? Sure, the piece was popular, but what did that matter? Addisyn frowned. "I don't think it's common enough to be—"

"You two talk, come up with something else. Something a lot more original." Trent flipped the page, signaling the next phase of the conversation. "Next up is the routine itself. Requirements are fairly straightforward for the short program. I need to see an Axel—double or triple—plus another double or triple jump. At least Level 3 on that one."

Addisyn blinked. "I'm sorry—Level 3?"

"Yes." Trent tossed her an exasperated look. "She needs to grab attention right from the beginning."

Falling right off the bat would garner attention in a different way. "Well—"

"And then either a layback or camel spin, no foot changes. Officially, six rotations are required, but I'd like to see that up at ten."

Was Trent kidding? Kenzie was in no way ready for this. Addisyn glanced at the girl, but her face was as impassive as ever. If she was shocked, she was hiding it well.

By the time Trent finished going over the paperwork with them, Addisyn was ready to rip his clipboard to shreds. Choreography requirements were one thing, but Trent was notching up the difficulty far above what Kenzie could attain. Good grief, even Eastern Regionals—her toughest competition—hadn't required a triple flip.

And Kenzie was still wobbling on crossovers.

"Okay, then." Trent tucked the clipboard under his arm and directed his next words to Addisyn. "Show me what she's got. Let's take a glide into a double toe and a combination spin, just to get the feel."

Her shoulders relaxed slightly. The sequence wasn't that challenging—a good way for Kenzie to gain some confidence. She nodded encouragingly at the girl. "Ready, Kenzie? Remember what we talked about." She could feel Trent's eyes on her, but she wouldn't look his way. "Keep your movements loose, and don't look down on the jumps."

"Right." Kenzie nodded, but her breath was already coming faster. Uh oh.

The glide was fine—although Kenzie's weight distribution was a bit off—but she completely missed the takeoff for the single toe. She stumbled over the step and threw a desperate glance at Addisyn.

"What happened there?" Trent crossed his arms with a scowl.

"She's getting it." Addisyn could hear the defensiveness in her voice. She turned back toward the rink. "It's okay, Kenzie! Just relax."

Kenzie nodded, but the panic was setting in. Even from the edge of the rink, Addisyn could feel the friction in her movements. This time, she made the jump, but immediately lurched on her landing with no momentum left to enter the spin.

"Come on!" Trent's voice frayed with frustration. "What's going on, Kenzie?"

Her eyes were wide with worry. "I'm sorry."

Trent scowled. "You need to focus here."

That was enough. Addisyn didn't know what Kenzie's problem was, but *focus* wasn't it. "Mr. Payne." She bit her lip. "Kenzie's just nervous, is all."

"Nervous?" His eyebrows drew together. "Yeah, well, she'll be more nervous when she gets laughed off the ice at her audition." He clapped his hands together and frowned at Kenzie. "Third time, Kenzie."

The glide was strong, and the jump landed well, and for just a moment, Addisyn believed that this time, Kenzie truly had it. Her form was flawless, going into the combination spin—

And then in a tilted blur, she was hitting the ice.

Addisyn sucked in a breath, secondhand impact gripping her. "Kenzie! Are you okay?"

To her relief, Kenzie slowly pushed herself back up. "I just—"

"Kenzie, what the *devil* are you doing?" Trent all but roared the words. "Are you messing around, or what?" He spun toward Addisyn. "I'm not impressed."

With the anger in his eyes, he looked so much like— She forced the comparison away, but sweat was stinging her palms. "She's just coming back from her season off. She needs time to—"

"Time?" Redness rushed into his face. "Time is what we don't have."

Darius was walking up now. "Uncle Trent—"

The man bulldozed over Darius's words. "Auditions will start in two months. Two months, you hear that? So regardless—"

A movement behind him caught Addisyn's attention. Kenzie had pulled herself back to standing.

And she was crying.

Addisyn blinked. She'd never seen, never imagined, the stone-hearted girl shedding tears. Yet on the other side of the rink, she was silently sobbing in a way that made Addisyn want to jump over the loose railing and rush to her aid.

"—much more dedicated than she is right now. Do you hear me?"

She heard him, but she couldn't listen to his words. Not now, because all she could see was Brian. The way he'd critiqued her mercilessly. The way he'd managed to make her feel like more of a failure after every practice.

The way she'd often stood on the ice and cried just the way Kenzie was doing now.

The memory stung her to action, and she took a step toward Trent. "Kenzie has been off the ice for a year, Mr. Payne. I don't think it's fair for you to expect perfection the moment she returns."

She hadn't realized how loud her voice was until she heard her words echoing off the ceiling of the rink. Trent's expression turned thunderous. "I'm not expecting perfection. I'm expecting focus." He threw her a withering glance. "Which I'm not seeing."

"Focus doesn't come from pressure."

Darius's hand rested on her shoulder. "Uncle Trent—can we just talk about this, and maybe—"

"Darius, let me handle this." Addisyn shook off his peacemaking and glared at Trent. "I know what it takes to be successful in this sport, Mr. Payne. Kenzie will be more than ready by her auditions. I can give you my word. But for today, she's done." She directed her next question to Kenzie. "Ready to go?"

She didn't wait for the girl to respond before she turned and strode out of the center, her insides still twisting from the encounters. With Trent. With Brian.

Footsteps jogged up behind her. "Addisyn, are you okay?"

She was the opposite of okay and definitely not ready to face Darius. She gripped her bag with shaking hands. "Sure."

"I don't know." His hands on her shoulders turned her to face him. Worry scrunched his forehead. "You seemed—really upset, back there."

She hesitated. Apparently no one except her had noticed Kenzie's breakdown, and the moment felt too intensely personal to share. "I didn't like how he was treating her, Darius." She searched his face for understanding. "Don't you think he was a little—harsh?"

"Yes, but—" He sighed. "Uncle Trent is just—he's just driven. You know, he's a coach. That's all."

"So you agree with him?"

"No! Of course not." Darius held up his hands. "He's—he's hard-nosed. Nobody knows that better than me." Pain flashed over his face for a second. "But just try not to react, okay? Give him a chance to—"

Oh, *she* needed to give *him* a chance? "Really?" She yanked her bag onto her shoulder. "He's determined to think the worst of me."

Darius's jaw locked. "That's not true."

"It is!" The frustration was unspooling. "Don't tell me his mind wasn't already made up before I ever came to this center."

"Whoa, whoa! Wait a minute." Darius shook his head. "He assigned Kenzie to you. That shows he trusts you."

No, that just showed he didn't trust her with anyone actively competing. Addisyn shook her head. "Darius, I need to get home."

"No, come on, Addisyn." He caught her hands before she could pull away. Concern wrote itself across his face. "Something more is going on, isn't it? And that's why you reacted the way you did."

Darius had always had a window into her heart, but there were some things she didn't want him to see. "No." The lie came easier than she'd expected. "I'm fine."

He opened his mouth, then sighed and rubbed the back of his neck. "Okay." He cleared his throat. "Can I drive you somewhere? And then maybe we could—"

"No, you have to get back to work, and I need to get Kenzie home." She lifted her chin, keeping the tears back. "I'll be fine."

With that she walked away, ignoring the feel of his gaze on her back.

Darius had always been her protector. Since the moment they'd met, she'd drawn on his steady strength. But this time, not even he could help her find her way back to okay.

CHAPTER 10

The problem was that Trent was right.

Addisyn dropped into one of the metal lawn chairs on the front deck of the guesthouse and groaned. Kenzie was failing. Which meant she was too. Trent was unimpressed. And Darius…

No, she couldn't start guessing what he thought about her right now.

She forced herself to retrace her steps, attempt to problem-solve. Trent would say she was lacking experience, but the explanation didn't fit right. She'd started skating at the age of seven, taking to the ice with skates—and dreams—that were still waiting for her to grow into them. And since that time, the ice had been her element. The one place where she never made mistakes.

And from the sound of things, Kenzie's skating experience wasn't too shabby either.

Addisyn glanced again at the file folder in her lap—details about Kenzie's competition history and prior coaching. The girl's scores were high enough to show some serious talent. She'd made it as far as Regionals last season, where she'd come in fifth with a combination that included a triple Axel and three Level 4 elements. Not half bad.

But after that, the details wore thin. Apparently, Kenzie really had sat out the entire season. No scores, no coaching record. Was it something to do with the doctor?

Or with why Kenzie had been crying today?

Darius's words floated back through. *Something happened back there, didn't it?*

Not really. It had just been a weird moment, taking her back to a much darker time, when...

Enough. She shook her head. She was wasting time, mulling over the negatives. She needed to be productive. And forging some way forward would start with Kenzie's choreography. Making up the routine was overdue. Especially now that Trent had blown all her half-formed ideas out of the water today by changing everything.

She pulled up Spotify on her phone and listened to Kenzie's new piece. It was an upbeat one with a definite pop groove. A little challenging to choreograph. "Blue Garden" had had a more lyrical feel. Too bad Trent had vetoed it. But then again, Brian had always picked fast-paced music too. Usually something uncomfortably suggestive.

Well, anyway. She skimmed the sheet of requirements. Pretty vague, as usual—since skating moves were divided into difficulty levels within each category, the sheet only called for, say, a Level 2 jump or a Level 3 spin. Choosing moves that fulfilled the requirements while making sense musically was up to the skater.

And the skater's coach, of course.

She listened to the opening hook again, tapping the rhythm on the edge of the table. Yes, okay. Start with some strong arm movements—then directly into a glide to—what? Triple loop? Or triple flip?

Better make it a loop. The easier jump. Kenzie's confidence would be shot if she messed up that early in the performance. It was a gamble—a more difficult move could net more points but also bring more deductions for a mistake.

What next? Well, Brian had once told her he always tried to follow a jump with a spin. Which did make sense. But which spin? Combination spin needed to be saved for later—camel spin didn't really make sense with the beat there. Did she dare try to insert an Axel? Difficult moves were worth more points in the second half of the program, but Kenzie would be more tired then. Another risk to weigh.

This was harder than she'd expected. Naturally. Addisyn rubbed her head. If not for the—incident—today, she'd call Darius for help. Although choreography was significantly different for men and woman. And he didn't have a feel for Kenzie's abilities the way she did.

Or maybe—

Why not draw some inspiration from one of her own performances? If nothing else, Brian had at least been a savvy choreographer. Of course, she'd have to make changes, but she could at least get an idea for the basic layout of steps. A template, so to speak.

She grabbed her phone and flicked open YouTube, then typed in her name. The first video that came up was from her last competitive performance. Eastern Regionals, at Lake Placid, a year and a half ago.

And there she was, poised in the middle of the ice, waiting for the music to begin. Surreal, seeing herself, the girl she'd been standing just on the other side of the screen.

Her music began—a snappy instrumental arrangement of Avicii's "Wake Me Up." She'd forgotten how suggestive the arm movements had been on that opening sequence. She grimaced. Not using those for Kenzie, for sure.

She needed to be taking notes, but she couldn't drag her eyes from the screen. There was something so—so tragic about it, somehow. She knew how many lies the girl on that screen believed. She knew how many tears she shed in the dark of the night. She knew how isolated, how frightened, how guilty, how—

The girl on the screen struck her ending pose. Applause washed over the arena, but the tightness in the girl's expression didn't ease. Because— as Addisyn knew now—she was looking for something that no score or medal could provide.

She tugged herself loose from the past, letting the video cut to the next clip as she scribbled down some ideas. Well, she could still use that jump in the middle, and the glide where—

"—definitely a strong performance for her tonight."

The voice grabbed at her gut. She jerked her focus back to the screen, where the next video had loaded. And there he was. Sharply groomed haircut, expensive suit, eyes that had always been a touch too hardened. Brian—talking to reporters after her performance.

"We spoke with Miss Miles earlier, and she seemed very disappointed by her low score. How do you feel about the results today?" The reporter shoved her microphone back in Brian's face.

He ran his fingertips lightly over his hair before answering. "She gave a very strong performance. The goal is to be constantly improving."

Spoken like a true coach, but the reporters hadn't gotten the whole story. They hadn't been there when he'd later cursed at her and accused her of ruining her career. When he'd used her score as an excuse to give up on both their professional and personal relationships.

He was still talking. "I'm very pleased with what we've been able to accomplish."

We. His favorite word, when all along, it had been only him he'd been thinking of.

Anger shook her, and she swiped the video away, cutting him off mid-word. How could she have ever been so stupid? She'd completely ignored Avery's warnings and Brian's red flags and the uncertainty in her own soul, and she'd run straight ahead into something that had destroyed her.

But of course, he'd played his part well. For the first year and a half she'd trained with him, he'd seemed gentle, kind, always ready to compliment her skating or give her encouragement on a bad day. It really wasn't until she was eighteen—until he'd persuaded her to move in with him—that she'd seen a different side of him.

She could still remember when his personality had seemed to shift. She'd been trying to master an especially difficult turn, and she kept losing her balance. When she'd hit the ice for the fifth time, he'd slapped his palm on the railing so hard that the pop echoed in the rink. *"For God's sake, Addisyn!"* He'd cursed, the words smearing across the air between them. *"Get it together, will you?"*

His tone had knocked the wind out of her more effectively than the fall. *"Brian—I'm trying—I—"*

"Try?" He'd sworn again. *"You've got to do more than try in this business, Addisyn. You've got to be good, or go home. Got it?"*

"You—you told me I was good." She'd all but whimpered the words, sitting up gingerly on the slickness of the ice.

His eyes had flashed cold sparks. *"You will be. I won't have it any other way."* He'd waved his hand in disgust. *"Do it again."*

The memory filled her with a broken kind of rage. Not because he'd made her do it again and again and again, until her legs were so shaky she could barely walk out of the rink at the end of the day.

But because she'd done it.

The same way she'd done—well, everything else he'd asked. And all the while, she'd never realized that he was making every decision based on his own interests and ego. Her success had never been important to him, unless it could stoke his own.

No, he'd let her dangle behind him for five crucial years until he'd sabotaged her whole skating career. And in the meantime, he'd scarred her soul beyond repair. So how was she supposed to know how to help Kenzie when the coaching style with which she'd been familiar came from a man who'd been the biggest mistake of her life?

Kenzie's face returned to her mind, past blurring with present. The tears shed in the corner of the rink, the look of failure weighed down with guilt.

Far too familiar.

△△　△△　△△

THE WINDS WERE lazy today, and the mountains basked in summertime serenity. Avery paused on the crest of the ridge and glanced back over her shoulder. Trees stairstepped down the sides of the valley from which she'd just climbed, fringing the blue comma of Cub Lake.

It was one of her favorite hikes, but today she couldn't concentrate on the scenery or the sunshine or the bird songs. Today, she could only think about Skyla's invitation.

She pulled her water bottle from her backpack. The offer itself had been unbelievable. Skyla had emailed her more information, which she'd studied for over an hour last night. The hours were more flexible than at the store, although she'd sometimes have to work Saturdays if they had a weekend group. The pay was generous—slightly more than what she earned now. The work was exciting—the grant would allow for classes, field trips, even guided hikes. And the official job title was outdoor educator—helping people understand and connect with the natural world.

She glanced again at the view. Trees and mountains and lakes and birds, and she was being asked to show forth the wonder and witness inherent in every corner of it. Sharing her story of how she'd met El Shaddai here, the God Whose love stitched all things together.

A perfect job. Right?

She shifted her backpack and plunged downward, following the steep, rocky trail that cut through Forest Canyon. After she'd read Skyla's description, she'd done her own research. Outdoor education was a fast-growing career choice. But every job she'd seen required a bachelor's degree in the field, paired with some elite concentration—wildlife biology, ecology, natural resources management. Just reading the qualifications had overwhelmed her. Six months of weekly volunteering and a love for the land couldn't replace formal training.

If she'd had a degree, it might have been different. Perhaps she could have supplemented her existing education with required core courses. But that wasn't an option for someone with no degree at all.

Someone who'd given up their chance at higher education to raise their younger sister.

Avery could still remember the pressure she'd felt that senior year of high school. At the time, she'd wanted to be a teacher—helping kids not only learn, but love the process. She'd spent hours on the computer investigating her options, determined to find the best school, driven to keep her grades high enough for a scholarship.

And she'd done it. Even before she'd begun her final semester, she'd received her acceptance letter from Penn State. The path had run straight before her, as clearly marked as the trail she walked now.

But there had been Addisyn.

The closer the deadline drew, the more concerned she became about leaving Addisyn alone with their father. His rages were becoming more frequent, his fists more free. And three months before graduation, the knowings had begun. Every night, she'd throbbed through the urgency, watched consequences she'd never imagined spill across her dreams. And she'd known that she would not, could not, leave Addisyn behind with their father.

She couldn't leave Addisyn behind, period.

And so she'd begun making her own plans. Different ones. After graduation, she'd headed not to a college in Pennsylvania but to an apartment in New York. And there, she and Addisyn had begun a life removed from the dysfunction of their family. She'd shoved her acceptance letter into some forgotten file and never allowed herself to consider all that she'd given up.

Until now.

The trail crossed a wooden bridge, a small waterfall splashing down the hillside. Avery paused for a moment, letting the spray splatter her.

All the memories seemed so far away, now. It was almost impossible to reconcile the serious girl who'd expected to be a teacher with the version of herself that she'd become instead. And until now, that version had been enough. She'd found enough joy in wandering the land and watching the mountains scrape the sky. She'd found enough purpose in running Laz's store efficiently and spending her Fridays jogging through a flight cage.

And that was another thought—Laz.

Avery set off again, watching her footing on the slick rocks. Education—or lack thereof—aside, she couldn't desert Laz. He'd been her lifeline when she'd first come to the mountains—the only employer willing to take a chance on a scared young girl running from her own broken life. She couldn't abandon him now, no more than she could have abandoned Addisyn back then. They'd both needed her in different ways. And she would do her best to be there for them.

The mountains peered down at her with timeless faces. They were unchanging, but she wasn't. She was twenty-five years old, eight years removed from the frightened teenager who'd made that move to New York. An entire decade, nearly. How could the river have run so many years since then? Since she'd first bought that rickety truck and rented that apartment and become the shield for her younger sister?

Eight years.

And all she'd done was survive. But hadn't she been in survival mode long before New York? From her first memories, her chaotic home life had already been training her to think small, to prize safety and stability and find comfort in cages.

But now—now what she'd set out to do eight years ago was accomplished, because Addisyn was okay. She was on a solid path, a path that would lead her higher and deeper into a future perfect for her.

And Avery—Avery was left behind.

△△ △△ △△

ANOTHER WEDNESDAY. KENZIE had been inside the doctor's office for half an hour already when Addisyn's phone lit up with a call from Avery. The tension from their last call kept her wary as she swiped to answer. "Hey, A."

"Hey." Avery sounded uneasy. "I'm sorry. I just realized you might be at work."

"Not till this afternoon." Addisyn leaned back in the seat. "What's up?"

"Um—well—it's just—"

Avery's voice stalled out. Addisyn frowned. "Are you okay?"

"Yeah—I wanted to ask you something."

Avery wanted to ask *her* something? "Um—okay."

"Do I—do you think I do a good job at work?"

Okay, that was the most random thing ever. "What? You mean, at the store?"

"Yeah."

Where had this come from? "Uh—well, yes, of course." Encouragement. Maybe that's what Avery was looking for. She'd always been prone to underestimate herself. "The way you run the place and organize everything—and keep Laz in line—it's a gift."

Avery was silent for a moment. "I don't know if Laz needs me anymore."

"Oh, of course he does." That kooky old guy could never run the store without Avery's efficiency. "I heard him say all the time what a help you are."

"But—should I be doing something—different?"

Why did none of her answers seem to fit Avery's questions? "Different?"

"Yeah. Something—more." Avery's words were slow, cautious, as if each one were a step on shaky ground. "Like, something that makes an impact. That's—bigger."

Works at an outdoors store and lives in the mountains. Boring. Addisyn frowned and brushed off Tina's words. "I think you're fantastic at what you do, A. It makes you happy, so stick with it." A thought made her blink. "You are happy, right?"

"Well—I mean, yes."

Then why did her words hold less enthusiasm than a two-day-old soda? Addisyn raised her eyebrows. "You sure?"

"Yes, it's just—don't you ever feel kind of, I don't know, unsure?"

"Well, yes." Of course *she* did, but not Avery. Addisyn's worries doubled. "A—are you okay?"

"Oh, yes." Avery's voice was still too drab. "I told you, I'm just wondering about some stuff."

"But—you've seemed kind of—off the last few days. I'm worried about you." If this weren't so weird, she could have laughed at the way they'd reversed roles.

"Well—" Avery paused, and Addisyn waited, expectation leaning into the silence between them. But then her sister sighed. "I just miss you."

Avery's words held the same ache Addisyn had felt. "Aww, A. I miss you too." She lightened her tone. "Nobody here can talk about hawks all day the way you can."

Her sister's laughter was quiet, but at least it was there. "Or take you hiking on inadequately marked trails?"

"Exactly." Addisyn thought of the white bear hike and winced. That was something she was definitely not ready to share with Avery yet. "Although I'm getting more familiar with the trails here." *Against my will.*

"I bet there are some great hikes."

The office door swung open, and Kenzie shaded her eyes, scanning the parking lot. Addisyn tapped the horn and waved to her. "Hey, A? I have to go. I'll call you back later."

And then she'd find out what was really going on.

△△ △△ △△

ADDISYN LOOKED UP as Kenzie slid into the car. "So? How'd it go?"

"Fine." Kenzie cleared her throat. "Could we make a stop on the way home?"

Addisyn glanced at the dashboard clock. She really needed to get home and call Avery back, but— "Well, if it's quick."

"I need to go by the ranger station. I want to see what they say about the bears. Recent sightings, or anything."

Addisyn bit back a groan. After the days of rain had kept them from going back into the woods, she'd allowed herself to hope that Kenzie might drop the whole thing. She should have known better. But at least the ranger station sounded safer than braving the ridge again. "Okay. But you have to give me directions."

They were almost across town when Kenzie slid Addisyn a glance heavy with curiosity. "Who were you talking to? When I came out."

It wasn't her business, but— "My sister."

Interest perked in Kenzie's expression. "You have a sister? Is she older or younger than you?"

"Yeah, Avery. She's four years older."

"That's cool."

"Uh huh. We're very close." Well, except for whatever weird stuff was going on with Avery, but they'd get through that. "We've had our ups and downs, but we're best friends. Always will be."

"Neat."

Something more than idle curiosity seemed to lie beneath her words. "What about you? Any siblings?"

"No." Kenzie squinted, even though the sun was behind them now. Her next words were soft. "But I always wanted a sister."

Well, that was surprising. You'd think a girl as antisocial as Kenzie would thrive on life as an only child. "Oh. Really?"

"Yeah." Kenzie pointed to a side street. "Go left here." She waited until Addisyn had maneuvered the turn before she sighed. "If I'd had a sister, things would have been different. I wouldn't have been—"

Her words stalled out, and Addisyn raised her eyebrows. "Been what?"

"Nothing." She frowned and crossed her arms. "I don't want to talk about it."

Back to her usual charming self. Addisyn had a sharp reply ready when she remembered the incident on the rink yesterday. She bit her lip

157

and focused on the downtown traffic. A bus roared by from the other direction with the stenciled logo of United Pacific College.

"That's where Tina goes to school." Kenzie's voice was back to normal now.

"It is?"

"Yeah. It's in Vancouver. She does some online and commutes when she has to." Kenzie watched the bus in the side mirror. "Tina's really smart. And it's a great school."

"Is that where you'll go to college?"

A door slammed shut in Kenzie's expression. "I—I don't know." She sank back into the seat. "I'm a little—a little behind."

"Behind in school?"

"Yeah." Kenzie bit her lip, her defenses suddenly down. "That's why I'm doing online studies this summer. To catch up. I missed some because of my—health stuff."

Health stuff serious enough to put her behind in school? A stir of sympathy caught Addisyn off guard. "Wow—I didn't—"

"It's okay." Kenzie shrugged awkwardly and nodded to a low building tucked under overhanging pines. "Here's the ranger station."

The building was empty except for a bored-looking young ranger slouching behind the desk. He raised his eyes listlessly. "Hi. Can I help you?" His tone wasn't eager to find out.

Addisyn nudged Kenzie forward, and the girl stepped up to the counter cringingly. "Hi." Talking to strangers was clearly hard for her. Her tone was next door to an apology. "Can you tell me—that is—I was looking for information about, uh, spirit bears."

"Spirit bears? The white ones?"

"Yes."

The disinterest on his face didn't lift. "Well, you're too far south for them." He shrugged and pulled an ink pen from his shirt pocket, tapping a laminated map of Canada's west coast. "Here we are"—he poked at Whistler. "And all the way up here—" the pen trailed up the coast—"is the only conservancy area for spirit bears. Kitasoo, on Princess Royal Island."

Addisyn squinted at the map. "How far away is that?"

"Over three hundred miles, as the crow flies." The guy tucked the pen back into his pocket. "The bears aren't as widespread as they were, anyway. No more than five hundred in the world. And last I heard, it was something like only fifty left in Canada."

Addisyn grimaced. The chances of this succeeding were even slimmer than she'd imagined. "Why aren't there more?"

"The genetic mutation that makes them white is a very rare double recessive gene. Only about ten percent of the bear population has it." The guy rummaged under the counter until he retrieved a handful of slick papers. "Here, see for yourself. These are photos from Kitasoo."

Addisyn leaned closer as Kenzie studied the first photo. Sure enough, a gleamingly white bear was paused on a cliff, as stark as a snowman in the rainforest. She sucked in a breath. "Wow. Cool." The words were inadequate to describe the mysterious creature. And Kenzie had actually seen one? She flipped to the next photo—a bear in a rushing stream—and blinked. "That one looks kind of reddish."

"The gene that makes them white is the same one that causes blond fur in dogs and red hair in humans. So sometimes they have a hint of that in the white. And as you can tell, they still have dark noses and eyes."

"Yeah." Addisyn pointed to the photo. "What's this one doing in the water?"

"Salmon fishing. A salmon-running river is the best place to see any bear, white or not."

"Okay, well, thanks." Addisyn took a step back, but the man's expression narrowed with curiosity.

"Why were you asking, anyway?"

"Um—well—"

"I saw one." Kenzie's voice was soft, but her expression was firm. "Several years ago."

Disbelief scribbled across the man's expression. "Here in Whistler?"

"Yes."

"Sorry, but they're not here." He stacked the photos back up. "Must have seen something else."

Addisyn frowned. She'd had her own moments of disbelief, but the dismissiveness in the man's tone rubbed her the wrong way. "Aren't you open to receiving reports of wildlife?"

"Ma'am, you'd be amazed at the reports we get here. People think they see all kinds of things out in the woods. Flying horses and Bigfoot and white bears." He rolled his eyes. "But science is science."

"This wasn't a flying horse or Bigfoot." Addisyn braced herself against the counter. "There haven't been any other reports of spirit bears here?"

"Well—" The man shrugged reluctantly. "About six years ago, some dude reported seeing one in the Callaghan Valley."

Same place, same time.

Kenzie grabbed Addisyn's arm. "Did they search—or find—"

"Sure. There was a big media circus. News networks ran the story and a thousand crazy tourists went tramping through the woods." Disgust twisted his face. "But the park service never found any evidence. Like I said, we rarely do in these types of situations."

Addisyn ignored his tone. "Where in the Callaghan was the report made?"

"Wildcrest area." The guy pulled out a paper map and circled an area the size of a half dollar.

Addisyn studied the region, a bullseye in the squiggly lines that marked the mountains. "Can we drive there, or—"

"Sorry." Although his tone sounded anything but. "That's the densest part of the valley. Hundreds of acres of wilderness."

Oh.

"Were you wanting to find it again or something?" He folded the map and handed it to Kenzie.

"Yes." Kenzie's voice was soft. She appeared to be studying the creases on the map.

The man's laugh held an edge. "Sounds like a wild-goose chase to me."

The same thing Addisyn had told Kenzie. Yet watching her wilt under the ranger's sarcasm, something uneasy squirmed in her chest. Had her own words sounded that uncaring?

"Come on, Kenzie." She shot the ranger her best scowl—the one that Avery had once claimed could wither a pine tree—and tapped Kenzie's shoulder protectively. "Let's go back home."

CHAPTER 11

They were not going to find a spirit bear.

Addisyn was sure of it now. She and Kenzie had finished their second trip up to the ridge yesterday, and the biggest animal she'd seen was a chipmunk. On the way down, she'd quizzed Kenzie until the girl admitted that she'd seen the bear only for a moment, down in the valley, stomping its way through thick brush that swallowed it from her view within seconds.

Not a promising witness.

Kenzie, of course, remained adamant that she knew what she'd seen. She'd spent the rest of the night scribbling down the facts from the ranger on the back of the paper map he'd given them. But meanwhile, Addisyn had done some research of her own. Reports of the *Whistler white bear* from six years ago abounded, but proof was hard to come by, and even the believers grudgingly allowed that it was an anomaly this far south. While the ranger had certainly had limited social skills, he apparently had done his homework on the region's wildlife.

The truth was obvious: either Kenzie was mistaken, or the bear she'd seen had moved on. Regardless, they weren't going to find it. And while the facts might be simple, the task of explaining that to Kenzie after their next trip up the ridge would not be.

Focus. Addisyn brushed her hair back and rearranged the papers in her arms. She still had a job to do. She'd just finished another practice with Kenzie, and while the girl completed her stretching regime, Addisyn was heading back to the office—she'd been needing to make some copies of a workout routine. If she could find the original, anyway. She fumbled with the papers as she stepped through the office door and immediately jerked against something hard. "Ouch!" The carefully stacked papers slid in an avalanche to the floor.

"Hey, watch where you're going!"

Tina. To make a good day better.

The girl scowled and examined her arm elaborately. "I hit my elbow."

"Sorry." Addisyn didn't try to make the word sound less curt. She bent over and started gathering her papers, including the workout routine, which was now resting innocently on top of the pile. Of course.

Tina sighed and knelt beside her. "Here, I'll help you." She reached for a paper and tilted her head. "Wait. 'Places to look for bears'? Is this yours?"

No, no, no! Addisyn ripped the paper out of Tina's hands to see the map from the ranger station. Kenzie's neat handwriting marched across the back. How had that gotten in here?

Tina was watching her. "Uh...yes." She cleared her throat and tucked it into the stack. "It's mine."

Tina sat back on her heels and stared at Addisyn as if she'd begun speaking French. "You're looking for *bears*?"

Her pitch on the last word nearly hit the ceiling. "Tina!" Addisyn made a *settle down* motion with her hands. "It's not a big deal."

"But that's what you're doing? That's weird."

She had started something she had no way of ending. Addisyn shoved the rest of the papers into a stack and headed for the reception counter.

"It's dangerous, too." Tina tagged behind. "Bears are big, Addisyn. Really big. I've seen them."

"My sister has too." Addisyn reshuffled the papers. Maybe if she seemed indifferent, Tina would lose interest.

"So do you have a thing about bears? Like, they're your spirit animal or something?"

"No."

"Your zodiac sign?"

"No."

"Your reincarnated relative?"

Addisyn slapped the papers onto the counter. "Look, Tina, it was

Kenzie's idea, not mine, okay?"

The words flew out before she gave them permission, rushing ahead of where she'd wanted to go, and now there was no turning back.

"Kenzie is looking for bears?" Shock rippled across Tina's face. "That's the dumbest thing I've heard yet."

"It's more complicated than that." Guilt lodged itself in her chest. Kenzie had trusted her with the secret, and here she'd unveiled it in front of Tina, of all people. Why hadn't she just kept her mouth shut? Did it matter, really, if Tina pegged her as a nature-worshipping bear seeker?

"Complicated? I bet." Tina rolled her eyes. "When Kenzie's in the mix, things are always complicated."

Well, now that she'd blown the secret…was there any harm in asking Tina for information? If she acquired any hints, maybe it would also appease Kenzie's wrath. "Actually, Kenzie's looking for a specific bear."

"Who?" Tina plopped down in her desk chair and studied her computer. "Sorry, but I don't think Smokey's been seen real often around here."

"She's looking for a white bear."

Tina's hand froze on the computer mouse. "What?"

"A white bear." Addisyn gauged Tina's reaction. "She says she saw a white bear when she was here before. Do you remember that?"

Tina blew out a breath. "Uh—no." Her eyes darted to Addisyn's face, and she tried to laugh. "A white bear? That's just crazy."

She didn't have to have Avery's intuition to know something was off here. Addisyn narrowed her eyes. "She says they're called spirit bears. Ever heard of that?"

Tina shifted her eyes. "Oh. Yeah. I remember that now, but they're not here."

"Have you ever seen one?"

"No." Tina snipped the word short. "I haven't seen one because they're not here."

"But Kenzie must have seen something." Tina didn't respond, and Addisyn cleared her throat. "Right?"

"I guess. I don't know." Tina drummed her hot pink fingernails on the edge of her keyboard. "I was a kid, Addisyn. I'm not going to remember every detail of some stupid game Kenzie was playing. There are a lot of deer in those woods, and they can look pretty light if the sun hits them just right. But there are no white bears."

"So Kenzie is lying?"

Tina hesitated. "I didn't say that. Kenzie's just—you know, she's very imaginative. She always has been." Her gaze drifted above her computer screen, toward the trees that tapped against the windows. "She used to love stories. Fairytales, you know. Gnomes and unicorns and fae and—well, all these legends that weren't possibly true."

"Like a white bear."

"Right." Tina shrugged and began typing. "The line of reality was always kind of blurry for her, anyway." Bitterness soured her tone. "I think she lives in a fantasy world."

So was the bear nothing more than a figment of a lonely girl's imagination? But would Kenzie have braved telling the ranger—and Addisyn, too, for that matter—if she'd known all along the bear was fake? Addisyn turned back to Tina. "Kenzie seems sure of herself. She doesn't act like it's make-believe."

Tina stopped typing and sighed elaborately. "Look, Addisyn. I don't have time for any more of this today, okay? I can't tell you what's going on in Kenzie's mind, but I can promise you that I've lived here my whole life. There are no white bears, and if Kenzie says otherwise, then she's crazy." Her tone hardened again. "Which is highly possible."

"You keep saying that."

"Because it's true."

Frustration yanked at the knots in her soul. "Look, don't you think that maybe Kenzie just needs this?" She kept going before she could ask herself why she felt the need to defend the younger girl. "Maybe she just needs something to do or think about or—"

"What's going on in here?"

Oh no.

Trent squared himself in the doorway, elbows jutting out. "I could hear your voices all the way down the hall. Not very professional."

"Sorry, Dad." Tina jabbed her finger at Addisyn. "It's her fault. Addisyn and Kenzie are looking for bears."

Addisyn didn't even have time to consider shaking Tina before Trent swung to face her. "Looking for bears?" His eyebrows shot up. "What's this about?"

Out of the corner of her eye, Addisyn saw a smug smile stretch itself across Tina's face. She cleared her throat. "It's—well—Kenzie and I did some hiking the other day." She tried to keep her tone casual. "Just something to do. And Kenzie mentioned seeing, uh, a bear when she was here before, and we were just wondering if we'd see it again." She gave a weak shrug. "That's it."

"Not just any bear, though." Tina leaned forward with a catlike smile. "A white bear."

"A white bear?" Trent glared at Addisyn. "Are you serious? Kenzie is looking for a white bear?"

The minute Trent walked away, Tina was a goner. "She says she saw it when she was here before."

"And you're encouraging this delusion?"

"I—uh—" Addisyn reached desperately for words. "I mean—you told me to be responsible for her, so I figured if she was really going to—"

"That's right!" Trent's voice bounced off the walls of the lobby. "I said *be responsible*. I did *not* say to take a teenager up into rough country in pursuit of a legend. In fact, that sounds very irresponsible to me."

"But I don't see how it could hurt, especially—"

"Don't see how it could hurt?" A vein was throbbing in Trent's temple. "Don't you realize that Kenzie needs to have her mind on her skating right now? If she's ever going to make a comeback, she has to be focused. *You* have to be focused." He jabbed his finger at her. "Her energy right now needs to go into her training. And you should not be distracting her by encouraging her to chase stupid myths!" He muttered something under his breath. "White bears? Really?"

His anger pounded in the space between them, pushing Addisyn back. "I—I was just trying to help—"

"Help?" Trent's eyes flashed. "If you want to help Kenzie, then help her stay in the real world. Don't keep distracting her with childish daydreams." He flung Addisyn an exasperated glance. "Did you really believe her, anyway?"

"Uh—no." The answer was a reflex. She forced a nonchalant laugh and swallowed the taste of betrayal. "Of course not."

A muffled sound from the hallway took Addisyn's focus from Trent, and the next instant, her heart dropped. Standing in the door, eyes wide with pain, was Kenzie.

Oh, what had she done? Addisyn shook her head, pleading with the frozen expression on Kenzie's face. "Kenzie—"

But Kenzie was looking at Tina, not Addisyn. "I know what I saw."

Tina's face was too pale. She shrugged with a shaky substitute for her usual bravado. "Why are you looking at me? I'm not—"

"Tina." Kenzie took a step forward, eyes begging for something. "You remember. Tell them."

Remember? Addisyn stared at Tina. "Remember what?"

Trent's brow creased. "Do you know something about this?"

Tina bit her lip. "Well—" An odd look flashed across her face with the suddenness of heat lightning. Some mix of hurt and pain and deep rebellion.

And then she huffed and swiveled to her computer, her back to the room. "Kenzie's making it up. We pretended there was a white bear. It was just a game."

For a split second, the words hung in the air. And then Kenzie's cornflower eyes were swimming in sudden tears. "Tina." The word was a rough whisper, heavy with hurt. The next instant she grabbed her fallen gym bag, yanking it back onto her shoulder. "I'm ready to go home."

She spun and raced down the hallway, her shoes slapping against the hardwood. Tina jerked to her feet with her face down. "I have to take care of something in the back." She muttered the words and brushed past Addisyn, heading down the hall in the opposite direction.

An uneasy silence hovered behind the counter. Then Trent sighed and shoved a hand through his hair. "See? That's what I'm talking about." He gestured the way Kenzie had gone. "Her mother sent her here to, uh, refocus. Not to lose herself in bizarre daydreams."

Whatever Addisyn had just witnessed between Tina and Kenzie had drained her concentration. "I understand."

"So see to it that she learns where to put her energy." Trent's tone was returning to normal. "Is that clear?"

"Yes, sir."

"Fine." Trent rolled his eyes and stepped out from behind the reception counter. He was still mumbling about white bears as he marched down the hall.

The intensity of the encounter worked its way through her, and Addisyn sank into Tina's desk chair. Now she'd have to go drive Kenzie home and try to explain how the secret had escaped.

Excuses chattered in her ears. Maybe it wasn't her fault. After all, Kenzie had contrived this whole scheme—a scheme that could have cost Addisyn her job. And Trent and Tina were right, weren't they? There were no bears, and the whole thing was ridiculous, and they didn't need to waste any more time on this senseless pursuit. In fact, she had a watertight reason to stop the project now. *I'm sorry, Kenzie, but your uncle said...*

Once again, Kenzie's face floated through her mind, and the guilt redoubled, pressing on her back with an iron thumb. It didn't matter what selfish rationalizations she gave, because one simple truth was staring her down.

She'd blown it. As usual.

Oh, Avery would have never made such a mess of things.

KENZIE WOULDN'T LOOK at Addisyn all the way home. The girl who'd blabbed the whole Project to Tina and Uncle Trent—of all people—didn't deserve eye contact.

How could she *do* that? What, had she just been humoring Kenzie all along, waiting for the perfect moment to snicker with Tina behind Kenzie's back? *"Kenzie thinks there's a white bear. I know! So stupid!"*

The whole thing was like a nightmare from the past year, every plot twist borrowed from real life. Girls who thrived on swapping secondhand secrets like trading cards. Conversations that paused awkwardly when you walked into the room. Phony friends who didn't pull down their masks until you were too deep not to drown.

Yes, she'd seen it all before. And she'd fallen for it again.

Stupid.

She swallowed a sob just as the car shuddered to a stop in front of the guesthouse. She still wouldn't look at Addisyn, but she heard the older girl sigh. "Kenzie. Can we—can we talk?"

"There's nothing to talk about." She didn't feel like going into the house, so she waited, keeping her eyes averted. Any moment, Addisyn would give up, get out of the car, and leave her alone.

Addisyn's seatbelt unsnapped. But then several seconds of silence dripped by. "Okay. Look. Can you just—can you please just listen?"

Couldn't Addisyn just leave her alone? Kenzie shifted in her seat.

"Kenzie—what I said back there—"

"You don't believe me."

Addisyn's hesitation was its own answer. "I didn't say that, but you know, it's sort of—well, it's unlikely."

She'd known all along that Addisyn didn't believe her, hadn't she? But still, it hurt more than it should have. Gradually, through the hike, and the doctor's visit, and even the days of practice, Addisyn had started to seem not so bad after all. Now betrayal rushed in over the walls she'd let down. Because everything she'd thought about Addisyn had been right all along.

Addisyn was still talking. "You know, I did some research of my own last night. And, well—the ranger is right. Spirit bears are incredibly rare, and they're only reported in the Great Bear wilderness. Eight hours away by car."

"It's what I saw." She locked her jaw and finally looked at Addisyn.

"I—okay." Addisyn tugged at the ends of her hair. "Kenzie, you've got to understand, I'm in a bad spot here. I'm responsible for you, and your family expects me to be watching out for you, not taking you on a wild-goose chase."

"So spilling my secrets is watching out for me?"

At least Addisyn had the grace to look ashamed. "I—I really didn't mean to. It just came out. I didn't think."

"When people trust you, you have to think."

"Look, Kenzie, I made a mistake—"

The old copout apology everyone tried to use, and it wasn't good enough. "Forget it. I should have known what kind of person you were."

Addisyn stiffened. "What do you mean by that?"

Her emotions were tumbling out, over the barrier she'd so carefully built. "You're the kind that doesn't care. And maybe trust doesn't mean anything to you, but it does to me." Her breath caught on the sharp edges of fathers who abandoned you and friends who betrayed you and secrets left to tremble naked in front of critical eyes. "You know what? Forget it. I know you want me to just go back home. Well, maybe I will!"

She scrambled out of the car and darted into the cabin. She didn't truly feel safe until she'd slammed and locked the door to her room and thrown herself onto the bed. Burying her face in her grandma's quilt, she closed her eyes and let the tears come.

Why would no one believe her? So much doubt was almost enough to make her question herself. She closed her eyes and cross-examined the memory again. The massive, lumbering creature. The crash of the underbrush beneath its broad paws. The glimmer of the sun on its snow-colored coat, and the way it had glanced up just when it reached the river, a wise expression on its furry face.

Yes, that was what she'd seen. The precious, sacred memory that she'd mistakenly trusted Addisyn with.

Her loneliness pulled tight, like a scar that wouldn't quite heal. Who was the last person she'd really been able to trust?

Not the man who'd fathered her and never looked back. Not her stressed mom, the busy single parent who usually treated Kenzie like a combustible science experiment. Not Uncle Trent, the businesslike coach who saw her as nothing more than neatly packaged talent. Not Tina—not after what had happened all those years ago.

And certainly not Addisyn. Addisyn was the kind of girl who could never be trusted. The kind who never had to ache in loneliness or face down fears or try to build a life on a foundation that remained shaky.

No, Addisyn only had to worry about one thing: how to shift responsibility and get rid of the sullen teenager. People always did that, shuffling her down the line so no one had to deal with her, help her, see her.

Coming back to BC was supposed to help. Wasn't that what Mom had said? *You'll have some peace...you won't have to go to school and see them...it will all be a nice rest for you...* And she'd thought so too, at the time. She'd foolishly believed that the magic of her childhood memories would be conjured by her return. But now, even this world where she'd once fit so nicely had forgotten her. And still, no one had time to see her heart.

What she'd told Addisyn was right. She'd be better off at home. At least there she expected to be hurting and lonely. Nothing new. Then maybe Addisyn would be sorry she hadn't believed Kenzie. Sorry that she'd been like everyone else.

The idea that had dangled idly in her mind began to slowly take shape. Well, why not? Kenzie sat up and scrubbed her sleeve over her face, glancing at the clock. Still a good two and half hours of daylight left.

If everyone wanted her out of the way...well, she could arrange that.

CHAPTER 12

Addisyn had no intention of trying to talk to Kenzie again. Not tonight. Maybe not ever.

She'd come in just in time to hear Kenzie's door bang emphatically shut. So she'd put a load of laundry in, made a quick sandwich, and then retreated to her bedroom to watch skating performances on YouTube.

But no matter how hard she tried to focus on the technical prowess of the competitors or the comments of the judges, she kept seeing Kenzie's face. Hearing her words. *You're the kind that doesn't care.*

Which was ridiculous. Of course she cared, but not about the bear of questionable reality. No, what she cared about was doing her job right—proving herself to Trent and not making any more mistakes. Not giving him any grounds to complain to Darius or throw her out of the center. The existence or not of the bear was completely immaterial. Addisyn would not be looking for it again under any circumstances. And if Kenzie couldn't understand that, well, that was her problem.

But she'd lost track of how many times she'd had to tell herself that.

Finally, she gave up on her videos and tossed her tablet aside. She glanced at the clock. Whoa, was it past eight thirty already? Over two hours since they'd arrived home.

She crept out into the kitchen, but the house was silent. Well, what had she expected? That after the conversation they'd had, Kenzie would be sitting at the table, ready to be friendly?

At Kenzie's door, she cleared her throat and knocked cautiously. "Kenzie? May I come in?"

No response.

No surprise there. "Kenzie. Please open the door."

Nothing.

"Kenzie, if you don't open this door, I'm coming in."

Still nothing, and a vague shiver of fear shot through Addisyn. It almost seemed as if—

She didn't wait any longer before throwing the door open. Her gaze darted around every corner of the room before she could accept the truth.

Empty.

"Kenzie!"

A search of the house took only a few moments to reveal some important facts. One, that Kenzie wasn't inside. And two, that her boots were gone from their place by the back door.

Kenzie was gone. Gone. And Addisyn had let her get away. Oh, what would Trent say to this?

Her pulse kicked into overdrive. Why hadn't she seen this coming? She should have known that Kenzie was upset enough to do something drastic. Now where was she? What if she ran into trouble or—

She glanced out the window. Already the valley was sinking into shadow, the last rays of sunlight polishing the tops of the peaks. She had half an hour before sunset. Maybe not even that.

Lights were on inside the big house, cars parked out front. Clearly the family was home. She should walk over there, find Trent or Tina, and explain the circumstances. But she'd rather jump over Alexander Falls.

What if—what if she could find Kenzie herself? And maybe they wouldn't even have to know. Better for everybody, right?

She pulled out her cell phone and dialed Darius's number. He answered almost immediately. "Hello?"

"Darius, I have a big, big problem." Her words slipped over each other. "It's Kenzie. She's taken off somewhere."

"Taken off? What do you mean?"

"What I said. She's gone." The urgency had whittled her patience down to nothing. "I was—uh—in my room, and when I came out, she was gone. I have no idea where she went."

"Did you call Trent?"

"No. I—I don't want him to know yet." Addisyn bit her lip. "Please, Darius. I need to find her without—without Trent knowing."

Silence. Would he insist they tell his family? Wash his hands of the problem? Scold her for letting Kenzie get away?

"Okay." His voice was still calm, still as reassuring as a flashlight in the dusk. "Just stay at the house, okay? Don't go anywhere. I'm on my way."

BY THE TIME Darius's Traverse pulled up in front of the cabin, Addisyn's racing thoughts had spun her straight to the verge of a meltdown. Her chest was tight as she slid into his passenger seat. "Darius, where could she be?"

"I don't know, but we'll find her."

His tone was still measured, calm. How did he do that? "I hope. We don't have much daylight." She glanced toward the big house. If someone was noticing, this hopefully looked enough like a simple date to not stir up suspicion. And then she and Darius could smuggle Kenzie back into the guesthouse before anyone was the wiser.

If they could find her.

The panic twined itself around her throat again. "I can't believe I let this happen."

"Hey." He paused at the end of the driveway and worked his fingers through hers. "Quit blaming yourself."

How could she not? Just like always, she'd blown it again. "What if we can't find her, or what if—"

"Addisyn." Darius squeezed her hand. "We'll find her, but we have to think. Help me out. Where would she go?"

The map of Whistler pieced itself together in her mind, a constellation of landmarks and roads and mountains and businesses. So much space to cover. "I don't know. Where should we start?"

Darius propped his chin in his hand and peered up and down the street. "Um...I'll head toward Spring Creek School." He flipped his blinker on. "Maybe she went that way. There's a park down there."

Addisyn grimaced. "I don't think she left to find a park. She was—uh, sort of upset."

"Upset?" Darius drove slowly down the narrow street. Shadows collected under the trees, but no sullen girl. "Do you have any idea why?"

She had more than an idea. Shame squirmed over her. "Well—it's a long story." She was too distracted to get into the details now. "At least we know she has to be on foot." This was one time she was grateful Kenzie didn't have her license.

Darius gave an uneasy face. "Unless she called a taxi."

Addisyn considered that for only a moment. "As shy as she is, I just don't think she would get in one. And if she called one to the house, someone would have seen. The same goes for Uber, and anyway, I don't really think she'd try that when she knows you drive for them."

"Yeah, and I was on the clock until eight or so. Right down here in Cheakamus."

"So even if she'd put in a ride request, it would have probably gone to you."

"Right. Okay, well—" Darius rubbed his chin. "Of course, there's the intracity bus too. She could have caught that from the stop right by Uncle Trent's house, gone downtown."

Oh. She hadn't thought of that, but— "Not likely. I've offered several times to take her into the Village, and she's never been interested."

Spring Creek School stretched in front of them, a low brick building with a school's summer silence. No lights, no movements, no figures in the parking area or sidewalks or basketball courts. Darius sighed and made a U-turn in the parking lot. "Well, it was worth a try. Let's head the other way. She could have walked toward Cheakamus. Like you said, she can't be too far."

But half an hour later, they'd patrolled a geometric maze of backstreets and seen only one person—a woman in a green hoodie jogging with a Jack Russell terrier. By the time Darius once again looped back to Spring Creek, panic was snagging Addisyn's breath. "Darius, what are we going to do?"

"We're going to find her." His voice was still even, but his expression was tightening. He glanced out the windshield at the fading daylight.

"Okay. Think. You said she was upset. Did she say anything—give any clues—"

Addisyn closed her eyes and forced her throbbing brain to focus on the possibilities. The bears—would Kenzie be looking for them at this time of night? Surely not. There weren't even any trails nearby.

The center was much too far away, and Kenzie had no reason to return there anyway.

What was left? She tried to replay their conversation, listen between Kenzie's words. Suddenly, a sentence jumped out.

I know you want me to just go back home. Well, maybe I will!

She shot upright in the seat. "Darius, how would someone get to Vancouver from here?"

"Vancouver?" Realization sank into his expression. "You think she's heading home?"

"I do." Addisyn's heart rate notched up as the idea grew into certainty. "Could she get a bus to Vancouver from the stop by the house?"

Darius shook his head. "That's intracity transit only. To get to Vancouver, you'd have to go to the plaza in Whistler Village. About—oh, probably five or six kilos."

So—three miles? Five? She wasn't the best with metric measurements. "Let's go."

Darius was already turning around in the next intersection. "All the buses around here run every thirty minutes." He glanced at the dashboard clock and winced. "So, if she left two hours ago…"

"Then she could have taken a bus to the plaza and caught the Vancouver bus from there." Why hadn't she thought of this sooner? "What times do the buses out of town leave?"

Darius shook his head. "I don't know, but we'll find out." He made the turn onto Highway 99 and pressed the gas until the dark trees blurred into the lights of the city. "The bus plaza is about a mile from here. We'll have to see if—"

The headlights flicked across a figure by the side of the road. Jacket with the hood pulled up. Purple backpack. Walking toward the Village.

"Darius!" Addisyn grabbed his arm. "There she is!"

Relief leaked through his sigh. "Oh, thank goodness. On foot? She walked all the way here?"

There was no traffic behind them. Darius pulled up beside the girl, and Addisyn rolled her window down. "Kenzie?"

Kenzie jerked and darted a glance at them. Even in the dim lighting, it was obvious that she'd been crying. But she kept walking without a word.

"Kenzie, we were worried about you." Darius coasted alongside her. "Ready to come home now?"

Kenzie's stride didn't falter. "No."

Darius sighed. "Kenzie, come on. These roads aren't safe in the dark."

"Then go back." Kenzie hunched herself deeper into her hoodie. "I'm not coming."

Darius looked at Addisyn helplessly. "What now?" His voice was barely above a whisper.

Why was he asking her? The idea that she might know her way past Kenzie's concrete walls and barbed wire was ridiculous. "I don't know."

"There's got to be some way to reach her."

Some way to reach her.

Hadn't that been what Avery said the other day? Something about building a connection. It hadn't made sense then, but now—now maybe it was something like—

And suddenly she wasn't on the dark road anymore. She was thirteen again, brokenhearted by some boy, and she'd run for refuge to the quiet city park near their house. But while she was sitting on the swings, Avery had found her. She could still remember how mad she'd been at the interruption of her isolation. "*Go away.*"

Avery hadn't been fazed. She'd slid into the swing next to Addisyn. "*Just thought you might need somebody to be sad with.*"

"*I don't want to talk to anybody.*"

Avery had shrugged. "*That's okay. I'll wait till you're ready.*"

The memory dissolved, but the truth of it remained. "Um, Kenzie—" She leaned out the open window. "How 'bout this? Can I walk with you to the bus stop?"

Kenzie set her jaw. "I'm going back home."

"I'm not stopping you. I just want to walk with you to the bus stop."

Kenzie's stride hesitated for the first time. "And then I can leave?"

177

"Um—well, we would need to call your mom and let her know. But then, yes."

"Addisyn, what are you doing?" Darius's voice was low but urgent.

"It's okay. Just let me try this." She glanced back out the window. "So?"

Kenzie tilted her head, then shrugged. "Okay."

Darius stopped, and Addisyn scrambled out of the car. "Drive on up to the bus plaza. We'll be there in a few minutes."

Darius frowned. "Addisyn, I don't like this idea. These roads are dark, and—"

"We'll stay on the sidewalk where we can." Addisyn glanced back at Kenzie. The girl was still walking, the distance between them stretching with every step. "Please, Darius."

He sighed. "All right. I'll see you at the plaza. You've got your phone?"

"Yes. Thank you." Addisyn waved to him one more time, then jogged to catch up with Kenzie. The maroon Traverse passed them just as she fell into step beside the girl. "So." What could she say? "You're heading home?"

"Yeah." Kenzie glanced ahead.

"Did you talk to your mom about it?"

"Not yet." Kenzie hesitated for a split second. "But she'll be fine with it."

Was she trying to convince herself or Addisyn?

Cars flashed by, a steady stream flowing into the Village. Addisyn shivered. Even in summer, the night was chilly. "Kenzie?"

"Yeah?"

"Did you walk all the way here?"

Kenzie shrugged one shoulder. "I waited for a while on the intracity bus. Then I realized it had left just before I got there. Didn't feel like sticking around for the next one."

"Why didn't you ask me to drive you?"

Kenzie slanted her a hostile glance. "You know why."

Silence prickled between them. Addisyn sighed and stuffed her hands into her pockets. "Look. I shouldn't have said anything about the bears."

"Yeah. I should have known not to trust you."

This was not helping either one of them. Addisyn rubbed one hand over her face. "Okay, can we just—"

"You don't have to do this, you know." Kenzie glanced at the pale shape of the mountains against the indigo sky. "I can get to the bus stop without a problem."

"No." Addisyn shook her head as they paused at a crosswalk. "I'm not leaving you."

"Why?" A challenge flashed in Kenzie's eyes. "Because Uncle Trent will be mad at you?"

The light changed, and Addisyn led them across the intersection. "No. Because—because I want to help you." She was surprised to find she meant that last statement.

Kenzie huffed. "I don't believe you."

The bitter words burned, but Addisyn couldn't find a way to defend herself. What had she been thinking of the whole time Kenzie had been with her?

Because Uncle Trent will be mad at you?

Guilt sloshed over her soul. Kenzie was right. Everything she'd done had been to try to win Trent's approval and prove herself. She'd treated Kenzie like a mission, a task, a chore—and she'd never once considered what Kenzie needed. Even tonight, when she'd realized Kenzie was gone, hadn't her first concern been keeping Trent from finding out?

Maybe trust doesn't mean anything to you, but it does to me.

Regrets rolled like rocks in her stomach. No wonder the girl didn't trust her.

Car headlights sliced by. Addisyn took a deep breath. "Look, Kenzie. You're right. I'm not good with people, I guess. I—I never have been. I've never even coached before. And I've been—not much help to you." Somehow on a dark road it was easier to say the things that clung stubbornly to the inside of her soul. "I've handled this pretty much all wrong. I didn't mean to tell Tina about the bears. And you're right to be mad at me for that. And I'm sorry."

Her words fell like dried leaves on the sidewalk. Too little. Too late. Addisyn bit her lip. She might as well call Darius and tell him to pick her up because—

"You've never coached before?"

Was Kenzie's tone a little less rigid? Addisyn glanced at her cautiously. "No. I competed, of course. I just—I was never on the other side of things."

The ghost of a smile flickered across Kenzie's face. "So maybe that explains the whole choreography problem?"

Hesitant laughter slipped out. "Yeah. I guess so." The thought of her mistakes made the laughter die. "I know I'm not doing so well."

"I think you're doing okay."

Simple words, but coming from Kenzie, they tasted like grace. "Well—thanks." Addisyn blinked away the stinging in her eyes. "You're— you're a strong skater, Kenzie."

Kenzie tunneled her hands into her jacket pockets. "Not anymore."

"You are. Your technique is there. You're just—afraid."

They were in the business district now, darkened store windows like sleeping eyes. Kenzie took a deep breath and pushed back her hood for the first time. "I—I used to love skating." She shrugged. "That's why we moved to Montreal. So I could train there. Seven years ago."

"So what happened?" Addisyn kept her tone gentle.

"I, uh—some of the other girls didn't like me."

A sick sense of foreboding washed over Addisyn. She could see around the curve of the story even before Kenzie spoke again.

"They did a bunch of stuff. Took my things, messed up my locker, called me—" Kenzie broke off abruptly. "I used to start shaking when I had to go to practice."

"You didn't tell your mom? Your coach?"

"My mom's not—we're not close." Kenzie shrugged. "My coach said to ignore them. That a true competitor should be able to push through."

Get over it, Addisyn. Brian's words, every time she'd dared to confront him.

"And then—" Kenzie fidgeted, adjusting her ponytail. "And then I got—sick."

"Is that why you see Dr. Drees?"

"Um—yes—well—" Kenzie hefted her backpack, shrugging some invisible weight on her shoulders. "After the girls—" She waved her hand. "I started having health issues. Because of, you know, the stress and everything. So I had to, uh, deal with that this past year."

"I—I didn't know." The words weren't an excuse. "Are you—okay now? Like, healthwise?"

"I'm better. I don't know if I'll ever be okay."

Oh, she knew that feeling, the hole that was left when pain ripped something precious straight out of your life.

How had she missed it? All these days with Kenzie, all this time of working with her and living with her and complaining about her, and she'd never realized the truth. Kenzie was just the way Addisyn had been at that age. Restless and wounded and driven to keep one step ahead of the hurt. Broken…just like Avery had said.

The disorienting sense of déjà vu grabbed at her, and she swallowed hard past the lump in her throat. "I understand." And for the first time, she truly did.

"Everything's different now." Kenzie's voice was almost too quiet to hear above the traffic. "My mom—when she wanted me to come here, I was excited. Things were always good here. But when I came—everything was different. Uncle Trent—and Tina—" She sniffed. "I'm different. I'm—not strong anymore."

And she knew that too, didn't she? Returning to safety only to realize that the shattered world had shattered you too. That you'd never be the same.

Kenzie was still talking, her words floating soft into the darkness. "So that's why—I really needed to find the bear. And I know it sounds crazy, I mean, I really do. It was just—it was something I needed. Because of the story."

And somehow, even the spirit bear project no longer sounded as crazy as it had. What if Kenzie had simply needed a distraction? Something to tug her back to a much more peaceful past? Yet Addisyn had threatened that for her too. "Kenzie—" She sighed. "I don't mean what I said today. I believe you. About the bear, I mean."

Kenzie studied her sideways. "Really?"

Addisyn glanced up at the ghostly shadow of the mountains, the way the stars danced just above the crest. So much more in the world than she'd once believed. And she—she'd been walking right past all of it. "Really."

A diesel-snorting vehicle rumbled behind them, and the next instant, a blue Vancouver bus lumbered into a wide plaza not a tenth of a mile ahead. Kenzie pointed. "There's the bus." But her tone sounded less certain than earlier.

Addisyn cleared her throat. "Tell you what. Come back with me, and I'll help you."

"Help me what?"

Addisyn paused in the golden halo of one of the streetlights, gauging Kenzie's expression. "Help you get better. And help you find the bear."

"Well—"

The bus lurched to a stop, passengers spilling out.

"I won't want to talk about it anymore. What I told you."

Addisyn shrugged. "Okay."

A parallel-parked maroon car flashed its headlights at them. Darius.

"Come on, Kenzie." Addisyn held out her hand. "Let's go home."

Kenzie glanced at the bus one more time, the fears Addisyn knew so well shifting over her face.

And then she reached for Addisyn's hand.

CHAPTER 13

Cousin or not, Darius was starting to get seriously irritated with Kenzie.

Since the moment the girl had stepped off the plane in Vancouver, it seemed all she'd done had been to brew problems for Addisyn. And at first, he'd tried to give her the benefit of the doubt. Typical teen moodiness, and all that.

But last night—last night was the final straw. He'd never seen Addisyn so panicked. Which in turn made *him* want to panic.

But then, somehow, she'd evidently talked Kenzie out of her impulsive runaway decision—how, he still didn't know. He'd been reluctant to leave Addisyn on the road with the difficult girl, but she'd seemed insistent. While the minutes waiting at the bus stop had trickled as slow as syrup, he'd fretted about the outcome. Would Kenzie take off into the woods? Or would Addisyn have to drag her bodily back to the car?

But when they'd come into view, they'd appeared to be having quite the conversation. And then, amazingly, Kenzie had actually taken Addisyn's hand.

Addisyn had maintained her grip on Kenzie while they climbed into the backseat—whether as a gesture of protection or to keep the girl from changing her mind, Darius couldn't say. All he knew was she'd shot him a *not now* look over Kenzie's head, and he'd swallowed all his questions and driven home in silence.

But apparently she was ready to talk now, because she'd texted this morning and asked him to meet her at the Village Park. Kenzie was in some doctor's appointment or something, and she had an hour, she'd said.

Darius glanced at his dashboard clock as he turned into the unrolling green space of the park. Right on time. It was good that they had this chance to debrief about last night. Together, they'd come up with some plan for dealing with Kenzie. This childish behavior had to stop.

He drove the loop until he saw the Jeep he'd let Addisyn borrow, and Addisyn herself at a picnic table just off the road, watching a group of teens playing disc golf. He parked the car and crossed the distance between them. "Hey, pretty girl."

She turned, tried to smile. "Hey."

"How's Kenzie today?" He slid onto the bench beside her.

She sighed and sagged slightly. "Better, I think."

Exhaustion ringed her eyes, and protectiveness surged inside him. Kenzie couldn't keep straining Addisyn like this. He simply wouldn't allow it. "So—about last night."

"Yeah." Addisyn fiddled with a strand of her hair. "Last night was—interesting."

Well, that was a mild way to put it. There was more worry than frustration in his huff. "Things definitely seem to get *interesting* whenever Kenzie's around."

But instead of agreeing, Addisyn looked slightly off balance. "Right—well—actually, things might be different with her than I thought."

Yeah, *different* as in *worse*. Darius frowned. "So did she have an explanation?"

Addisyn nodded. "She was really upset."

Really upset? That was the best excuse she could conjure for her immaturity? "Have you told Uncle Trent yet?"

"Uh, well—no."

"When are you going to?"

Addisyn studied the disc golfers with an intense concentration. "Well, I—I'm not sure I see a reason to."

She didn't see a reason? Darius planted his elbows on the table. "The reason is that he needs to know how Kenzie is acting. I mean, I know she's been difficult, but this is a whole new level."

"Well, yes, but—I mean, what did she actually do wrong?"

Was this some weird version of *The Twilight Zone*? "Yelling at you, running away, planning to leave, being stupid, making us chase her all over the—"

"Okay, okay." Addisyn held her hands up. "But, you know, pretty much all she did is just go for a walk."

"A dark, dangerous, and unauthorized walk."

"Maybe she didn't think about that."

Any minute Rod Serling would rise from the bushes. "You don't have to make excuses for her, Addisyn. I thought you were pretty fed up with her yourself."

"I was. But last night—" Addisyn sighed and rubbed at a scratch on the tabletop. "She's—she's different than I thought."

Different. The second time she'd used that word. "How so?"

"She's really struggling."

Struggling to make everyone's life miserable, yeah. "What makes you say that?"

Addisyn hesitated a long moment. "She's had some health issues. Last night she told me they were caused by stress from some—some hard things she went through. And I think she still—" She angled herself to face him. "I don't think she's past all of it."

"Does Uncle Trent know about this?"

Addisyn shrugged. "I guess. I don't know. I didn't ask. Darius?"

"Yes?"

Her eyes searched his, pleading for understanding. "I don't want to tell Trent what happened last night."

Oh. He should have seen this coming. Darius drew a deep breath, his obligations pulling crosswise. "Addisyn—I understand, but—I really think we need to. If she does something even worse next time, then—"

"She's—difficult, yes. But she's not a bad girl. She's scared and hurting, and so she's making some bad choices." She glanced toward the disc golfers again, squinting in the sunshine. "I understand that."

Well, Kenzie's struggles added more color to the picture, but they didn't redraw the lines. "Being scared and hurting is still no excuse for people to make poor decisions. They only end up hurting themselves. And usually those around them too."

Addisyn's spine stiffened slightly. "I don't think that's fair, Darius."

Her tone had dropped fifteen degrees. What had he said wrong? "Addisyn—"

She lifted her chin. "Look, Darius. I'm asking you not to tell Trent. That's all. I'm the one responsible for her, and I'll keep her out of trouble."

Now, that sounded like an impossible promise. "And how will you do that?"

Addisyn fidgeted on the narrow bench. "I have a plan."

But in a year of knowing her, Darius had discovered that she usually only said those words when she most definitely did *not* have a plan.

"Please, Darius."

Oh, this was exactly what he'd hoped to avoid. Caught in the crossfire between his loyalties. And really, Addisyn was asking for trouble, taking matters into her own hands like this. Trent would find out and be mad, or something else would happen, or—

"Darius, do you not think I can handle her?" Indignation scorched her words.

"No, of course not!" He shook his head. "I just think if there's a problem, Trent needs to know."

"Why?" Rebellion flashed in her eyes. "So he can beat Kenzie up for her mistakes? The way he does with you?"

She was upset, striking shots, and she didn't know how deep that one could go. Darius clenched his jaw to hold back the hurt. "He's just a little stern sometimes."

"And his version of *stern* is not what Kenzie needs right now."

Everything in him wanted to brush Addisyn's argument under the picnic table. She was already stressed enough, after all. And she didn't need the extra distraction. They were supposed to be finding their footing as a couple. Moving forward in their relationship. The last thing he needed was for Kenzie to siphon still more of her focus.

But she did have a point about Trent. And besides…there was a strength to her words that he'd never heard before. Even now, he could see the conviction in her eyes. Was it worth making her angry with him?

He shoved down his misgivings. "Okay. If you think you've got things worked out with her, then—yeah, Uncle Trent doesn't need to know." Foreboding pulled tight. "Unless something else happens."

Her face relaxed ever so slightly. "Thank you. And it won't."

"All right."

"So? What about the other part?"

"The other part?" The conversation was exhausting him. And he still had whiplash from Addisyn's change of heart.

"That Kenzie's struggling."

"Addisyn." She was taking too much on herself. The very thing she always complained about Avery doing, and here she was in a full-blown imitation. "She'll have to work that out on her own. I mean, didn't you tell me she's already seeing a doctor?"

Addisyn shook her head. "This isn't a doctor situation. She's really hurting, Darius. On a deep level. I think she needs more help."

"Therapy or—"

"No, something—something *warmer* than that. More like just—some friends. Some fun things. Some things that are easy and normal and make her feel more—" Addisyn gestured vaguely—"safe."

"So you're saying—"

"I think we should figure out some ways to help her." Addisyn pressed her palms together like a prayer. "Try to get her some normalcy. Maybe we can find some activities for her, things that would help her find her confidence again."

Her words spiraled hopefully, her whole being caught up in this plan she'd fabricated. He hated to splash cold water, but she'd gotten far too carried away. "Addisyn." He reached for her hands, brushed his thumbs against the back of her fingers. "Kenzie is just your client. That's it." He kept his voice kind. "I know you have sympathy for her, and that's wonderful." *And strange.* "But, well, I don't want to see you have to take on another burden."

"But I want to help her."

The compassion that broke in her voice was one of the reasons he loved her so much. "I know that." He slid closer to her on the bench. "But you just need to worry about her skating. Which is enough." He leveled a reminding gaze at her. "Do you really think Uncle Trent would be happy if you were doing extracurricular things with her?"

Uncertainty burrowed beneath Addisyn's confidence for the first time. "Well—probably not."

"Right." Relief soaked through him. Finally, she was going to listen. "And I don't want him blaming you for interfering. Or thinking you're trying to overstep your bounds."

Addisyn seemed to ponder this for a moment. "I—I really wanted to help her, Darius."

"I know you did." He wrapped his arm around her shoulders, pulling her closer. "But the best way you can help her is just to make sure her skating is top-notch. She's a smart girl. She'll sort the rest out on her own."

"Well—" She gave a tiny shrug and relaxed into his arm. "Okay. I guess you're right."

Darius tugged her closer with a breath of relief.

Crisis averted.

△△ △△ △△

ADDISYN WALKED OUT of Village Park with no intention of taking Darius's advice.

She managed a shiny smile as Darius drove away, then slumped into the driver's seat of her car. Family politics? Really? When she was asking him for help, he was going to tiptoe around what *Trent* wanted?

But whether she liked it or not, he was right—irritatingly so, but still. Trent would have a holy fit if he thought Addisyn was "*distracting*" Kenzie from her skating. Plus, she couldn't really share the full story without bringing up the spirit bear again. And *that* wasn't going to happen.

So yes, the whole thing was bringing more problems than she knew how to solve. A wise and reasonable person would back away now. But Addisyn had certainly never claimed to be either of those things.

NMP. Tina's famous acronym drifted into her mind, but this time it didn't sit well. They'd all worked hard to look away, but where did that leave Kenzie? If she was no one's *problem*, then who would ever help her?

Well, she couldn't go along with Tina's hands-off view any longer. Couldn't stay where the footing was firm. Not when Kenzie was slowly sinking, scared and lost and pounding with a pain she couldn't outrun.

The same way Addisyn had been.

So she'd nodded along with Darius's words—no reason to worry him any more about her—but she'd walked away from the conversation with her goal clearly set. If she could help Kenzie, somehow, someway—then maybe the younger girl wouldn't repeat Addisyn's mistakes. Addisyn dug her cell phone from her purse. She knew just where to go for backup this time.

The phone rang only twice before Avery's voice came over the line. "Hey, Ads."

"Hey." For once, she'd calculated the time zones correctly. "You're on lunch, right?"

"Yeah. Just stepped outside for a minute."

"Guess you're busy this time of year." Why was it so hard to touch the topic?

"For sure."

Silence crackled awkwardly between them. Why had this seemed like a good idea? As strangely as Avery had been acting, she probably wasn't interested in helping.

"Is something wrong, Ads?"

"I, uh—" Did she really only call Avery when she had a problem? Guilt burned through her. "I—no. Never mind. I actually needed some help, but—"

"Help?" Her sister's voice warmed with something oddly like—*hope?* "With what?"

"Uh—" Addisyn took a deep breath. "A, how do you find a bear?"

The line was silent for a painfully long beat. "What?"

"How do you find a bear?" Avery had to be thinking she'd lost her mind. Deservedly so. "Like, when you're hiking, or whatever."

The sudden surprise of her sister's laugh rang out. "Um, I don't find bears, Ads. I try to keep bears from finding me."

The joke was too near reality to be funny.

Avery's tone turned more serious. "Why are you asking about bears?"

"I, well, I sort of became caught up in the hunt for a spirit bear."

"A spirit bear?" A hint of amusement still lurked behind Avery's confusion. "Do Canadians celebrate Halloween in the summer or something?"

"A, it's not funny." She'd meant to sound properly indignant, but her sister's reaction was tickling her too. She launched into an explanation, and by the time she finished the tale, both of them were laughing harder than they had in months.

"Wow." Avery was still gasping from the fun. "I would not have expected this."

"Me neither. And it's all your fault."

"*My* fault?"

"Yeah." Addisyn planted her free hand on her hip as though Avery could see her. "You're the one who told me to try to talk to Kenzie, connect with her. Well, I did it, okay? And now I have to find a spirit bear."

"And you're wanting my help?"

"Well—yeah." Just like always. The last traces of lightheartedness fled, and Addisyn bit her lip. This wasn't Avery's problem. "But I mean, if you don't—"

"I'd love to help you."

Addisyn blinked. Unless it was her hopeful imagination, Avery sounded like herself again—more open than she had the whole time Addisyn had been gone. "Well—thanks."

"No problem." Avery's tone shifted to her classic older-sister executive mode. "Let's make a plan."

They discussed the possibilities, ideas ping-ponging back and forth. Addisyn suggested more frequent trips to the ridge, but Avery was certain that the bears would be deeper in the wilderness area than that. "They need a lot of territory. They're big animals."

Addisyn didn't care to be reminded of just how big. "Yeah. And I haven't seen any sign of bears the whole time I've been here. White or otherwise. So they could very well be farther back in the mountains."

"Yeah, especially this time of year." Avery hummed thoughtfully. "Even at altitude, they should be coming out of hibernation by now. That's when they're most active."

And hungry. Addisyn forced the thought away. "So where should we go?"

"Um—well—have there been any other sightings?"

"Oh, I forgot to tell you that part." Addisyn quickly filled Avery in on the ranger's information. "He was pretty vague, though."

"Still, there might be trails in that area."

"Maybe, but I'm not up for any more hiking."

"Oh, you could do it." Avery's voice rang with confidence. "Just get an early start, pack plenty of water—"

"Nope. Not for me. Now, if you were here and could go with us, that'd be different." She hesitated. "Are you ever going to come visit?"

"I don't know, Ads. I want to. It's just—" That strange shadow crept back over Avery's tone. "You know, I can't really leave the store."

What had she said to make Avery sound sad again? "Okay, but—maybe later in the summer?"

Avery seemed in a hurry to brush past the topic. "Yeah. Maybe. But in the meantime, you should totally take Kenzie hiking up there."

"I'll think about it." Actually she had no intention of taking a teenager deeper into the wilderness alone.

"But be very careful." Avery's tone turned more older-sister. "Bears are nothing to play with."

"Yeah, I know." *All too well.* She tried to infuse some levity into the moment. "If I see one, I'll run, I promise you."

"No, you can't run from them. That activates their chase instinct." Avery sounded worried now. "Anyway, they can run thirty-five miles an hour."

"Oh. Great." Addisyn leaned back in the seat. "Thanks for the encouragement, Mountain Girl."

"Ads, I'm serious." Her sister was using the same warning tone with which she'd taught Addisyn about hot stoves, busy intersections, and men who offered candy to children. "They're not naturally aggressive, but they're still wild animals and need their space."

Well, if it were up to her, she'd happily leave their whole mountain undisturbed. "Okay. I'll remember that." She glanced at the dashboard clock. Only ten minutes until she needed to be back at the clinic. "Hey, I've got to run. I'll talk to you later."

As she pulled out of the park, misgivings worked their way through her. It should be Avery here now, helping Kenzie and looking for bears and navigating the backcountry. Anything Addisyn could do to help would just be a feeble imitation of what she'd seen her older sister do.

The memory rushed in. How old had she been that summer evening? Ten? Eleven? Their dad had been working late at his office, giving them a rare moment of peace. Avery had spread a blanket outside on the sweet summer grass, and they'd lain on their backs examining the stars.

"*There's Andromeda. The princess.*" Avery had elbowed Addisyn playfully. "*Like you.*"

Addisyn had giggled, delighted with the magical way her sister could spin stories from the stars. "*What's that one?*"

"*Oh, that's Gemini.*"

"*The twins.*" Addisyn remembered that one. "*Like us, right, Avery? We're twins because we're the same.*"

Avery had laughed softly and squeezed Addisyn's hand. "*I guess we are.*"

The summer quiet had settled around them, and then Avery's voice had turned more serious. "*Ads, see that star right there?*"

"*The bright one?*"

"*Uh huh. That's Polaris. The North Star. It doesn't move like all the other stars. And it will always show you the way to true north.*"

"*Hmm. That's cool.*"

"*It's important you remember that.*" Even in the dusk, the intensity on Avery's face had been obvious. "*Remember that when you're lost, you can find your way again by looking at the things that don't move.*"

At the time, the idea had been entertaining but not meaningful. But now—now she could see the pattern, clearer than any constellation. Avery had been her north star—the unmoving one who had always pointed to what was good and true. She'd believed in Addisyn through every betrayal. She'd loved her even when Addisyn had given her every reason not to. And when Addisyn had been lost, it had been Avery's prayers and love, the strength of starlight, that had led her back home.

Whistler Holistic Health came into view. Kenzie was already waiting outside. Propped against the side of the building, she looked frighteningly fragile, as if the world had broken her so many times that the cracks were beginning to crumble.

Addisyn took a deep breath. Never mind her misgivings. This was her chance, and she had to try. To be for Kenzie what Avery had unfailingly been for her.

A north star.

⋀⋀   ⋀⋀   ⋀⋀

"ALL RIGHT." ADDISYN tunneled her hands into the pockets of her nylon jacket, accidentally jiggling the loose railing. "Ready?"

Kenzie nodded, but the familiar fear was working its way back into the corners of her eyes. Addisyn frowned. "Hey. Don't be scared."

"But—" Kenzie's breaths were coming faster. She tugged her sleeves over her hands. "I have to do better than this if I'm going to have any chance at the auditions for Skate Six. And if I keep getting scared every time, then—"

"Kenzie." Addisyn tapped her shoulder, cutting off her unspooling worry. "Today is going to be different, okay?"

Kenzie still looked wary. "Different how?"

"Because I've had an idea."

"Really?"

"Yep." She'd racked her brain all weekend, trying to contrive a solution for Kenzie. Finally, it had hit her. Now, if she could just convince the girl.

"You found a way to help me not be scared of falling?" Kenzie's face lit with a heartbreaking hope.

"Yes. I think I did." Addisyn took a deep breath. "It occurred to me that I've neglected to practice a really important skill with you."

Kenzie cocked her head. "What's that?"

"Falling."

Confusion twisted Kenzie's expression. "What?"

"You heard me."

Kenzie stared as if Addisyn had asked her to skate upside down. "But the whole goal is to not fall."

"Wrong." Addisyn pointed at her. "The goal is to know how to fall. To fall over and over until you can't be scared of it even if you try."

Alarm worked itself through Kenzie's expression, and Addisyn couldn't blame her. The idea did sound crazy out loud. "Look at it this way." She paused, rolling the explanation together. "Falling is a skill, okay? Just like any other. You have to know how to fall without getting hurt, and then you won't be afraid of it. And once you're not afraid, then you can quit holding yourself back."

Kenzie still looked uncertain, but she nodded. "Um—okay. I guess we can try it."

The best she could hope for, under the circumstances. She pointed toward the skates Kenzie held. "Put those back in your bag for a minute. If we're going to practice falling, we should do it on a more forgiving surface than the ice."

She led Kenzie over to the cushioned practice mats and held up a finger in mock sternness. "Okay. Welcome to Falling School, lesson one. Watch me carefully. This is your basic fall. When you're gliding or doing crossovers or whatever."

Worry still creased Kenzie's forehead, but at least she was watching.

Addisyn took a deep breath and bent her knees slightly. Practice mats or not, she'd still feel this impact. "Okay, see that I have my knees bent, right? That's something I've noticed you're struggling with. I don't think you're keeping your weight forward."

"On the balls of my toes?" Kenzie shifted slightly.

"Yes. Exactly. That will help you with your balance and speed, obviously, but it also helps when you fall. It's always better to fall forwards than backwards." Addisyn blinked. That statement was true in a lot of ways. "Anyway, when you feel yourself start to go down—"

She pushed off, stretching her arms forward and pulling her legs toward her chest, and then she'd landed on her hands and knees with an impact not nearly as bad as what she'd expected. "See?" She nodded toward her hands. "The trick is to stay on your hands and knees. Don't go all the way down. And if possible, hit your hands first and use your arms to stop yourself."

"But then what's the best way to get back up?"

That was the question, wasn't it? Addisyn bent her knee and pulled one foot under her. "Just dig this foot into the ice and use this knee as leverage and that—" she pulled herself back to standing—"will get you up."

"Okay." Kenzie still didn't look convinced.

"So." Addisyn brushed her palms together and nodded toward the practice mats, trying to analyze Kenzie's expression. "Are you ready?"

"I—" Kenzie bit her lip and stepped back, dropping her head. "I can't."

Addisyn took a deep breath. "Okay. If you don't want to do it today, I won't push you. But please listen to me first." She focused on what she could see of Kenzie's face. "You're going to fall when you skate. It's unavoidable. You're going to lose your balance, or you're going to miss a step, or you're going to get dizzy on a turn. You can put off falling today. But you can't put off falling forever. Not unless you're willing to never take another risk."

Kenzie was still looking down, but Addisyn could feel her listening, feel her reaching for the words. "But what's important is that you're ready. That you know that even when you've fallen hard and been hurt—" was she talking to Kenzie or to herself?—"you can get back up."

"I've never been good at getting back up."

"Then let's change that." She squeezed the girl's thin shoulder and waited until she had Kenzie's full attention. "We all get hurt, Kenzie. But none of us can afford to stay down."

Kenzie held her eyes a heartbeat longer. Then she took a deep breath, squared her thin shoulders, and stepped up to the mat.

Addisyn gripped her fingers into fists. "That's right. Okay. Lean forward—and—"

Kenzie tipped forward, her knees crumpling, and then she was on the mat, sliding forward until she almost hit her chin. She sat up quickly. "I didn't do it right."

"But you did it." Addisyn squatted down next to her to demonstrate. "Look. I keep most of the weight on my hands, see? Really reach with your arms." She stood and offered Kenzie a hand. "Try it again."

Kenzie fell more readily this time, landing solidly on her hands and knees. When she glanced up at Addisyn, a flicker of excitement undergirded her expression. "I did it."

"Absolutely!" Addisyn grinned. "Let's try again."

After only a few more tries, Kenzie was more than comfortable with the basic fall, and Addisyn moved on to more positions for jumps and turns.

"That's it!" She pumped her fist in the air as Kenzie fell into a roll. "Right there!"

Kenzie pushed herself into a sitting position on the mat and brushed her hair out of her eyes. "I think I'm getting it."

"I think you are too. Ready to call it quits for now?"

"Yeah." Kenzie pulled herself up with Addisyn's offered hand, then ducked her head. "Addisyn?"

"Yeah?"

She glanced up with a hesitant smile. "Thanks."

Addisyn blinked. "Sure. No problem." She patted Kenzie's shoulder. "You're doing great."

Kenzie didn't say anything else. Just a quick nod, and she slung her bag over her shoulder and headed out of the rink. But it was more than enough.

Kenzie was smiling not because she was learning to fall, but because she was learning to finally get up. Was it possible that Addisyn could learn the same?

CHAPTER 14

After five Wednesdays, the drive to Whistler Holistic Health was as routine as a well-worn path. Addisyn had even memorized the way there. The way Kenzie probably had as well.

Addisyn adjusted her sunglasses and searched for something to fill the silence in the car. "Your appointment's still at ten thirty, right?"

"Yeah."

Only one syllable, but enough to show Kenzie's strain. When they stopped at a red light, Addisyn studied the girl from behind her sunglasses. As usual before these appointments, Kenzie was shrinking into the seat, arms hugging her middle as if holding herself together.

The light turned green. Addisyn cleared her throat. "So, Kenzie, I was wondering something."

"Uh huh?"

"Are you—" There was no tactful way to ask this. "Are you—sick?"

Kenzie dropped her eyes. "Because of the doctor?"

"Yeah."

Silence, and another red light. This section was stop-and-go.

"I mean, it's none of my business." She should have never asked. "I knew you had some health stuff from the stress, but you never told me what exactly was wrong, and I—I wanted to make sure you were all right."

The light turned green, and again they inched their way forward with the rest of the downtown traffic. They'd gone another block when Kenzie finally spoke. "I'm not sick, not like that. These are just checkups." Her voice was soft, distant. "It's just—follow-up stuff. To make sure I'm okay."

"And—are you?"

"Am I what?"

"Okay."

Kenzie's fingers were wrapped white around her seatbelt. "Well—" Deliberately she relaxed her hands, folded them across her lap. "I will be."

The medical center stretched before them, the tinted windows glazed over like disinterested eyes. A strange kind of guilt nibbled at Addisyn as she let Kenzie out at the door. Why was she trusting Kenzie to that indifferent building? If this was truly a *health center*, how come Kenzie seemed farther from well every Wednesday?

As she found a parking space and pulled out the fitness magazine she'd brought, the uneasiness swarmed in her soul. What if something was really wrong? And what if the doctor wasn't helping? She frowned toward the building. Maybe she should go in with Kenzie sometime. See what exactly—

But she didn't want to pry. And anyway, the girl was an athlete, after all. Surely Trent wouldn't allow her to train if her health problem were truly serious. Maybe it was some preexisting condition—asthma or diabetes. Something manageable that just needed some monitoring.

She pushed the worries from her mind and forced her attention back to her reading. She was in the middle of an article about the five best sources of protein when the car door jerked open. Addisyn blinked and lowered the magazine. "Are you back already? I didn't—"

Her words dropped off the edge of disbelief. Tears were tracing down Kenzie's cheeks—tears that the girl who'd spent so much time polishing her pride now didn't bother to hide.

"Kenzie? What's wrong?"

Kenzie shook her head and slumped into the seat. "I'm done." A sob caught the end of her words, and she pressed her lips together. "It was a bad day."

"Tell me what happened." Addisyn rubbed Kenzie's shoulder soothingly and dug through the console with her free hand. Were there really no tissues in this car?

"Nothing, it just—" Kenzie drew a shuddering breath and scrubbed her sleeve awkwardly over her cheeks. "I want to go home."

Addisyn glared accusingly at the smug little health center. "Look, do I need to talk to your doctor? Did somebody say or do—"

"No, no!" Alarm joined the other emotions in Kenzie's voice. "Nothing like that."

"Then what's wrong?"

Kenzie glanced out the window for a moment, where the puffy summer clouds bobbed in the blue sky. When she looked back at Addisyn, her face held the raw sorrow of a soul stripped bare. "I just *hate* this."

Addisyn was still preoccupied with the idea of finding Kenzie's doctor and demanding some serious answers. "You hate what?"

"All of it." Her arm circled, sweeping the car and the center and the uncaring clouds into her statement. "The doctors. The—the sickness. The worrying. Having to come here and deal with this every week. Not being— normal." A fresh wave of tears skated across her blue eyes. "Never being normal."

The desperate brokenness in her voice cracked straight through Addisyn's heart. What could she do to help?

Avery would have some kind of perfect compassionate response. And Addisyn didn't even have a Kleenex.

Awkwardly she angled in her seat and gripped Kenzie's hand. As if by hanging onto the girl, she could keep the despair from submerging her. "Kenzie—I'm sorry." Such weak words. "Is there anything I can—"

"No." Kenzie was studying her jeans, idly picking at a loose thread. "I just want to go home."

Her face had turned dull and flat, her pain once more packed away. Addisyn sighed and released her hand. "Okay. We'll go home."

Traffic was lighter by now. Fortunate, since Addisyn couldn't concentrate on her driving. Frustration wrapped itself around her compassion. There had to be something she could do. Something more than just helping Kenzie with her skating and ferrying her back and forth to see these stupid doctors who really didn't seem to be doing their job.

Good grief, Kenzie hadn't even had any fun since she'd been with Addisyn. She'd spent her days practicing in the ice rink or slumped on the couch with earbuds or traipsing through the woods looking for spirit bears. Not the way for a sixteen-year-old girl to spend a summer.

I hate this...never being normal...

Never mind what her diagnosis was or how these appointments were supposed to be helping. Whatever was going on, Kenzie had to feel helpless. Powerless. Good grief, she couldn't even drive herself to her own appointments. Which was also weird, come to think of it. Why didn't she have a license by now? And why hadn't Tina or Trent arranged to help her with that over the summer, instead of just assigning Addisyn to be her chauffeur?

Unless she was easier to control that way.

Brian's face flashed to the forefront of her memories again. Living with Avery less than a block from a subway stop, she'd had no need of her own vehicle—even if they could have afforded it. Then, after she'd moved in with Brian, she'd begged him to help her find a car of her own. But he'd always had some excuse. Public transport was easier, or his townhouse had limited parking, or he didn't want her driving in the city's chaotic traffic. It had all been lies, of course. Just another way he could keep her under the shadow of his power.

Addisyn rubbed her thumbs across the smooth leather of the steering wheel. When she'd finally gotten her own car after her years with Brian, it had been a satisfying moment of victory. Nothing like driving to give someone a feeling of independence, of being able to control their own—

The idea darted into her rambling thoughts and scattered them in every direction. That was it! The very solution.

They were out of downtown now, the trees beginning to cluster more thickly. The Spring Creek turnoff appeared to her left, but Addisyn kept going. "Kenzie?"

"Yeah?" She glanced up and leaned forward. "Hey, where are we going?"

"We're finding a different road." Addisyn slowed and scanned the surroundings. A side street would be best.

"A different road?"

"Yup. You'll see." What about that one? It looked—no, it was unpaved. She wasn't taking Darius's shiny little car off-roading, even if it was a Jeep. "Kenzie, you said you didn't have your license."

"License for what?"

"Your *driver's* license, Kenzie." Yeah, they were definitely at square one. "But do you have a learner's permit? Or how does that work in Canada?"

"Well—" Bewilderment still draped itself over Kenzie's words. "I mean, yeah, I have a provisional license. The kind you get to practice with."

Must be the same as a learner's permit at home. "When did you get it?"

"Last year, but it's about to expire. I'll have to retake the written test unless I can learn to drive and get my real license in the next two months." From the doubt in her voice, you'd think she had to pull off a lunar landing or a transatlantic swim instead of simply learning how to keep a car between painted lines.

"So then, you can legally drive as long as an adult is in the car." She was nailing down that point for sure. Wouldn't Trent love a phone call from the jail?

"Yeah, but *why?*"

"Because, believe it or not, I'm considered an adult." The intersection for Cheakamus Lake Road appeared, and Addisyn assessed the possibilities. Two-lane layout, thirty-kilo speed limit, generous shoulders. Perfect. She pulled to the side of the road, gravel crunching under the tires, and swung out of the car. "Well, come on. Trade places."

Kenzie's expression morphed from confused to horrified. "Wait. What are you doing?"

"I'm going to ride home this time."

"No." Kenzie's words tumbled out frantically. "I can't drive. I've never practiced, and I hate going fast, and I don't even know where the gas pedal is, so—"

"Gas pedal is on the floor next to the brake. And it's like skating. You learn by doing." Addisyn tapped her fingers on the hood of the car. "Come on, Kenzie. Take us home."

Kenzie had no sooner settled into the driver's seat—if *settled* could begin to describe her on-edge state—that the reality of what she'd just done slammed itself into Addisyn's mind. What on earth was she doing, turning over her car—no, *Darius's* car—to an emotionally unbalanced teenager who'd already admitted her lack of driving experience?

Oh boy. This could be a capital-D disaster.

Kenzie was staring at the dashboard as if a poisonous snake might leap out. "I can't do this." Her breath was coming short again, panic clearly just under the surface. "I'll hit someone or I'll drive off the road or I'll—"

"Or you'll learn to drive and get your license." Hopefully her voice projected a calm she didn't feel at the moment. "Come on, Kenzie. You've got this. Hold the wheel at ten and two."

"Like this?" Kenzie gripped it as if preparing to wrangle a rodeo steer at the Calgary Stampede.

Addisyn sighed. "Not that tight, but yes." She tapped Kenzie's shoulders, which were nearly connected to her ears. "Loosen up, Kenzie. Driving tight will give you a headache. Okay?"

"Okay." Her shoulders dropped. Slightly.

"Now." They'd start with the barest basics. Headlights and blinkers and windshield wipers could all wait. Addisyn pointed into the floorboard. "That's the gas on this side. And the other is the brake. Use your right foot for both."

"The brake is the bigger one."

"Right." Maybe this wouldn't be that hard.

"So now what?"

"Well." She tapped the gearshift. "These are your gears, okay?" Kenzie had it easy, driving an automatic. Addisyn had been forced to learn on Avery's ratty stick-shift. "Put the car in drive first."

"How do I know where drive is?"

"The D." Hopefully her voice didn't sound too impatient.

Kenzie touched the gearshift so timidly that it took her two tries to move into drive.

"Now turn your wheel—that's it—"

The car lurched back onto the road at an awkward angle and rolled slowly down toward another side street through its own momentum.

"Okay, now, you're going crooked. Stop and—"

The car shot forward with a sudden urgency, the street sign seeming to leap in front of the windshield.

"Kenzie, the brake!" Addisyn lunged for the steering wheel and yanked the car away from the metal post just as Kenzie—finally—slammed the brake with a force that shoved Addisyn into the dashboard and undoubtedly shortened the life expectancy of Darius's tires.

"I'm sorry." Kenzie slowly released the steering wheel, a tremble beneath her voice. "I got the gas and the brake mixed up."

Addisyn gingerly rubbed a hand over the throbbing in her side. Was this how a broken rib felt? "Kenzie—you've got to keep that separate for sure."

"I know."

The sharp scent of burning rubber was leaking into the car. Never mind. This was not a good idea. No matter how noble Addisyn's intentions had been, she couldn't risk a collision. Next time, it might be something worse than a street sign.

Before she could find the words to gently let Kenzie down, the girl shook her head. "Don't say it. I know. I told you I couldn't do this."

Defeat dragged down her voice, and Addisyn paused. If she let Kenzie quit now, the darkness and its lies would only gain power. "Nope. That was just a—an adjustment." She glanced over her shoulder. The little car was still stuck crosswise across both lanes. Thankfully the road wasn't very popular. "You can do this, Kenzie. But do straighten us a little bit."

Kenzie's face was still whiter than normal, but she gripped the wheel and hesitantly maneuvered them to the correct side of the yellow line.

"Okay. Good job." Addisyn buckled her seatbelt across her still-aching side. For a ride like this, she should have been wearing the strap from the beginning. She glanced up at the road sign on which they'd nearly been impaled.

HAZARD ST.

She sighed and waved her hand toward the road ahead. "All right. Let's go."

KENZIE WAS QUITE familiar with fear.

She lived with it every day, like a poisonous pet she couldn't get rid of. It slid beside her across the ice and prodded her when she tried to sleep and hissed its haunting words when she swallowed the orange pills every morning. But in five minutes behind the wheel of a car, she was learning the word in a whole new way.

What was Addisyn thinking, tossing her into the deep end like this? She'd never be able to drive them home. She could already see the police report. *Stupid teenager confused the gas and brake. Car totaled. Two casualties.*

She'd spent her life walking the razor-edge of perfection. Staying on the balance beam, refusing to fall onto the sharp teeth of mistakes waiting on every side. But now—a mistake here wouldn't be just embarrassing or disappointing or frustrating. It would be deadly.

Oh, what was she doing?

"Loosen up." Addisyn shook her shoulder gently. "You're too tense."

Tension had knotted itself into every corner of her body. Her fingers were locked onto the steering wheel so tightly that they'd probably have to be pried away by Addisyn. Or by the coroner. "Am I doing okay?"

"You're doing great."

Addisyn's voice sounded miraculously calm. What was her secret? Even when they'd almost hit that street sign, Addisyn hadn't seemed troubled.

"I feel like I'm driving down the middle of the road."

"You're not. It just looks that way at first."

A diesel-snorting truck loomed around a curve in front of them. Kenzie's heart rate spun into overdrive. "What do I do?"

"Just keep going."

The truck was chugging closer. Close enough now to see the sunshine glinting wickedly off its blue paint. "Addisyn, it's going to hit us!"

"It's not, Kenzie. You're in your lane. Just stay there."

This was it. This was how they died. Kenzie braced for a collision as the truck barreled toward them—and then it was passing them. Obnoxiously close, but still.

Kenzie glanced in the rearview mirror and blinked at the disappearing tailgate. That was it? They'd survived?

"See?" Even without taking her eyes off the road, Kenzie could hear the smile behind Addisyn's voice. "Good job."

Good job. The knots were relaxing now, the tension slowly loosening its fist. "Thanks."

The road was opening up now, the fields unrolling on either side. Sunlight dappled through the trees. In the late afternoon, the shadows on the mountains were stronger than usual.

"This reminds me of when I learned to drive." Addisyn's voice sounded farther away than before. "My sister taught me."

Her sister again. Kenzie kept quiet, leaving empty space for the rest of the story.

"She did it just the way we're doing it now." Addisyn gave a quiet laugh. "Drove me out to a rural area and turned me loose on the farm roads. I think we almost hit the ditch twenty-six times that day."

In spite of herself, Kenzie laughed. "Was she mad about it?"

"Avery? No. She never got mad." Addisyn was quiet for a minute. "She still has the same truck. And it's a stick-shift, by the way."

"What's that?"

"Be thankful you don't know." Addisyn chuckled. "That big old truck. I felt like a gnat behind the steering wheel."

"Were you scared?"

"No. I was always up for a challenge." Addisyn paused. "At that time, anyway."

Somehow questions seemed easier here, when she could look at the road instead of at Addisyn. "How did you keep from being afraid?"

Addisyn's silence stretched longer this time. "Well—I don't know. Things were—very different then." Her tone seemed shadowed now. "Maybe I wasn't afraid enough."

What did that mean? Before Kenzie could ask, Addisyn pointed ahead. "Pull in that driveway there and turn around." She nodded at where the road dissolved into dirt just ahead. "No four-wheeling for you yet, young lady."

Half an hour later, Kenzie had made it back up Cheakamus, practiced turns in a spiderweb of small streets, and even followed the highway to the Spring Creek turn that would take them home. And most amazing of all, she was still alive. She'd been behind the wheel of a three-thousand-pound machine, and the only thing she'd run over was an old shoe.

Funny, when you thought about it. She'd made plenty of mistakes, big ones, like almost hitting that sign and messing up the gas and brake and accidentally running over a curb by the plumbing place. But still, she was on the road. After each mistake, she'd just learned and adjusted and kept on driving.

What if that were true in other ways too?

"You're doing great." Addisyn squeezed her shoulder proudly as she passed a bus on Spring Creek without even flinching. "Almost home now."

Home. Her enthusiasm leaked slightly. "Actually—uh—you better take us the last bit."

"Nonsense." Addisyn shook her head. "We're less than ten minutes away, Kenzie, and these are easy roads."

"Yeah, but—my uncle."

"Oh." Addisyn stretched the word out slowly.

She didn't want to be disrespectful, but at the same time— "He's very—protective."

"He wouldn't be excited to know you're learning to drive?"

"You know him. What do you think?"

The silence filled with Addisyn's answer. When Spring Creek School came into view, the older girl pointed to the parking lot. "Pull off there. I'll take us on home."

Kenzie pulled over and put the car in park just as Addisyn had shown her. She shouldn't have mentioned Uncle Trent. Her fears from earlier were inverted now. What if Addisyn didn't let her drive again? What if she lost this exciting new skill, this ability that made her feel capable for the first time in so long? "Addisyn?"

"Yeah?" Addisyn paused halfway out the passenger door.

"Will we—" She laced her fingers together, the request sticking awkwardly. "Next time—I mean—when can I try again?"

A smile slowly warmed Addisyn's expression. She glanced down the road toward home, then nodded once at Kenzie. "How 'bout tomorrow?"

△△ △△ △△

A REAL DATE. That's what Darius had called it when he'd phoned her yesterday evening. Addisyn had laughed. "What, were all the other dates fake?"

He'd joined her laughter. "No, but this is my fancy side, okay?"

"Your fancy side." She'd tried unsuccessfully to picture him in something besides his typical lumberjack style.

"Yeah. I'm keeping you indoors for a change." She could hear the teasing in his voice. "We'll get dinner somewhere nice."

Somewhere nice. Surely nothing like the upscale restaurants Brian had always taken her to. She'd picked at unpronounceable food while he'd droned about the merits of his alcoholic beverage, hobnobbed with any acquaintances he saw, and usually watched the waitresses with a little too much interest. She'd swallowed the sour taste of the memory. "We don't have to go anywhere expensive—I don't really have the clothes for a place like that—"

"Addisyn." He'd given a soft laugh. "I'm not taking you to the ball. Just wear something comfortable."

She'd never stop being grateful for how unlike Brian Darius was. Relief had absorbed her concerns. "Okay."

Now she glanced at the clock. Darius would be here any minute, but she was nearly ready. "Kenzie?"

"Yeah?"

Addisyn stepped into the living room, where Kenzie was stretched on the couch, and displayed two pairs of earrings. "Which ones?"

Kenzie laid her phone aside and sat up to study the options. "Um— the loopy ones."

They were the prettier pair, but did she really have the confidence to pull them off? "You sure they're not too big?"

"Nope." Kenzie stretched out again and reached for her phone. "They frame your face. The other ones get lost behind your hair."

Well, then. Who was she to question a teenager's fashion advice? "Sounds good." She threaded the earrings in and glanced at the clock again. "Do you need anything before I go?"

"Nope." Kenzie offered a small smile. "Have a good time tonight."

"Thank you." Addisyn returned the smile. Over the last few days,

Kenzie seemed to be slowly stabilizing. Whether it was the nontraditional skating practices or the undercover driving lessons, Addisyn couldn't say, but something was helping her. Shadows still hung in her eyes, but at least the light was starting to break through.

Tires crunched on the driveway outside. "That must be Darius." She grabbed her purse and opened the door just as he stepped onto the porch.

"Addisyn." His crooked smile tipped up shyly. "You look lovely."

Her cheeks heated under his lingering gaze, and she brushed her hands down her rose-colored skirt, acutely aware of Kenzie's witness to the scene. "Thank you. You look nice too." He was actually wearing khaki slacks and a buttoned shirt, and his hair was neatly pulled back.

"I clean up well when I need to." He took her hand and drew her through the doorway. "Let's go."

The restaurant he'd chosen was a rustic steakhouse that fronted Lake Alta, thankfully the exact opposite of the stuffy clubs to which Brian had dragged her. After they'd finished their meal, Darius folded his hands expectantly. "You know what tonight is?"

She scanned her mental calendar. Thursday. June 20. "Uh—"

"It's the summer solstice. The longest day. And I think we should be outside for sunset." He pointed out the window. "There's a little path that leads by the lake. Want to take a walk?"

She'd go anywhere with him. "Absolutely."

As they stepped out of the steakhouse, the hum of conversation died, replaced by the rhythmic whirring of summertime insects. A deepening purple dusk draped itself across the landscape as the longest day dissolved behind the horizon. Addisyn took a deep breath of the warm air, relaxing into the peace of the evening. "This is beautiful, Darius."

"Mmhm." His hand found hers in the twilight. "Years of living here, and it never gets old."

Lights were glittering on the rippling waters, homes across the lake glowing with welcome. "It's a special place."

"Yes. But—" he paused, gathered both of her hands in his. "What makes a place special is who you share it with. Don't you think?"

"Yes." She breathed the word into the soft serenity of the summer night.

Behind them, guitar music from the restaurant filtered into the stillness. Darius pulled her closer. "Care to dance?"

"Dance?" Her laugh sounded nervous even to her. She glanced down at the brick path beneath them. "I haven't been dancing since—" Since she'd hung off Brian's arm at cocktail parties. "Since forever."

"Well—" His arm encircled her waist. "Some things you never forget, right?"

If only that weren't true. But she allowed him to pull her closer anyway. "Right."

The guitar strains throbbed a lovely kind of longing. He gently settled her hand along his shoulder, drawing her into the dance. "Good?" He whispered the word near her ear.

"Yes." No surprise that Darius was a wonderful dancer. Strong but gentle, guiding her without demands.

An ideal partner. Just as she'd always known.

"Have I told you lately—" his hand smoothed across her shoulders— "how beautiful you are?"

Beautiful. The word was a tender touch on the places in her soul that Brian had left so bruised. He'd tossed the word around flippantly every time he was satisfied with her makeup or neckline or hairstyle. But Darius—Darius was speaking to something much deeper. "Thank you."

"I mean it. Don't forget that."

The fading sunset struck sparks against the sky, and she shivered suddenly like the shimmering lights on the water. How long had it been since she felt this way, as if she belonged in the beauty of this night? Lovely and desired and special. As though she might truly deserve Darius one day.

And he'd been willing to bring her here even after the way her fear had wedged between them. He had to be confused by her reactions over the last few weeks.

"We've been needing more time like this." His voice was still gentle. The guitar ended to a smattering of faint applause, but the scuffing of their shoes on the walkway was its own kind of music.

"Yes." This was her chance to tell him, to open her heart in the best way she could. "Darius, I need to talk to you about—about the way I've been acting." She rushed on before he could answer. "I—I know I've been—well, distant. And I'm sorry."

"Hey, it's no problem." His voice filled with pure understanding. "You've had a lot on your plate. I know you haven't had much extra time."

"No, Darius, it's not just that." She hesitated, balancing her words against her secrets. "I've just been—I guess I've been feeling the pressure lately. But I think I'm starting to realize something."

"What's that?"

Again, the careful choosing of words. "Something happened that made me realize I really can do this job. I think—I think maybe I was just trying too hard."

"Ah. That can happen sometimes."

"Yes." The guitar started a new song, a brighter one this time. "So— I think things will be better now."

"I'm glad." He brushed back a strand of her hair. "I don't want you to feel any pressure, Addisyn. Of course you'll do well. You're an incredible skater. And the most amazing person I know."

The words should have lifted her up, but they bent her down. He was still seeing her through a warped window that camouflaged her scars. Her throat pinched. "I don't want you to be sorry you invited me here."

"Are you kidding?" He released her hand and wrapped her into the warm strength of his embrace. He whispered the next words beside her ear. "I would never be sorry I invited you here."

Tears stung her eyes, and she slipped her arms around his neck, clinging to him like a promise. "Never?"

"Never." He was close enough now she could smell his wonderful scent—like the ocean-tang of the Pacific inlet and the deep green mystery of the mountain winds. "You'll forever be the best thing that ever happened to me, Addisyn Miles."

"Forever is a long time." The words were a whisper straight from the place of her fear.

He brought one warm hand to the side of her face, brushing his thumb gently over her cheek. "Not long enough."

The love in his touch was like the golden gleam of the lake houses, throwing their light across the waters and guiding safely home. She let herself feel its pull, closing the inches between them. "Are you sure?"

"Absolutely."

In a moment as natural as the sunset, his lips met hers in the kind of kiss that soothed and stirred her soul at the same time. When he drew back, his voice was softer than the wind that ruffled the lake. "I love you, Addisyn. Don't ever doubt that."

She rested her head on his chest, breathing in time with the steady tempo of his heartbeat. "I love you too."

Fear still lurked in the shadows, but it would have to wait. Because tonight, as the seasons turned, she only wanted to be in this moment, with this man, dancing on the edge where the light met the dark.

CHAPTER 15

"Here you go, sir." Avery handed the receipt to the latest customer—a bearded man with a Denver Broncos ball cap—and offered her best professional smile. "Have a great day."

"Thanks." He touched the cap brim. "You too."

As soon as the door swung shut behind him, Avery drooped against the counter. Laz was in the back room, so she didn't have to hide her exhaustion. Only Tuesday, and she was already tired. Not from customers or inventory or the long hikes she'd been taking more and more often, but from tugging unceasingly on every corner of Skyla's offer.

Over a week now, and she finally had the answer. Five little words she'd mentally rehearsed like an unwilling understudy, ready for the moment when she'd stand before Skyla and say them in person.

I'm sorry, Skyla. I can't.

Five little words, but she'd had to practice them over and over, had to train her tongue that so badly wanted to say *yes*.

I'm sorry, Skyla. I can't.

The door chime jangled. "Avery, hey!"

She yanked herself from her thoughts. "Tyler! What are you doing here?"

"Just came in to grab a new pair of hiking socks." He made his way to the counter. "We missed you at the center on Friday."

"Yes, I know." Avery glanced away from his concern. "I was, uh, busy here."

"Well, I was hoping to show you the latest banding results. One of our birds was found."

"Oh!" Every bird released from the rehab center wore a thin metal band on its ankle, inscribed with a unique ID number. Banding was a process Tyler coordinated as part of his studies, registering the numbers with the U. S. Geological Survey and tracking all the sightings in the database. "Which bird?"

"KZ98. That American Kestrel from December, remember?" He cleared his throat. "The one that you went with me to release?"

"Oh, yeah!" Skyla had been busy with something at the center's gift shop, so Avery and Tyler had driven the raptor back to where he'd been found, on the border of the national forest near Fort Collins. "Where was he?"

"Berthoud. A ranger there made the report."

A sudden fear pulled at her gut. "Was he—you know—"

"Alive and healthy." Tyler grinned. "He flew into a mist net at their banding center. They entered the new coordinates and released him again."

"That's awesome." The hawk she'd held, now free to roam the whole frontier of the heavens. Such rewarding work. If only...

"So, uh—" Tyler rested his arms on the counter. "Chay was mentioning that Skyla had offered you a job."

Avery's heart rate jolted into double time. She glanced over her shoulder, but Laz was still out of sight. Out of earshot, too, hopefully. "Oh, well, yes. She did."

"That's wonderful." He smiled, his eyes bright with encouragement. "You'd be great at that. Have you decided yet?"

The words wedged back into her mind. *I'm sorry. I can't.* She opened her mouth, but a different answer forced its way out. "Well, um, not yet."

Now why had she said that? Postponing her refusal was nothing short of cowardly.

"Well, I hope you decide to do it. We need you over there."

She had to land the conversation before Laz came back out. "Well, thanks. And thanks for letting me know about the bird." At least something was flying free.

"What bird?" Laz's voice boomed over her shoulder. He stepped beside her and nodded at Tyler. "Howdy, son."

"Hey, Mr. Jobe." Tyler smiled. "Just letting Avery know about the bird she and I released in December. He was tracked in Berthoud."

"Well, ya don't say." Laz raised his eyebrows. "I 'member when you two took that fella. Kestrel, wasn't it?"

"Yes, sir."

The conversation stalled into an awkward moment, but Tyler made no move to leave. Avery bit back a groan. Tyler was a nice enough guy, but his social skills had never been one of his greatest strengths. Today, of all days...

The bell over the door jingled again, and Laz turned away to assist the next customer. Tyler shifted his position. "Hey, Avery?"

"Yes?"

"That was a fun day, wasn't it? The day we took the raptor."

"Oh. Yes." *Patience.* She donned a smile. "It's always fun to see the birds go free."

"Right, well—" There was an odd searching in his gaze. As if she might answer a riddle for him. "The Christmas carols were fun."

"Christmas carols?"

His expression drooped slightly. "The radio was playing classic Christmas carols. We sang along on the way home, remember?"

They had? Avery rummaged through her memory. Yes, she could dredge up something like that. "Oh. Right." She smiled at him politely, trying to put a period on the conversation. "Yeah. A fun day."

He sighed and pushed away from the counter. "Well—see you later."

"See you." Avery waved as he headed out the door, then turned just in time to see Laz studying her. "What?"

"Nothin'." He shrugged. "He's a nice young fella."

Nice, but not good with social cues. "Yes. He does a great job with the birds." A thought suddenly struck her. Tyler had left without once looking at the hiking socks he'd supposedly come to buy.

"Yep, a nice young man." Laz's eyes slanted at her wisely. "You'll be findin' yerself some nice young fella like that one of these days."

Oh, not again. "Laz, we've been over this." Her boss had been hinting about *nice young fellas* for as long as Avery had known him. "I don't have the time for that right now."

"You sure?" He narrowed his eyes at her.

"Of course." There was more to why she kept men at arm's length—much more—but nothing he needed to hear.

"Waalll…you never know. Yer sister sure found herself a right nice boy."

"My sister and I are different." The words were out before she realized how sharp they'd sliced. "Laz…" She shook her head. "I'm sorry, that—"

"Now 'pears to me I asked for that, stickin' my nose in." Laz shrugged, smiled. "Don't worry none 'bout it."

He was being gracious, but she'd never responded that harshly to his matchmaking before. Avery sighed and ran a hand over her hair. "No, I'm just—" What could she tell him about the war within her? "I'm just stressed lately."

Laz's eyes crinkled with compassion. "Been noticin' that." The store was devoid of customers, the only sound John Denver singing about sunshine that brought tears and joy together. "Wanna tell me 'bout it?"

What could she say? That she was living a story her younger self wouldn't have recognized? That she was aching from being set aside by the sister who'd always needed her? That all the expectations had dragged her miles off course? She sorted through the statements and reached for the shallowest one. "I'm just busy. And—I miss Addisyn."

"Wondered if you was gettin' lonesome without her." Laz smoothed his beard. "Figgered you had to be."

"Yeah." Avery sighed. "She's fine without me, though."

His shaggy eyebrows lifted. "She say that?"

"Well—no. But I can tell. She's on her own now. She doesn't need me anymore."

"Hmm. I dunno if we ever outgrow needin' each other."

Avery just shrugged and turned back to the order form she'd been putting together before customers interrupted her. The silence stretched long enough that she'd given up on the conversation when Laz cleared his throat. "I saw Miz Skyla t'other night down at Safeway. She was sayin' how she missed you this week."

Another weight pressed against her chest. "I know. I hated skipping

Friday. I just—I just have too much here right now."

"Waalll, yer missed over there. Miz Skyla said you've got a real gift with them birds."

Again, the older woman's praise fit awkwardly, like clothing she'd never grow into. "Well—that's kind of her. I don't know about a gift—"

"Eh, course you do." Laz waved his hand in the air. "I been watchin' that ever' since I first saw you grippin' Isaiah like yer life depended on it."

Avery laughed at the memory of the first hawk she'd helped Laz care for—and the determination she'd had to see him heal. "Isaiah was special."

"That he was." Laz leaned his hip against the counter. "You had a— a spark when you was around him. An' yer missin' that now."

He'd noticed. Of course he had. "I know." She tried to sort through her emotions, selecting her words with care. "Sometimes—with Addisyn gone, and my life so busy—I just feel, well, lost."

"Know that feelin' right well." Laz folded his arms. "So whaddya do when yer lost?"

"What?"

"When you lose yer direction up in them hills." He jerked a thumb over his shoulder, toward the High Country. "Whaddya do?"

Avery paused. "Well, I guess I would find where I left the trail, and I would get back on it, and—"

"Yer forgettin' a step, girl." Laz shook his head. "First you gotta decide which way yer headin'."

"Which way—"

"You listen to me, Avery girl." His eyes took on the piercing look of a hawk, the expression that told her his next words would matter. "Trails run forward an' back an' all over them mountains. If yer jes' lookin' to get on a trail, then yer gonna end up headin' who knows where. Don't you just go followin' any path you see. You figger out where you wanna be headin', and then—" He jerked his head in a nod. "Then you find yerself a path to take you there."

Avery blinked, the words landing squarely on her soul. How was it Laz could always roll wisdom together from the rough-edged experiences of his life?

"An' in the meantime—" He thumped a fist lightly on the calendar

216

taped to the counter. "I'm givin' you some time off."

"Wait—not in the middle of tourist season and—"

"Yep." His tone breezed past all her objections. "I been thinkin' on it ever' since I seen Miz Skyla. She says I'm workin' you too hard, an' I'm shore 'nuff inclined to agree with her. Take a couple weeks, go up north, see yer sister."

Would it really be that easy? Hop a plane in Denver and see Addisyn again? Her sister had been begging her to visit for a while now, after all. And she still had a valid passport from her senior trip to Mexico.

The next instant the responsibility wagged its finger at her again. She was dependable, trustworthy. Not someone who ran off from their job on a whim. "No, Laz—you need me here—"

"Avery, girl. Now, neither of us has time to waste bickerin'."

"I'm not—"

"Yes, you are. Do it for me, will ya? Take a break from all that thinkin' and have some fun with that crazy sister of yers." He rolled his eyes. "Who knows what kind of trouble she's got herself into without you watchin' her, anyway."

Well, he had a point there. "Laz—if you're sure—" She exhaled, the release rolling off her shoulders. "Thank you."

"No problem." He brushed off her gratitude, a glint returning to his eyes. "An' who knows? Mebbe you'll find yer trail. Or even—even a nice young fella."

He ducked just in time to avoid being smacked with the order form.

△△　△△　△△

IT WAS UNUSUAL that ideas occurred to Addisyn before her morning coffee. Usually it took a jump-start of caffeine to kick the cogs of her brain loose. But this morning, a thought struck her before she'd even put the pod into her Keurig.

Where did Kenzie go every morning?

The pattern the girl had set on the first week of her stay with Addisyn had continued unbroken. Every morning, Addisyn would fumble drowsy into the kitchen, and while she was making breakfast, Kenzie would come in the back door. Apparently after having already eaten, since she rarely joined Addisyn for the meal.

Addisyn frowned and glanced out the kitchen window. She'd never thought to ask before, but now it wasn't a matter of idle curiosity. It was a chance to gain another of the disconnected puzzle pieces that made up Kenzie's character.

She stepped onto the little porch, into a morning still caught in the twilight of the valley shadows. "Kenzie?"

The two lawn chairs were empty. No one moving around the big house or in the yard that separated them. But around the corner of the house, smudged footprints in the dew-drenched grass led to the trees behind the house. And a tiny trail that Addisyn hadn't noticed before.

Surely Kenzie wasn't running off again. Addisyn tucked her hands into her jacket pockets and ducked beneath the shadowy skirts of the pines. The trail—just a worn crack in the forest—burrowed into the woods for maybe a tenth of a mile. And then the trees parted like theatrical curtains to reveal a grandfatherly old oak standing alone in a clearing. Its silver trunk was twisted with age, but its limbs spread with strength.

And in a fork of the branches, Kenzie was perched on a platform treehouse complete with a rope ladder.

"Hey, Kenzie." Addisyn strolled to the base of the tree and shaded her eyes to squint up at the girl. "Couldn't find you."

Kenzie seemed to shrink into herself, as if fearing a reprimand. "I come here every morning—I didn't—"

"No, it's okay." Addisyn ran a finger over the gnarled knobbiness of the bark. "Mind if I come up?"

Kenzie studied her a moment, then shrugged. "Okay."

Addisyn grabbed the scratchy rope ladder, ignoring the pitching of her stomach as she swung unpleasantly above the ground. She pulled herself up the weathered rungs, then crawled onto the creaky boards next to Kenzie. "Wow. Cool place up here."

"Thanks." Kenzie hugged her knees to her chest, resting her chin on top. "Uncle Trent built it for me and Tina."

The girls who were like oil and water now? "You and Tina?"

"Yeah. We came here all the time." Kenzie pressed her lips together.

"We used to be friends."

Another sad chapter in Kenzie's story. "Used to be? What happened?"

"I guess you'd have to ask Tina. But back then—" Her breath was foggy with sadness. "We were always together."

Oh, she'd definitely be asking Tina. Addisyn frowned. "Well—it's a really cool treehouse. Were you watching for the bear?"

"Sort of." Kenzie picked at the moss on one of the boards. "Just thinking, mainly."

"What about?"

She kept fingering the moss for a long moment. "My mom called yesterday."

The parent Kenzie rarely mentioned. Addisyn angled herself to face the girl. "Yeah? What'd she say?"

"Usual stuff." Kenzie shrugged again. "She's really busy. She works at a law firm."

Avery would have had the perfect words, stepping effortlessly into Kenzie's pain. But Addisyn's own empathy never seemed to fit into comforting phrasing. "And your dad—"

Kenzie lifted one shoulder. "I don't remember him that well. He left when I was five." She flicked a piece of moss off the edge of the boards. "I remember I called him on the telephone after that and asked him to come to my birthday party. He said it was a waste of time."

The comment burned anger through her veins. "He was wrong."

"Well—" Kenzie's voice was soft. "He didn't come. He didn't ever come again."

Addisyn swallowed matching pain. Her own father hadn't been absent. But it would have been better if he had been.

She could still see his face, carved against her worst memories. The eyes like gun barrels, the close-pinched lips, the veins that throbbed in his temples when he raged in fury. And she'd longed for him to be proud of her, to love her, to even hint—just once—that he cared about her.

And he never had.

"You're lucky, you know."

The words were random enough that Addisyn blinked. "What do you mean?"

"You've got a great family. Your sister, and all."

"No." How much should she share? "I, uh—my family was—not good. My dad was—" *Troubled. Angry. Hateful. Bitter.* "Very broken."

"Oh. I didn't know that." Kenzie peered at her. "Did your dad—love you?"

Flying fists and cursing and Avery telling her to keep her bedroom door locked. Addisyn cleared her throat. "Um—" She'd spent most of her teenage years trying to convince herself otherwise, but the answer was as stark as the stone shoulders of the mountains. "No."

Kenzie nodded slowly. "My dad used to say things. When he got mad."

They were reading between the lines of each other's stories. "My dad did that too."

"Do you still talk to him?"

"No. He's dead." The words came out more harshly than she'd intended. Addisyn shifted on the boards. "And actually, I didn't see him again after I was fourteen."

"Did your parents get a divorce?" Kenzie blinked suddenly. "I'm sorry—it's not my business—"

"No, it's okay." These wounds were old now. "My parents split a long time before that. When Avery graduated high school, she took me to the city with her, got an apartment, and finished raising me. Did a much better job, for sure."

"Wow." Kenzie looked impressed. "She didn't go to college or anything?"

"No." The stack of all Avery had given up for her hung heavy over her shoulders. "She got a job—well, several jobs. Kept me in school and skating, made sure I was okay. Taken care of."

"She was your guide." Kenzie glanced away. "Because she loved you."

Guide. Yes, that was the perfect explanation of what Avery had done. "Yeah. You're right." She nudged Kenzie's elbow. "You're going to get to meet her. I guess she got some time off work finally. She says she's coming up next week."

"Cool." Interest sparked in Kenzie's eyes. "She sounds neat."

"She really is."

"I never had anybody like that. I guess my best friend is skating." Kenzie's smile looked weak. "I've got to do great at my fall auditions." The nervous, edgy look was back in her eyes. "If I can beat my scores from last year, I know I'll get accepted to Skate Six. And only one other girl in my skating club tried out, but her scores were lower than mine last season, so I'm expecting to get the fall audition."

Her pitch was rising, like a teakettle nearly ready to boil over, and the desperate drive in her face was uncomfortably familiar. Addisyn took a deep breath. "Well—it's good to have goals—but, you know, if you don't make it, it's okay."

Kenzie made a soft sound of scorn. "It's not okay. I've worked really hard, and—I have to make this happen. I just have to." She paused. "And anyway, Uncle Trent has always said I'm really talented. I don't want to disappoint him or my mom."

For just a moment, Addisyn thought of her dad again. The only time she'd ever seemed to please him was when she skated. For some reason, her skating ability had caught his attention early on. He'd driven her to practices without complaint and watched her every performance with an odd, grimly triumphant pride in his eyes.

Sometimes she wondered if that was why she'd tumbled into Brian's web of cutthroat competition in the first place. Because she'd been taught early on that only her accomplishments could make her worthy.

She sighed and studied Kenzie. Oh, that restless, anxious look broke her heart, because she knew where it led. "I understand, Kenzie. I was like that too, when I was competing."

For a moment, she considered spilling her entire story. Showing Kenzie the dreary destination that lay at the end of a path of perfection. But then again, what happened with Brian was too painful. Too personal.

Some scars you kept hugged tightly to your chest.

She sighed and settled for generalities. "I know it's tempting to push things. But don't be too hard on yourself, okay?"

Kenzie's smile was sad. "I can't be any other way. Not now."

And she knew what that was like too.

"Well, I'm here." She shrugged awkwardly. "If you ever, you know, need to talk. Or whatever."

Kenzie glanced at her with a soft sort of surprise. "Well—thanks."

The morning melted over the treehouse, the sun finally peeking from behind the mountains, and Addisyn considered her own words.

I'm here.

Maybe that statement was truer than she realized. She had no guidance, no wisdom, no magic pearls of advice that could solve Kenzie's problems.

But she was there.

And in the arms of the oak, with the day drenching them in sunlight, it almost seemed like enough.

△△   △△   △△

ADDISYN HAD BARELY stepped through the center doors when Tina flashed her a conspiratorial grin. "Heard you had a big date with Darius last night."

Addisyn sighed and plopped her gym bag down. "And just how did you hear that?"

"I have my ways." Tina smirked. "Darius told Grant a couple days ago he was taking you to Wallace's Steakhouse. And Grant told me."

"Hmm. News travels fast."

"Yeah, we have a regular grapevine here."

Addisyn couldn't find it in her to be annoyed. Kenzie was truly starting to find her rhythm on the ice, and even Trent had seemed impressed with her progress today. And of course, last night had kept her spirits buoyant all day.

"So?" Tina glanced over her shoulder, at where Canuck was blissfully asleep in a sunny patch on the floor. "How did it go?"

"It went well. We had a nice time."

Tina rolled her eyes. "Come on. You sound like you're describing a business meeting. Give a girl more details."

Addisyn laughed. "We had dinner and went dancing. No more details."

"Okay, okay." Tina cocked her head with a curious gaze. "I've been wondering. How come you didn't just move in with Darius when you got here?"

Brian leaped to her mind. The way he'd wasted no time cajoling her under his roof. And what he'd done once he'd had her there. Addisyn shook her head. "I don't think it's right, Tina. Or healthy." She kept her tone light, but there was truth behind her words. "Next time I move in with a man, I'll have his last name."

"Boundaries, huh? I can get behind that." Tina glanced back down at her computer. "So, if that's what you're waiting for, you just need to marry that boy already."

Marry? Good grief, they were a long way from that, but still all her fears leaped from the shadows. "Um—well, I mean—" She laughed weakly. "He hasn't asked me."

"So? Ask him." Tina shrugged. "I would, if I were dating a guy who dragged his feet."

Somehow Addisyn had no problem envisioning that. "I'm sure you would." She cleared her throat. "I don't think he's planning to ask me anytime soon. And I'm fine with that."

Tina sighed and propped her elbows on the desk. "Listen, Addisyn. I'm helping you out, okay? Darius is—" she waved her hand—"slow. Cautious. You know? Always has been. You need to spur him on a little."

Tina didn't understand that she was far from ready for a proposal. "I—I'll keep that in mind."

"Also—" Tina shoved a paper across the counter toward her. "You can get that railing replaced now."

The typed words leaped at her. "Budget request form? What's this?"

"It's a little-known fact that the budget does have wiggle room."

"What do you mean?"

"I mean you need to figure out what it will cost to have that railing fixed. But bring the form back to me when you're done. Not Dad. Okay?"

"I—okay." Somewhere underneath the girl's frosty exterior, something was thawing. "Thanks, Tina."

"Huh. Don't thank me. I'm just sick of hearing you gripe about it, is all."

Addisyn grinned and tucked the paper into her bag. "Gotcha." She glanced around. "I guess I need to find Kenzie. She finished her practice a little bit ago. I thought she was coming in here."

Tina's expression closed off. "I saw her out the window. She's on the walking trail by the lake."

She was using the hardened tone she reserved for discussing Kenzie. Addisyn frowned. "Kenzie said you two used to be friends."

For a moment, Tina blinked, off-balance. Then she huffed and glanced away. "Forced friends. You know, we were cousins, and we were close in age. So our moms got the idea we should play together."

"I saw the treehouse."

"Oh." Tina's voice dipped, as if the word sagged under the weight of many memories. "The treehouse. Yeah. Dad built that for us."

"So…" Addisyn let the word dangle. Across the room, Canuck blinked into wakefulness and began rhythmically grooming his front paws.

Tina sighed. She pulled off her glasses and scrubbed them with her shirt. "Okay, yeah. We played together a lot when we were kids. Mostly we just got into stuff and made our moms crazy." A reluctant smile pulled at the corner of her mouth. "Kenzie and her mom lived in that guesthouse for a while, you know. After her dad left. And one time, she and I tie-dyed shirts in there. Look at the tile sometime, in that south corner of the kitchen. The stains are still there."

"So—what happened with you two?"

Canuck paused in his washing, as if waiting to hear the answer too. Tina frowned and shoved her glasses back on. "Circumstances. Change. We got older, and we didn't have much in common anymore. Plus, they moved." The desk phone shrilled a ring, and she grabbed for it without another glance at Addisyn. "Hello, Bearstooth Athletic Center, this is Tina speaking…"

Addisyn slipped out the door, the impact of Tina's words lingering. Two cousins forced together by nothing more than familial ties and separated by nothing more than distance? No way. Something had happened to break them apart. Certainly something more than divergent interests and a cross-country move.

The summer sun danced off the water, the lake shimmering like a disco ball. Addisyn shaded her eyes and started down the dirt walking trail. Less than five minutes from the office, she saw Kenzie slumped on a bench, staring at her phone. Addisyn slid onto the bench next to her. "Hey."

Kenzie jerked and shoved the phone in her pocket. "I didn't hear you coming." Her expression was unreadable behind her sunglasses.

"Sorry." Addisyn studied her rigid posture. "What were you doing?"

"Just looking at Instagram."

"Oh, okay." After growing up under Avery's technology aversion, Addisyn had never jumped on the social media bandwagon. She hadn't posted on Facebook in over a year, come to think of it. "Checking on your friends?"

Kenzie shrugged. "I don't really have friends."

Again, Kenzie's words were echoing her own story. As a kid, she'd been too preoccupied with hiding the secret of her family's dysfunction. And as an adult—well, she'd assumed Brian's friends were hers too. Ha.

"Lots of skaters I know are doing really well this season." Kenzie picked at her chipping nail polish. "Marie—one of them just came back from the provincial training camp."

"Really?"

"Yeah." Kenzie scuffed her toe into the dirt. "I could have done that, Addisyn. I missed my chance this year."

"Sometimes when you miss a chance—" She was back in Chicago again, walking away from the biggest opportunity Brian had ever offered her, feeling his chains cracking—"you find something better."

Kenzie looked at her suspiciously. "Is that something your sister would say?"

Had she really quoted Avery that many times? Addisyn laughed. "Yeah. Probably so."

Kenzie gave a faint smile and stood reluctantly. "All right. I've got to get back to practice if I don't want to mess up next season too. Strength training this afternoon, right?"

She was tense again, her expression taut with an anxious determination. The same look Addisyn had worn to every practice. All while Brian's bottomless demands sucked her deeper into the spiral.

She cleared her throat. "Tell you what. We're done practicing today."

"What?" Kenzie stared at her.

"You heard me." Trent would have a fit if she deviated from Kenzie's training schedule, but he'd never know. She jumped up. "Come on. Let's do something fun."

Kenzie lifted her sunglasses. Confusion peered from her expression. "I can't miss my extra session."

"Of course you can." Addisyn rubbed her hands together. "Tell you what. Let's drive into Whistler and get something to eat. But something fun and ridiculously unhealthy."

"No, I can't. I'm training and—"

"I'm older, so I make the rules, okay?" Avery's standard playful reply. Weird to hear it coming out of her own mouth. "Come on. Where's a good ice cream shop around here—or bakery—or—"

That ghost of a smile passed over Kenzie's face. "There used to be this place called Love You a Latte. Coffee shop and bakery next door. It was on—"

"Martin Street. I worked there." She vaguely remembered a bakery section connected to the little coffee shop where she'd worked during her first trip to Whistler. But her coworker had managed that. She'd only been responsible for the coffee.

"Really? They made the best Nanaimo bars ever. We used to go there all the time."

We? Her and Tina? Addisyn focused on the first part. "What's a nano bar?"

"Nanaimo bar." Kenzie looked at her incredulously. "You've never had a Nanaimo bar?"

"No." The word sounded familiar, though. "What's that?"

"Chocolate, and wafer, and icing all made together into a—"

"Stop." Addisyn raised her hands. "I'm sold. Let's go."

△△ △△ △△

THE FAMILIAR PINK-AND-WHITE awning of the coffee shop still swung over Martin Street, and Kenzie pointed out the windshield. "There it is."

"Yeah, here we are." Addisyn maneuvered into a curbside parking space and grinned. "Parallel parking. I'm teaching you that next."

Kenzie felt a smile coming. "Let's wait until I don't gasp every time a car passes me."

Addisyn laughed and grabbed her purse. "All right. Deal. Now, these nano-whatever bars better be as good as you described."

The inside still had that cute retro vibe. Pink tile countertops, Polaroid prints splashed across the wall, bubbly pop music for ambiance. And the sugary smell in the air.

"Addisyn!" A frizzy-haired blonde girl waved from behind the counter. "Cuban?"

"Hey, Chelsea!" Addisyn grinned with an easy confidence. "No coffee today. This is my student, Kenzie. She's Darius's niece. Kenzie, this is Chelsea."

"Nice to meet you." Chelsea probably couldn't even hear her soft formality over the pop music. Why did talking to people always have to be so hard? She took a deep breath and tried to strengthen her voice. "I wanted to show Addisyn the Nanaimo bars."

"Oh, yeah!" Chelsea scurried across the shop to a partially enclosed bakery section behind the corner booths and gestured toward a display case stacked with fluffy pastries.

Kenzie bent over, peering through the smudged glass. "Yeah." She tapped the case and glanced at Addisyn. "That's a Nanaimo bar."

"Wow. It looks like a cross between a s'more and a brownie." Addisyn studied the decadent treat. "And what are they made out of again?"

"The base is a wafer with coconut and almonds, and the center is custard icing topped with chocolate ganache." Chelsea raised her eyebrows. "Basically, they're Heaven in a single dessert. Oh, and we have specialty flavors too. Peanut butter, mocha, pineapple."

"Pineapple?" Kenzie had never heard that flavor before.

Chelsea shrugged. "Okay, so that one was more of an experiment."

Addisyn was still examining the bar like a scientist discovering a new species. "Why do I never see these in America?"

"Because they were invented right here in BC." Kenzie took a step away from the case. The smell of sugar was already giving her a headache. "On Nanaimo Island."

Chelsea straightened slightly, as if she'd been the one to create the recipe. "That's right. There are plenty of stories about what happened

227

after that, but now they're our trademark."

Addisyn dug out her wallet. "I'll take the mocha. Kenzie, which flavor do you want?"

The delicious treat that had seemed so wonderful to her childhood self now might as well be wearing a poison warning. The rules she'd read in fitness magazines wagged their fingers at her. *Insulin problems. Inefficient metabolism. Blood sugar dysregulation. Reduced performance.*

Reduced performance she couldn't afford. And especially...

"Kenzie?"

Addisyn was waiting. "Uh—" The last time she'd eaten this much sugar was—before. Before the rules. Before the doctor visits. Before the orange pills. "I—I don't want one."

Addisyn stared at her as if she'd done something much worse than decline a sugar bomb. "Kenzie, you're the one who talked me into this. Come on. It's my treat."

"I—I—" She couldn't explain in a way that wasn't beyond embarrassing, especially not with Chelsea watching the whole exchange. "I don't eat that much sugar when I'm training."

A strange sadness dropped over Addisyn's expression. But she sighed and shrugged at Chelsea. "Okay. One mocha, please."

Kenzie kept her eyes fixed on her scuffed white sneakers while Chelsea wrapped Addisyn's bar in paper and managed to ensnare her in a torturous ten-minute conversation about some guy named Jeffrey who was back from Ottawa and what his latest texts had said and whether Addisyn thought he liked Chelsea as a friend or as *something more*—Chelsea's voice dropped to a reverent hush on those words. Kenzie barely listened, all the memories hovering around her shoulders. Tina and her, rushing through the doors, buying a stockpile of Nanaimo bars to eat later in the treehouse. How could she have known then that happiness took its own kind of courage—a courage she wouldn't have one day?

As they drove away, she braced herself for Addisyn's questions, for an insistence on explanations she didn't want to give. But to her relief, Addisyn just dug into the bakery paper. "Okay. Time to try this thing." She took a big bite and raised her eyebrows, nodding as she chewed. Then she swallowed and grinned. "Kenzie, you were right. This is amazing."

Addisyn's reaction made her smile in spite of herself. "They are good, aren't they?"

"Out of this world." Addisyn took another bite, driving with one hand. They went a block in silence before she cleared her throat. "What happened at the store—do you want to talk about it?"

She sighed. "It wasn't the same."

"The store or the bars or what?"

That answer was easy. "Me."

Another silent block. The sugar scent was less overpowering now. More like an enticing invitation to step over the boundaries she'd built for herself. A reminder of a time when joy had come more freely.

What was she thinking? Only lazy and undisciplined people let a momentary craving disrupt an entire training regimen. And she was neither of those things.

She closed her eyes and pictured the plain green bottle, the orange pills that were so much a part of her story. They were working, right? But—why was there no joy in that anymore?

The car coasted to a stop, and she looked up to see a red light. Beside her, Addisyn broke off the uneaten half of the bar. "Here."

"Wait—"

"It's yours. Just take it. You can eat it, or hold it, or throw it away when we get back home. But it's yours."

The bar was still warm in her hands. "Why would you—"

"Simple." The light turned green, and Addisyn pulled forward, licking the melted chocolate from her fingers. "You're my friend."

Friend.

The word turned the entire situation on its head, and suddenly everything she'd believed about Addisyn crumbled like the coconut crust of the treat she held. All along, she'd kept her walls stacked high, refusing to offer Addisyn a single sliver of trust. But the older girl had stubbornly refused to be repelled by the prickly persona she showed the world. She'd helped her with skating. She'd taught her to drive.

And she'd called her a friend.

Her throat tightened, and she blinked hard so she wouldn't break down in front of Addisyn. She'd had doctors and nutritionists and physical therapists. She'd had medicine and counseling and supplements and workouts and meditation courses.

But she'd never had a friend. Not since Tina. Not since before.

The melted chocolate was squishing onto her fingers, and suddenly there was no reason to wait. Just a little bit couldn't hurt, could it? She took a tiny bite off the corner, and the flavor exploded in her mouth—the taste of the world she'd thought was gone forever.

"Still like you remember?" Addisyn grinned. "I bet that's what you've been missing all these years."

"Yeah." Kenzie took another bite, the flavor of friendship dancing on her tongue. She glanced over at Addisyn and didn't have to fake her smile. "I think it is."

CHAPTER 16

The parking lot of the church was still empty. Darius pulled to a space not far from the door and slipped out of the car. He was almost half an hour early for the weekly men's prayer group, but it made more sense for him to come straight from work. And he didn't mind waiting in the empty church. In fact, it was one of the most peaceful moments of his whole week.

He headed into the foyer and glanced around. Time froze in this place. The floor was still laminated in the vinyl squares that had been trendy a few decades ago, and the brass light fixtures were a bit cloudy with age. He couldn't begin to guess how many cups of joe had been brewed in the ancient coffeemaker.

The building was quiet, soaked through with a silence that had always felt sacred. He poked his hands into his pockets and wandered down the hall, peeking into the sanctuary. In the darkened room, the mellow sunlight glowing through the stained-glass windows was nothing short of otherworldly.

Addisyn had been coming to church with him faithfully and seemed to be settling in more every Sunday. She was making her faith her own, taking hold of the same rock to which he'd been clinging since childhood, and watching her journey filled him with pride. She'd taken the long way back to this stained-glass shelter, but didn't that make the destination all the more special?

He passed the sanctuary and continued into the classroom they'd be using tonight. He flicked the light switch, found a bottle of water in the little refrigerator, and was just heading for a chair when he noticed it. A photo by the door? Someone had actually updated the decor in here? No way.

He stepped closer for a better look and blinked. The picture was of the man who'd first begun the church, the man for whom he'd been named.

Darius Andrew Payne, Sr.

His grandfather was standing in front of the little building, beaming with a smile that the decades couldn't deny. Without a doubt, Grampy had been the most joyful man Darius had ever met, his smile constant across both halves of his life. He'd first been a successful figure skater for several seasons, and then he'd left the ice behind, enrolled in seminary, and planted the church. By the time he'd died, he'd given almost fifteen hundred sermons from the old wooden pulpit.

Darius squinted at the date on the far left corner of the photo and calculated the years. Yes, this picture had been taken well after Grampy's diagnosis, into his last few months when the cancer was winning on a tilted playing field. Yet still the man had smiled. Still he'd been strong. All the way home.

He'd been more than Darius's grandfather; he'd been his inspiration. So much so that when he'd passed away, Darius's skating dreams had practically died right alongside the man.

His jaw clenched, but he could still remember the headlines of the sports columns the year after his grandfather died, the year when there'd been no one to help him hold up the toppling weight of expectations. *Andrew Payne—one-hit wonder?...Vancouver's golden boy struggles in second season...Andrew Payne: great expectations fizzle out.*

Footsteps sounded in the hall. Darius turned away from the photo and flinched. "Uncle Trent?"

"Darius." His uncle cleared his throat. "Didn't know you came to this group."

"I started about six months ago." When Addisyn had helped him break free from the shame that had kept him far from others. But in all that time, he'd never seen his uncle here. "Are you visiting tonight, or—"

"Yes, thought I might need—" Uncle Trent stopped, rubbed his eye. "Thought I'd see what it's about."

His uncle seemed more—human, somehow. Like any other guy after a long day of work. "It's a good group. It's helped me."

But Uncle Trent's gaze had landed just over Darius's shoulder. "That's your grandfather's picture."

His defenses shot back up, and he quickly stepped away from the wall. "Uh, yeah."

Uncle Trent peered at the image. "A great man."

Here it came. The insinuation of Darius's inferiority. The reminder of how he'd let the legacy topple. Darius braced himself, but instead Uncle Trent pressed his lips together. "Seems weird still, not having him at the church. Sure do miss him."

Brief as it was, the remark was the most vulnerable comment Darius had ever heard his uncle say to anyone, let alone to him. "Yeah. Me too."

"He poured his soul into this place." Uncle Trent was still staring at the photo, as if it were a window to some long-ago reality. "He'd get here on Sundays at six o'clock in the morning. Praying, waiting to talk to people when they arrived."

Darius could still picture Grampy shaking hands in the foyer. "I remember. I spent every Sunday here with him."

"We did too, growing up. Me and Tracy and—" He rubbed a hand over his chin. "And Zach."

Darius's throat tightened at the mention of his dad. "Yeah."

"I know you grew up here too." Uncle Trent folded his arms and leaned against the doorframe.

"I'd say so." The church had been a second home, a haven where peace and acceptance replaced the rigor of competition. "I loved being here with Grampy. He was my hero." The instant the words tumbled out, he cringed. Reminding his uncle of the greatness of his namesake could only be a bad idea.

But Uncle Trent just nodded. "I know. Been thinking some lately about that."

His uncle's voice was less gruff than usual, but Darius still eyed him cautiously. "About…"

"Well—" His uncle coughed as if the words were caught in his throat. "I guess it was probably harder for you than we realized. With him to live up to."

Understanding from Uncle Trent? His expectations skewed sideways. "Uh—" What could he say? "Yeah…it was. I never wanted to disappoint him." He took a deep breath, his past needling uncomfortably. "Or anyone."

Uncle Trent studied him thoughtfully. For a moment—just a moment—there was a flicker in his eyes. Understanding? Sympathy? "I know that, Darius."

More footsteps and voices echoed down the hall. The next moment, Terry poked his head into the room. "Hey, Darius!" He chuckled. "Now didn't I just see you?"

Darius laughed. "Seems like it." It was a running joke between them—that Darius left work on Tuesdays just to attend his boss's Bible study. But Terry had become more than just an employer in the past year; he was a mentor now as well.

"And Trent! Glad you could make it." Terry clapped Trent on the back. "Good to see you here, man."

Uncle Trent shrugged. "Thought I'd come try it out." He took the chair across from Darius. Not beside him, but still a start.

"Absolutely." Terry flipped open his worn Bible with a smile. "Great things happen when we come together in unity."

As the other guys filed in and Terry bowed his head for the opening prayer, Darius couldn't help but feel more hopeful than he had in a long time. Because great things did happen when people came together.

And for the first time in years, it seemed that he and Uncle Trent might be doing just that.

⛰ ⛰ ⛰

AVERY HAD HOPED to avoid Skyla until after she returned from Whistler. Until she could put some distance between herself and Skyla's offer, until she could turn down the position in a firm and calm manner that was untainted by regrets and emotions.

She'd done a good job of dodging the woman, too. She hadn't gone by the raptor center. She hadn't stopped at Skyla's gift shop downtown. She'd kept an eye out while shopping in Safeway, and when Chay had come into the outdoors store on Wednesday afternoon to shoot the breeze with Laz, she'd busied herself in the back room until he'd left.

But with fewer than twenty-four hours until her departure, she was rolling T-shirts to tuck into her roomiest backpack, maneuvering around a sleeping Mercy on her floor, when a firm knock on her front door echoed through the house. She froze. Maybe it was Laz. Or more likely—

Oh no.

She shuffled the armload of clothes to the bed and crept to the window, peering out with the secrecy of a spy. Sure enough, a blue Bronco was pulled into her driveway. Which meant Skyla was at her front door.

Avery shrank back from the window and considered her limited options. Her truck was parked in front, a telltale sign that she wasn't in town—but then, she often wandered up into the woods behind her house. If she simply stayed quiet long enough, Skyla would surely assume she was out for a walk and give up.

The knocking came again, more insistently, and this time, Mercy bounded up, ears pricked.

"Mercy, no!" Avery hissed the warning and lunged for the dog, but Mercy skidded out of the room and down the steps. And then eager barking ricocheted from the hall.

Great. Just great. Skyla knew that Avery never went anywhere without Mercy. Avery trudged downstairs. "Coming!" Her shout probably sounded less than thrilled. She yanked the door open and squinted in the sunlight. "Hello, Skyla."

"Greetings, Avery." Skyla was wearing khaki shorts and a T-shirt with a feathered wing stenciled over one shoulder. Undoubtedly she'd come straight from the center. Mercy fawned around her feet, and Skyla gave a slight bow. "And to you, Mercy."

Avery ignored her traitorous dog and focused on Skyla. "Is something wrong?" The sooner she could end this conversation, the better.

"Not in the usual way. May I come in?"

As if she had a choice. Clearly Skyla Wingo would walk into her life with or without permission. Avery sighed and stepped aside. "Of course."

Skyla swept into the living room. "I went first to the store, thinking to see you there. Laz kindly told me of your upcoming journey. He expected you would be here to prepare."

Had he now. Avery forced a smile. "Well. That was—*helpful* of him." She'd pick a different adjective when she discussed this with Laz. Which she would.

"Indeed." Skyla turned, the sunlight splashing over her face, and crossed to one of the picture windows. "You have a lovely view from here."

"Yes. Very majestic." Skyla hadn't come to her house in the middle of a workday to admire the view.

"Do you know why your view is so exquisite, Avery?"

She was on guard, ready to see around Skyla's rhetoric the moment her words turned the inevitable symbolic corner. "Um—no."

"It is because you are in the hills. This land is higher than the level of the town."

Come to think of it, the road was a consistent climb from Estes Park. "Oh—yes, I guess so."

"And from the heights, one can see far." Skyla turned penetrating eyes on her. "What is it you see, Avery?"

"I'm sorry?"

"Please, Avery." Skyla took a step toward her, the sun flicking across her profile again. "Your heart is set on high, and so you have a clearer view. What do you see when you look across the days which will come?"

The days which will come. The empty days in which she was no longer needed. In which raptors eagerly flew from her hands and Laz's store hummed without her help and her sister spun a whole new life fifteen hundred miles away. Avery swallowed the sudden ache in her throat. "Nothing." The word was little more than a whisper. "I see—nothing."

Skyla pressed her lips together. "You saw enough to avoid me for many days."

Avery dropped her head. She'd taken the cowardly way out, and Skyla was right to be disappointed in her. "I'm sorry. I—I needed time."

"Time?" Skyla's brows arched. "It is something to do with the request I made of you." Her gaze probed as sharply as always. "Is it not?"

"Well—I—"

"Perhaps I was wrong to make the offer?" Surprisingly, Skyla's tone was saddened, not angry. "Perhaps it is not what you have seen for yourself.

I thought I saw—but my vision is not always clear." She pressed her palms together. "If this is true, please forgive me."

She couldn't let Skyla blame herself. Avery swallowed and steeled herself for the truth. "Oh, Skyla—please don't apologize. It's a wonderful offer—and so generous—but—" Her heart twisted. "I don't have any training, or education. After I graduated high school, I was caring for Addisyn. I never went to college, and I read that a job like this requires at least—"

"Is this all?" Skyla waved her words into insignificance. "This does not concern me. *Education*—" the word seemed to hold a sour taste in her mouth—"is not learning. And learning is gained here." Her gesture encompassed the cabin and the blue sky beyond. "Of course, there are some classes you would need. Certifications that are offered. But that is a small thing and one with which I could help."

The barriers were falling, so why did she feel pure panic instead of freedom? "I can't leave the store." She grabbed desperately for the one excuse she had left. "Laz—he needs me." True enough.

"Avery, focus your gaze." Skyla's voice tightened with a rare urgency. "What is the calling you bear?"

"The calling?"

"All of us are born with a burden in the shape of our hearts. What is yours?"

"I told you." She couldn't give herself a single moment to examine Skyla's words. "The store."

"And this is what you are led to do? What you see laid before you?"

"It's—I mean—" Avery squirmed away from the penetrating gaze of the farsighted woman before her. "I want to help Laz. He's been very good to me."

Silence settled between them, heavy and thick and uneasy. Then Skyla sighed. "Very well." She rubbed her eyes and ran a hand over her hair as if the conversation had somehow wearied her. "It is different from what I saw—from what I believed I saw. But if it is your path, I know you will walk it well."

"Thank you." The words were stiff, holding her soul rigidly in place.

"And I will let you return to packing." Skyla nodded and started toward the door, then suddenly paused, her eyes caught on the corner table.

Avery followed Skyla's gaze. Nothing important there, just a pinecone she'd found in the woods and an old brass compass and a framed photo of her and Addisyn. But Skyla remained frozen, staring as if she'd found the final clue to a riddle.

"Your sister." Skyla breathed the words with an undercurrent of knowing.

Her sister? Addisyn? "Wait—what do you—"

"It is your sister, then, who holds the next thread." Skyla's eyes fixed with focus, her voice a sleepwalker's murmur. "And thus—"

"Skyla?"

Another moment, and then Skyla seemed to snap free of the connection. She let out a heavy breath and blinked at Avery as if momentarily surprised to see her. "You go to visit your sister—yes. Even as Laz has said. And this is good and holy. Your sister will help you to see."

Addisyn would help her see? And see what? Avery frowned. "I don't know that—"

"You were the guide unto her trail. And it may be that she will now do for you what you have ever done for her." Skyla raised a hand in an unmistakable gesture of blessing. "Go in grace, Avery. Call me when the path is plain."

And with that, she opened the door and stepped into the shimmering summer day.

△△   △△   △△

TONIGHT. DARIUS WOULD find the ring tonight.

He blew the dust off another box and peeked under the lid. More books? Good grief, he'd known his parents loved to read, but he hadn't realized they'd had the equivalent of a library in their possession. He slid the box aside and reached for the next on the stack.

That stack had shrunk considerably over the last few weeks. He'd managed to sort through almost everything. Addisyn had helped him several evenings, organizing items and making notes and listening to the stories he'd never forget. The boxes they'd sorted were now neatly labeled and arranged in two orderly stacks: one for his storage building and one for Goodwill.

But somehow, he still hadn't uncovered the one treasure he'd been hunting since the beginning of the project: his mother's jewelry. Tonight, though, had to be the night—because he had only three boxes left.

The first one was a scrambled mess of odds and ends. He sifted through the contents, struggling to assess if there was anything of greater value than some tabletop knickknacks. Memories rose with every item he unwrapped, but over the last few weeks, peace had come along with them. The closure had brought its own kind of comfort, because at last, he wasn't looking over his shoulder. Instead, he was looking forward. Into a future that was nothing but bright.

Everything seemed better now, really. Addisyn had excitedly reported to him that Kenzie was doing better. Her practices were apparently more productive, and her confidence had greatly improved. Just the thing to put Uncle Trent in a better mood.

Maybe because of the reduced stress, Addisyn was much happier—more open, more at peace. As a result, things between them were good, their relationship running smoothly with no uncertainty dragging them down. They'd been to see a concert last night in Meadow Park, and once Avery arrived this weekend, she'd be able to stay with Kenzie some and free Addisyn up even more.

Yes, things were good on all fronts. Which was why it was time.

For a moment, he was back there in the coffee shop downtown, coming in for his morning Cuban and ending up behind a girl with long brown hair and a smile like a held-out heart. He was watching the way the early morning sun struck her face, and he was caught in an irresistible current. He smiled and closed his eyes, savoring the magic of a memory he'd treasure for the rest of his life. One single moment. One magical instant. And from then to now, the girl in the coffee shop, the girl who'd smiled with a simple courage that morning, had been rewriting his story into the truest happy ending.

His heart swelled, and he brushed his thumb under his eyes. It had all built to now, and he wasn't waiting any longer. He'd already planned his next steps. First was this weekend. His whole family would be heading to Alta Lake for a Canada Day celebration, and there, in the footprint of the glacier with the fireworks overhead, he'd let her know his intentions. The actual proposal would come in a couple of weeks, while Avery was still in Whistler. He wanted his future sister-in-law present for that kind of pivotal moment.

Now he just needed to find the ring.

The second box was a dusty crate of clothes so old there was no point in even sorting through them. He set it aside and blew out a breath. Last box. For the first time, anxiety squiggled through his certainty. What if—what if it wasn't there?

But when he opened the box, relief hit him down to his knees. There it was. The very last box. The worn white leather of his mother's jewelry case.

Tears sprang immediately to his eyes, but these were a different kind of tears. Tears that came from his breathless love for Addisyn, from knowing that they'd have a marriage rich with the kind of love that his parents had shared, from believing that somehow Mom and Dad were still part of the story—that they'd be cheering him on when he went down on one knee.

He unlatched the delicate doors of the case, unsurprised by the sparse contents. Mom hadn't worn jewelry often. The pieces she owned were carefully curated—heirlooms from his grandmother or gifts from Dad or mementos from places they'd traveled.

A few necklaces dangled from pegs in the center, their intricate chains puddling on the velvet beneath. He tugged open the little drawers on each side. A few pairs of earrings, a silver bracelet, an Alpha Chi pin from college. More bracelets, a couple of brooches he recognized as his grandmother's, and a pair of silver cufflinks that were undoubtedly Dad's.

He lifted out the bottom tray, and his heart plummeted. There were only two rings pushed into the velvet spacers. A tarnished silver one with a missing stone, probably another heirloom, and his mother's class ring from college.

He shook his head, denying the sick sense that coiled around him. Her engagement ring had to be here. He went through the jewelry case again, shuffling as quickly as he could through the pieces. Closed the door, stared at it. Opened it back up and did the entire thing a third time. Then he felt around the inside of the cardboard box in which he'd found the case.

Nothing.

A feeling barely shy of panic was pounding in his chest. He blew out a breath and scrubbed his hands over his beard. He could still picture the ring. A dainty silver circle with a single solitaire diamond. Elegant, lovely, feminine.

And now—it was gone?

He pushed against the idea with all the strength of his denial. Again, he opened the jewelry case, scanning through the contents that were already familiar. When he finished, he sat back on his heels and let his head drop to his knees. What was he thinking? That the ring would appear from thin air?

No, he might as well face it. The beautiful ring that had been a promise of his parents' love—the one he'd hoped to see sparkling on Addisyn's finger—was gone.

The loss settled like a rock in his gut. How could he have lost his grip on such an important part of his parents' story? He'd failed his mother. And Addisyn too, for that matter. Oh, it would have looked so beautiful on her delicate hand. And it would have been a double promise—a symbol not only of his love for her, but of the heritage and story that was bigger than them both.

C'mon, Payne. Think. He propped his forehead on his fist and tried to peer into the past. His memories of those early days after the accident were still wrapped in foggy grief. He remembered being given his parents' wedding rings, in a box he still had upstairs. And he remembered throwing things into these cardboard boxes with a reckless kind of sorrow. But details—details he didn't have. Had he even seen the engagement ring after the accident?

But where else could it be? Darius blinked as a sudden hope materialized. Did Uncle Trent maybe have the ring? Perhaps he'd asked for it during the arrangements. At the very least, he might remember better than Darius did what had become of it.

He squirmed at the thought of discussing something so personal with Uncle Trent. But after all, the man had seemed so much friendlier at the

Bible study. And really, finding the ring was worth any amount of personal discomfort.

Yes. That's what he'd do. He'd talk to Uncle Trent at the first opportunity, and somehow he'd find that ring.

And then he could ask Addisyn the question that burned on his heart every day.

CHAPTER 17

Avery had always hated airplane travel, but as she squeezed onto the skybridge along with the jostling crowds to board the flight from DIA, her excitement far outweighed her nerves.

She was going to Whistler! Finally, after weeks of pixelated FaceTime sessions and hurried phone calls, she'd see her sister again. And for the first time, she'd experience her sister's world, the mountain town that had captured Addisyn's heart. The thought was enough to banish her usual pre-flight jitters.

The plane roared to life, taxiing down the runway and then shooting skyward with a force that left Avery clutching her seat. It wasn't until they'd leveled and the scenery was sliding slowly away beneath them that she released her aching grip and grinned wryly.

Okay...so maybe some of those jitters remained.

How long had it been since her last flight? Almost a year now. She'd flown all the way to New York to reunite with Addisyn and bring her hurting sister back to the safety of her mountains. How much had changed since then to complete the circle of the story. Now Addisyn was the one waiting eagerly in an airport.

And Avery was the one who felt so lost.

She watched her mountains dwindle to nothing more than a white patch on the continent. And somewhere in the center of that white dot, she'd chosen to live her one insignificant life. A life that had shrunk to a pinprick on an enormous landscape.

You have the eyes to see...what do you see when you look across the days which will come?

She closed her eyes, tried to forget her answer.

Nothing. I see nothing.

She hadn't told Addisyn about Skyla's offer, and she had no plans to. Why bother? She knew exactly what Addisyn would tell her to do—pick up the phone and call Skyla and be working with the wings as soon as she arrived back in Colorado.

But Addisyn didn't understand all the tangles that could keep feet from moving forward, and how could she? Addisyn had somehow stumbled right into a life that was perfect for her. *Whistler. Skating. Darius.* They all fit together, the trifecta of Addisyn's tomorrows, and something like envy twisted oddly inside Avery's heart. She'd poured so much of herself into forging Addisyn's future. No wonder she'd forgotten to give any thought to her own.

The flight was far more boring than she'd expected—a good thing, of course. So she pulled out the magazine she'd brought—a back issue of *Field & Stream*—and lost herself in articles on trails and trees and wildlife and wandering. By the time a staticky voice announced that they were descending to Vancouver International Airport, she'd left all her dark thoughts between the pages.

She stuffed the magazine back into her carryon and peered out the window as the plane circled into a descent. Her breath caught at the aerial beauty of her first glimpse of Canada. VIA was an intricate web centered on an emerald-green island that sank into an unbelievably blue sea. And as the plane banked lower, the northern horizon rippled into something steeper than the sea.

The mountains.

And then she was off the skybridge and into the glass-and-concrete bowl, a mad weltering dome where people crawled and clung like bees in a hive. Every centimeter of the enormous building vibrated with the chaos, and the same anxiety she always felt in crowded conditions began itching up her back.

Addisyn. For Addisyn. She tugged her baseball cap lower, shielding her senses from the chaos, and studied the bilingual signs until she found the one for CUSTOMS/DOUANE.

By the time she'd undergone X-rays, passport inspection, and security under the grim faces of the border patrol agents, her nerves were stretched to their fullest extent, her hands trembling like turbulence. She ducked into the concourse and leaned against the wall for a moment, squeezing her eyes shut. But the noise was increasing, the din throbbing against her eardrums. She needed just a moment of quiet—a breath of mountain air—

"Avery!"

She jerked back to attention, scanning the crowds, and there was her sister, sprinting toward her across the crowded airport. And just like that, the panic relaxed its grip. Avery ran to meet her, boots squeaking on the tile flooring, and then Addisyn flung her arms around her in a crushing hug that sent Avery's ball cap tumbling to the terminal floor. "A!" She tightened her arms around Avery's neck the way she'd done since she was a little girl. "I've missed you so much."

Avery pulled her sister closer and brushed a hand over her hair, working her words past the thickness in her throat. "Oh, Ads, I missed you too!" The joy of the encounter righted her world. She was back with Addisyn—the person whose story would be eternally bound with hers, across any barrier of time and space. Her confidante. Her best friend.

Her sister.

"So, I've been waiting for you for, like, forever." Addisyn pulled back, talking fast, no doubt to cover the shimmering emotion in her eyes. "We got here almost an hour ago, because I thought, you know, what if the flight was early?"

"Which I told her they never are."

Avery turned at the voice to see Darius waiting patiently off to the side. "Darius!" She stepped over to give him a hug as well. "It's good to see you."

"Likewise." His expression still shone with the faith and strength that had won her trust last fall. He held up her cap with a grin. "Saved this for you."

Avery reached for it, but Addisyn snagged it first and tugged it over her own ponytail. "All right, Mountain Girl." She linked her arm through Avery's, guiding her toward the glass doors through which the foothills were visible. "Let's pick up your luggage and get you to Whistler."

△△　△△　△△

AVERY DRANK IN pure wonder as they drove across the Lions Gate Bridge. The stacked concrete of the city was shrinking behind them, the inlet chopping its way underneath the road. And in front of them, the mountains rose.

Addisyn's mountains.

"Addisyn, this is gorgeous." She turned and smiled over her shoulder at her sister—Darius was driving, and Addisyn had insisted that Avery ride shotgun for the best view.

"I knew you'd love it." Addisyn grinned in return from beneath the bill of Avery's cap.

"And this isn't even the best part yet." Darius flipped on his blinker, and a moment later the road soared sharply up between heavy fringes of trees. "Welcome to the Sea-to-Sky Road."

The road was well-named, curving between pine-pointed mountains on one side and the restless waters of the inlet on the other. About half an hour into the drive, Addisyn leaned forward. "Darius, let's stop at Nch'ḵay̓."

"I was thinking the same thing." Darius pulled over into a gravel area, and Addisyn scrambled out of the car.

"Come on, Avery! This is an amazing view."

Avery climbed out of the car and stretched her arms over her head, breathing in the evergreen incense of the mountains—comfortingly familiar, yet also excitingly new. She followed her sister to the viewpoint and took a breath. "Oh. Wow."

Sunlight shimmered like sequins against the turquoise ruffle of the inlet. And behind the water rose the mountains—glacier-sheared peaks holding the blue sky upon their backs. Tears suddenly prickled behind Avery's eyes, for no reason except she was so weary, so worn, and she hadn't expected this release, hadn't guessed she'd find so much peace in this place her sister had found.

"You like it?" Addisyn bounced slightly on her toes like an excited kid showing off a new toy.

Avery cleared her throat to steady her voice. She wasn't in the habit of allowing Addisyn to see her cry. "Yes. I love it."

"Right there is Mount—" Addisyn stopped abruptly and peered at her. "A, are you sure you're okay?"

What, was Addisyn the soul reader now? Avery forced a smile, thankful for her sunglasses. "Yes."

Darius nudged Addisyn with a reminding glance. "She's probably tired from her flight."

"Oh! You're right." Addisyn hopped off the rock she'd been standing on and grabbed Avery's hand. "What time was your flight this morning? Six, right? You should probably sleep on the way to Whistler. We can sightsee later."

Avery passed the rest of the ride in the backseat next to Addisyn, Darius's '80s music crooning comfortably as the car swooped around mile after mile. She was almost asleep when Addisyn jostled her arm. "A? This is Whistler."

Whistler! Finally! She straightened and peered out the window as they passed a decorative sign capped with two Canadian flags. Colorful banners stretched from lampposts, and a midsummer abundance of flowers adorned the roadsides. Evergreens bristled along the streets, parting to reveal rustic lodge-style buildings pressed together in the safe embrace of the mountains.

The town had a feel of home, and in many ways, it reminded her of Estes Park. The two places were different, yes, but similar at the core.

Rather like her and Addisyn.

Darius turned down a quiet street lined with mansions that seemed to turn up their noses at the road. Addisyn waved her hand as they slowed in front of a wrought-iron gate. "Here's the house." Her tone didn't sound particularly enthusiastic. "The guesthouse is behind."

Avery had been prepared somewhat by Addisyn's description, but the house was still grander than she'd expected. "Wow." She leaned forward and glanced at Darius. "And your family owns this?"

"Yeah. My uncle." A shadow passed over Darius's face. The next instant he shrugged. "It's impressive. But I still say, give me a cabin any day."

Avery grinned. "Amen."

As she and Addisyn stepped out of the car, Darius held out his hand. "I've got to get to work, but it's been great seeing you again, Avery."

She squeezed his hand. "You too, Darius."

He turned to Addisyn, and his expression changed to a hopeful sort of longing. "So—see you later?"

"Right." Addisyn leaned in the car window and gave him a quick kiss. "Bye."

Hmm. Looked like things were going very well. As he drove away, Avery slung her backpack over her shoulder and grinned at Addisyn. "Well, Ads, what—"

The guesthouse door creaked open behind her, and she turned. A slender ghost of a girl was peering cautiously onto the narrow guesthouse porch. The shadows on her face pulled at Avery's compassion. She glanced at Addisyn.

Addisyn nodded, answering her unspoken question, and turned toward the girl. "Hi, Kenzie. This is my sister, Avery. Avery, this is Kenzie."

"Hi there." Avery gave her most disarming smile and held out her hand. "I've been looking forward to meeting you. Addisyn says you're a fantastic skater."

Kenzie's face eased ever so slightly, and she took Avery's hand. "Nice to meet you." Shyness softened her tone.

"Avery, let's get your stuff inside." Addisyn nudged Kenzie. "Did Trent bring that folding bed over?"

"It's in the bedroom." Kenzie edged toward the porch steps.

"Okay." Addisyn glanced toward the woods. "Heading to your treehouse?" She waited for Kenzie's nod. "All right. I'm going to help Avery unpack, but call me if you need anything, okay?"

Avery watched the girl's hunched shoulders as she scurried toward the tree line. "Her treehouse?"

Addisyn waved her hand. "Long story. Let's get your stuff inside."

The inside of the guesthouse was simple but comfortable, with big windows in the kitchenette and an overstuffed couch in the front room. Avery braced herself for a mess when Addisyn led her into the bedroom, but amazingly, everything was relatively neat. Maybe Addisyn was outgrowing her scattered ways. Or, more likely, she'd crammed the chaos out of sight before Avery arrived.

"Here we are." Addisyn parked Avery's luggage by the folding bed wedged in the corner and flopped backward onto the twin bed opposite. "So? Do you love it?"

"I totally love it." Avery stretched out on her back beside her sister and studied the knotholes in the wooden ceiling.

"I've been counting down the days till you got here. Ask Darius."

"Darius." Avery turned her head just enough to catch her sister's eye.

"What?" Addisyn's face was already flushing.

"Come on." Avery kept her tone light. "What's the latest on you two?"

"Oh, well—we're good."

"Uh huh." Avery nudged Addisyn playfully. "Very good, I'd say. He'll be pulling out a ring any day."

Something uncertain flickered over Addisyn's face. "No." She cleared her throat. "We're still a long way from that."

From the way Darius looked at her sister, she wasn't so sure about that. But okay. "All right."

"So—Kenzie."

The image of the shy girl on the porch returned, and Avery propped herself up on an elbow to face Addisyn. "Yeah?"

Addisyn sighed. "We still haven't found the bear. We've made a few more trips to the ridge, but we haven't seen anything bigger than a squirrel."

Avery frowned. "I wonder why it's so important to her." How tightly was that wary girl clinging to her secrets?

"I have no idea." Addisyn spread her hands helplessly. "All I know is it's something to do with a story, or a legend, or something. She won't tell me anything besides that. But it has to be important."

She wanted to care as much as Addisyn did, but the last month of worrying over Skyla's offer had drained all her energies. She shrugged. "I don't know what else you could try, though."

"Come on, A." Addisyn folded her hands with a pleading expression. "I mean, you're the mountain girl. So now that you're here, can't you help us?"

The conversation was making her even more tired. "You said Kenzie was doing better, though. Even without finding the bear."

"And she is, but—" Addisyn took a deep breath and picked at a thread on the blanket. "She really wants to find this bear. And I want to help her."

The whole idea still sounded just a little impossible. Avery sighed. "I don't know, Ads. Maybe you should just let it go."

Hurt replaced the hope in Addisyn's expression. "I'm not going to let it go, A." She sat up. "It's important to Kenzie. I want her to—"

"Want her to what?"

Addisyn was quiet for a long moment. "I want her to find what she's looking for. I want her to have something to hang onto."

Why was there such sadness on her sister's face? "Well—" Avery sighed. She'd come to Canada for a respite from her own problems, not to get roped into whatever circus Addisyn and Kenzie had created. But if Addisyn needed her help—even just a little bit—

"Okay." She lay back and studied the ceiling again, the boards marching like trails. "I'll help you find the bear."

△△   △△   △△

THE LITTLE ORANGE pills stared from her palm like two accusing eyes. Kenzie shook away the idea, but her discomfort remained.

She unscrewed the cap of her water bottle but hesitated. Somehow over the last few days, the pills had started feeling a little—weird, sort of. So much was pulling her forward now, into a light she hadn't expected to find again. But the pills were left over from the darkness. In fact, over the last couple of days, she'd glanced at the idea of forgetting the pills altogether. But quitting now couldn't be a good idea, not with auditions coming up.

She shrugged and gulped them down before she could think about it anymore. Maybe in a couple of weeks, she could reconsider her dosage. Just not today.

She waited until the dizziness settled and her heartbeat felt more even before she headed into the kitchen. Addisyn and her sister were already sitting at the kitchen table, the aroma of coffee swirling with their conversation.

"—and so I'm walking Mercy outside the cabin, and I'm already late for work." Addisyn's sister took a drink from her mug. "And she's, you know, just sniffing around and won't do her business, so I'm getting kind of grouchy, right?"

"Yeah." Addisyn was nodding, fully engaged in whatever story Avery was telling. "And then what?"

"Then—" Avery set her mug down, her hands entering the storytelling—"this squirrel flashes out of nowhere, and Mercy's off like a shot. So of course, I run after her."

"Where did she go?"

"To where those four big pine trees are, you know? Up by the back corner. And then—" Avery rolled her eyes. "She couldn't figure out which tree it was in. She just started running these figure eights around all of them."

Addisyn tossed back her head in a burst of laughter. "So where was it?"

"That's the best part." Avery grinned, pausing for the punchline. "It had jumped from the tree to the roof of the house, and it was just sitting up there by the chimney, watching Mercy make a fool of herself."

Kenzie couldn't contain her own laughter at the image. Avery turned in her seat and lifted her mug in welcome. "Oh, hey, Kenzie! Good morning."

Avery had remembered her name? "Good morning." Kenzie perched in the seat next to Addisyn. "Who's Mercy?"

"My black Lab." Avery pulled out her phone and held it out. "See?"

A sweet charcoal dog with an eager expression peered from the screen. Kenzie smiled. "She's pretty."

Addisyn smirked. "She's Avery's guard dog. Trained to defend."

Avery rolled her eyes. "Yes, she's quite scary. Especially when she's sleeping on the porch in a sunny spot, which is her favorite activity." She slipped the phone back into her pocket. "Which reminds me. Ads, I finally got the porch railing redone."

"Oh, really?" Addisyn leaned forward. "Did you use the cedar?"

"Well, Laz figured—"

Kenzie studied the two of them as they volleyed the conversation back and forth. Avery had shorter hair and lighter eyes than Addisyn, plus her fashion style was definitely a lot simpler. But regardless of the surface differences, it was obvious they were sisters. Not just because of their facial shape or vocal pitch, but because they shared the same light in their eyes, the easy joy of two people whose stories had always fit together.

They were still talking about things and people that meant nothing to her, the conversation slowly shutting her out, and Kenzie sank slightly. What had she expected? That Addisyn would still have time for her once Avery arrived? No, she was an awkward third party to their sisterhood. She stood and backed away. "I, uh, I'm going to clean my room."

Addisyn broke off in the middle of a sentence to stare at her. "Clean your room? We're getting ready to leave."

"Leave?" She glanced at the clock. "I thought I didn't have practice today."

"You don't." Addisyn drained the last of her coffee and stood. "We're going to show Avery the town."

"Yeah, I want to see this place." Avery swooped up the coffee mugs and set them in the sink. "Ready, Kenzie?"

They wanted her to go with them? Kenzie blinked between the two of them. "Are you sure—I mean—"

"Of course. In fact, you're driving us." Addisyn scraped the chairs in and grinned at her. "Grab your bag and let's go."

Fifteen minutes later, Kenzie was driving downtown. Riding shotgun beside her, Avery fiddled with the dial on the radio until she found some old-sounding music with a twangy guitar. "Hey, John Denver!"

Kenzie stopped at a red light and frowned. "Who's that?"

"You don't know who John Denver is?" Avery raised her eyebrows and glanced into the backseat at Addisyn. "Well, I can tell Addisyn has left some big gaps in your education."

"Whatever." Addisyn shrugged and grinned at Kenzie in the rearview mirror. "Avery only likes vintage country music or these weird indie bands that nobody else has ever heard of. She's behind the times."

"Um, says the girl who used to think the lyric was 'Country roads, make me foam.'" Avery turned the radio up. "Listen closely, Kenzie.

We're going to develop your musical taste."

The easy banter warmed like sunshine, driving away the dark clouds that so often rolled over her life. By the time they reached downtown, Avery had taught her all the words to "Country Roads" and promised to let her listen to "Rocky Mountain High" next. "Matter of fact, I have his *Greatest Hits* CD with me. I can let you borrow it."

"CD?" Addisyn rolled her eyes. "What did I say? Behind the times."

Thankfully, the traffic was light in Whistler Village. At the next red light, Kenzie glanced in the mirror at Addisyn. "Where are we headed?"

Addisyn leaned forward over the console. "This afternoon, we're heading to the cultural center. Avery had the idea that someone there might know about the bears."

Excitement fizzed within her. "Really?"

Avery nodded. "It's worth a try."

"Exactly." Addisyn jostled Kenzie's shoulder. "So that's this afternoon. This morning, I thought we'd let you pick."

The choice landed in her lap, and she had no idea how to hold it. "Well—no. I mean, whatever you two want to do is—"

"No, Kenzie. Really, you pick."

Avery nodded at her encouragingly. "Yeah, you're the local. What should we do?"

They were watching her, waiting for her words. How long had it been since anyone had cared about her opinions? "Well—" Theater was too ordinary. Shopping was boring. Gardens would be empty this time of year. What about— "Axe throwing?"

"Axe throwing?" Addisyn's eyes widened slightly. "That's a thing?"

"Yes." Her confidence in the idea was growing, the fun memories from years ago flooding back. "There's a place a few blocks from here. They teach you how, and then you try to hit the targets with these really cool axes."

Addisyn laughed suddenly and shook her head. "Well, then what are we waiting for?" She slid Avery a look of mock suspicion. "Did you put her up to this?"

"No, she's just got good ideas!" Avery high-fived her at the next red light. "Let's go!"

The axe-throwing place was pretty much as Kenzie had remembered—an industrial vibe with classic rock music that echoed from the concrete floors. A guy with spiky black hair and a lumberjack beard led them to an empty lane and demonstrated the principles for them. "Just hold the haft like so—dominant hand on the bottom—and then throw it—" He swung the axe back between his shoulders, then lunged forward and released it. The tool whirled through the air and struck the target almost exactly on the bullseye.

Addisyn blinked. "Well, you've done this before."

"A time or two, yeah." He laughed and backed away. "The lane is yours for an hour. Let me know if you have any questions."

As soon as he left, Addisyn grabbed one of the axes. "I'm going first."

Avery leaned against the chain-link barricade and raised her eyebrows. "Is it too much to ask for you to not decapitate one of us?"

"Quit distracting me." Addisyn lined up the way the man had directed, adjusting her stance with an expression of fierce determination.

Avery cleared her throat. "Other hand on top, Ads." She squeezed Kenzie's shoulder. "Back up, Kenzie. No telling where this will go."

"Oh, honestly, A." Addisyn took a step forward and let the axe fly. It veered erratically into the target, handle first, and bounced against the barricade.

Kenzie's laughter overflowed, and she sagged against the chain-link, her giggles colliding with Avery's. Addisyn shot them a mock glare, but then her smile broke through. "Okay, so I already knew this wasn't my strong suit." She collected her axe and clapped Avery on the shoulder. "Show us how it's done, sis."

"He said if the axe hits handle first, you're too far away." Avery scooped up her own axe and moved closer to the target. "Pure science, Ads. This is easy."

Her aim was much straighter than Addisyn's, but her axe only weakly clipped the edge of the plywood. Addisyn coughed. "Easy, huh?"

"Hey. I still did better than you!"

By the time the session was almost over, they'd all proven their inability to axe throw, and Kenzie had laughed more than she had in years. But it wasn't just the fun that filled her heart. Joining in the competitive banter, watching Avery duck every time Addisyn touched an axe, it was easy to pretend. Like maybe she was the third sister, and maybe she really did belong, and maybe the scowling sky she'd lived under for so long was about to break like dawn.

"Well, another skilled shot from the mountain girl." Addisyn deadpanned as Avery's axe hung in the outermost ring of the target. "What were you aiming for that time?"

"You, if you keep harassing me." Avery yanked her axe free with a grin. "Show me you can do better."

"Well, I guess we're almost out of time." Addisyn glanced at her watch and handed Kenzie her axe. "Here. You go."

"No, it's your turn."

"Yeah, but I've already proven my incompetence." Addisyn made a funny face. "Come on, Kenzie. Just try one more time."

"Well—okay."

She took her place at the end of the lane, the axe heavy in her hands. The target loomed in front of her, and suddenly it all came clear.

Hadn't she always been facing a target? Hadn't she spent her life desperately taking shots at elusive bullseyes she could never quite nail?

Her hands trembled, sweaty palms slipping on the axe handle. The pursuit of perfection—it was paralyzing her. The way it did when she stepped on the ice or looked on Instagram or took the orange pills.

"Kenzie?" Avery's voice reached through the fear. Gentle, calm. "Take your shot."

She drew in a breath and glanced at Avery and Addisyn. Then she raised the axe. Surprisingly, it wasn't as heavy as she'd expected.

One step forward, and the axe went whirling, straight and true. It hit in the upper right quadrant with a satisfying *thunk* and bit into the wood less than ten inches from the bullseye.

"Whoa!" Addisyn sprang to her side. "That's the closest any of us has come today!"

"Yeah!" Avery draped an arm around her shoulders. "Way to go, Kenzie!"

Kenzie smiled. "Thanks." She glanced at the target again. Okay, so she hadn't hit the bullseye.

But for the first time in years, she was finally back in the game.

CHAPTER 18

"This is the place?" Addisyn flipped on her blinker and glanced at Kenzie for confirmation. The cultural center was in the heart of downtown, so Kenzie had readily agreed to let Addisyn navigate the traffic.

"Yes." Kenzie nodded at the sweeping modern building, all curving beams and expansive glass that reflected the blue of the sky.

Avery pointed at the sign. "Squamish Lil'wat Cultural Center." She tipped up her sunglasses and nodded approvingly at the building. "This looks neat."

The center was filled with traditional artifacts, as if heritage hung in the very air. Addisyn glanced at the many exhibits as she followed Avery and Kenzie. A carved wooden totem pole towered in the far corner, and life-size canoes were mounted by the windows. And behind that—

"Check it out!" She grabbed Kenzie's hand and pointed. A taxidermied bear—a brown one, but still—rose on his hind legs beside some of the artwork, an intricate tasseled covering draped over his torso.

"Wow." Kenzie's eyes brightened. "Has to be a good sign, right?"

Avery nodded. "Definitely!"

Did no one but her notice the ferocious fangs on that bear? "Yep." Addisyn forced a smile as she led the way toward the information desk. "A good sign."

"Hi there." A man with a long silver braid and sharp eyes encircled by wrinkles nodded to them. "Welcome to the cultural center."

Addisyn glanced at Avery and Kenzie, but both of them were watching her expectantly. Apparently she was the unofficial spokesperson for the group. "Hi." She fiddled with her bracelet. "We're, uh, hoping for some information on spirit bears."

"Spirit bears?" The man's eyes shadowed slightly. "The *mooksgm'ol?*"

"Um—I don't know. The white bears—some people call them ghost bears—" She trailed off and bit her lip at the evident hostility on the man's face. What had she said wrong?

"Why do you ask about the spirit bears?"

"Well—" Addisyn glanced at Kenzie. "Um, well, um, they're just—interesting."

"Interesting?" The man tasted the word as if it had been an insult. "The bears are more than *interesting* to us. They are very sacred."

Oh. Leave it to her to trespass on holy ground. Addisyn took a deep breath. "I'm sorry, I—"

"They are the protectors of the forest." The man's voice rang with authority. "Traditionally, our people saw them as guiding spirits. They symbolize healing and renewal and unity among the people of earth."

Healing. Renewal. Unity. Exactly what Kenzie needed. And what she was seeking herself.

She gripped the counter. "And—where are they found?"

"The Great Bear Rainforest in the far north. And that is tribal land."

The conversation was ramming into dead ends. "Wasn't there a bear in Whistler?"

And just like that, the man's stony gaze flickered. Only for a moment. But the moment was long enough for Addisyn to read the truth.

He knew something.

"Of course not." He'd recovered his lofty tone. "They are only found farther north."

Addisyn leaned forward, the desperation in Kenzie's gaze driving her onward. She could be just as stubborn as this grouchy old man. "Look, I know there was a bear here in Whistler. We've been searching for two months, and we really need to know where to find—"

"And I am not able to give that information." The man's voice was downright chilly now. "The *mooksgm'ol* are the guardians of the forest. And we are the guardians of them."

"But—" Addisyn glanced at Avery, but her sister just shrugged slightly and tipped her head toward the door.

Well, no answers here. Addisyn glared back at the man, whose expression was still as immovable as the carved faces on the totem. "Okay. Fine." She squeezed Kenzie's shoulder. "Let's go."

They were halfway to the door when the old man's voice echoed behind them. "Wait!"

What now? Addisyn halted and warily turned toward him. "Yes?"

He crossed the room toward them, his braid swinging over his shoulder. "Why do you ask about the spirit bears being in Whistler?"

"Well—uh—"

But before Addisyn could stammer out a decent explanation, Kenzie stepped suddenly forward. "I saw one in the woods here." Her voice was soft, but sure. "Years ago. But I wasn't—I couldn't come back before now, and I need to—to see it again."

The man's eyebrows twitched. "You saw a spirit bear? Are you sure, child?"

"Yes, sir."

"And why do you need to see it again?"

Kenzie's voice dipped whisper-soft. "I—I know the legend. And I really need it now."

He studied her for a few moments more with a look not unlike Avery's soul-reading gaze. And then he nodded slowly. "In that case—to be visited by a spirit bear is a different matter."

Kenzie's face flushed. "I—I didn't say I was visited. I just—saw it. In the woods."

"A visit nonetheless. Nothing is an accident." The man sighed and glanced around the group, his face now drained of defiance. "I'm sorry. Most of the inquiries we receive are from people interested in the bears for very wrong reasons." His face darkened. "Poaching has become a serious problem."

Anger flashed in Avery's eyes. "People can be so cruel."

"Yes." The man's tone was shadowed with sadness. "And you see, we believe that the bears are very much needed." He glanced out the window at the tall pines pressed close around the building. "The forest is incomplete without them." His drew a paper map from his pocket. "Now.

It is true what you have said. The bears were seen six years ago in this area." His finger circled a point on the paper.

Addisyn drew in a breath. "Wildcrest."

"Yes. And it was said that they were seen again there. Only three months ago now."

"Three months?" Kenzie leaned forward. "That recently?"

"Indeed." He held up a hand. "Now, this is not confirmed. But if you do need to see one—" his eyes flicked to Kenzie again—"you could hike up."

Avery leaned over the map. "There are trails?"

"Yes, a network, in fact. A lovely path leads to the top. Only eight miles round-trip."

Only eight miles? Addisyn coughed. "Is it—steep?"

"Yes, certainly, but the view at the top is well worth it."

The view didn't interest her, but the chance at finding the bears—at helping Kenzie—now, that was worth whatever it took. "We'll look at—"

She blinked. Avery was still studying the map, but her expression had changed to clear disapproval. Addisyn forced herself to refocus. "Uh—yes, so, thank you again."

"You are welcome." The man smiled finally, his skin creasing into friendliness. "If you do see the bear—" He was speaking to Kenzie now. "Please let us know."

The girl who'd hung her head perpetually a few weeks ago now met the man's gaze fearlessly. "I will."

Addisyn glanced at Avery again as they headed out of the center. "A, what's wrong?"

"It's a bad idea." There was kindness in Avery's tone, but there was big-sister firmness too.

"Why?" Kenzie took the map from Avery and slid into the backseat.

"Yeah, why? You're the one who had the thought in the first place." Addisyn ducked into the driver's seat and narrowed her eyes at her sister.

"I didn't realize it was backcountry."

Her sister would need to translate the mountain lingo. "Which means—"

"Rough terrain and isolated areas. Much more dangerous."

Addisyn started the car and headed out of the parking lot. She wouldn't let Avery see how much that description worried her. "We can manage it."

"Ads, I'm serious. And for that distance? An eight-mile hike?"

"So? Eight miles isn't that far." Kenzie jumped into the brewing argument. "I used to hike here all the time."

"Exactly." Addisyn set her jaw. "A, aren't you always telling me that eight miles is nothing?"

"It's nothing for me because I hike all the time. You two just aren't as experienced."

She couldn't really argue with that. She ran a hand through her hair and sighed, trying to think of another way to convince Avery. "You said yourself that you wanted to hike while you were here."

"Not on backcountry trails in a remote area." Avery glanced over her shoulder at Kenzie. "Anyway, should you really be wearing yourself out, with your training and all?"

"It's not going to wear me out."

"Trust me, backcountry will." Avery pressed her lips together and glanced at Addisyn. "Ads, I know you mean well, but I don't think this is a good plan."

She tightened her grip on the steering wheel. "Well, *I* think we should do it."

Kenzie leaned forward from the backseat. "I've been looking at the map. According to this, it's a popular hike, so it shouldn't be too impossible."

"Popular with survivalists, maybe…"

Kenzie ignored Avery's interjection. "And it's eight miles if you start from the Aspenwalk Basin, but you can actually join via a spur trail from Bearstooth."

Addisyn blinked. "From the center? Really?"

"Yeah, and it cuts off a mile and a half each way."

"So only a five-mile hike." Addisyn watched Avery out of the corner of her eye. "Pretty easy, right, A?"

"Let me see that." Avery took the map from Kenzie and studied the dotted lines. "Yes. You're right."

How perfect was this? "Then I don't see why we can't do it."

"See?" Kenzie's voice was brimming over with hope. "Addisyn thinks we can do it."

"Yes, well, she and I need to talk about it some more, okay?" Avery passed the map back to Kenzie. "Here. Look this over again and see if you find any more connecting trails."

Kenzie bowed her head over the map, and Avery leaned closer, keeping her voice low. "What will Trent say about you taking his niece on a strenuous hike in rough terrain?"

"He won't care." Addisyn tossed her hair over her shoulder, trying to believe her own words. "Anyway, he won't know." She narrowed her eyes at Avery. "Unless someone tells him."

"You think *I* would say something?" Avery tossed her an irritated look. "Okay, tell me this. What happens when we don't find this bear? She's going to be very upset."

Addisyn gritted her teeth. Avery was so aggravating when she got like this. "You don't know that we won't find it. And maybe she just needs to look for it. To know she's tried."

Avery took in a breath. "Ads—look, I don't know what you're thinking, but if you take my advice, you won't do this. It's rough country up there, by the looks of the map, and—well, I just don't have a good feeling."

If you take my advice...

Irritation rankled along her spine. Had there ever been a time when Avery thought Addisyn had a good plan? No, she was the naive one. The weak one. The unwise one.

The mistake.

Well, she wasn't backing away from this. Not when she had the chance to help Kenzie in the biggest way yet. Not when she finally had her moment to prove that she could bring healing instead of hurt, that she could be something more than the disaster she'd always been.

"I'm responsible for Kenzie. And I say we do it." The words were harder than she'd intended.

Avery crossed her arms. "And if I don't want to go?"

Wait, Avery might not go? Her stomach lurched, but she kept her face stoic. "Your choice, I guess."

Five silent minutes leaked slowly by before Avery sat up and sighed. "Okay. I'll go with you. If something happens, you'll need me there."

She hid her relief, keeping her tone businesslike. "Okay. Thanks, A."

Avery shrugged. "It's what I do."

What was that behind her sister's words? Addisyn frowned and glanced over her shoulder. "Kenzie?"

The girl's head snapped up, her gaze brimming with hope. "Yeah?"

Addisyn donned a bright smile and tried to ignore Avery's serious expression. "We're going to Wildcrest on Saturday."

△△   △△   △△

"THIS IS AMAZING!" Avery grabbed the seat as the swaying red gondola lurched to life. "Good idea, Ads."

"Thanks." Addisyn slid closer to her sister on the bench seat and grinned. She'd known Avery would love a ride on the Peak-to-Peak gondola. Their glass-enclosed car would be swinging over the valleys between Whistler and Blackcomb, and the views would be amazing. "There's even a restaurant up top where we can get lunch."

"Sounds perfect."

"And you're sure you didn't want the glass-bottomed car?"

"No." Avery shook her head vigorously, her shoulder-length hair swirling around her face. "I'd get sick."

Addisyn laughed and settled back into the seat. The gondola was surprisingly quiet today—only a few other passengers engaged in quiet conversation across the car.

Avery was already snapping pictures on her phone. "Look at this, Ads. It's gorgeous."

"For sure." The mountains fell away below them, tree-roughened shoulders spreading to the horizon. Addisyn glanced up at the clouds close enough to touch.

"I see why you love this place."

Addisyn drew a deep breath. "Yes." How scared she'd been when she'd first come to Whistler—alone and uprooted and running from Brian.

263

And she'd never forget how the mountains had wrapped their peace around her.

"You've built a great new life here."

A great new life that still had fault lines from the past. "Well—"

"I'm serious." The reflective lenses of Avery's sunglasses kept Addisyn from seeing her eyes. "You've got skating and Darius and the mountains."

That undefined tightness was in her chest again, the tightness that reminded her how quickly everything could crumble, but she just shrugged.

"It's the kind of life I always wanted for you, Ads."

The odd mix of joy and pain in Avery's voice squeezed at Addisyn's heart. "I—I am happy here. But—I don't know." She hesitated, looking for words that would keep her fears hidden. "It still feels—it doesn't feel quite real to me, I guess."

"You're just getting used to it. Give it some time."

Time wouldn't put her back to the way she'd been before Brian or give her the skills to ever become more than who she was now. "I guess so."

"And Darius is wonderful."

Could they talk about anything else? "Yes. Of course."

"It's good to see you with him." Avery's words were slow, soft, filled with something almost like—longing? "I'm glad you have him. Someone who will protect you and care for you and—and love you like that. It's— sweet. And romantic."

What? Addisyn peered at her sister. "*Romantic?* I don't think I've ever heard you use that word in my life."

Avery's laugh halted self-consciously. "Oh, you know what I mean. It's just nice to see that there are still good guys out there. That's all." That strange wistfulness was back behind her words. "He loves you. I can see it in his eyes when he looks at you."

And she loved him, with an intensity that frightened her, but her love could never build anything lasting. "He's—he's a great man." Her cheeks stung hot, and she tried for a laugh. "His family is a piece of work, though."

"So I've noticed." Avery's mouth dipped down. "Nothing like ours, though."

Addisyn swallowed. "No."

Silence seeped between them, and Addisyn knew they were both wandering the dark hallways they never discussed, the shattered story of their childhood. Yet another reason she was clueless when it came to loving Darius the way he deserved.

When they disembarked from the lift at the top of the mountain, the altitude-cooled air was chillier than Addisyn had expected. She shivered and pointed at the restaurant. "Right over there."

"Okay." Avery shrugged her bag off her shoulder and handed it to Addisyn. "Find us a table, would you? I'm going to refill my bottle at the water fountain."

"Sure." Addisyn hurried into the restaurant and found a corner table with a big window—Avery would love the view. She slid onto the bench seat and plopped Avery's bag beside her, but it capsized, the contents tumbling to the restaurant floor.

Seriously? She couldn't even guard her sister's bag without causing a disaster? Addisyn groaned and crawled under the table—where she was tempted to stay—to retrieve Avery's belongings. Wallet, car keys, a pocket Bible—Addisyn stuffed everything back in the bag, already knowing she'd never replicate Avery's intricate organization system. She grabbed her sister's phone last, intending to tuck it on top, when it lit up. An unread text slid across the lock screen. *New message from Tyler.*

Tyler? *Tyler?* Who the heck was Tyler? Addisyn's mind whirled into high gear. Avery was getting texts from a *guy*? No way. Had her romance-averse sister finally turned the corner?

Of course, she wasn't going to actually read the text. That would be a nosy younger sister move. And she was not a nosy younger sister.

But—well, it was right there on the lock screen. Right in plain sight. Could there be any harm in just glancing quickly at it?

Hey, Avery! Just thinking about you and wondered if you'd told Skyla anything yet about the position. I hadn't heard the latest on that. Hoping to have you on board!

The situation had too many loops now for her to keep up. *Position?* What position? *Hoping to have you on board?* Did that mean—

"Addisyn, is that my phone?" Avery yanked the device out of Addisyn's hand and pinned her with an exasperated look. "What are you doing, snooping on me?"

"Well, maybe I should be!" Addisyn crossed her arms and glared back. Avery didn't intimidate her. Not much, anyway. "Who's Tyler?"

"Tyler?" Avery's expression altered slightly, and she glanced at her phone. Her eyes darted over the message before she sighed and dropped into the seat across from Addisyn. "Tyler is a guy who works at the raptor center. I met him through volunteering there."

"Okay…" She'd come back to that one. "So what's he talking about, a position?"

Avery scowled and shoved her phone into her pocket. "You were reading my texts? Seriously, Addisyn? Did you go through my bank info while you were at it?"

"Look, it just came up on the screen after your bag—anyway, it was right in front of me, okay? It's not like I went through all your messages or something." Although after reading that text, she totally would have if she'd remembered the password. "So—what's going on?"

"All right." Avery tossed her hands in surrender. "Skyla offered me a job."

How had she not known about this? "What do you mean? What kind of job?"

"She's expanding the rehab center to be an outdoor education venue. Classes, exhibits, field trips, all kinds of ways to connect people to nature." Avery shrugged. "She wanted me to work there."

The job sounded as if it had been custom-made for her sister. Addisyn laughed, breathless with the excitement. "A, that's terrific! Why didn't you tell me? When do you start?"

Avery made an uneasy face. "I didn't take it."

She didn't take it? A job like that had come her way, and she'd let it go? "Oh—okay." She paused, trying to choose words that wouldn't reveal how crazy she found that idea. "Um—why did—"

"Because of the store." Avery laced her fingers together on the table. "I can't leave Laz, Addisyn. He's done so much for me, and he needs me at the store."

"But—Avery—" Loyalty was one thing. Sacrificing your whole future was another. "This job sounds perfect for you. I'm sure Laz would understand—"

"I don't want to put him in that spot." Avery looked away, rearranging the condiment packets on the table.

"He ran the store fine before you got there."

"Addisyn, there's more to it than that." Avery paused with her hand above the stack of flat squares. "I do well at the store, okay? It's something that comes easily to me, and—"

"And you won't try something new?"

Avery's eyes flashed with a dangerous light for a moment. "That's not it. The store—it's my path."

Retail was no long-term path for Avery. Avery, who had a heart bigger than the horizon, whose eyes could see beyond the blurred edges of the spiritual world, whose life had always been lived as a gift to those around her. "Avery—" She kept her tone level. "I think you should try the job. I can see you being really good at something like that."

"Addisyn." Avery's voice held a faint pleading. "I already told Skyla no, okay? I'm not doing it. I understand that you disagree, but it's my life."

This still felt all wrong. But Avery was right; it was none of her business. And what did she know about life choices, anyway?

She sighed. "Well. If that's what you want."

"The store is where I belong." Avery sighed and rotated her shoulders. "Look, can we talk about something else?"

Addisyn waited all the way through lunch and sightseeing from the top—all the way until they had boarded the gondola back down Blackcomb—before she cleared her throat. "How old is Tyler?"

"Oh, I don't know." Avery was staring out the window, her voice still heavy. "Early twenties, I guess."

Early twenties. The perfect age. Addisyn angled for a creative way to ask the next question. "Does his wife work at the center, too?"

"He's not married. He's still pursuing his master's degree. Wildlife veterinary."

Single and smart. And interested in wildlife. This was getting better and better. Only one pertinent question remained. "Is he cute?"

"Cute?" Avery stared at her. "Um, may I remind you that you're dating someone?"

To be so farseeing in most areas, her sister was certainly thickheaded when it came to men. Addisyn sighed. "I'm thinking of you, A." She tipped her sunglasses up, trying to catch her sister's eye.

"Oh, no. No, no, no. You are not going to start this with me." Avery waved her hands wildly as if trying to shoo away the very idea. "He's just a coworker."

"A coworker who has your number."

"Because he texts me when he needs help with a bird release." Avery's tone was becoming more clipped.

"Oh, I bet he does." Addisyn grinned and nudged Avery playfully. "Come on, A. Show me his picture. I bet he's cute. And if—"

"Addisyn, stop it right now." Avery's tone sliced across her words with a frustration that instantly shriveled her teasing. "Look, why does everything come back to guys for you? Ever since you started dating Darius, you think you're my personal matchmaker. But not all of us are waiting on Prince Charming, and—"

"Whoa, whoa, okay!" A couple in the opposite corner of the lift was staring at them curiously. Addisyn winced and lowered her voice. "I'm sorry. I just assumed—"

"You'd be best off not *assuming* again."

Addisyn felt her eyes widen. Avery was never that short. Especially not with her.

Good thing the gondola was enclosed so Avery couldn't throw her off.

The silence wedged itself awkwardly between them. Then Avery suddenly slipped her hand into Addisyn's. "I'm sorry, Ads." Her tone was calmer now. "I shouldn't have snapped at you."

Relief rolled off her shoulders. "I'm sorry too." She squeezed her sister's hand. "I was just giving you a hard time."

"No, I know. It's just—I'm not looking to date."

Avery's standard answer. Addisyn frowned. She'd watched Avery shun boys in high school and skip prom every year and work at whatever job she held as if productivity were far more important than relationships. As far as she knew, Avery had never even been on a single date. But she'd also seen her sister cry over romantic movies and gaze with a vague longing at couples on the street.

I'm not looking to date. The kind of clear-cut explanation Avery liked to hide behind. But there was something far more complicated going on.

"I know you think that." How much could she say without riling Avery up again? "But, I mean—don't you hope that, someday—"

"Just because you found a great guy doesn't—" Avery stopped. Drew a deliberate breath. "I hear you, Addisyn. But I'm okay on my own. Really."

The inevitable conclusion to any conversation she'd ever tried to have with her sister about dating. Addisyn sighed. "Okay." Maybe someday she'd find out what her sister wasn't saying. But not today.

The ski lift was lower now, the trees rising above them again. When it bumped down on the platform, Avery stood with a lukewarm smile. "I know you're trying to help, Addisyn. But it's my life, okay?"

"I know."

But as Addisyn followed Avery out of the gondola, she couldn't help but wonder.

If it was truly Avery's life...who was Avery living it for?

△△   △△   △△

AVERY GLANCED AROUND as she stepped through the office doorway at the Bearstooth Center. She'd driven up early in the afternoon with Addisyn and Kenzie and had been walking the trail around the lake while they practiced. But dark clouds were looming over the lake, and she was ready to be inside before a possible storm could hit.

"Can I help you?"

The voice didn't sound all that helpful. Avery glanced up and smiled hesitantly at a bored-looking girl behind the information desk. "Uh—I was just—"

The girl's eyes suddenly flashed with recognition. "Oh!" She grinned and stood. "You're the sister, aren't you?"

"The—"

"Addisyn's sister, right?" The girl marched around the end of the desk and examined Avery with the curiosity of a scientist who'd found a new specimen. "From Colorado?"

"Yes. That's me." The pieces clicked together. "You must be Tina. Addisyn's told me a lot about you." Although she wouldn't be sharing exactly what Addisyn had said.

"She talks about you all the time." Tina propped her hip against the edge of the desk. "She said you live by yourself in the middle of nowhere and work at a little store."

Avery sucked in a defensive breath. "I—I live in Estes Park. It's a small town in the mountains. And I do work at an outdoors store."

"Hmm. Sounds boring to me. But to each her own, right?" The phone jangled, and Tina scurried back toward the desk, tossing a conclusion to the conversation over her shoulder. "Addisyn's in the rink if you're looking for her. Big gray building that way." She snatched up the phone. "Bearstooth Athletic Center, Tina speaking..."

A glance out the window revealed even more wicked-looking clouds. She had no desire to hang around Tina any longer, so she ducked out of the office and hurried across the gravel parking lot toward the gray building.

Live by yourself. Middle of nowhere. Work at a store.

Anger lit a match in her chest. Seriously? There was more to her life than that. Much more.

A rush of refreshingly cold air—a welcome contrast to the humid day outside—hit her as she pushed open the door to the ice rink. She blinked, waiting for her eyes to adjust from the glare of the daylight.

Addisyn was standing beside the ice, watching Kenzie work through some complicated-looking turn. In a moment she nodded and clapped her hands once. "You're doing much better with that, Kenzie, but you're still under-rotating just a little. Be sure to keep that forward foot steady."

Avery slipped as unobtrusively as possible into a row of seats off to the side and glanced around the rink. She'd been in her share of these over the years to see Addisyn compete. But watching her sister as a coach—that was a whole new experience.

Addisyn was on the ice now, next to Kenzie, gesturing while Kenzie nodded. In a moment, she extended her outside leg, showing Kenzie something about the jump she'd just done. She said something that brought a smile to Kenzie's face.

An aching kind of pride swelled Avery's heart. Addisyn had come so far. In the past, skating had dragged her down, into Brian's snares and schemes. But now—now skating was a path that took her up, that helped her connect with Kenzie in a way no one else could.

"Try it one more time, okay?" Addisyn was backing off the ice, snapping on her skate guards. She glanced over her shoulder and waved exuberantly at Avery. "Hey! Come up here."

Kenzie was marking through her routine as Avery stepped up next to Addisyn. "Ads, she looks good."

"Yeah—she's getting there." Addisyn nibbled the eraser end of a pencil, scrutinizing Kenzie's moves. "Her rotations are much cleaner." Kenzie launched through a jump sequence, and Addisyn scribbled something on the clipboard she held. "Although she's got to stay on the outside edge of her blade. She's got a bad habit of under-rotating."

None of that made any sense, but she'd take her sister's word for it. "If anyone can help her, I know you can."

An uneasy look passed over Addisyn's face. "I don't know."

Avery shook her head. "What do you mean? You're doing a great job."

"Trent doesn't think so."

Avery pressed her lips together. Addisyn had told her a little about Darius's family. "Still?"

"He's not convinced." Addisyn hesitated. "She's still not as strong as she could be. As she was last season."

Avery studied Kenzie again. Her moves were sweeping, beautiful, but her face was taut with tension. Landing out of her next jump, she stumbled and immediately glanced at Addisyn.

"It's okay!" Addisyn's voice was upbeat. "No problem, keep going!" Once Kenzie had found the rhythm again, she sighed. "See?"

"What's holding her back?"

"She's too tense still." Before Avery could respond, Addisyn stepped forward and paused the music. "Kenzie, that's looking so good. We just need to talk about these landings one more time."

Avery retreated to her original seat, not wanting to distract Kenzie, and watched the skilled way Addisyn gestured and explained and adjusted

Kenzie's stance. A bit of guilt needled at her. All along, she'd rather expected Addisyn to fail, hadn't she? Not because she didn't believe in Addisyn's ability, but just because she couldn't see her as anyone besides the haphazard younger sister she'd always known.

But now—now she was seeing something on Addisyn's face she'd never seen before.

Strength.

Her sister had changed over the last year—transforming from the restless, rebellious girl she'd always been into a woman ready to hold her own. She'd fought her way through every struggle with a tenacity Avery hadn't realized she had. And now, she'd come full circle.

Crazy, wasn't it? Addisyn—the scattered, sporadic one—had carved this wonderful life for herself. A life with love and family and purpose and joy. She'd skidded from one wrong choice to another for most of her life, but somehow she'd stumbled into success, the life she was designed for seeming to spring up all around her.

Here on the ice that had always been her element, she was helping someone else make their own journey. She'd found a place where she could use all her deepest soul to reach out to others. And she'd had the courage to take the opportunity in the face of all odds.

The way Avery had not.

She thought back to their conversation on the ski lift. Addisyn hadn't brought up the job offer again since then, but the subject remained tense and silent between them.

She glanced across the ice, where Addisyn was talking Kenzie through some elaborate spin. "Right, so keep your arms overhead for the extra feature points. That's it, you've got it! Elbows in—"

Tina's words jabbed at her again.

Live by yourself. Middle of nowhere. Work at a store.

So that was how Addisyn had described her? As an isolated introvert trapped in a dead-end job?

The image taunted her with its truth, and a sick feeling wrapped around her stomach. Suddenly she could see her low-level life exactly as it would appear to people who had purpose and passion for their callings. People who were on trusted trails into boundless futures.

Was Addisyn embarrassed? The thought that her sister might be ashamed of her made her want to sink into the floor of the rink.

The next moment a sudden flash of something harder than loneliness flared in Avery's heart. It was for Addisyn she'd sacrificed everything, after all. She'd laid down her future to build a bridge for her sister. If she'd been on her own, she would have—

She blinked back the sudden surge of resentment. Ridiculous, to feel that way. So what if her life had revolved around Addisyn? She would have made the same choice a dozen times before she would have abandoned the younger sister who'd relied on her.

But still, somehow, it just wasn't fair. After all, she'd spent her life being the responsible one, the steady one. She'd turned her back on all her own dreams. She'd forced herself to cling to faith even in the darkness. She'd even helped Addisyn navigate through all the fallout of her own wrong choices.

She'd done all the right things, made all the right turns, but still, she was reminded of a hike she'd done last summer, when she'd lost the main trail and ended up on some side path without realizing it. She'd hiked a steep mile and a half into the rocks before she suddenly hit a dead end.

And wasn't that true now too? Somehow, she'd veered off the trail for her life. She'd walked the plain path of duty and expectation right to the rocks, and now she was staring at a destination of nothingness. She was an empty nester three decades too early. She had a predictable job that had long ago stopped firing her soul with excitement. And the only people who were genuinely glad to see her were some broken birds on Friday afternoons.

Yes, it was a dead end in every sense of the word. And she had no idea how to get back to the path she'd always hoped she might walk someday.

She was so tired. So tired of always being the reliable one, the steady one, the dependable one. So tired of lending her strength to everyone else and leaving none of it for herself.

And in all the time she'd spent helping others find their wings, she'd completely lost her own.

CHAPTER 19

Darius waited until his lunch break to drive to the athletic center. Uncle Trent was always busiest in the mornings. Maybe by later in the day, he'd be more free to talk. Besides, Addisyn should be busy practicing with Kenzie then. The last thing he wanted was for her to walk in on him while he was talking with Trent about a ring. It would spoil every aspect of the surprise.

He parked near the front door and hurried inside, glancing around for her just in case.

"Looking for Addisyn?" Tina was chewing a wad of gum with an almost frightening intensity. "She's in the rink with Kenzie. And her sister."

Perfect. "No, actually I was looking for your dad. Is he busy?"

Tina stopped working the gum just long enough for the answer. "Probably."

Darius sighed. "Can you check and find out?"

Tina cracked the gum one more time. "Guess so." She plopped down in her desk chair and smacked an intercom button. "Dad, Darius wants to see you. I told him you were too busy right now."

A moment of hesitancy crackled over the line before Uncle Trent's voice came through. "No. Send him on in."

Darius followed the hall to his uncle's office. "Hello, Uncle Trent."

"Afternoon." His uncle swiveled away from his desk and gestured at another chair across the room. "Have a seat."

"Thanks." Darius awkwardly perched on the edge of the chair.

"Something on your mind?"

Now that he was here, why was it so hard to approach the subject? "Um—sort of." He focused on the pines outside his uncle's window. "So, I've been going through my parents' stuff. Trying to sort it, figure out what to keep and what to toss."

"Thought you'd already done that."

"No." His uncle would view the depth of his grief as weakness. He took a deep breath. "Anyway, I can't seem to find one thing in particular. Mom's ring."

Uncle Trent's brows creased. "Her wedding ring?"

"No, her engagement ring." Darius sighed. "I found her jewelry box and went through it, but the ring wasn't there. And now I can't remember when I saw it last."

"And you thought I had it?"

"Well, no, just—" This couldn't sound like an accusation. "I just thought maybe you remembered seeing it—or knew what had happened to it—"

Uncle Trent frowned thoughtfully and reached for a pen, tapping it in that maddening habit. "Remind me again what it looked like."

"Silver, with a big solitaire diamond, and I think it had some engraved design around it. Lines or swirls or something."

His uncle nodded. "I do recall it now, I think. But I don't remember what happened to it after the accident." His eyebrows tucked closer together. "Matter of fact, I don't remember ever really seeing any of their things. You boxed them up."

If there was something deeper behind that statement, Darius wasn't lingering to find out. "Well—I don't know. I actually wanted it for Addisyn."

"For Addisyn?" The pen stilled in his uncle's hands. "Pretty valuable ring just to give to a friend."

Did Uncle Trent still not realize the depth of their relationship? "She's not just a friend, Uncle Trent. And this is not just a gift." He straightened in the chair. "I'm going to ask her to marry me."

An odd expression crossed his uncle's face. "Huh." He cleared his throat. "Didn't realize you were that serious about her."

"I am serious." Maybe now Uncle Trent would stop downplaying their relationship. "I want her to be my wife."

"Are you sure you're not making a mistake here?"

His uncle's words were like a plunge into the fjord on an icy day. "What?" He leaned forward in his chair. "Uncle Trent, I'm not making a mistake. I love—"

"Hold on a minute." Uncle Trent raised a hand. "Addisyn is—she's a nice girl. She's done fairly well with Kenzie." His tone held a grudging concession. "But, you know, you two have significantly different backgrounds."

What did he mean by that? "If you mean being from different countries, that's not a—"

"Different countries, different cultures, different—" Uncle Trent hesitated. "And you haven't known her very long. A year, I think you said?"

"A year is long enough." In those twelve months, the landscape of Addisyn's heart had become more familiar to him than the profiles of the mountains that had watched him since childhood.

"Have you talked to her about her feelings?"

"No." He took a deep breath. His uncle was trying to protect him, probably, but still, his frustration was struggling for release. "But I know she feels the same way. We're on the same page."

"Hmm." Uncle Trent pinched his lips together for a moment. "If you're sure."

"I am."

Tension stretched the silence between them, and then Uncle Trent sighed. "Well. Anyway." He was hiding behind his business tone. Again. "Back to the ring. Have you considered the fact that your mom may have been buried in it?"

The thought punched a hole in his heart. "What?"

"I remember she was buried in some jewelry. I don't recall which pieces."

No way. He'd made all the arrangements, and he'd never have allowed a ring with that much significance to be buried with his mother. Or had he? He'd been on such a grief-fueled autopilot that he could barely remember the ceremony. Had he somehow—

He shifted in his seat. "I don't recall picking out any jewelry for the funeral home."

"You didn't. Myrtle did that."

"Great-aunt Myrtle? How did—"

"As I recall, Myrtle wanted to pick out the jewelry for your mother to wear." Uncle Trent rubbed his nose and squinted slightly. "Didn't you give her your mother's jewelry box?"

Oh. Now it was coming back. He'd had so many details to coordinate anyway, so when Great-aunt Myrtle had made the offer, he'd given her permission and the jewelry box. But he'd pulled out all the sentimental pieces first.

Hadn't he?

The nightmarish conversation was opening a sinkhole in his soul. "But you don't remember if Mom was wearing that ring?"

"I didn't pay that much attention. She had a ring on her hand, I'm pretty sure. And if that's the ring that's missing—" Uncle Trent shrugged slightly. "I'm just saying it's a possibility."

His throat pinched. The ring that had meant so much to his mother was gone. And all the hopes it had held were dead and buried.

Just like his parents.

"Thank you, Uncle Trent." He stood quickly. No way would he let his uncle see him cry. "I appreciate it."

Thankfully, Tina was on the phone when Darius hurried through the lobby, and there was still no sign of Addisyn. He ducked into his car and gripped the steering wheel. Holding onto what he could, when he'd let so much else slip through his hands.

The ring was gone. The word ricocheted through his thoughts. *Gone. Gone. Gone.*

He dug into his memories, desperately fighting to extract the details. He'd given Myrtle the jewelry box, yes, but she'd brought it back to him at the ceremony. Anyway, he could have sworn he'd removed all the important jewels. Unless he'd overlooked that one somehow.

He shouldn't have left this up to Myrtle, really. Her mind had started slipping soon after, and she'd passed away not even a year after his parents. So who knew what she could have done in a muddled moment. The ring might even have been in her own belongings—which had been immediately swarmed by her children in a bitter estate feud as soon as she passed.

He had to get out of there before he broke down or saw Addisyn. All the way down the Callaghan Road, he tugged at the options, running a dozen different scenarios through his brain. But in the end, every road led back to the same disastrous conclusion.

The ring was gone.

But by the time he pulled up at the climbing center, he'd forced himself to rearrange his perspective. It was a disaster, yes. But it couldn't derail his plans. He'd simply buy a ring at the jeweler's the way every other guy did. It wouldn't hold the history of his mother's ring, but he could still find something beautiful.

He took a deep breath, releasing the disappointment as best he could. After all, there was still one very wonderful truth he could cling to. The truth that neither a missing ring nor his uncle's disapproval could ever shake.

The truth that one day soon, the girl he loved with his whole heart would be his wife.

△△ △△ △△

"READY FOR A great time?" Darius squeezed Addisyn's hand as they headed up Spring Creek Road.

"So ready!" Addisyn balanced the bowl of pasta salad she'd made that morning on her lap. She'd been in Whistler for Canada Day last year, but she'd been preoccupied with her own problems and dealing with an upended life. This year, though, she could fully enjoy the experience.

Avery leaned forward from the backseat. "So, Addisyn said we'll be boating today."

"Yeah, on Alta Lake. It's really beautiful. And the water is super clear from the glaciers. My family has a party barge."

"Sounds fun." In the backseat next to Avery, Kenzie actually smiled.

Except for the part about Darius's family being there. But after all, Addisyn had Avery and Kenzie for backup. It couldn't be that bad, right?

The traffic thickened as they approached downtown, tourists

funneling into Whistler Village. Oversize maple leaves dangled from the light poles, and the red and white of the Canadian flag draped itself from every corner. Even with the crowds, it didn't take much longer than normal to arrive at Alta Lake. Darius found a parking space in a lot next to Wallace's Steakhouse. A stone's throw from where they'd danced the other night.

"This is beautiful." Avery drew a deep breath and gazed over the sun-spangled water.

"Glad you think so." Darius took the bowl of salad from Addisyn and pulled out his phone. "I'll try to call Uncle Trent and see where they are."

A movement down the beach caught Addisyn's eye. "No need."

Tina marched toward them in a pair of cutoff denim shorts and a tank top splattered with fluorescent maple leaves bright enough to send Addisyn fumbling for her sunglasses. "I'm supposed to show you where we are or whatever." She pointed vaguely down the beach. "That way."

Avery whistled softly as they approached the dock and leaned closer to Addisyn. "Some boat."

"For sure." The sparkling red party barge could have held at least fifteen people, with a fringed canopy and wraparound seating surrounding a built-in galley. Of course, had she really expected any less?

Darius took her hand and helped her on board, where Vera was waiting, as usual all fluttering smiles. "Happy Canada Day! And Addisyn, this is your sister? Yes, so nice to meet you too. And you brought a side dish? Oh, you didn't have to, but thank you so much. If you'll just take that to the galley."

Addisyn escaped to the rear of the boat and ducked under the canopy. "Where should I set this?"

"Here." Tina opened a miniature fridge and plucked the bowl from her hands, pausing to lift the aluminum foil from a corner. "Pasta salad. Ick. I hate that stuff."

Then don't eat it. Addisyn kept her voice calm. "Well, hopefully someone will like it."

"Oh, Mom likes it okay." Tina grabbed a bag of snack food and ripped into it, then held it out. "Jalapeño Cheetos. Want one?"

"No, thanks." Avery loved spicy foods, but they usually made

Addisyn have a sneezing fit. Not a great impression for Darius's family.

"Okay, then. You don't know what you're missing." Tina popped an orange crunch in her mouth and spoke around her mouthful. "Ready to do the family lake day thing?"

"You don't like boating?"

Tina shrugged. "The only good part is watching the hot guys on the stand-up paddleboards." She paused with another orange crunch halfway to her mouth and grinned. "Only thing worth risking bugs, sunburn, and heat for."

A roar ripped through the air, and the boat shuddered to life, the momentum sliding Addisyn off balance. Tina grabbed her arm with a laugh. "Always like that at first. Where do you want to sit?"

On the other side of the boat, Avery was apparently still entangled in Vera's looping conversation. Darius wasn't to be seen anywhere. But Kenzie was tucked into a corner of one of the bench seats, an almost visible isolation encircling her. Addisyn pointed. "By Kenzie?"

A gate seemed to close behind Tina's eyes. "Oh." But somehow the syllable held something quieter and heavier than her usual disdain. She frowned and rummaged in the Cheetos bag. "You go on over there. I, uh, need to clean up a few things here."

Addisyn shrugged and crossed the boat, attempting to time her steps with the pitching of the floor but still landing less-than-gracefully next to Kenzie. "Hey." She smiled at the younger girl. "Looking forward to today?"

"Yeah." Kenzie adjusted her sunglasses and glanced back toward the galley, where Tina was busily wiping down the already-spotless countertop.

Someday, she'd find out what had happened between those two. Addisyn glanced up as Darius slid into the seat on her other side.

"Hey, Addisyn? Remember me telling you about the glaciers?"

"Yes!" She scanned the white patches on the nearby mountains. "You said we'd see them from here."

"Right, well, there's Armchair Glacier." Darius pointed at a milky whiteness tucked into a bowl-shaped valley between two of the taller peaks. "Around nine thousand feet."

"Wow!" Addisyn squinted at the snowy brightness. "And that's thousands of years old?"

"It is." Darius shrugged. "Even after the Ice Age, some things never thawed."

Hard to imagine, in the warmth of the July sun.

There was a kind of calm to the afternoon that Addisyn hadn't expected. The blue of the lake caught the blue of the sky, and in between the peace hovered like a prayer. When the sun lowered itself behind the mountains, Trent cut the motor in front of a tree-crowned island.

"This is where we're cooking." Darius squeezed Addisyn's hand and stood up from the bench seat, wobbling slightly on the rocking boat. "Uncle Trent and I will go start the grill."

Vera recruited Tina and Kenzie to help her carry the food, but Avery lingered for a moment beside Addisyn. "This is a beautiful place, Ads. I can see why you love it so much."

"Yeah." Addisyn took a deep breath. The briny smell of the lake mingled with the incense of the pines, and the waves gently sloshed against the boat in a rhythm like a peaceful heartbeat. Ahead of them, the mountains welcomed the sun to its evening home.

Was it possible she was finally home too?

"I'm going to go take some pictures. See you in a minute."

Avery hurried onto the land, and Addisyn cocked her head. Pictures for Tyler, maybe? Hmm. She should really try to catch a glimpse of Avery's phone again before—

"Hello there, Addisyn."

She startled and squinted up at Trent. "Oh! I didn't hear you."

"Just came for a minute to get the briquettes while Darius sets up the grill." Trent fumbled with the package of charcoal in his hands. "Enjoy the ride today?"

"Yes. It was—" She searched for a more sophisticated-sounding word than *cool*. "Very pleasant."

"This boat is a high-end model. Aluminum hull instead of fiberglass, you know. Makes all the difference for a smooth ride." He stared at her as if daring her to disagree.

"Yes. I'm sure."

Trent shaded his eyes and glanced at the shore. "Kenzie's been doing better the last couple of weeks."

"Yes, she has." Why didn't Trent take the charcoal and go? Where was this conversation heading?

"Although still shaky on her rotations, I think."

"Yes. That's something we're working on." If only she weren't alone on the boat, but she couldn't see either Avery or Darius from here. Even Tina would have been welcome.

"So, Addisyn." Trent hefted the charcoal. "I did a little digging this week."

Her pulse increased. "Okay…"

Trent smiled, but the creases around his eyes didn't change. "I'm a straightforward man, Addisyn. So, forgive me if I call it like I see it."

Some shadow prickled over her. "Go on."

"I discovered that your previous coach was a man by the name of Brian Felding. Is that correct?"

And just like that, every peaceful thing about the day plummeted overboard. Panic slapped against her. "I—uh, yes." What had Trent found about her? And what had he been looking for in the first place?

"Interesting." Trent squinted toward the sun. "I understand he's been suspended by his agency for some conduct violations."

She linked her fingers together, swallowing her stuttering heartbeat. "Yes. So I understood as well."

"Apparently he had an *inappropriate* relationship with one of his clients."

Inappropriate. The word weaved through her thoughts like a poisonous vine, strangling all her newfound hope. And next Trent would ask—

"Would that skater happen to have been you, Addisyn?"

If only she could say no. If only she could tell Trent that she had no idea what he was talking about, that she would never make such horrible choices. Instead she clung to the tiny shred of dignity she had left. "I—I don't see how it is your business, Mr. Payne. With all respect."

"Yes. Exactly what I thought you would say." His tone frosted with a sudden shadow. "I will tell you why it is my business. Because you are dating my nephew." He paused for emphasis.

He was bringing Darius into this? Addisyn's heartrate notched higher. "Mr. Payne. Darius and I—our relationship is between us." She gripped the edge of the seat, her sweaty palms sliding on the leather. "Why do you—"

"Because Darius is—naive, shall we say. He always sees the best in people."

The truth of Trent's words slapped against her soul. Hadn't she worried about the same thing all along? That Darius was seeing her through the glowing lens of his own emotions, when really—

"Which is—touching. But also dangerous."

Dangerous. But what he meant was—s*he* was dangerous.

Trent was still talking. "He ruined his career and broke our family legacy with a single mistake." His gaze narrowed with a merciless intensity. "I don't want to see him make another one."

A mistake.

A nausea that had nothing to do with the rocking waves twisted her gut. That's how Trent saw her? As Darius's next disaster?

A mistake.

She'd been right all along. Every fear had told her nothing but the truth: she knew nothing about the kind of love Darius deserved, and she would only bring him down. And now—

Trent stepped back and tugged the brim of his ball cap, as if they'd just had a cordial conversation. "I told Darius at the beginning, and I'm telling you now." He narrowed his eyes at her. "No more mistakes."

And with that, he turned and headed onto the shore, his elongated shadow sliding after him as the boat pitched in waves far rougher than she'd realized.

△△   △△   △△

SOMEHOW ADDISYN MADE it off the boat. Somehow she filled a plate with grilled chicken. Somehow she made conversation with Avery and Kenzie while she pretended to pick at her food.

But Trent's words roared through her mind. *A mistake. A mistake. A mistake.*

No more mistakes.

Just as dusk deepened, Darius came up behind her and settled his hands on her shoulders. "Hey."

"Hey." She kept herself rigid.

"The fireworks will start in a minute." He pointed across the lake. "Let's walk down to the water. We'll see them better."

"Yeah, you two go ahead, Ads." Avery was gathering paper plates. She glanced skeptically toward Tina, withdrawn to the edge of the group and hunched over the glow of her phone screen. "Kenzie and I will help pick up here."

She'd rather swim back to the Village than be alone with Darius right now. But she allowed him to take her hand and lead her down to the margin of the beach. Sand squished into her shoes, the tree line now a dark shadow serrating the sky.

"Did you have a good time?" Darius tugged her closer to him, his arm across her shoulders.

"Yes." She tried to keep her voice normal.

"So—" He glanced across the silver sheet of the lake. "I want to talk with you about something."

His voice was suddenly taut with apprehension, and Addisyn blinked. "What's going on?"

"I—well—"

Foreboding tunneled through her stomach. She ducked from under his arm and turned to face him, struggling to analyze his expression in the dim light. "Darius, is something wrong?"

"No. No, not at all." He rubbed the back of his neck. "I want to talk about—about—us."

Us. The word twisted a knot in her already churning stomach. How many blows could she take today? "What do you mean?"

He reached for her hands with fingers that were far too cold. "Addisyn." He paused, swallowed. "I—I need to talk to you about where—where this is headed."

Where they were headed?

A mistake. A mistake. A—

Her heart thudded against the inside of her ribs. This was it. She was losing him. Trent was right, and Darius was getting ready to leave her alone in the dark where—

"I love you. I—I want to spend my life with you. And—and I need to know if you feel the same way."

Her expectations flipped upside down as her brain struggled to catch up. "Darius, are you—"

"I'm not proposing." His laugh was soft. "Trust me, I'd pick a more romantic spot. But I'm just—I'm letting you know." The sincerity in his eyes shone even through the dusk. "I want you to know what my intentions are. Where I'm planning for this—for us—to go."

But she was a mistake.

"Darius—" Her words were gone, completely ripped away by the surprise.

His expression was faltering now, his confidence fading to something more tentative. "Are you—are you okay? Should I not have—"

"Wait." She pulled her hands free. The shock was still spreading, her heart beating in triple time. "I need a minute."

She turned and almost ran to the other end of the beach. Then she sank to her knees on the scratchy sand as trembling raced through her body.

Darius wanted to marry her. *Her.* He wanted to *marry her.*

The trembling was getting worse, working its way deep into her core. She spread her palms on the sand, desperately grounding herself in some semblance of stability.

Tina had said something like that, hadn't she? And Avery? But Addisyn hadn't believed them. She'd never seen this coming. Never dreamed that Darius, her larger-than-life hero, would ask her to marry him. Why would he? She, who'd been so broken by all that she'd gone through?

The first firework exploded in the sky, a cascade of shimmering colors, and two strong hands brushed her shoulders. "Addisyn—I'm sorry—"

"No, Darius." She blinked and scrambled to her feet, the colors smearing behind her tears. "It's not your fault."

"So, does this—" He stopped, cleared his throat. "Are we not—not headed where I thought we were?"

Two fireworks whistled skyward, popping on each other's heels. Applause and cheers drifted from where the others were gathered.

"I don't know."

The silence between the explosions was loud. "I—I thought we were on the same page."

She couldn't listen to the pain in his voice—the pain she'd put there—one more second. "Darius, we are. I mean—" She stood and turned to him, watching the remnants of the fireworks in his eyes. "I'm sorry. I just need—" *To not be so broken. To not be so afraid. To rewind the clock to before I ever met Brian.* "I just need more time."

"Right." Confusion cracked his expression, but no anger. "I mean—sure, of course."

Addisyn watched the reflection of three more fireworks in his eyes before he spoke again. "I shouldn't have brought it up. I'm sorry. I didn't want to ruin this evening for you."

She'd just broken his heart, yet it was her he was thinking of. The realization shattered her soul a little bit more. "Darius, don't. This is my fault."

"But—I mean—" He looked down, scuffed his sandal over the beach. When he looked back up, his expression was more raw than she'd ever seen it. "You do—care, don't you?"

Care? Did he think the lukewarm word was all she felt for him? "I don't just *care*." Tears were trembling in her eyes, but she was powerless to hold them back. Instead she went to him, wrapped her arms around him, clung to his warmth and strength. "I—I love you, Darius. I've never felt about anyone the way I—" The intensity of her feelings was pulling her off balance, here on this dark beach with the sky exploding over their heads. She forced herself to take a breath before she let the desperation talk her into words and actions that would only confuse both of them more. "I love you." She stepped back, begging him to read the truth in her eyes. "I'm sorry I can't—not yet—"

He shook his head, then gently lowered his lips to meet hers. The kiss was heavy with the sorrow they both felt and left her aching when he pulled away. "Addisyn, it's okay." He swallowed, brushed his thumb over her tears. "I understand."

But he didn't understand. She could see the questions hanging in his eyes. Questions for which she had no answers.

"I'm, uh, I'm going back with the others." He stepped back, rubbing his hand alongside his face the way he did when he was weary or confused. Or both. "Are you—"

"I'll come. I'm staying here a minute."

He gave a single nod, then walked away, never once glancing up as the fireworks display exploded in its grand finale.

The smoke hung its heavy head over the beach, and Addisyn watched the last of the fireworks fade into cloudy remnants. The color was all dead now.

And all that was left were the ghosts.

△△   △△   △△

OF ALL THE places for everything to fall apart, it had to be on an island, trapping Addisyn into the rest of the evening. Somehow she'd talked with Vera, dodged the tension between Tina and Kenzie, avoided Darius's wounded look, and ignored the questions in Avery's eyes. All while feeling as empty as the discarded shells of the fireworks.

Then had come the tense ride home in the car. With Kenzie and Avery in the backseat, there was no chance that her earlier conversation with Darius might revive. Instead, they'd both kept things on the surface, plowing diligently through dialogue about the boat, the fireworks, the center, the decorations downtown. Anything and everything to keep the dangerous subject stuffed down.

But Darius hadn't reached across the console for her hand.

Back at the house, she told him goodnight and got out of the car without waiting for the kiss she no longer expected. His car idled behind her while she fumbled to unlock the door, but she stepped inside without looking back.

"Where do you want this?" Kenzie cradled the still-mostly-full bowl of pasta salad.

Darius's tires slowly crunched over the gravel outside. He'd given up. "Just—on the counter." She'd have to find room in the refrigerator. She set her bag down, washed her hands, and grabbed a mug from the cabinet.

Avery narrowed her eyes. "What are you doing?"

"I'm making coffee."

Kenzie blinked, stifling a yawn. "Isn't it too late for coffee?"

Addisyn glanced at the microwave clock. 10:18, but who cared? She'd be up all night anyway, caffeine or not. "It'll be okay."

"I'm not supposed to drink caffeine after supper."

"Well, I'm a grown-up, so I can do whatever I want." Ha. If only. She popped a pod in the Keurig and turned around just in time to see Kenzie yawn again. "Kenz, why don't you go on to bed?" She infused a brightness she didn't feel into her tone. "Remember, we're hiking tomorrow."

"That's right." Kenzie's tired eyes sparked to life again. "I wanna get up early. G'night."

"Night."

Her footsteps had barely faded down the hall when Avery folded her arms. "Okay, spill it. What's going on?"

"Nothing." The Keurig beeped. Addisyn pulled out the pod and watched the thick, dark liquid run into her cup. A Cuban. The drink Darius had introduced her to. The one she'd forever know as his.

"I don't believe you."

If she allowed the tiniest crack in her dam, her emotions would surge past her barriers. "A, it's fine. It was just—" She searched for a more general explanation to placate Avery. "Darius's family, you know."

"See, I don't believe that." Avery planted herself by the coffee maker. "Look, I'm not going to bed until you tell me—"

"Avery, I said I'm fine!" She banged the mug onto the table harder than she'd intended, and a few stinging drops splattered on her hand. She sighed. "I'm just tired tonight, okay? And you need to go to bed too." She forced a smile. "Kenzie will have us both up at the crack of dawn, you know."

The questions didn't leave her sister's eyes. "Can we talk more about it tomorrow?"

"Sure. Yes." Anything to get Avery gone before Addisyn's straining stamina couldn't hold back her emotions any longer.

Avery gave her one last uncertain, reaching glance. Then she sighed and turned toward the hall. "All right. I'm going to bed."

"Okay. I'll try not to wake you up when I come in."

But Avery was already gone. Addisyn slumped down in a chair. She took a sip of the strong, sweet coffee, but it didn't begin to warm the cold place at the core of her being. The one that had frozen to ice from the moment she'd watched Darius break beneath that exploding sky.

She could look back now, read their relationship backwards, and everything he'd said made sense. He'd been planning this all along, doing everything methodically, honorably. He'd been her friend, then asked her to start dating. He'd invited her to his home for the summer and made arrangements for a job and housing for her. He'd introduced her to his family and showcased every detail of his life. In fact, he'd walked a path straight to this moment. Letting her know his intentions was simply the next right step, the next milestone on the journey he'd unwaveringly traveled.

So why hadn't she seen it coming? What *had* she thought? That they would date for a while and then just stop? That their relationship wasn't deepening every day in a way that could only lead to one foregone conclusion? That Darius would simply be content to be her permanent boyfriend—hovering forever just outside her vulnerability?

No, the truth was she simply hadn't thought ahead at all. Exactly what Avery always accused her of doing. She'd just been so caught up in the moment. What with the worry over Kenzie and the frustration with Trent and the anxiety of trying to measure up, she hadn't once thought ahead to what might happen.

Or maybe she had. She stared down into her coffee. In the back of her mind, hadn't she sort of expected that Darius would walk away? That one day, he'd see her the way she really was?

Had she held herself back all along because she'd believed there would be an end?

Even now, Darius's words couldn't sink through her disbelief. Out of all the girls he could have chosen, he wanted *her*? He thought *she* was the one for him to link his life with? The idea would have been exhilarating if it weren't so terrifying.

A mistake.

The accusation scalded across her soul like a branding iron. A mistake. Just what she'd always been, and it hadn't taken Trent's words to remind her of the truth. So she couldn't let Darius take a risk on her. He'd already been wounded by her broken pieces. If she committed to him the way he asked, she'd have to invite him into every dark corner of her soul. And she wasn't ready for that.

In the silence of the house, the ghosts raised by Trent's words peered mockingly from the corners. Every one of them with Brian's sarcastic sneer.

Brian. Again, she was back there, in the dark corners of their relationship. For sure, Brian had never been interested in commitment—the one time she'd hesitantly brought up the topic of marriage, two years after she moved in with him, he'd laughed. "*What, turning traditional on me?*"

"No." That answer had been quick. *Traditional* meant Avery and rules and morality. All the things she'd tried to dodge, back then. "*But, Brian—*" She couldn't explain her yearning, her need to receive his promise, to know that he hadn't made her life a minefield just to abandon her in the shrapnel.

"*Not trying to tie me down, are you, Addisyn?*" His eyes had narrowed with the warning she knew all too well. "*What, you don't trust me or—*"

"*No! No.*" She cringed now to realize how quickly she'd waved her white flag. "*I was just thinking it might be—nice.*"

His laugh was caustic. "*Well, your holy-roller sister thinks we're married already, living how we are.*"

As angry as she'd been with Avery at that time, she'd still flinched.

"*Come on, baby.*" He'd pulled her toward him with a grip that was a little too tight and pressed a forceful kiss on her lips. Then he'd drawn back and smirked. "*See? Who needs a piece of paper?*"

His kiss had felt like contamination, but she'd never brought up the subject again.

Her hand was shaking on her mug. She carried the now-cold coffee to the sink, watching it swirl down the drain. She was shivering now, as if the glacier they'd seen today had lodged itself in her chest.

The glacier. What had Darius said?

Even after the Ice Age ended, some things never thawed.

The terrible truth of his words doubled her shivering. Because he was right. She'd escaped from Brian, yes. But she'd never be able to escape what he'd done to her. Like the glacial lake itself, the terrain of her heart had been forever reshaped.

The microwave clock blinked at her. 11:09? Had she really just spent almost an hour mourning what could never be changed?

She turned the water on hot and rinsed out her coffee mug, the steam rising against her shallow breath. She brushed away the tears she hadn't realized she was crying. She couldn't let herself fall apart the way she wanted to, because tomorrow she had to be ready to take Kenzie up Wildcrest.

Kenzie. The faintest flicker of hope brushed its timid wings against her heart. Things were too late for her—Brian had made sure of that. But if they could find the bear tomorrow, then Kenzie would call forward a courage she'd buried until now. And maybe—maybe she wouldn't make Addisyn's mistakes.

And that would have to be enough.

CHAPTER 20

Pre-dawn gray was just beginning to wash around the edges of the landscape. Kenzie frowned at the digital clock on her nightstand. 4:08 in the morning. Still at least two and a half or even three hours before Addisyn would get up. Somehow, even with all the excitement that lay ahead, she and Avery were apparently sleeping soundly.

But for Kenzie, anticipation had carbonated her blood, jerking her awake almost an hour ago and sending her thoughts chasing circles. So she'd been quietly readying her backpack and gathering her belongings, looking for some outlet for the pent-up adrenaline.

She glanced at the lumpy backpack on her bed, and the excitement tingled over her again. She hugged herself with a whisper-squeal that wouldn't wake the other girls. After all this time, she was finally going to see the spirit bear again! She just knew it.

But she wasn't finished packing yet. She aimed the flashlight around her room until she found the paper map from the cultural center. What else? Her portable cell charger and earbuds were already in the front pocket. Oh! Her camera. This time, when she saw the bear, she'd be capturing proof that even Tina couldn't doubt.

Tina. Kenzie bit her lip and remembered her mom's words before she'd left. *And Tina will be there…you'll have so much fun with her. You two are best friends!*

Kenzie rolled her eyes. The statement had only confirmed what she'd already known—her mom truly had no clue what was going on in her life. Not if she still thought her daughter's best friend was a girl who hadn't spoken to her in the last five years. Mom didn't realize that the cousin who'd been more like a sister was gone now, stuck somewhere inside the shell of a sarcastic girl who'd long ago left Kenzie behind.

Oh, Tina. Where did you go?

She glanced into the monochrome world outside. There was a faint spark of light on the eastern horizon now—enough to see the shadowy outline of Tina's window.

What if—what if she tried to talk to Tina before they left? Reminded her of the spirit bear and invited her to come along and tried to find their way back to friendship?

Nonsense. Of course she couldn't do that. Tina had already made her disdain of Kenzie clear. She had no interest in a spirit-bear search. Anyway, she might tell her parents.

Kenzie squirmed uncomfortably. She knew exactly how big of a fit Uncle Trent would throw if he had any idea of what they were doing. He'd been trying to keep her under lock and key because of—well, everything that had happened. With the doctors, and all. And a five-mile hike in the wilderness wasn't at all what Dr. Drees would recommend.

So what? She clenched her jaw defiantly, silently daring the darkened room to stop her. This was her last desperate chance to reclaim what was left of her. If the legend was true—then every part of her nightmare would end, and she'd finally walk free.

But what if the legend was just that—a myth?

Icy fingers of anxiety slid down her neck. Was she risking all this for nothing? Or what if it didn't work? Or maybe—

Stop. Wasn't that one of the reasons her health had spiraled out of control? Too many *what ifs*? And did her concerns matter now, anyway? She had to take this step. Had to trust that the story was true, and that she'd see the bear, and that everything would happen just as she'd dreamed.

She rolled up a jacket, tucking it on top of the other things in her backpack, then zipped up the bag and stared at it. Everything was ready, and she still had to wait at least another two hours. Maybe she could hop on Instagram.

She crawled onto her quilt, propped her back against the headboard, and reached for her phone, squinting at the brightness of the screen. The airbrushed photos flicked by, a hypnotic river of unreality. She kept scrolling half-heartedly, her hand growing heavy, and she was in some twilight place on the fringes of sleep when Marie's face was suddenly on the screen—holding—

In an instant, she jerked back to alertness. Surely that wasn't—

Her eyes darted over the caption. Got my letter today! @montreal_skate_six, here I come! Soooooo excited to be performing in Ottawa this fall!

The disbelief drained to her stomach, knotting itself inside her. No. No, it wasn't possible! She pinched on the photo until she could see the official logo at the top of the paper Marie held.

Skate Six. Marie was going to Skate Six. Marie, who deserved no opportunity as golden as this. Marie, who had…

She closed her eyes, but she could still see the girl. See her the way she'd looked on Kenzie's first day at the Montreal Skating Center, when Kenzie had still been confident and calm.

And fifteen pounds heavier.

"*Hi there.*" Marie had approached her outside the lockers. "*What's your name?*"

She'd been lonely enough to interpret Marie's words as an outstretched hand, and hope had buoyed her heart. "*I'm Kenzie.*"

Marie's smile had stretched acidic. "*Well, Kenzie, I'm afraid you're misdirected.*" Her eyes had flicked over Kenzie with an evident judgment. "*The weight-loss classes are down the hall.*"

The other girls had snickered, and a coldness shivered in Kenzie's chest. But she'd lifted her chin. "*I'm a skater.*"

"*Really?*" Marie had raised her perfectly stenciled eyebrows. "*I thought whales liked to be under the water. Not on top of it.*"

Looking back now, the worst part hadn't been what Marie had done. No, the worst part was what everyone else didn't do. The way all those watching eyes shifted away from her silent cry for help.

And it had only gotten worse from there. For months and months of her dwindling bravery, it had only gotten worse.

The tight fist of the memories closed around her heart, and she threw the iPhone with a scarlet surge of wounded rage, Marie's smug smile thudding to the floor.

Marie had stolen so much from her already. And now she would have this too?

And Kenzie would be left in second place. As always. Chasing that elusive target through a labyrinth where every choice demanded more perfection than she could produce.

But wasn't she to blame too? She'd gotten sidetracked, just as she'd promised herself not to. The hiking and the driving and the fun times downtown with Addisyn and Avery—she'd tricked herself into thinking that all of it might help. Instead, it had only fractured her focus, made her forget how important it was to keep her brain trained only on success. And while she'd been having frivolous fun, Marie had been stealing her chance at a comeback.

Panic was overtaking her anger, her breath coming in snatches again. She dropped her head into her shaking hands. She'd gotten careless, but she wouldn't do it again. And she knew just what the moment needed. She rolled off the bed and fumbled through her bag until her sweaty fingers closed on the little pill bottle.

She yanked frantically at the cap, the urgency screaming in her ear, and then the little orange pills tumbled into her palm—five of them. She picked out two, intending to dump the rest in the bottle, but hesitated. Well—why not? A double dose wouldn't hurt, right?

Some warning began pounding in her chest, but she hurled her reasoning its way. The pills were all natural, or mostly. She knew lots of girls who took far more than she did. It was just for this week, to make up for her laxness.

And Marie…

The mental image of Marie gripping that acceptance letter with that smirky smile decided it. A few gulps from the bottle of water on her nightstand, and the pills were gone.

But Marie's words were not.

△△ △△ △△

295

AFTER A NIGHT of spinning circles around the whole mess with Darius, exhaustion—on every level—had stolen every trace of Addisyn's enthusiasm. But for Kenzie's sake, she'd kept her act together. Even though the girl actually hadn't said that much on the drive over to the trailhead.

"All right." She put the car in park in the center lot—Avery had found some spur trail that would keep them from having to drive that bone-shaking dirt road. She glanced at the dashboard time. Just after nine o'clock. Not as early a start as she'd hoped for, but still good. She climbed out of the car and rubbed her hands together with what she hoped was an eager expression. "Let's do this."

"All the way to the ridge up there." Avery's expression was grim.

That impossibly distant ridge was the top? Addisyn swallowed hard. "Oh. Right."

Avery swung her backpack onto her shoulders and walked beside Addisyn toward the trailhead. "We don't have to do this, you know."

"No, A." The words came out a little more forcefully than she'd intended. She relaxed her tone. "This will be fun. Right, Kenzie?"

No answer, so Addisyn glanced over her shoulder. Kenzie was still leaning against the car, downing a bottle of water. Had she not been behind them? "Kenzie!" She waved to the girl. "Come on, we're starting!"

"Sorry." Kenzie pushed off the car and trudged their way, slowly twisting the water bottle in her hands.

"Are you excited? This is the big day."

"Uh—yeah." The corners of Kenzie's mouth lifted slightly in an expression that might have been intended as a smile.

Well, if Kenzie was no more excited than that, maybe Addisyn would take Avery's advice after all. "Everything okay?"

Kenzie rotated her head, as if her shoulders were stiff. "I—I feel a little carsick."

Not surprising, on that curvy Callaghan Road. "Well, that should wear off with the hiking."

"Okay, let's go." Avery unfurled the map and studied it one more time as they started up the trail. "It looks like our first intersection is in about a mile and a quarter. We'll take the Everhill Trail."

Despite Avery's dire predictions, the trail wasn't that bad. Narrow, yes, but still easy to follow and not as steep as Addisyn had expected. But Kenzie still looked a little unsettled, and Avery was watching trees and clouds with a preoccupied expression devoid of the peace her face normally held in the woods. And the silence that sank over them all didn't feel like the usual restful quiet of nature.

Addisyn sighed and watched a raven circle overhead. Maybe she was just imagining things. Or projecting her own angst on the situation. Especially since Darius's words were still hovering over her thoughts like the dark shadow of the bird.

You do care, don't you?

Oh, she cared. She cared far too much.

She was so wrapped in the worry that she nearly ran into Avery when her sister stopped in front of her. "Well, here's the first intersection."

"Already?" Had she really let her thoughts spiral for over a mile?

Avery glanced at her watch. "Thirty minutes, yeah. Let me double-check our route here." She fumbled for the map. "Seems like it was the Clear Creek Trail, but—" She glanced over her shoulder and frowned. "Kenzie? Are you okay?"

Kenzie looked up from the log she'd slumped onto and tried to nod. "I just—I still feel sick."

"Still?" Concern creased Avery's brow. "It might be the elevation here."

Altitude sickness. Darius had talked about that before, how the body could rebel at high elevation. And if anybody knew the signs, it ought to be her mountain-girl sister.

Avery pulled a bottle of water out of her own backpack and tossed it to Kenzie. "Drink some of this and take some deep breaths, okay?"

Kenzie nodded and opened the bottle obediently, and Avery angled the map toward Addisyn. "Anyway, what I was saying was that we can take this trail to the North Forest Crest and then join onto the ridge, or we could also go through the Sherman Trail, which would make the distance a little—"

Addisyn nodded along, but a weird feeling was starting to itch deep inside. Like something was more wrong than Kenzie was letting on. The girl's face was chalky, even paler than normal, and her eyes were oddly clouded.

"Hey, A." She kept her voice low and nudged her sister's arm. "I think Kenzie really is sick."

Avery glanced at Kenzie over the edge of the map. "It really could be the altitude." Her words were hushed as well. "We're a thousand feet above the valley."

"Yeah, but she already felt bad down at the trailhead, remember? And that's the same level as the center."

Avery pressed her lips together. "You're right."

"I'm going to talk to her." Addisyn crossed the trail and perched on Kenzie's log. "Hey." She kept her tone casual. "You don't look so good, Kenz."

Kenzie shook her head and swiped a sheen of sweat off her forehead. "I'm okay."

"What all feels bad?"

"Just my stomach, and—and that's it." Kenzie edged away from Addisyn. "I'm fine. Really." She stood but lurched suddenly forward.

Addisyn leaped up and grabbed her arm. "Are you dizzy?"

Kenzie closed her eyes and gave the slightest nod.

"Then it is the altitude." Avery was at her side. "Okay, just take some deep breaths. And then we should go back down."

Kenzie's eyes flew open. "No! I want to find the spirit bear."

Addisyn hated to disappoint the girl, but she had to agree with Avery. "Look, Kenzie, if you're already sick—I mean, the altitude is going to get worse."

"I promise. I'm fine." Kenzie stepped away from Addisyn's grip and shrugged her backpack on, her movements sure and steady again. "I feel better now. Honest. Maybe I was dehydrated too."

Avery glanced at Addisyn, her eyebrows raised. Addisyn hesitated. Boy, she hated decisions like this. She probably shouldn't risk taking Kenzie higher in elevation. But on the flip side, how could she cancel something that meant so much to the girl?

"Come on." Kenzie planted her hands on her hips and jerked her head toward the trail. "Aren't we going?"

Addisyn shrugged and fell into step behind her. "Okay." She ignored the disapproving stare Avery was sending her way. "But let me know if you start feeling bad again, deal?"

"Deal." Kenzie was hiking fast, as if to make up for lost time.

Avery fell into step beside Addisyn. "Ads, don't you think–"

"It's important to her." Her resolve was too flimsy to push against Avery's scrutiny. "Do you think she might get better hiking? Like, her body might adjust?"

"It's not likely. And it probably didn't help that she had such a big day yesterday either."

Yesterday. The ghosts she'd sidestepped momentarily invaded her mind again. "Yeah."

"Speaking of—" Avery kicked at a rock and slid Addisyn a sideways glance—"are you ever going to tell me what happened?"

Addisyn kept her eyes fixed on Kenzie's purple backpack. "Not right now."

"Why not?"

"Because I don't want to." Why was Kenzie hiking so quickly? The gap between them was widening rapidly.

Avery adjusted the bill of her ball cap. "But if you would tell me what happened, then maybe—"

The tension of the last two days boiled over. "A, can we just wait until we're off the mountain before you keep prying into yesterday? It's not like we don't have more pressing—"

A slipping, scraping noise suddenly tumbled down the trail. Addisyn glanced up just in time to see Kenzie crumpling, her legs melting beneath her. And then she slammed into the packed dirt and lay still.

"Kenzie!" The word was a shriek, but Kenzie didn't move.

Addisyn flung herself forward, churning up the trail faster even than Avery. Just as she ran up, Kenzie rolled onto her back with a moan.

"Kenzie, what's going on?" She dropped to her knees, frantically scanning the girl for injuries, illness, anything. "Why—"

Kenzie was panting, her breath dipping shallow in and out of her chest. She gripped Addisyn's arm with sweaty palms, her expression wracked with a fear Addisyn didn't understand. "I—don't—"

"Addisyn, here." Thank goodness, Avery was there beside her. She pressed Kenzie's wrist, her face tightening for six slow seconds. "Her pulse is around one eighty." She gripped Kenzie's shoulders. "Kenzie, talk to us. Do you have any food allergies? Were you stung by anything?"

Kenzie shook her head. Her eyes were darker than normal. "I—I just—" She was shivering now. Goosebumps prickled on her arms and legs even in the summer heat.

"Kenzie, it's okay." Addisyn wrapped her arm around Kenzie and blinked at the sharpness of the girl's shoulder blades. Gosh, had Kenzie always been that thin? She glanced at Avery. "What should we do?"

"This has to be some kind of allergic reaction." Avery shook her head and slipped her cell phone back in her pocket. "I don't have service up here. We've got to get her down."

Her own pulse was probably as fast as Kenzie's. "How on earth can we do that? We're a mile and a half from the trailhead. Look, you'll have to hike down and get help, and I'll stay with—"

"Addisyn." The mask of calmness her sister wore in emergencies was slipping. "We may not have time to do that."

Wait. Did Avery mean—

The thought redoubled her panic, so she shoved it away and refocused on Kenzie. "Okay, Kenz." She tried to steady her own voice, to project a measure of Avery's calm. "We need to get you down, all right? You've gotta try to walk."

"I can't." Kenzie's voice was pitched high, her words pushing against panic. "My legs—everything feels too—too shaky."

"You have to." She could be as stubborn as Kenzie if she needed to be. Addisyn slung Kenzie's arm over her own shoulders and stood, nodding at Avery. "Okay, so Avery's going to help you from the other side."

"That's right." Avery ducked beneath Kenzie's other arm. "Come on. We're going to help you."

"It's—my fault." The words wheezed out. "I—messed up—"

She wasn't making sense, but no wonder. Addisyn shook her head. "Hey, don't try to talk, okay? Let's just get you down."

The trip down was a nightmarish blur. Slippery rocks and powdery dirt and tree branches that slapped her face. Kenzie's desperate grip on her shoulder and the snatching sound of her breaths and the terror trapped behind Avery's frozen face. The awkward stumbling of a three-legged race and the faster flutter in Kenzie's wrist.

And then they were a quarter of a mile from the end, and Kenzie was sinking once more to the ground, and Avery was shoving Addisyn forward. "Get Trent. Go!"

She sprinted down the mountain, the rocks and roots rising to meet her frantic footfalls. What if Kenzie—

The dirt road opened before her. Oh, why hadn't they parked at the trailhead? She tore down the road, momentum catching her on its wings as the way tunneled into the campus of the center. "Trent! Trent!" She screamed his name without slowing her pace.

The office building loomed before her, sickeningly silent.

"Trent! Help! Someone—"

The door flew open, and Tina appeared. "Addisyn, what's going on?"

"Kenzie!" She stumbled to a stop, gasping out fragments of the explanation. "We were hiking—she's sick—needs hospital—"

Tina took the steps in one leap. "Where?" She grabbed Addisyn's arm, dragging her toward the parking lot and the spotless Lexus.

"The trailhead. She collapsed." Addisyn tumbled into the passenger seat. Her boots stamped dusty prints across the floormats, but Tina didn't seem to care anymore.

"God." The cry behind the word could have been a prayer or a swear. Tina shoved the little car into reverse. "Where's your sister?"

"With Kenzie." The panic she'd held in for so long was bubbling for release. She dug her fingernails into her palms as Tina lurched over the rutted road. "There!"

Avery was just stumbling off the trail, Kenzie's arm stretched over her shoulders. Addisyn rolled down the window. "Avery, how is she?"

"Her pulse is faster." Avery half-dragged Kenzie to the backseat and fell in beside her as Tina's wheels screeched in a U-turn that slung them into each other.

Addisyn glanced over her shoulder. Dark circles were sinking around

Kenzie's eyes, and her shaking was getting worse. And still, that raw panic on her face. Did she know what was wrong?

"It's okay, Kenz." Avery pulled Kenzie close to her side, rubbing the girl's bony arm soothingly. "You're going to be okay."

But the helplessness on her sister's face didn't match her words.

△△　△△　△△

ADDISYN SLUMPED ON the vinyl chair in the waiting room. The last hour had been both too slow and too fast, and the whiplash of the emotions was draining through her.

Tina had called her parents on the way, and they had been waiting when she screeched into the hospital parking lot on two wheels, somehow completing a thirty-minute trip in nearly half the time. Avery and Addisyn had all but carried Kenzie into the waiting room, and she'd been taken back to a room immediately, flanked by her relatives.

Leaving Addisyn in the waiting room with Avery.

"What on earth could have happened?" Avery's tone sounded as exhausted as Addisyn felt.

"I don't know." She leaned forward over her knees. "Do you think she ate something bad? Maybe yesterday at the picnic?"

"We all ate the same thing, and nobody else is sick." Avery shook her head. "It looked more like an allergy to me. Does she have any allergies?"

"She's allergic to cats. Nothing else that I know of." She swallowed. "Will she be okay?"

Avery paused a moment too long. "I hope so."

Why didn't they have any news yet? She shifted on the hard chair. "Thanks for helping me get her down. You knew exactly what to do."

"Comes with living in the mountains. I'm glad I was there to help." Avery bumped Addisyn's shoulder gently. "But you could have done it without me."

Her sister was wrong. Addisyn would probably still be standing helplessly on the mountain if Avery hadn't been with her. Just as unprepared as usual. If only she'd listened to Avery's misgivings in the first place.

"I can't just sit here." Avery stood, shuffling her feet restlessly. "I'm going to walk around. Want to come with me?"

"No. I want to be here if—you know."

"I do." Avery squeezed Addisyn's shoulder and headed toward the exit. "I have my phone. Call me if you have any news. I'm going to be praying."

Prayer. Of course her sister would be the one to think of that. Why hadn't she remembered? Addisyn bowed her head. *Dear God*—

The words stalled there. This was all her fault. God would know that. She'd seen Kenzie acting oddly at the trailhead. She should have never taken her up the mountain.

"They're still running tests."

Addisyn blinked and looked up just as Tina plopped into the seat next to her. "Oh."

Tina cleared her throat. "Um—why were you guys in the woods?"

Did it matter? "Hiking." She kept the word short.

"Were you, uh—looking for the spirit bears?"

Tina had remembered that? Addisyn shrugged. "Yes. It was important to Kenzie."

"And you thought that would help her?"

Seriously? In the middle of everything, Tina was still going to inject her snarky self? She who'd ignited the entire mess simply because she wouldn't part with her stupid cat for six weeks? "Yeah, I did, okay? What is this, Twenty Questions?"

"Whoa, whatever!" Tina's eyes flashed hard. "I was just asking."

Fear and frustration snarled together in her soul. "Yes, well, I think you've done enough when it comes to the bears. Kenzie was really upset you didn't believe her, you know."

Tina's expression changed slightly. "What? You mean—"

She'd regret it later, but for now, the words tumbled out recklessly. "I mean that when you found out what she was doing, you made her feel stupid. In fact, you went out of your way to harass her in front of your dad."

Something broken dropped over Tina's face. "Look, it's not that—" She took her glasses off and rubbed her eyes, then clenched her jaw.

"Never mind. Believe what you want." She jammed her glasses back on and stalked toward the restrooms.

"Tina?" Addisyn scrambled up and started the same direction when rapid footsteps tapped along the tile hallway. She turned to see Darius hurrying into the waiting room. "Darius?" Every awkwardness from last night reignited. "How did you—"

"Uncle Trent called me." Worry had written its way across his forehead. He glanced over her shoulder. "There he comes."

"Darius. Addisyn." Trent nodded curtly as he marched up. "We have news."

Every other concern fled. "How is she? Is—"

"She's overdosed."

The floor melted beneath Addisyn's feet. "What?"

"Just what I said." Trent scraped a hand hard across his chin. "There's evidently a—I don't know, some kind of supplement she's been taking."

Why would she have been taking some strange supplement? And how come she'd never mentioned anything?

"Was this—a prescription, or—" Darius sounded as confused as Addisyn felt.

"No, she ordered it online, apparently." Trent hesitated. "It's for weight loss."

Weight loss? A good gust of wind could have blown Kenzie away. Why—

Trent took a deep breath and focused on something over Addisyn's head. "She's—she's had some trouble with her eating before."

Trouble with her eating?

But then the memories were returning, filling in the details of the sickening story. All those little things that hadn't made sense. A painfully thin girl with a white-knuckle grip on life. That permanently half-full bowl of cereal she picked at in the mornings. Her refusal to eat the Nanaimo bar at first. Addisyn shook her head. "So—Dr. Drees—"

"Is her therapist." Trent's jaw was grim. "Counseling, weigh-ins. It was supposed to be follow-up. She was—rather bad off last year. She spent six months doing an outpatient program. We thought she was better now, but—"

Darius shook his head. "Uncle Trent—I didn't know."

"Yes, well." Trent shook his head. "She admitted she took over double the dose this morning. The doctor looked up the name, and it has sibutramine."

"What's that?"

"Some kind of drug that messes with metabolism. Causes low blood pressure and fast heart rate too, because it speeds up your system. And anxiety and headaches and all other kinds of complications." The weight of his words reflected from his face. "It's illegal in drugs in the U.S. I guess she heard about these somewhere, figured out how to get them online. She's been taking them for almost a year."

"Will she be okay?"

Trent rubbed his eyes. "She feels pretty bad right now. Her heart rate is still elevated and irregular. Fortunately her liver tests came back normal. Still waiting for the kidney results. She's on an IV for now."

The ramifications spun through Addisyn's mind. All this time… Why hadn't Kenzie told her any of this? "Does she need—"

"I think it's obvious you don't know what she needs."

His tone was like a slap. "Mr. Payne, I—"

"Kenzie says you all were in the woods." Twin creases furrowed his brow. "What was that about?"

There was no denying it anymore. She hung her head, the words like a white flag. "We were looking for the spirit bears."

Darius blinked. "For *what?*"

Trent huffed out a breath, ignoring his nephew. "Are you kidding me right now?"

"It was important to Kenzie." Addisyn tried to keep her voice steady. "I thought it might help her."

"Well, it obviously didn't." His tone was rising, a storm gathering on his face.

Darius cleared his throat. "Now, Uncle Trent, I—"

"Don't start with me, Darius." Trent spun to face his nephew. "We had this conversation, when Addisyn first arrived. Remember? I told you I didn't think she was competent enough for this position. And you—" His tone was a wagging finger. "You assured me she would do a fine job."

"Hold on a minute." A reckless kind of rage was rising, and Addisyn stepped in front of Trent again. "This isn't Darius's fault. Don't you think I should have known about her health history when she came? That was pertinent information that I wasn't provided with." She took a deep breath, meeting his steely eyes. "Maybe because you hoped I would fail."

"Hoped you would fail?" Trent's eyebrows shot into stiff peaks. "That's ludicrous, Addisyn. Kenzie was—sensitive about the whole issue. She didn't want it told to everyone, and I respected her privacy."

Darius stepped forward again. "Addisyn, let's—"

"Darius, don't." This was her fight. She locked her jaw and stared at Trent. "You asked me to help her. How was I supposed to help her when I didn't know what was going on?"

"Well, you've helped her straight into a terrible situation." Trent flung his arm toward the hospital room. "She needed to be supervised and monitored. Not left to wind up in dangerous situations."

"She needed a *friend*." The words were louder than she intended. "Don't you think that's part of her problem? That everybody has treated her like—like she's broken? She needed someone who—"

"She needed a leader." Trent's tone wilted her words. "A guide. A— a mentor. Which I hoped—and Darius promised—you could be for her." He paused just long enough to slide an accusing glance at Darius. "Kenzie was in a delicate place when she came here, Addisyn. She needed support. But you didn't provide that for her."

His words were like a blow to the gut. Addisyn sucked in a reflexive breath. "Mr. Payne—"

"Instead of trying to keep an eye on her, to make sure she was okay, you let her drag you all over the woods looking for a stupid legend that was never true anyway. Don't you realize that's the last thing she needed? Her body was already under stress, and you added to it." He paused to deliver his final blow. "You can stand here all night and tell me you wanted to help Kenzie. But you see her now? All you did was make things worse."

She couldn't breathe. Couldn't move. *A mistake.*

"You were already untrustworthy when you came here. Against my better judgment, and on Darius's recommendation, I gave you the benefit of the doubt. But now—" He glanced toward the hospital rooms, and suddenly, worry and weariness replaced his anger. "You just allowed my niece to nearly kill herself."

He turned and marched off down the tile hallway, his words hanging like swords around her soul. He was right, wasn't he? If not for her, Kenzie would be—

"Addisyn?" Darius's hand was on her elbow. "Talk to me. What's going on?"

More than she'd realized. Obviously. "I—I don't know."

"Okay…" He shook his head, as if unsure which conversational thread to tug first. "What's this about—bears?"

"It was something—" She was too tired to explain the whole rigmarole right now. "Never mind. It was just something I was trying to help her with."

"But—Uncle Trent told you not to?"

His words snapped like a dry stick in her soul. "Trent? Seriously, Darius? All you can think of is Trent?"

"No, no!" He shook his head. "It's just that we talked about this. At the park that day. About how you needed to make sure you didn't—"

"Didn't what? Didn't step on his toes?" The anger was racing away faster than her words could catch up. "Well, guess what? Kenzie's the way she is because of him and people like him."

"People like what?"

"People who make success their god." She all but hissed the words. "People who have pressured her and prodded her and tried to squeeze her into their box. I didn't know about the pills, Darius. So I was trying to do anything I could to reach her."

"But I thought we decided—"

"That it was a bad idea. Of course you did." Her words tumbled over each other. "Because all you care about is making your uncle happy. Everything comes back to him for you. Even that first night—when he was so harsh to me—you just let him."

His expression tightened. "Addisyn, I wish you wouldn't keep saying stuff like that. You don't understand—"

"I understand that you'd rather placate him than try to reach someone who needs help. Or take a stand." Her voice caught, but she pushed forward. "It's like I said. You're afraid of him. Plain and simple."

"Take a stand? I thought we agreed—" He broke off, spread his hands. "But clearly, I don't know what you're thinking anymore."

She flinched. "Darius—not here."

"Then where?" His expression changed, the brokenness shimmering through his eyes. "You won't ever fully open up to me. Every time I think you're about to, you shut yourself away again. I just can't seem to get through to you anymore." The fire in his eyes cooled somewhat. "Come on. Let's talk about this. Tell me what's going on."

Talk about it? What was there to talk about, when everything she'd hoped had hit concrete and shattered like delicate glass? She'd made so many mistakes, but this was her worst one yet. And all this time, while she'd been hoping to save Kenzie from choosing the wrong road—well, the girl had detoured long ago.

Darius was waiting for her answer. She stepped back. "I'll never be Avery."

His face wrinkled with confusion, but before he could respond, Tina trudged up. "Addisyn, uh, I can drive you and Avery back to the center to get your car." She shrugged one shoulder. "We've done enough here."

"Okay." Addisyn turned away from Darius without looking back and followed Tina out of the waiting room.

Because she was right.

Addisyn had already done enough.

CHAPTER 21

She hadn't found a spirit bear. And she'd lost the last bit of herself.

The night was dark, the moon a dull scrap over the mountains. Kenzie slid down farther into the car seat and glanced at the dashboard clock through eyes scratchy with exhaustion. It was nearly midnight. The hike this morning seemed as if it had happened in a past life.

Since all her tests had come back fine, the hospital had let her go after a twelve-hour observation period. Uncle Trent had signed her discharge papers without a word and maintained his echoing silence all during the car ride home. Not that she could blame him.

The bars of the gate slid shadows across the car as they turned in the driveway. Uncle Trent cleared his throat when they reached the house. "Obviously, you know I have no choice but to call your mom."

He didn't need to bother. Mom had always been too busy for even simple homework help. She certainly wasn't going to carve time in her schedule to deal with an unruly daughter. But Kenzie just nodded and slipped out of the car.

Cicadas stroked their rhythmic song over her head as she crossed to the guesthouse. Her legs were still shaky, her body aching as if she'd just recovered from the flu. And then a flicker of movement in the second-story window of the big house caught her eye.

Tina. Peering from her bedroom window into the night. She was still awake?

Their eyes caught, and for a moment, Kenzie could almost—*almost*— see through her cousin's uncaring armor. As if the friend she'd once known was still hiding inside.

And then in the next moment Tina turned away and let the curtain swoop back into place.

Kenzie jammed her hands into the pockets of her shorts and crept into the guesthouse. Her hopes of avoiding the sisters were smashed when she noticed Avery sitting on the couch with a book.

"Hey." Avery laid the book facedown on the cushions and stood, her eyes soft with compassion. "You scared us today."

The kindness in Avery's voice brought another wave of guilt. "You stay up this late?" Her plastic hospital bracelet was still on her wrist. She tugged it off and stuck it in her pocket.

Avery laughed, but there was a weariness under it. "Not usually. I wanted to make sure you were okay."

Her throat pinched unexpectedly, and she shrugged. All she could manage without breaking down.

Avery studied her for another thoughtful moment, then suddenly stepped forward and pulled her into a gentle hug. Kenzie squeezed her eyes shut and held herself rigid. She didn't deserve Avery's compassion.

Or maybe Avery didn't know the truth about what had happened. That was more likely.

She shrugged away from the older girl's embrace and cleared her throat. "Where's Addisyn?"

Avery's face drooped slightly. "In her room. She was—tired tonight."

A delicate evasion, but she could see through to the truth: Addisyn didn't want to deal with her. She rubbed her throbbing head. "Okay."

"Do you feel like sitting with me for a moment?" Avery's smile turned hopeful. She waved her hand toward the book. "I was just reading about hawks. I can show you some of the photos if you'd like."

"No, thanks." Kenzie inched toward the hallway. Her headache was definitely getting worse. "I need to lie down."

"I hope you feel better soon." Avery's voice floated after her, still rich with an unexplainable empathy. Clearly, she didn't realize that Kenzie was at fault. Otherwise, wouldn't she be lecturing her? Avoiding her?

Like Addisyn was.

Kenzie didn't bother to turn on the lights in her room. Instead, she sank back onto the bed and pressed the heels of her hands against her eyes. Somehow the thought of Addisyn was hardest to take. Addisyn had believed in her and tried to help her—even when she'd held Addisyn at arm's length, the girl had relentlessly broken through her barricades. She'd kept reaching out when it would have been much easier to turn away.

The only person who had truly befriended her. And she'd let her down with a crash.

How could she have been so stupid? The girls had told her the pills were totally safe. Just natural stuff like herbs and essential oils and whatever. She'd never dreamed they had something as dangerous as that whatever-it-was drug.

But she should have known. She should have done more research. She should have asked for more details. Matter of fact, she should have thrown out the pills altogether. And she certainly shouldn't have been careless with the dosage.

Stupid, stupid, stupid. All her bad choices had followed each other like train cars on the Englewood Railway. And now she'd tumbled into a predicament she'd never get out of.

The consequences of what she'd done burned through her aching brain. Uncle Trent had already called Mom, no doubt. She'd almost certainly be sent back to Montreal. She wouldn't be able to skate this year. She'd probably have to go back into treatment, which meant she'd fall further behind in school. And Mom would once again watch her with uncertain eyes and probe for answers she didn't have to give. *What were you thinking? Why do you act this way? Don't you realize the harm you're doing?*

As if on cue, her phone rang, the catchy melody shattering the stillness in the quiet room. Kenzie slipped it out of her pocket and squinted at the too-bright screen. Yep. Mom.

Ignoring the call would only get her in more trouble later. Kenzie swiped. "Hey, Mom."

"Kenzie." Her mom's voice sounded more strained than usual. "Your uncle told me what happened."

Kenzie closed her eyes and pressed the phone closer to her ear. "Yeah."

"He said you'd taken some—" Her mom hesitated, as if the words wouldn't cooperate. "Some pills."

"Diet pills. Just natural—" Well, clearly they hadn't been. She sighed. "Yeah."

"So—uh—how do you feel?"

"Pretty bad still. Tired."

"I'm sure." Her mom was quiet again, silence digging its trench through the conversation. "So—have you been going to your appointments? With Dr. Drees?"

"Yes. Every week."

"She's not helping?"

Yet another thing her mom had never understood—that talking about her feelings for an hour a week in a sterile therapist's office couldn't fix problems in the real world. "She's nice. Mom, I promise you, I'm fine. I just—"

"It doesn't sound like you're fine, Kenzie." Mom hesitated. "I think it's time for you to come home and go back to treatment."

She'd seen it coming, but her heart still fell through a funnel. "Mom—"

"No arguments, Kenzie." Her mom's voice was more weary than angry. "I thought BC would be good for you. It always helped you before, but…"

Before. When Tina was still spinning tales about ghosts and goblins. When she could still eat sugar without a panic attack. When Marie's lies hadn't yet burrowed into her brain.

"You'll be coming home next week. Your uncle said he'd make the arrangements with the therapy program."

Arrangements. Like a funeral. Which it was—the death of everything she'd once been and could never be again. "Mom, please." She sat up on the bed, ignoring the dizziness. "I'll do better—I'll—"

She'd *what?* Her words faded into uncertainty. She was alone—drowning in the darkness she'd chosen. There was no one to take her hand. To show her the path she was too weak to walk on her own.

Mom was using her lawyer voice. "You can't seem to get a handle on this, so until you show me you can make better choices, I don't have any other options. I don't know what else to try."

What else to try? Her mom hadn't *tried* anything. She'd just shuffled Kenzie down the line—to Uncle Trent, Dr. Drees, Addisyn even.

"How about you try being a mom?" The words burst out with more force than she'd expected. "How about you try loving me and talking to me and—and understanding me?" She bit her lip. Now she'd be in even more trouble.

"Kenzie—" Mom's voice still wasn't angry. "I don't know what to do. You're—you're just more than I can handle right now." Soft sniffling came over the phone line. "You're right. I—I could have done more. It's just that I don't know—"

Her mom gave a small sob, and tears pricked to Kenzie's eyes too. "You were such a happy little girl." Mom's words were a whisper, as if the memory might vanish. "Such a sweet, happy little girl."

She could see the girl her mom was talking about. And the ever-widening distance between who she'd been and who she was now was enough to destroy what was left of her. She fought to keep her voice steady. "I have to go, Mom. Bye."

She swiped off the call, but the words were still there, the desperate ache behind her mom's voice.

Such a happy little girl...

The darkness pressed in around her, and all the pain of the day overflowed. Her mom was right, and that girl was gone, and who she'd once been was never coming back. No hospital stay, no therapist, no supplement could lead her back to who she'd been all those years ago when she'd stood on the ridge and watched the spirit bear. The bear with the legend she hadn't needed then.

The bear she'd almost seen again. If her own stupidity hadn't wrecked everything. And now she wouldn't have another chance before she left BC.

Unless...

The barest sliver of hope presented itself, and she grabbed on with the strength she had left. It was reckless, she knew. And crazy. And rebellious. Three things she definitely was not.

But it was also her only hope.

WHEN ADDISYN HAD seen Trent's headlights splash over the darkness last night, she'd gone to her room immediately. What did she have to say to Kenzie? Nothing that would help. That much was obvious.

A few minutes later, Avery had slipped in tentatively. "Kenzie's back."

"I saw that."

"She said she still doesn't feel well."

"Yeah, well, I'm sure she doesn't after stuffing a bottle of diet pills down her throat." The words had sounded harsher than she'd intended.

Avery had taken a deep breath. "Don't you think you need to go talk to her?"

She'd already proven how inadequate she was at handling any of this. "No. Why don't you do it?"

"Why me?"

"Because." Addisyn had folded her arms and tried to keep the resentment out of her voice. "You're good at helping people."

Avery had given her a hard-to-read glance. "You're the one she has a relationship with. The one she trusts."

Well, Kenzie hadn't *trusted* her enough to let her know what was really going on. "No."

"Fine." Avery had sighed and sunk onto the rollaway bed as if dragged down by gravity. "We'll just leave her alone this evening. She probably needs rest anyway."

Addisyn slept in snatches, nightmares twisting through her mind. When the velvet darkness finally faded into gray, she dressed and tiptoed out of the room, careful not to disturb Avery, who was still breathing peacefully on the rollaway bed. Then she slipped into the coolness of the early morning and wandered through the dew-drenched grass toward the trail in the woods.

In the first hints of dawn, the treehouse was shadowy. But the tree stood strong. Addisyn rested one hand against the furrowed bark. All these years of standing. And no signs of weakness.

The roots must run deep.

The scratchy rope ladder was no easier to climb this time, but she managed to scramble her way up to the platform. The mossy boards were cold against her legs. She leaned back on her elbows, ignoring the empty space next to her where Kenzie had sat that day.

The shadows were slow to melt this morning. She angled herself toward the east to wait for the sun.

She couldn't be angry with Kenzie—not really. No, the real person to blame was herself. She was supposed to be the responsible one. She was supposed to provide guidance and leadership. The way Avery had for her.

And for a time there, she'd thought she was doing it. But who was she kidding? It had been ridiculous all along to believe that she could touch a life with the same power Avery did. She, the weak one, the helpless one, the reckless one—who was she to guide or direct anyone else?

No, she'd failed. Just as she'd known she would. But she'd so wanted to help Kenzie. So wanted to help her find her way through the familiar pain.

An eerie déjà vu sifted on the breeze. At Kenzie's age, she'd been just as lost. Just as willing to sacrifice her soul for skating. Their choices had worn different masks, but the same desperation—the same pain—lay under them both.

No wonder the strain on Kenzie's face had looked so familiar. It was the same fear she'd had no answer for then. No answer for now. How could she, when the dark road Kenzie was walking had forever left scars upon her own soul?

And now she was limping through life just as disastrously as Kenzie was. She'd never be the girl she once was—the one who wore her innocent heart upon her sleeve. She'd never be on Darius's level—never able to open her soul to his gaze. And she'd never walk with Avery's holy purpose—never dwell fully in the love of the God Who was as real to her sister as the surging shoulders of the mountains.

The weight of it pressed her down, and she closed her eyes, but the tears leaked out anyway. She'd utterly failed at everything she'd come to Canada for. Trent had been right all along. Darius had seen her for the flawed failure she really was.

And Kenzie had been caught in the crossfire.

"Thought you might come here."

The voice jerked Addisyn from her thoughts, and she peered over the edge of the boards. There was Avery, hands on hips at the foot of the tree.

So here was her sister to rescue her. As always. The irritation was irrational, but she made no attempt to brush it aside. "You can't come up."

Avery shrugged, unfazed. "Okay."

"Why are you here?"

"Because we need to talk." The genuine compassion in Avery's eyes disarmed her defensiveness. "I can tell you're hurting."

Of course she was, but talking wouldn't change anything. "Nothing left to talk about."

"That's not true, Ads." Avery pressed her lips together. "Come on. Let me up."

Knowing Avery, her sister would scale the tree with her fingernails if she had to. Addisyn sighed and scooted over on the boards. "All right."

Avery scampered up the rope ladder with twice Addisyn's dexterity. Of course. She settled in on the platform and tucked her knees against her chest. "The morning is beautiful."

"Yeah." The sun was burning over the ridge now, a crystal-blue sky unfurling overhead. The moment seemed held in a brief breath of peace.

"Hey, Ads?"

The peace popped like a bubble. "Yes."

"Don't be so hard on yourself." Avery leaned against the tree trunk. "You're finding your way forward. And that's never easy, but—"

"No." She wasn't in the mood for her sister's wise-woman discourse. Addisyn laced her fingers together and stretched her hands in front of her. "I've failed at everything, Avery. Don't you realize that?" Through the trees, the eastern windows of the big house were glittering in the sun. "The whole family hates me."

"What about Darius?"

Her throat tightened, but there was no point in faking anymore. "Darius—we're actually—" How could she classify the snarls in their relationship? "We had a—well, an argument, I guess."

"So?" Avery's expression didn't change. She picked at a patch of moss on one of the boards. "Happens in every deep relationship."

"He—he wants to marry me."

Avery's fingers froze on the moss. "Isn't that—a good thing?"

It should have been, and the way her longing dangled just out of reach pricked tears to her eyes. "No. I can't, Avery. I'm not—" *Not like you. Not a good girl. Not the woman he deserves.* "I make a mess of everything. I can't wreck our relationship too."

Avery raised her eyebrows. "Turning your back on him is not wrecking your relationship?"

Oh, so now the sister who'd never dated was going to weigh in on her love life? Her irritation doubled. "I'm not turning my back on him. I just need time." Okay, that sounded like a bad rom-com cliché.

Avery looked unconvinced. "Don't you think you should talk to him?"

"Not right now." Time to share the decision she'd made this morning while she'd sat in the quiet woods. She took a deep breath. "I'm coming back to Colorado."

Stillness stiffened every inch of Avery's body. "You're what?"

"I'm coming back to Colorado." The words dragged heavy with defeat. "This—" her gesture circled the mountains and the sky and the abandoned treehouse—"didn't work out."

Two heartbeats passed. Three. And then Avery's measured voice. "Where will you live?"

She blinked. In Avery's cabin, right? "Well—uh—with you. I thought."

Avery was fingering the moss again. "Sorry, Ads. You can't."

What? Addisyn stared at her sister, but Avery's expression was ironclad. "Avery—" She'd never imagined this plot twist. "If you're joking, now is not—"

"I'm not joking." Avery squinted at the horizon instead of Addisyn. "You can't live in my cabin. I won't let you."

So even Avery didn't want her back.

"Avery." She heard the tears in her voice. "I—I thought you would be happy to—"

"Listen to me, Addisyn." Finally Avery turned to her, her expression hard with the same granite-carved resolve she'd worn only at the most decisive moments of their lives. "You always run, do you realize that? Always. Every time things are hard, you take off. To me, to Darius, to

Whistler, whatever. I'm not letting you do that this time."

"I'm not running." She hissed her denial, looking away from the truth of Avery's words. "I'm just coming back home."

"Home?" Avery's eyebrows arched. "Colorado is not your home. It never was. *This* is your home."

No, it was the home she could have had, if she'd never met Brian. "Avery, you're not being fair!" She heard the rebellious teenager in her words, but she couldn't stop it. "Look, I need to come back. I can't believe—" Her words caught. "I can't believe you won't help me!"

"I am helping you!" Avery's words were fired with an unmistakable intensity, her eyes burning with the flame of whatever gave her the gift of seeing inside souls. "You've run your whole life, Addisyn. From yourself, mostly. But at some point, you've got to stop running. You've got to dig in and do the brave thing."

"Brave?" Addisyn lifted her chin in challenge. "Says the woman who was too scared to take her dream job?"

Avery flinched, her expression tightening. "That's not true. I told you. I'm really not qualified, and Laz—"

"And Laz needs you, and he's been your friend, and you owe him. Right. I've heard it all." She jabbed her finger at Avery. "But you know what? You're just scared. Like it or not, you're running too."

"Well, maybe it's just that I've never been able to have a life apart from you." Avery was angry now, the glow in her eyes like heat lightning. "Have you ever considered that, Addisyn? From the time you were born, everything I did was centered on you. Because I wanted you to have a good life. The kind I'll probably never have." Her voice wavered, but she kept going. "And you know what? You have that here."

Why couldn't she make Avery understand? "Don't you realize? I don't know how to help Kenzie. I don't know how to—to do anything right." The shame soaked over her again. "Not like you."

"That's what you think?" Avery shook her head. "You think I don't ever lose my path?" She blew out a breath. "You're selling yourself short, Addisyn. I've watched you with Kenzie. You were so good with her. And Darius—whatever lie you're telling yourself about the two of you is ridiculous. He worships the ground you walk on, and you glow like a lantern whenever he comes in the room."

"It doesn't matter." Brian's face, Brian's voice in her mind. The glaciers that had reshaped her soul.

"What's it going to be, Addisyn? Are you going to run this time? Or are you actually going to do the thing you were born to do?"

"Avery, it's not fair that—"

Her catchy ringtone invaded the air between them. Addisyn huffed and dug for her pocket.

Tina? What did she want?

She threw Avery one last angry glance and swiped on the call. "Hello?"

"Addisyn, Kenzie's gone."

Kenzie was gone? Addisyn pressed the phone closer to her ear. "What do you mean, she's gone?"

"She's not in the house."

Avery leaned closer and mouthed, *Kenzie?* Addisyn nodded and put the phone on speaker. "How do you know?"

"I went up to the guesthouse because I needed to—" Tina cleared her throat. "I had something I needed to say to her. I knocked on the door and nobody came, so I tried the knob and it was unlocked. So—" Her voice was slightly sheepish. "I went in."

Of course she had, but Addisyn was too worried to be mad. "And you're sure she's not there?"

"I'm sure." Tina sighed. "So, where are you right now?"

"Here at the house, back in the woods."

"Wait—you're not in town?"

"No." Addisyn glanced back at the snatches of the big house she could see through the trees. "Why?"

"Because your car is gone."

The car was gone? How—

Oh, no. No, no, no.

Addisyn scrambled up on the creaking boards. "Kenzie. She has my car."

"Wait, she can't drive!"

"It's a long story, Tina. I'll be right there."

"But if she's driving—" Tina groaned. "She could be anywhere. Do you know where she might have gone?"

Addisyn glanced at Avery. Her sister nodded. "Yeah. I have a good idea. Look, I'll be right there, okay? Just wait at the house for me."

She ended the call and looked at Avery. "Wildcrest?"

"No doubt." Avery was already swinging onto the rope ladder, the fight forgotten. She scrambled down and jumped the last couple of feet. "Let's go get her."

WHEN DARIUS STARTED his car, the radio was blaring some song about a broken heart. He switched off the music and took the turns out of downtown with no real destination in mind.

He'd been awake all night—reliving the whole sorry story. Somehow he'd made it through work. Now he needed a destination. Somewhere to take his confusion and pain.

Not home. He couldn't stand to walk into the empty house, the house that he'd hoped would be the epicenter of his life with Addisyn. Not to his family's place, where Aunt Vera would badger him with questions and speculation about Kenzie's condition. Not to the center, where the tentative bridge he'd built with his uncle had burned out.

But there was one place yet. One place that had never failed him.

He flipped on his blinker and made the turn onto 99. In fifteen minutes, he was there. At the little church that contained a grace bigger than the whole world.

He parked and jogged across the lot. The wind was rising, the Christian flag in front snapping in the breeze. He glanced toward the cemetery, where the pine limbs thrashed over the gate as if waving away intruders. He looked away. He couldn't face his parents today.

He'd failed again. Just as he had before. But this time, it was Addisyn he'd hurt.

As usual, the sanctuary was unlocked. He slipped into a pew in the shadowy back corner, uncertainty hanging around him. Why was he here?

He listened, as if he might hear a whisper from Heaven floating over the threadbare carpet and scuff-marked pews. But all he heard was silence. A condemning silence.

He cleared his throat. "I've messed up."

The words he'd been saying all his life. All the years when he hadn't been as strong or brave or wise or successful as everyone had expected him to be. As he had longed to be.

And now he'd ruined things in his biggest way yet.

The pain on Addisyn's face flooded his mind, and he dropped his head into his hands. He'd never meant for her to be hurt. The whole time she'd been in Canada, he'd wanted to prioritize her in every way. He'd longed to show her that she could trust him, that even after the nightmare Brian had put her through, he would be her steadfast rock.

Instead he'd just wounded her. Her words trickled back to him.

All you care about is making your uncle happy....You'd rather placate him than try to reach someone who needs help. Or stand up for what's right.

A sick taste wrapped around the memory. She was right, wasn't she? He'd spent the last few months obsessed with his uncle's opinion. Trying to fit himself into the man's predetermined mold. Longing for approval from the person who was the closest substitute for his own dad.

Good grief, he'd even pulled Addisyn into his charade. He should have drawn boundaries the first moment Trent had jabbed her at the dinner table. Instead, he'd convinced himself that both of them would be better off playing defense. Why had he never seen things from Addisyn's perspective? Never considered how betrayed that had to have made her feel?

Ironic. He'd longed to protect Addisyn from his uncle, but he'd been the one to wound her most deeply. In trying to atone for his past mistakes, he'd made his biggest one yet.

You're scared of him. Plain and simple.

Why had he even sought a love like Uncle Trent's? A love that had to be earned? Why had his uncle's approval meant so much to him that he would sacrifice everything else to achieve it?

He'd scoffed at her words yesterday, but the truth of them hit him squarely. He had lived his life with fear. It was that fear that had held him back, and it was that same fear that had led him to lash out at Addisyn.

Thinking back on his behavior in the hospital, he shook his head. Who was he to scold her? Okay, so maybe she'd made some mistakes with Kenzie. But at least she'd tried. She'd put her job and her convenience and even her relationship with Darius on the line to try to help the girl. She hadn't let Uncle Trent's words stop her from doing what she thought was the right thing.

Shame trickled down his back. Kenzie was his cousin, for crying out loud. But when he'd had the same choice Addisyn did, he'd taken the easy way out. Blaming the girl and judging her actions and shuffling responsibility. All to make things easier on him.

Addisyn was much stronger than he was.

He closed his eyes. He'd had such different visions for his life as a teenager. He'd been sure he'd become a great skater. He'd longed to live up to the legacy his family had left for him.

Instead, here he was, a thousand miles from that bright-eyed boy. He was wounded and battered in so many ways, and the worst part was his chances were over. He could try to trick himself, try to carve out a life of meaning in this little town, but he would never achieve the greatness his family had wanted for him.

And all he'd ever wanted was to be a great man.

"I'm sorry." He whispered the words to the ghosts who lurked in the corners and the God Whom he had tried to follow. But the words were too small, too broken. Too fragile to hold the weight of a new beginning.

A gentle glow of sunlight illuminated the stained glass at the front of the church. Darius squinted at it, watching the way the colors splashed over the wooden cross that stood beside the pulpit.

The cross. Where he'd hesitated, God had taken action. But try as he might, he couldn't envision his failures stacked on the Son of God. Couldn't imagine how he was supposed to walk the broken path that lay before him.

If only his grandfather were here. His hero. Darius studied the empty pulpit and could almost see the man in his forty-dollar suit, his face ringed with joy as he harvested truth from the pages of his worn Bible and delivered it like manna to his hearers. He'd been a down-to-earth man— a man who'd rolled up his sleeves and held out his soul instead of hiding behind eloquent preaching or cloaking himself in his calling.

A man who had been…great.

The truth rose slowly in his heart, materializing out of the shadows of his mind until it stood as strong and solid as the wooden cross at the front of the church.

Darius sucked in a breath. How had he missed it?

Yes, his grandfather had been a fantastic skater. But that was only a chapter of his life. The things that had made him great hadn't come from his performance. His greatness had come from the Word he preached and the way he lived and the witness he bore to all that was yet unseen. He'd lived out greatness not in a gym or on an ice rink, but around the dinner table and behind the pulpit and beside his young grandson.

And in so doing, he'd touched lives. Far more than he had as a skater. He hadn't chased achievement. Instead, he'd taken time to tend hearts.

All this time…how had Darius missed the meaning? He would never compete again, never push himself through another routine on the ice. He would never be rich or famous or honored. He couldn't bring back his parents or please his uncle or force himself into the athletic line of his family.

But he could still be great. The way his grandfather had been. In the power of his faith and the hope in his heart and the light in his smile. And he could start now. Today.

With Addisyn.

The light through the stained glass was stronger, the cross standing in silhouetted witness against it. Was that not his calling too? To let the light shine around him?

He turned and made his way out of the church, away from the empty pulpit from which the memory of his grandfather had just preached one final sermon. The tears were coming, but they were healing now. He'd do this. He'd head to the athletic center right away, and he'd do what needed to be done. What he should have done a long time ago.

He opened his car door, resolve still rushing him forward, and suddenly blinked at the boxes of clothing sitting in his passenger seat. He'd loaded them into his car three days ago, intending to donate them this week—but hadn't he put them in the trunk? Had he moved them without remembering?

Well, regardless, he did need to get rid of them. Maybe he could run by Goodwill after the center. In the meantime, they needed to go back in the trunk. It wouldn't do for the precarious stack to slip while he was driving.

He hurried to the passenger side and yanked open that door. Before he could react, the boxes tumbled out, the one on top sloshing its contents—a jumble of clothes—onto the asphalt.

Great move, Payne. He shrugged and knelt, scooping up items by handfuls. This was just a minor interruption, after all. Soon enough he'd be—

Wait.

What was that?

His hands froze on the item he held—a silk blouse of his mother's. Something hard had poked him through the fabric. Something that felt almost like—

His heart hammered into triple time.

He reached into the pocket. Yes. He could feel it.

But it couldn't be—

He waited, half-afraid to look, and then he slowly drew out an object he knew well.

A delicate silver band with a single solitaire diamond. A ring that reminded him of all that was good and noble and eternal. A ring that had been there all along.

Just waiting for him to find it.

He bowed his head, the sacredness of the moment falling over him like rain, and then he suddenly laughed out loud. He tucked the ring carefully into the inner pocket of his billfold and grabbed up the boxes.

He had to get rid of all the pent-up past. And then he could start on the next chapter of his life.

Being a great man.

CHAPTER 22

Tina was waiting for them on the steps of the guesthouse, clutching an envelope in one hand. "She's gone to look for the spirit bear, hasn't she?"

Her usual heavy makeup was missing, making her look more vulnerable than normal. Still, Addisyn eyed her warily. "Most likely."

Tina's head dropped. "I thought so." She jerked her chin toward the Lexus. "Hop in. I'll drive."

Avery raised her eyebrows. "You don't even know where we're heading."

"Wildcrest."

Addisyn blinked. "How did you—"

Tina shrugged, still fingering the envelope. "I know more about the spirit bears than you think I do. Now get in."

When they arrived at the trailhead, relief loosened Addisyn's insides at the sight of the little Jeep. So Kenzie was here, and at least she hadn't driven off the road on her way. She grabbed her backpack and glanced at Avery, who hadn't said a word to her since the treehouse. "What do you think? Same trail we were on the other day?"

"Definitely." Avery pointed to a muddy spot near the sign. "Her footprints. I noticed yesterday that her boots have that squiggle tread."

Of course Avery would have seen a detail like that. And at least she was finally talking. Addisyn peered at the tracks more closely. "They might be from yesterday, though."

"Too fresh. She's come this way today." Avery brushed her hair behind her ears and nodded at the trail. "Let's go."

The mountain that had been so warm and welcoming yesterday seemed to watch them with suspicious eyes today. It pulled a robe of fog from the inlet and wrapped the silver around its shoulders. Every sound was muffled, the air heavy with humidity. And then, after an hour and a half of scrambling up the tunneling trail, Avery's voice broke the silence. "That must be it."

Addisyn brushed the mist from her eyelashes and followed her sister's pointing finger. In front of them, a stony outcropping jutted into the fog like an island reaching into an unknown sea. Addisyn blinked. "Wildcrest."

Avery turned a slow circle. "And she's not here."

Addisyn groaned. "You've got to be kidding me." Panic pulsed again. "So where else could she have gone?"

"Well, she could have taken the North Forest Crest back there at the first intersection. Or she could have turned onto the Sherman Trail. Or she might have gone past the second—" Avery pulled off her ball cap and ran a hand over her hair. "She could be anywhere."

"But that doesn't make sense." Addisyn paced a circle around the rocky overlook, as though Kenzie might materialize from the fog. "This is where the bears were. She should have come here." She glanced at Tina, suddenly realizing the other girl had yet to weigh in. "Tina, what do you think?"

Tina hung her head for a moment. When she looked up, every trace of her calloused armor was gone. "I think it's my fault."

Her fault? Since when had she ever heard Tina admit wrong? "What—"

"About the bear." Tina bit her lip, seemingly struggling with her words. "I shouldn't have told you and her that I didn't believe her. It's just—well, here." She unfolded the envelope she still clutched and held out a slip of paper.

What was this? A grainy photo, blurry on cheap paper, of—trees and brush?

"Right there. In the middle."

And then she saw it. Almost hidden by the forest, but obvious enough to leave no doubt.

A white bear.

Addisyn gripped the photo and stared at Tina. "Where did you get this?"

"I took it." Tina stared down at her feet, pushing the toe of her boot into a crack between rocks. "Kenzie—she wasn't alone when she saw the bear."

Addisyn blinked. In all the time Kenzie had rehashed the sighting, she'd never mentioned anyone else. "Who was with her?"

"I was." Tina raised her head with a watery smile. "Kenzie and I— we were best friends. More like sisters. When I see you two—" she tipped her head to include Avery—"it makes me think about me and Kenz. The way we used to be."

Avery shifted. "So you saw the bear?"

"Not that well." Tina cleared her throat. "I saw movement, but I just didn't get a good look at it. After she left for Montreal, I started going up there to look, taking my camera, and about a month later I got this picture. I thought I would give it to her when she came back. A surprise." Her mouth wobbled slightly. "But that was the year she got really serious about skating. She had a bunch of training and stuff in the summers. Didn't come to visit anymore."

The pieces were filling in. "And so you kept it?"

"I was mad. Mad and hurt." Tina swiped at her eyes. "I missed her, and Dad—he'd always wanted me to be athletic. Once all he could do was rave about how talented Kenzie was, it just—I guess I blamed her. And I lied about the bears to get back at her." Her expression crushed with the confession. "I didn't realize how—how badly she was hurting. Not until I saw her in the hospital."

Here in the shifting fog, Addisyn was suddenly seeing Tina more clearly than she ever had. How much pain had been hiding behind her savage snark? "So—when you came to the house this morning—"

"I was going to bring Kenzie the photo." Tina sniffed, shifting position uncomfortably. "I knew what the bears meant to her. And the legend." She peered at Addisyn. "Did she tell you about that?"

"No. Just that there was some story—a myth—do you know it?"

"Yeah. I'm the one who told it to her." Tina's mouth twisted in a sad half-smile. "I doubt she remembers this now, but I always used to tell her stories. Crazy, outlandish stuff I mostly dreamed up. But this was real. I heard it at a cultural celebration downtown, and I never forgot it."

Avery was watching Tina, her soul-seeing look on her face. "Would you tell us the story?"

Tina nodded and took a deep breath. "So…it starts with the Ice Age. It almost destroyed everything, you know. Reshaped the whole world. But—the bears lived."

Her voice was shifting into a storyteller's lilt, and the trees and rocks and clouds were listening. Addisyn stepped closer.

"The bears were the survivors, defying all the odds. And so, to remind them of what they had undergone, the Maker of the universe created the spirit bears. One bear out of every ten was white. Like the ice. Scarred to remind them of their strength."

Wind whispered through the shadows of the trees.

"But the really fascinating part—then the bears were supposed to be guides. According to the story, they were guardians, befriending the lost and leading them from darkness to light."

The full impact of the story burst into bloom, and Addisyn sucked in a breath. "Is that—"

"That's what Kenzie was looking for, I guess." Tina's mouth trembled, but she pressed her lips together. "A guide. A—a friend."

Addisyn blinked back her own tears. "She was lonely."

"Yeah. That's why I picked you, you know."

Addisyn frowned. "Picked—"

"What, you really think I have separation anxiety over my cat?" Tina gave a shaky smile, her signature snark creeping back into her voice. "If anything, it would have given me a break from cleaning out his litter box."

"But—you said—"

"Yeah. Because I thought it would be better if Kenzie was with you. I knew she needed a friend. And I knew it couldn't be me, after everything that happened." The brokenness flashed behind Tina's eyes again. "So I figured you were the one to help her. And you were."

"No." The word caught on every insecurity she'd ever had. She looked up where the glaciers groaned against the mountains. "I—I messed everything up for her."

"Well, you got one big thing right." Tina shrugged one shoulder. "You loved her. Because you never left her alone."

"Tina—"

"Don't argue, okay? I'm right. I'm always right." Tina cleared her throat and blew out a breath as if shedding the emotions. "Okay. What next?"

"Uh—" Addisyn blinked, trying to transition from the personal to the practical. "Well, I guess we could…"

"Over here!"

She turned at Avery's cry. Her sister was pointing at a trail narrow enough that they'd overlooked it. "Where does this go, Tina?"

"I'd forgotten about that." Tina hurried over. "Along the eyebrow to another overlook, maybe a quarter of a mile. You think she's there?"

Avery nudged an impression in the dirt with her toe. "These are her footprints."

"Then here." Tina stuffed the photo into Addisyn's hand. "Take this to her. Please?"

"Don't you want to—"

"No." Tina scuffed her boot against the rock. "She probably—she won't want to talk to me. But she'll listen to you."

Addisyn swung beseechingly to Avery. "Avery, don't you think you should go? You're the one who—"

"No way. You're her friend, Addisyn." Avery nudged her forward, a world of meaning in her eyes. "Go on. Go show Kenzie the white bear."

△△   △△   △△

THE LITTLE TRAIL was so overgrown that Addisyn wasn't sure how Kenzie had found it. She squeezed between the trees, clutching both the bedraggled envelope and the last scraps of her courage.

Go show Kenzie the white bear.

The trees ducked aside, and she was standing on the overlook. Clouds rolled over what must usually be a breathtaking view. Rocks stacked themselves against the edge. A raven rasped its throaty cry from a pine tree.

And Kenzie huddled on a fallen log.

The worry shrugged off Addisyn's shoulders. Thank God. Whatever else happened, at least they'd found her. She cleared her throat. "Kenzie?"

Kenzie's head whipped around, and then the fright in her expression hardened into something much more rebellious. "Leave me alone."

Okay, not a promising start. Addisyn kept her voice steady. "Sorry, I can't do that." She crossed the rocky area and perched on Kenzie's log. "I hiked almost three miles up here. I don't intend to leave before I at least enjoy the view."

Kenzie shrugged. "Everything's foggy today."

"Seen any spirit bears?"

Kenzie shook her head. "There aren't any." Her voice was flat, defeated. "They're gone now, I guess."

Addisyn held out the envelope. "Tina sent you this."

Kenzie's expression didn't change when she saw the photo, but her fingers tightened. "Tina—had this picture?"

"She took it. Not long after you left here the last time, I guess. And she wanted me to give it to you." Addisyn hesitated. Tina's story wasn't hers to tell, but Kenzie needed to know that her cousin wasn't as hostile as she'd seemed. "She loves you, Kenzie. She's been worried about you."

Kenzie was still staring at the photo, gently tracing her finger over the outline of the bear.

"So, see there?" Addisyn swallowed, searching for words to fill the gap between them. "You finally have your bear."

Kenzie slid the photo back into the envelope. "It's too late."

"What do you mean by that?"

Kenzie drew her shoulders up. "I had a reason for finding the bear."

"Guidance?"

Her eyes darted toward Addisyn. "Tina told you the legend." At Addisyn's nod, she sighed, shrugged. "Yeah. I thought, maybe, if I saw one—I'd know how to get out of all the mess I'm in. But now—" The wind whipped loose strands of hair across her face, but she didn't brush it away. "I've ruined it all."

Kenzie's pain was like a forcefield around her. Holding everyone back. Addisyn reached toward her. "Kenzie, that's not—"

"And don't you try to tell me!"

The outburst was so forceful that Addisyn jerked back. "What?"

"Don't start telling me all the stuff you think you have to." Kenzie jumped to her feet, glaring down at Addisyn. "Don't tell me that it will be okay and I'll make it through and blah, blah, blah. Everybody says that, but they don't know!" Her voice was rising, the emotions flashing in her eyes. "They don't know what it's like when everything is ruined and there's no going back."

Addisyn scrambled up. "Kenzie—listen—"

"And you don't know either!" Her voice was gathering force, her pain echoing off the rocks. "You have a great boyfriend and a really cool sister and friends and talent and—and everything. You don't know what it's like to lose yourself!"

The wind gusted again, whipping the shreds of Kenzie's tantrum around them both. Kenzie stared with challenging eyes, but all Addisyn could hear was the despair in the words.

You don't know what it's like to lose yourself...

For the first time, she saw in Kenzie more than the reflection of the teenager she'd been. She saw the woman she was now.

And here on a windswept mountain, with Kenzie's wounds so raw and open, any words she might have spoken tumbled to the ground like dried leaves. She shrank beneath the stare of the ice-carved peaks looming over her head. She couldn't rewrite her own story. She couldn't change Kenzie's either.

No, because their lives had both been reshaped by the unmelting glaciers. And they'd cried out for guidance, but no white bears had come to lead the way. Not anymore.

Unless...

Tina's story floated back, the beauty of the legend slowly breaking through.

To remind them of what they had undergone, the Maker of the universe created the spirit bears...white like the ice...scarred to remind them of their strength.

She'd been through her own ice age, hadn't she? The fact that she'd survived—it was more than chance, more than luck, more than grit. So what if the wounds she still carried were no accident either? What if, there in her scars, something sacred had been slowly taking shape?

Then the bears were guides…befriending the lost and leading them from darkness to light.

Out of everyone in Kenzie's life, only Addisyn had walked her road. Only Addisyn had earned trust by marching every weary mile.

Go show her the white bear…

The wind whipped around her, but she straightened her shoulders. "Kenzie." She held out the girl's name, a prayer, a plea, a request for permission to tell more. "I am—I am just like you."

Kenzie didn't respond, but she didn't interrupt either.

"I gave up everything I believed to try to succeed. Be the best I could be at skating." She took a breath, bracing her balance before she let the floodgates loose. "When I was younger…I had a really bad coach."

The tightness wrapped her chest, the same old bands of shame with which Brian had bound her, but this time she was pulling away, breaking his rules of silence to reach a girl so desperately in need.

"He told me a lot of things that were untrue about myself and the people around me. And he—he made me believe him." She wanted to hold back, hoard the truth to herself the way she'd done for so long, but she forced herself forward. "I started training with him when I was sixteen." She paused, the ghost of the girl she'd been floating before her. "Your age."

Kenzie was listening. She could tell.

"I moved in with him when I was eighteen. He became even more controlling as time went on, but I didn't know how to leave him. Last year, I finally did."

Again, she waited, breathing fresh strength from the wind. The urge to run yanked at her, but she forced herself to stand. Strong and solid, the way she imagined a spirit bear would do.

To remind them of what they survived…

"But since then, I've been—" She caught her breath. Tears were running down her cheeks, but she hadn't realized she was crying. "I've thought that—that I couldn't be okay. That what I went through broke me forever. And I was right. I'll never be the same." The ice-carved peaks bore witness, the ones that would have never risen without the pain of the glaciers. "I'll be stronger."

"I've messed up everything, Addisyn." A cry tore at Kenzie's words.

The intensity of the moment consumed her, pushing aside her own fears and failures. "Kenzie, you know what Darius told me once? The glaciers covered this valley thirty feet thick." She could imagine it, there in the valley, the great groaning mass of ice. "But it melted."

"What if it doesn't?" There was so much fear in Kenzie's eyes.

"It will." A truth she could stand on, and the joy of the statement burst forth in her own thawing heart. "It will melt, Kenzie!" She reached toward the girl, begging her to accept the words that hung ripe for release. "And when it leaves—there's beauty behind it."

The promise of the peaks ringed them both. This high country to which she'd climbed, the world of the Maker of the universe, Who so lovingly marked His spirit bears. Transforming glaciers to glory and scars to story. Spilling the sacred over their paths.

"I'm here for you, Kenzie." The power was rising in her own soul, the light she'd always seen in Avery burning beneath her words as well. The wind whipped wild, and she was no longer afraid. She held out her hand. "Come on. I can help you. Let me walk you through this. Just take the first step for me and come home."

She waited on the cliff edge for the choice that only Kenzie could make. She watched the thousand different emotions pass over the girl's face. She waited while her friend wrestled down the same lies she herself had believed for so long.

And then she smiled as Kenzie gripped her hand.

She led Kenzie away from the perilous rocky ledge, back on the sure footing of the trail that would lead both of them home. Avery and Tina were waiting at the intersection, matching expressions of worry carved into their faces. But it was Tina who made the first move. Trudging slowly toward them, hunched beneath regret. About ten feet away, she stopped and shrugged. "Kenzie—I've never been good at saying sorry. But—" She studied the ground. "It's been pretty lame. Not having my best friend. I know I've been a jerk, but maybe—"

Her words broke off as Kenzie grabbed her in a hug.

AS THE FAITHFUL little Jeep wound up the Callaghan Road on Tuesday, Addisyn rolled down her window and breathed in the warm summer air.

Trent had asked her to come by his office today *"for a meeting,"* and she could guess what was about to unfold. No doubt, she'd leave the center today officially unemployed.

But the important thing was that Kenzie would be okay. She'd talked to her mother again, who'd decided to let her stay in BC a bit longer. Even better, she'd agreed to join a support group that Dr. Drees had recommended. When Addisyn had dropped her off for the first meeting this morning, she'd had a hope on her face that had been missing for far too long.

Addisyn flipped on her blinker and turned in the driveway, smiling slightly at the white bear on the sign. Who would have thought that the search for the spirit bears would lead them all home?

"Hey." Tina glanced up from behind the reception counter when Addisyn pushed through the doors. "I hear you have a meeting today."

Addisyn winced. "Yeah."

Canuck trotted across the lobby with his tail quirked in eagerness, and Addisyn hesitated. "Do you think he'd let me pet him now?"

"Probably. Maybe. Or not." Tina grinned. "He's a cat, Addisyn. Keep that in mind."

Addisyn laughed and gingerly brushed her fingertips between Canuck's shoulder blades. Amazingly, he arched his back slightly as if enjoying the attention.

"You like that, huh?" His fur was softer than she'd expected.

A warbling purr vibrated from his ribs, and Tina grinned. "Oh, yeah. I think he just made a new friend."

He wasn't the only one who'd made new friends recently. "See?" Addisyn straightened and flashed her ice-rink smile, Canuck still snuggling against her ankle. "I know how to win friends and influence people."

"Except maybe Dad?"

Tina's words invaded her moment of triumph, and Addisyn grimaced. "Except for him, yeah." She shrugged and turned to head back toward his office.

"You did a good job."

Addisyn swiveled back toward Tina, but no sarcasm lay beneath the other girl's smile. "Really?"

"Yeah. You helped Kenzie. So don't listen to Dad, okay?" Tina pulled a snarky face. "I quit doing that when I was about twelve, anyway. But go on before you're late. That'll tick him off for sure."

Addisyn had a distinct lions'-den feeling as she rapped at Trent's office door. Sure enough, when he swung it open, his face was grimmer than she'd ever seen it. "Have a seat."

She tentatively perched on the edge of one of his chairs, twisting her hands together, clinging to Tina's hard-earned praise.

You did a good job...

Trent sat heavily in the chair across from her. "Well. Is Kenzie at her new support group?"

"Yes. I dropped her off on the way here."

"Seems like a good idea for her."

"I hope so."

She was waiting warily for the conversation to detonate, but for the first time, Trent seemed at a loss for words. He finally sighed and scrubbed a hand over the back of his neck. The way Darius sometimes did. "Addisyn—"

Had he ever called her by name?

"I feel that my response in the hospital was less than—was somewhat misguided."

Misguided? "I'm not sure I understand."

"I suppose what I'm trying to say is—" He shifted and met her gaze squarely. "I owe you an apology."

An apology?

"At the hospital, I was—a bit harsh, shall we say. I was—this is no excuse, but I was extremely stressed." His gaze faltered. "Kenzie is very dear to me, and I knew her mother was also trusting my care of her, and to find out that she—" He broke off and shook his head.

Addisyn felt as dazed as if she'd just come out of a combination spin. "Um—well, I understand. I was very upset too."

"Well, I'm also aware that I have been somewhat—ungenerous to you since you arrived." He scooped a pen off his desk, tapping his palm in what seemed like a nervous habit. "The truth is that I was simply—well, to put it frankly, I was concerned you would not meet my expectations, especially given your—history."

Now was when Trent would send her packing for good. "I can understand that, sir. But—I do want you to know that I tried." She took a deep breath, searching for the right words. "I wanted to help Kenzie. I truly did. And I know that things didn't go the way they should have, but in everything I did, I wanted to—"

"Please let me continue."

She snapped her words off. "Yes, sir."

"As I was saying—" He firmed his mouth once more. "I feel that your—uh—approach possibly did more good than I initially believed."

The tiniest crack of hope opened in her heart, but she wouldn't let herself look at it yet. "Oh?"

"Actually, I was—well, it was Darius who got my attention. He came to see me yesterday, and he—" Trent coughed. "He was quite blunt, as a matter of fact."

Darius had defended her? Against Trent? The sliver of hope widened. "Darius came to see you?"

"He did indeed." Trent raised his eyebrows. "We had a long conversation, actually. About many things. He is a wiser young man than I perhaps gave him credit for. And apparently quite a fan of you."

Heat burned to her cheeks, but fortunately Trent kept talking.

"Darius seems to believe that you helped restore Kenzie's confidence through befriending her." He rubbed his nose. "He spoke quite passionately about that, as a matter of fact. Said that you had told him on numerous occasions how hard you were working to draw her out, help her find herself, so to speak."

"I—I did."

"Yes, well, I then called Dr. Drees. To inform her of the changes in Kenzie's situation, you know. She was quite—enlightening, as well. While she couldn't breach privacy, all that, she did let me know that Kenzie had apparently spoken of your efforts in quite a favorable way." He shifted his weight awkwardly. "In fact, it was her professional opinion that the sort of support you were providing Kenzie was key to her recovery. I reminded her that part of it included hunting for legends—" his voice soured slightly—"and she simply informed me that in her view, the world needed more people to believe in legends. Clearly that may be more of a disputable point, but the general truth remains that she considers your help as having been very valuable."

She couldn't have bitten back her smile even if she had wanted to. "That's—that's amazing to hear."

Trent folded his hands. "One of the opinions Darius expressed was that I have perhaps placed too strong an emphasis on performance metrics." He shifted his weight uneasily. "Which made me realize that there are likely other athletes undergoing the same stresses and challenges Kenzie faced, and—" He shrugged. "You seem to be an ideal candidate to connect with them."

Addisyn shook her head, the words blurring in her mind. "So are you saying—"

"That I would be interested in continuing your contract with us even after Kenzie's return to Montreal." For the first time, a faint warmth softened his expression. "I believe I misjudged you, Addisyn. As a businessman, I recognize a good idea when I see one. And you are a good idea for this industry, for the center, and—" He shrugged, a faint smile penetrating his seriousness. "For Darius."

He was holding out much more than a job offer, and the hope in her heart expanded into a full sunrise. Addisyn squeezed her hands together to keep from screaming in excitement right there in Trent's office. "Thank you so much, Mr. Payne. I really appreciate that—and I would love to keep working here—"

"Yes, well." He gave a curt nod, but his smile didn't leave. "We can discuss details in the coming days. And one last thing." He plucked a folded paper from his desk and held it out. "Darius left this for you."

The paper was unsteady in her hands. She pulled apart the folds to find a message far better than even Trent's offer. A message that sent her heart singing again.

The sun sets tonight at 9:20. (Late, I know.) It looks really pretty from Alexander Falls. I took a girl there once to watch it, and I'm wondering if she'd want to see it again.

By the way...I love you.

△△ △△ △△

THE LAST COUPLE of days had worn her out worse than a twenty-mile hike. Avery set her book aside and relaxed deeper into the lawn chair on the guesthouse porch. She closed her eyes and turned her face to the sun, watching the shifting light on the insides of her eyelids.

The crunch of tires on gravel snagged her attention. She sat up and opened her eyes just as the Traverse pulled up and a familiar figure swung out of the driver's side.

"Darius!" Wasn't he supposed to be at work right now? "Hey."

"Hey, Avery, how are you?" He leaned against the railing, propping one foot on the steps.

"Good. Tired."

"I bet."

She tilted her head, trying to read his reasons for showing up. "Addisyn's over at the center with Kenzie."

"Yeah, I know." He dipped his head. "I'm on lunch, and actually, I—I needed to talk to you."

To her? "Is something wrong?"

"No, not at all." He shuffled up the steps. "Uh, may I sit down?"

"Sure." What was going on? She hadn't seen him this awkward since the night she'd met him.

He took his time settling into the chair, then ran a hand over his face. "I—it's about Addisyn." He took a deep breath, then seemed to gather his courage and met her eyes. "I love her, Avery. And, well—I want to marry her. I'd like to ask for your blessing."

A bittersweet swirl of emotions rushed through her, nostalgic longing mixed with fiercely pounding joy, and the love shining in his eyes was enough to break anyone's heart. "Oh, Darius!" Avery leaned forward and squeezed his hand, biting her lip to hold back the brimming tears. "That's—that's the best news."

"Really?" His face relaxed.

"Really." Her laugh was shaky, a sob behind it. She wiped her eyes, her emotions scattering all over her soul. "I'm sorry, I—" She sniffed and found his face again. "So—you two worked things out."

"Yes. We did." His grin spread, slowly sheepish. "We were both scared, Avery. But now—things are different."

Avery pictured her sister's face, the way she glowed like a mountain sunrise at the mere mention of his name. "I'm so glad. She loves you, Darius. From her deepest places."

He flushed slightly. "She's wonderful, Avery. She's beautiful and special and—" His voice broke. "I just love her so much."

So this was it. Soon Darius would tell Addisyn how much he loved her, how he couldn't wait for her to be his wife. She could see it in his eyes, the kind of love that would last the two of them a lifetime. It would all go so fast, just as the years leading to this point had. But against the bittersweetness of change was the joy of knowing the truth.

Addisyn had found her home.

Avery swallowed hard. How thankful she was for this man with the sterling soul and the gentle hands and the ocean eyes—this man who would love Addisyn with the same faithfulness that held up the mountains. She rested her hand on his again. "Darius, do you know what your name means?" It was something that had struck her when she'd first met him.

"Uh—no—"

"'Upholder of the good.' It's a very ancient name, and it was given to someone who protected well the treasure entrusted to him." Tears pricked her eyes again. "I'm entrusting Addisyn to you, Darius. She's the greatest treasure I have. And you truly are an upholder of the good."

He squeezed her hand, his eyes shimmering too. "Thank you, Avery."

He could truly offer Addisyn a rare kind of love. A love Avery had never seen as a child or believed in as an adult. And somehow, seeing that love in his eyes brought a hollow sort of ache. What would it be like to receive that kind of love? To know that a man was willing to lend you his strength, to walk beside you along the winding trails?

Ridiculous. That kind of love would never happen for her—she'd determined so long ago. But it had come to Addisyn—her precious sister who deserved every joy. And seeing Addisyn happy would be enough for her.

She smiled and refocused on the moment at hand. "So? When are you going to ask her?"

"Before you go home. I want you there."

Oh, how thankful she was that he wanted her to bear witness to the moment. "That sounds good. Not one to waste time, are you?"

"Nope." He gave a bashful grin. "Not where a beautiful girl is concerned."

"Have you decided how you're going to ask her?"

"Well, I don't exactly know yet. I thought you could maybe help me plan." He shrugged awkwardly. "I'm not great at this, Avery. I've never done this before, you know."

His uneasy smile made him look like an uncertain little boy. "Don't worry." Avery smiled at him encouragingly. "We'll plan the best proposal ever. Do you have a ring yet?"

"Oh, yes." He glanced up at the buoyant blue sky with a grin. "I definitely do."

CHAPTER 23

Kenzie had solemnly given permission for Avery to visit the treehouse whenever she wanted—a privilege Avery didn't take lightly. She stretched her legs across the sun-warmed platform and leaned her back against the comforting roughness of the tree.

Strange. The last time she'd been up here, she'd been lecturing Addisyn about giving in to fear. And without her sister's help, she might have never seen how the words flipped back on herself.

She watched the clouds float across Addisyn's mountains. Somewhere up in those mountains was Wildcrest, where her sister had found the courage to take her bravest step yet. And if she could do that— then Avery had her own next step to take.

The wind whispered around her as she dialed the familiar number and waited for him to answer. One ring. Two rings. Halfway through the third ring, Laz's drawl boomed over the line. "Miz Avery! Thought you was still in Canada, girl."

"Hey, Laz. I am." Her heart rate accelerated some. There was no easy way to approach the subject. "I'm calling you from Whistler."

"Waalll, my first internat'nal phone call." Laz guffawed. "That makes me feel purty darn special. Everythin' okay up there?"

"Oh—yes."

"That sister of yers stayin' out of trouble?" Laz's voice took on the shape of a smirk. "An' that feller done popped the question yet?"

"Well—not yet." The memory of Darius's bashful face asking her permission still made her smile. "But I have it on good authority that it will be very soon. Before I come back home."

"Waaalll, I'm right happy for 'em." His voice sobered. "What's on yer mind, Miz Avery? I'm thinkin' you didn't call this old man up to tell him 'bout yer travels."

"Well—" She couldn't walk around the perimeter of the subject any longer. "I—uh—I need to tell you something."

"You got yerself a feller now too?"

"*Laz*." Impatience fought with her nerves. "I'm serious, okay?"

"All right, all right. What's on yer mind?"

She opened her mouth, closed it again. Switched her phone to her other hand and wiped her sweaty palm on her pants. "It's—about me. Um—" Every word she'd planned to say had swooped out of her mind. "I—this is hard to ask you about, because I'm afraid you'll be— disappointed in me." The idea stung tears to her eyes. "And please—don't take this the wrong way. I have loved working at the store, and I'm so honored you trusted me with it, and it was just what I needed when I first came, but now—and I know this is—"

"Miz Avery." Laz's voice didn't sound angry or frustrated, but— amused?

"Yes?"

"If yer tryin' to tell me that yer goin' to work for Miz Skyla up at her place—" now she could definitely hear the smile behind his words—"why dontcha try tellin' me somethin' I don't know?"

And just like that, the situation she'd dreaded turned itself upside down. Avery blinked. "Wait—how did you—"

"Miz Avery, you can't get nothin' past an old mountain goat like me." Laz snorted with enjoyment of his own joke. "Got eyes ever'where, girl."

She was still too dazed to laugh. "But—what do you mean—"

"I mean I knew from the get-go. Afore Miz Skyla ever asked you, she come in here one day when you was out gettin' an order and talked to me 'bout it. Said she was fixin' to expand her place and did I think you'd do well there."

Avery couldn't breathe. "And—"

"An' I told her straight up she'd be a fool to pass you by. Yer the best worker I've ever seen, an' that's jes' a fact."

"But, Laz—" She shook her head. "You've known—all this time?"

"Yep, since afore you did." He made an exasperated noise in his throat. "Although, I was startin' to think you might never tell me 'bout it."

Her laugh was still weak with surprise. "I thought—I thought you'd be disappointed. I didn't want to let you down—"

"Let me down? Good Lord, Miz Avery." He laughed again. "Sure, I'm not thrilled to be losin' the best worker I ever had. But I always knew you weren't at the store for good. You've got far too much to give for that."

"But—" She pressed the phone closer to her ear. "Are you sure you're not upset with me?"

"An' you think I'm gonna be mad at you for doin' jes' what the Good Lord done put you on this earth to do? Say, what kinda feller you think I am?" His voice turned serious. "Fact is, I couldn't be prouder of you. You've got head and heart, and the Good Lord only knows how rare that pair is. An' all these years you've been livin' for ever'body but yerself." The warmth of his smile came through his words. "Time for you to go find yer own path now. You've got us to a good place, an' we'll all be fine."

"Thank you, Laz." Her emotions squeezed the words small. "I—I'll miss you, you know."

"Miss me?" He snorted. "An' whaddya think, that I'm not gonna be around? Fact is, Chay's been askin' me to do some volunteerin' over at that place. So you'll probably be seein' more o' me than you hope."

The relief washed over her, and Avery laughed. "Maybe you can keep an eye on me. Make sure I'm doing things right."

"More like the other way around." Laz coughed. "All right, now, that's enough yakkin'. Call Miz Skyla and tell her yer comin' afore she finds some city slicker to take that job an' we have a boy-howdy mess on our hands."

When they ended the call, Avery waited for a moment, gazing to where the mountains rose in limitless ranges, all the way to the infinity of the Pacific Ocean. Her future would be like that—not a straight and boring street, but a narrow and winding trail. A trail that would take her up peaks and through valleys, all along the unpredictable mountain range of her life. A trail that she would walk with footsteps of faith, following the sweeping glory of El Shaddai. The God of the mountains…the God of her life.

And for the first time, she couldn't wait to see where that trail would lead.

Her smile came easily as she punched the number. And then the familiar voice. "Greetings to you, Avery."

"Hi, Skyla." She breathed in the crisp mountain air. Who knew what all her story held? "I'm ready."

∧∧ ∧∧ ∧∧

"I STILL CAN'T believe I let you two talk me into this." Addisyn pretended to scowl at Avery and Darius as they drove the dark roads out of Whistler.

"Oh, come on." Avery leaned forward from the backseat to poke her shoulder teasingly. "After what Darius told me about the sunrises from Alta Lake, I wasn't about to leave Whistler without witnessing one for myself."

"You watch sunrises every day in Colorado, A. I don't know that one more—" a yawn split her words—"was worth getting up at five o'clock for."

"Quit complaining." The headlights of a passing car flashed against Avery's grin. "I'm training you to become a morning person like me."

"Oh, good luck with that." She rolled her eyes and covered another yawn. Only for Avery would she have dragged herself out of bed before the day was even awake. But given that it was her sister's last day in Whistler, it seemed only right to let Avery choose the agenda.

And really, sunrise watching was less stressful than spirit-bear hunting.

Darius cleared his throat. He'd been unusually quiet on the drive. Probably just as tired as she was. "I promise, we'll take you straight for coffee as soon as this is over."

"Coffee." She rubbed the edges of exhaustion from her eyes and grinned at him. "I guess I can survive until then."

The eastern edge of the sky was just fading to a soft gray when Darius pulled up to Alta Lake. "The pier will be the best place for sunrise." He rubbed his hands together. "Why don't you two head on over there? I, uh, need to check on something real quick."

"Yeah, come on, Ads." Avery scrambled out of the car and grabbed Addisyn's hand, towing her toward the pier Darius had pointed out.

344

Addisyn laughed but followed. "Why the rush? Afraid the sun will rise without you?"

Avery pulled a look of shock. "Surely it wouldn't dare."

The morning was chilly, pine-pungent air floating like incense. Fog filtered above the murmur of the water kissing the shoreline. Addisyn hugged herself and crossed to the edge of the pier, her sneakers squeaking on the damp boards.

"Holy, isn't it?" Avery's voice was reverent.

Addisyn breathed in the strange silver hush that came before the dawn. "Yes." She peered at her sister's face, reading her expression in the shadowy light-to-be. "I'm glad you took the job."

"Me too." The promise of the new day lay in Avery's eyes. "I know it will be a big adventure. And—" She glanced over her shoulder at the car, then back at Addisyn. "I'm ready for it now."

"You'll do great."

"Thanks, Ads."

Light was gathering, a pastel pink smudge above the waters, as if the morning would burst from that single point.

"I love this." Avery's words were soft. "You know, the day has to break to let the light in." She squeezed Addisyn's shoulder. "The same way you did."

The truth settled into her soul with the gentle whisper of the fog. "Yes. You're right." And suddenly in the holy hush with her sister, there was too much she wanted to say. "Avery?"

"Yeah?"

"All these years—" The unseen wind ruffled the water and stirred in the exalting arms of the pines. "I never told you *thank you*. For protecting me and guiding me and—"

The magnitude of all her sister had done stacked above the peaks, but one phrase could hold the story.

"For being my white bear."

"Oh, Ads." Avery's hand wrapped warm around hers. "You've got it wrong. You were mine."

"But you were the one who fought for me and—"

"And you were the one who gave me something to fight for." Avery's voice wobbled slightly. She cleared her throat. "Don't you see, Addisyn? You gave me something to live for. Someone to protect. And without you, I—I would have given up. I would have never escaped what we grew up in."

And suddenly, the truth glowed in her soul like the sparks in the eastern sky. All this time. All the time that Avery had pulled her higher, she in some small way had done the same. And the weaving together of their journeys had led them both to mountains they could have never climbed alone.

"I'll miss you, A." Her throat pinched tight.

"Ads, I'll be here." Avery's hand tightened. "No matter where we are in the world, we're sisters forever. El Shaddai has tied our stories together."

El Shaddai. The mysterious and miraculous One, the mighty God Whose Spirit had hovered over them both with the exultation of the breaking dawn. She could finally see His footprints. The way Avery always had.

The first gold gleamed along the horizon just as Darius stepped up behind her. "Ready for the sunrise?"

She smiled, watching as the courageous joy of the light beat back every ounce of the dark. "I think I've been ready for a long time."

A bird song trilled from the tip of one of the pines as if all eternity were a celebration, singing the hymn of the bright and laughing light. And the new day pulled itself over the rim of the world until it burst forth in undoing power, until the mountains burned with the radiance.

The bird was still singing when Avery touched Addisyn's arm and turned her around with a knowing look. And then the sky of her own soul swiped strong with the gold of a thousand new days.

Because there, kneeling on the dock with the sun splashed across his face, was Darius.

And the new day was burning from the diamond ring in his hand.

△△ △△ △△

THROUGH ALL HER own years of performances, Addisyn wasn't sure she'd ever been more nervous.

"Now, just don't forget your Axel, all right?" She poked a slipping bobby pin back into Kenzie's bun. "Double rotation, coming down in the Salchow."

"Right." Kenzie nodded, her eyes enormous. "Keep my weight forward."

"Yes. All the way." A burst of applause filtered down the hallway. The third skater must have just finished.

Tina leaned in the corner of the room, flicking through her phone. She looked up and grinned. "And you know we'll be cheering you on. I even turned on the livestream at home so Canuck can watch."

Kenzie giggled. "He doesn't care, Tina."

"Are you kidding? He's your biggest fan." Tina pocketed her phone and jostled Kenzie's shoulder playfully. "After me, of course."

Addisyn smiled. Their reconciliation had been almost as much of a miracle as the fact that Kenzie was able to perform at all. After starting the support group and finally being honest with Dr. Drees, she'd taken six weeks away from skating. But the love of the ice had drawn her back. Just as it always had for Addisyn.

She'd missed her chance to compete this season, but when Addisyn had found the local showcase instead, she'd known it was an ideal fit. Here where perfection took a backseat to passion, Kenzie could skate for the sheer joy of it again. And almost three months after the spirit-bear hike, Addisyn couldn't believe how much progress the girl had made.

More muffled applause. The fourth skater must have finished, and Kenzie was sixth in the program. Addisyn zipped the nylon jacket that marked her as a Bearstooth coach. "Okay, let's line up. Tina, you better go grab a seat. Avery and Darius are in there somewhere." Her sister had insisted on coming back to see Kenzie perform.

Waiting beside the rink with Kenzie, she searched the stands, and there they were—her fiancé and her sister, both flashing her thumbs-up. She waved back just as Tina scampered into a seat next to Trent and Vera.

The fifth contestant hit her ending pose in a crash of applause. "Addisyn?" Kenzie leaned closer, her face drawn with a trace of the old worry. "I'm nervous."

"No, don't be. You've worked hard in every way. You'll do great.

Just have fun."

"But what if I fall?"

The question she'd grappled with her whole life, and she finally had an answer. "If you fall—" She glanced again toward the stands, filled with everyone she loved. "You'll just get back up."

And then the announcer was crackling to life…"McKenzie Howard"…and Addisyn squeezed Kenzie's hand one last time, and the girl was off.

She took her position in the middle of the rink, and in the hush of the breath-holding moment, Addisyn could feel it, the soul strung tight, the way she'd felt so many times on that ice.

And the music started, and like magic, Kenzie was in motion. Her first glide was a bit tight, her first turn slightly under-rotated. "Come on, Kenzie." Addisyn gripped the railing, muttering to herself. "Find that courage. You've got it."

And then she saw it. Like a blessing, like a daybreak, the power was returning. It was there in the lightening of Kenzie's face, the lengthening of her strides and the extension of her moves—and yes, yes, there she was! Skating the way Addisyn had always known she could.

She spun through her first toe loop, and suddenly Addisyn was snagged in the seams between past and present. Oh, she could see herself, Kenzie's age, flying over the ice with power and passion but no purpose. She'd poured every bit of herself into her skating until her very soul had frozen.

And since then she'd been on a journey to melt her own glaciers.

Could it be that all this time, her life had been like a skating performance? Not a charade to be choreographed, but a wild rejoicing in the true and right and beautiful.

It was the sweaty practices, the aching muscles, the will to press forward. It was the ability to fall a thousand times and still rise up. It was the passion to fling emotions into the wind, to leap onto the breaking balance of the knife-edge and literally walk upon water with unshaken trust.

But most of all, it was the dance. The following of the rhythm, the facing of the fears, the defiance of grace over gravity.

Just how faith was meant to be.

And she was here to witness it all. The realization shivered over her of how carefully her life had been planned. How lovingly every event had been choreographed by higher hands, in a pattern as intricate as a skating routine. How unwaveringly His love had been poured through her, over and above her every misstep.

She was not forgotten. She was not brushed aside. And she was no longer frozen.

She ran a finger over the stitching on her jacket. All her life, she'd strive to help others know the same. The others who would come in the years ahead, just as she'd once been—lost, broken, unsure. She'd be there to help them hear the music. To shine the thawing light on frozen souls. To show them how to dance again and turn their scars to songs.

Her tears were coming even before Kenzie whirled through her double Axel, even before she finished in her dramatic final landing and stood in the shower of applause with a wild and exultant joy leaping in her face. As she bowed to the judges, her eyes were on Addisyn, and as soon as she reached the edge of the ice, the question came. "Was it good?"

Well done, good and faithful one.

Addisyn squeezed her tightly, the emotion catching them both. "Yes." She blinked upward, where the lights of the rink shimmered against her tears, then pulled back to squeeze Kenzie's shoulders. "It is very good."

Very good. The words circled completeness around her as they waited for the judges' announcement, as Kenzie burst into tears at the magnitude of her score, even as the program ended and their family poured down from the bleachers carrying congratulations. *Very good.*

It was indeed.

Addisyn was standing in the dispersing crowd when someone tapped her shoulder. She turned to see a woman biting her lip with timid uncertainty. "May I help you?"

"I—I'm looking for—"

And then Kenzie's voice behind her, fragile but filled with trembling hope. "Mom?"

Her skating bag fell to the floor as she sprang into the arms of the woman with her own blonde hair and blue eyes. "What are you doing here?" Her voice hitched over a sob.

"What I should have done a long time ago." Her mom brushed a trembling hand over her hair. "I came to watch you skate."

Addisyn quietly scooped up Kenzie's bag and stepped back. And then Avery was beside her. "You called her, didn't you?"

Addisyn shrugged and grinned sheepishly at her sister. "Just thought she might like to know when Kenzie was skating. And that she needed a mom."

Avery's smile held all her sister's soul-knowings. She slung one arm over Addisyn's shoulders as they headed out of the rink, into the slanting gold of the September afternoon. "I'm proud of you, sis."

The dance and the faith and the walk upon water was still pounding in Addisyn's soul. "You know something, Avery?"

"What's that?"

Beside his car, Darius waved. And behind him rose the mountains, the peaks that had never ceased to welcome her home.

"This story is just getting started."

The sun struck warm, a light with the power to melt any ice. They were all moving forward—over the ridges and ranges of their stories, deeper into the heart of the mountains where they all belonged. And no matter where their trails led from here, Addisyn was sure of one thing.

They'd all be climbing higher.

Keep Reading!

Thank you for joining me on this journey, dear reader! I hope you were blessed by this story. If you enjoyed this book, would you please consider taking a few moments to leave a rating or review? Reviews are one of the best ways you can support my writing as well as help other readers find books they might enjoy. Thank you in advance!

Now, I have more exclusive content for you—the Climbing Higher Library on my website! This virtual library contains all the exclusive content from the Climbing Higher series—including a prequel scene from Addisyn and Avery's escape to New York, a scene of Skyla's backstory from before *Where the Wings Rise*, and even a collection of gorgeous mountain-themed phone wallpapers. Just scan the QR code below or visit **www.ashlynmckaylaohm.com/climbing-higher-library** to download all the special content today!

THANK YOU!

Dear Reader,

As an author, there's a particular kind of pressure that comes with creating the last book in a series whose writing has spanned over six years. In approaching this final book, I was forced to prayerfully examine what it is, exactly, I've been trying to say all this time—to put my finger on the pulse of the single story that has arched over three books. And as I prayed and pondered, one realization slowly unfolded: this book would hold the *why* of the entire series.

You see, this book is Addisyn's "full circle" moment. In *When the Ice Melts*, she commenced her redemptive journey. In *Where the Wings Rise*, she committed to it. But in *Why the Mountains Stand*, I wanted to push her beyond commencement and commitment to something deeper...consecration. I wanted to give her the opportunity to learn that the very events that had reshaped her soul—the scars she felt so desperately disqualified her—were in fact the connection point to her calling.

But what I wasn't prepared for was how deeply personal this story would become to me.

As I was writing the pages of this manuscript, I was wrestling with God as well. Beset by chronic health struggles, an unshakable sense of isolation, and the deceptive whispers of despair, I'd unwittingly come to see myself as broken. Somehow, the truth shining forth from my manuscript hadn't yet spread into the shadowy corners of my heart. I had become Addisyn, focusing only on all the ways I was disqualified from service to God and others. I had become Kenzie, cowering beneath the voice of anxiety that told me I was never quite strong enough, brave enough, good enough.

I'm beyond thankful for the ones who have come beside me to hold my hands and my heart and to cheer me on as I write forward in faith. Because I know that this story isn't unique to me. It's the story of us all.

All of us have broken places—cracked souls and rough edges and wounds that are still tender. All of us have seen unexpected hardships reshape the terrain of our souls in ways that left us bone-deep grieving.

And all of us, if we're honest, face a choice. We can hide our scars away, tucking everything painful beneath an artificially glossy façade. We can cling to the scars, tracing their outlines until they swallow every other part of our identity. Or we can make the choice that is both the hardest and the holiest: to see our scars as survival symbols, and our stories as light meant to be shared.

And if we do this…then everything changes. Suddenly, we're no longer victims, no longer trapped in a maze of meaningless pain. Instead, we're the spirit bears—the ones who were led through suffering by the hands of a Love deeper than any heartbreak.

The glaciers may have reshaped our souls, but the landscape has a breathtaking beauty. The scars may be written upon our hearts, but they tell only of the Maker of the universe, Who still brings us through our own ice ages. The darkness may have hissed a taunt of our unworthiness, but now we shout our Savior's story: how His grace never left us, how His Presence led us forward, and how we can now invite others to experience His light.

The whole song of the series built to this note, and so that's my prayer for us all. Even in our frozen fears, may we look for the thawing sun. Even in our own despair, may we reach for the hands of those around us and together walk forward with the strength of spirit bears. And even in the darkest times—when our souls are being forged by a Love too pure to be painless—even then, may we remember why the mountains stand.

– Ashlyn McKayla Ohm
April 2024

CLIMBING HIGHER

Don't miss the other two installments of the Climbing Higher series!

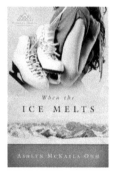

When the Ice Melts (**Climbing Higher #1**)
Losing her dreams may mean finding herself.
Competitive figure skater Addisyn Miles erased her older sister Avery from her life years ago. But when her dreams crumble and an old threat resurfaces, Addisyn must find Avery again…and the faith her sister followed.

Where the Wings Rise (**Climbing Higher #2**)
The flight of freedom starts with letting go.
In Colorado's Rocky Mountains, Addisyn struggles to find common ground with Avery, the sister she once betrayed. But an encounter with an injured hawk forces her to confront the fears that have left her just as wounded—or to allow her darkest enemy to sabotage her future.

Find out more about the Climbing Higher series and read the first four chapters of each book for free by scanning the code below or visiting **ashlynmckaylaohm.com/my-writing/** today!

More by the Author

Enjoy more writing by Ashlyn McKayla Ohm!

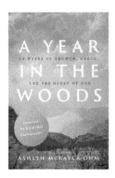

A Year in the Woods: 52 Weeks of Growth, Grace, and the Glory of God
What if encountering God in a fresh new way is as easy as stepping outside?
Step away from a stressful world and enjoy a full year of inspiration with this peaceful book—fifty-two nature-themed devotionals complete with full-color photography and space for journaling.

Find out more by scanning the code below or visiting **ashlynmckaylaohm.com/my-writing/** today!

ABOUT THE AUTHOR

A worshiper of the Creator and a wanderer of creation, Ashlyn McKayla Ohm is most at home where the streetlights die and the pavement ends. She is passionate about shaping stories that weave together unfailing truths, vivid characters, and dramatic natural settings—bringing readers face to face with not only the mountains but also the God Who still moves them. If she's not daydreaming about her next book, you'll find her hiking, birdwatching, or otherwise getting lost in the woods.

Follow Ashlyn's writing at the links below!

Website: **www.ashlynmckaylaohm.com**
Instagram: **www.instagram.com/wildernessashlyn**
Facebook: **www.facebook.com/WordsfromtheWilderness**

ACKNOWLEDGMENTS

A story may start as an idea tucked away within the author, but it takes so many hearts and hands to bring it to the light. It is with humility and immense gratitude that I acknowledge all who have helped me along the way.

For my friends who prayed for me, believed in me, and never laughed when I told them I was going to be a writer. If I began to list names, I could fill this entire book, but please know you are all so dear to me.

For my fabulous cover designer, Hannah Linder. Thank you for taking my sketchy vision and translating it to a cover that captures the spirit of the story.

For my extraordinary beta readers: Sonya Chittum, Erin Mifflin, and Alan Robinette. Thank you for the patient reading, the stellar suggestions, and the love for the story that bolstered my own.

For my amazing parents, Ralph and Derri Ohm. I would never be able to fly if you hadn't been my wings. You have given me strength in weakness, light in darkness, courage in the face of fear, and always, always, a love beyond measure. If I could count the stars or weigh the wind, I might be able to tell you how much I love you.

For my Savior, Jesus Christ. No words I could command would come close to describing the glory of Your infinite gift. Thank You for spinning this story in me and for guiding me through Your grace. On every night of *not-enough* or day of *don't-know*, Your love has never let me go. May You continue writing Your story on the pages of my life, and may Your fire fall on this altar where I offer it back to You.

Milton Keynes UK
Ingram Content Group UK Ltd.
UKHW022040290324
440241UK00015B/623

9 798985 334463